"What are you waiting for?"

He raised his other hand to her jaw, angling her face. This close, he could make out each individual eyelash and the gold striations in her rich irises. Her nostrils flared as though she took in his scent just as he took in hers.

Or perhaps she was so frightened, she struggled to breathe.

"The question is whether debauching my enemy's sister-in-law has quite the same cachet as debauching my enemy's wife," he murmured.

"You bastard," she hissed, her breath warm across his face.

He smiled as dread lit her eyes. "Precisely, *belladonna*."

Slowly he bent to place his mouth on hers...

"Readers beware: do not start reading *Midnight's Wild Passion* late at night. You'll stay up, as I did, telling yourself you'll only read one more chapter before putting it down for the night. Next thing you know, you've finished this marvelous book and discovered that it's nearly dawn."
—JoyfullyReviewed.com

My Reckless Surrender

"4½ stars, Top Pick! Campbell's 'slice of life' portrayal of society provides an intriguing glimpse at the inner workings of the ton's members. Her characters exhibit a depth of personality, moral fiber, and emotion, defining them as the best of all people. The enthralling story is complex and passionate and readers will experience a delightful sense of satisfaction from watching Campbell's characters grow in stature and emotional understanding. Quite a book!"
—*RT Book Reviews*

"Enchanting characters, sizzling sparks flying between Ashcroft and Diana, and a dark, ruthless villain lurking in the background make *My Reckless Surrender* a terrific read."
—RomRevToday.com

"Prepare yourself for Anna Campbell's most sultry, tempting tale yet! *My Reckless Surrender* wraps itself around readers like the most sensual of silks, Ms. Campbell's gorgeous writing a true thing of beauty."
—JoyfullyReviewed.com

Captive of Sin

"Smart Regency romance...delightful insight and... luscious love scenes. Readers will cheer for these lovable and well-crafted characters."
—*Publishers Weekly*

"*Captive of Sin* is an intensely passionate story of battling emotions. Anna Campbell has superbly captured the strong feelings and actions of her characters...I can't wait for Ms. Campbell's next book."

—NightOwlRomance.com

Tempt the Devil

"She's done it again, Gawd love 'er. Anna Campbell's *Tempt the Devil* is a triumph—a paean to sensuality, love, and the indomitable human spirit. Like Campbell, it's smart and a little bawdy. But also, it's devastatingly intimate, as well as the kind of romance that'll ruin you for others for a while."

—Michelle Buonfiglio,
RomanceBuytheBook.com

"4½ stars! Vibrantly refreshing and sizzling with sensuality and a depth of emotion that takes your breath away, Campbell's latest delivers an unforgettable powerhouse romance. The intensity comes from her comprehension of our deepest desires and our need for love and compassion. You won't be immune to this remarkable writer or the unconventional stories she creates."

—*RT Book Reviews*

Untouched

"Rising star Campbell's second emotionally intense novel is reminiscent of early Laura Kinsale. Her flair for sensuality and darkness, wounded heroes, and strong women, appeals to readers yearning for a powerful, sexy, and emotionally moving addition to their keeper shelves."

—*RT Book Reviews*

"Her writing and characters drew me in—held me riveted actually as I wanted to see the end of this dark but touching love story...one of the best reads I've read this year."
—TheMysticCastle.com

Claiming the Courtesan

"4½ stars! This fresh, vibrant novel launches an exciting new historical voice: a don't-miss author whose talent for bringing back the classic Avon style and melding it with a twenty-first-century voice ensures her place as a fan favorite."
—RT Book Reviews

ALSO BY ANNA CAMPBELL

Seven Nights in a Rogue's Bed

ANNA CAMPBELL

FOREVER

NEW YORK   BOSTON

Copyright © 2012 by Anna Campbell
Excerpt from *A Rake's Midnight Kiss* copyright © 2013 by Anna Campbell

Forever
Hachette Book Group
237 Park Avenue
New York, NY 10017
www.HachetteBookGroup.com

Printed in the United States of America

First Edition: September 2012
10 9 8 7 6 5 4 3 2 1

OPM

Forever is an imprint of Grand Central Publishing.
The Forever name and logo are trademarks of Hachette Book Group, Inc.

The Hachette Speakers Bureau provides a wide range of authors for speaking events. To find out more, go to www.hachettespeakersbureau .com or call (866) 376-6591.

The publisher is not responsible for websites (or their content) that are not owned by the publisher.

ATTENTION CORPORATIONS AND ORGANIZATIONS:
Most HACHETTE BOOK GROUP books are available at quantity discounts with bulk purchase for educational, business, or sales promotional use. For information, please call or write:

Special Markets Department, Hachette Book Group
237 Park Avenue, New York, NY 10017
Telephone: 1-800-222-6747 Fax: 1-800-477-5925

Seven Nights
in a
Rogue's Bed

Chapter One

South Devon Coast, November 1826

Storms split the heavens on the night Sidonie Forsythe went to her ruin.

The horses neighed wildly as the shabby hired carriage lurched to a shuddering stop. The wind was so powerful the vehicle rocked even when stationary. Sidonie had seconds to catch her breath before the driver, a shadow in streaming oilskins, loomed out of the darkness to wrench the door open.

"Here be Castle Craven, miss," he shouted through the sheeting rain.

For a second, terror at what awaited inside the castle held her paralyzed. Castle *Craven* indeed.

"I can't leave the nags standing. Be 'ee staying, miss?"

The cowardly urge rose to beg the driver to carry her back to Sidmouth and safety. She could leave now with no damage done. Nobody would even know she'd been here.

Then what would happen to Roberta and her sons?

The remorseless reminder of her sister's danger prodded Sidonie into frantic motion. Grabbing her valise, she stumbled from the carriage. When the wind caught her, she staggered. She fought to keep her footing on the slippery cobbles as she looked up, up, up at the towering black edifice before her.

She thought she'd been cold in the carriage. In the open, the chill was arctic. She cringed as the wind sliced through her woolen cloak like a knife through butter. As if to confirm she'd entered a realm of gothic horrors, lightning flashed. The ensuing crack of thunder made the horses shift nervously in their harness.

For all his understandable wish to return to civilization, the driver didn't immediately leave. "Sartain 'ee be expected, miss?"

Even through the howling wind, she heard his misgivings. Misgivings echoing her own. Sidonie straightened as well as she could against the gale. "Yes. Thank you, Mr. Wallis."

"I wish 'ee well, then." He heaved himself onto the driver's box and whipped the horses into an unsteady gallop.

Sidonie hoisted her bag and dashed up the shallow flight of steps to the heavy doors. The pointed arch above the entrance offered paltry protection. Another flash of lightning helped her locate the iron knocker shaped like a lion's head. She seized it in one gloved hand and let it crash. The bang hardly registered against the roaring wind.

Her imperious summons gained no quick response. The temperature seemed to drop another ten degrees while she huddled against the lashing rain.

What on earth would she do if the house was uninhabited?

By the time the door creaked open to reveal an aged woman, Sidonie's teeth were chattering and she shook as though she had the ague. A gust caught the servant's single candle, making the frail light flicker.

"I'm—" she shouted over the storm but the woman merely turned away. At a loss, Sidonie trailed after her.

Sidonie entered a cavernous hall crowded with shadows. Muddy brown tapestries drooped from the lofty stone walls. Ahead, the fire in the massive hearth was unlit, adding to the lack of welcome. Sidonie shivered as cold seeped up from the flagstones beneath her half-boots. Behind her, the heavy door slammed shut with a thud like the strike of doom. Startled, Sidonie turned to discover another equally geriatric retainer, male this time, turning a heavy key in the lock.

What in heaven's name have I done, coming to this godforsaken place?

With the door shut, the silence within was more ominous than the shrieking tempest without. The only sound was the sullen drip, drip, drip of water from her sodden cloak. Fear, her faithful companion since Roberta had confided her plight, settled like lead in Sidonie's belly. When she'd agreed to help her sister, she'd assumed the torment, however horrid, would be over quickly. Inside this dismal fortress, the horrible premonition gripped her that she'd never again see the outside world.

You're letting your imagination run away with you. Stop it.

The bracing words did nothing to calm spiraling panic. Bile rose in her throat as she followed the still-silent housekeeper across acres of floor. She felt like a thousand malevolent ghosts leered from the corners. Sidonie tightened numb fingers around her bag's handle and reminded herself what agony Roberta would endure if she failed.

I can do this.

The stark fact remained that she'd come so far and still might fail. The plan had always been risky. Arriving here alone and vulnerable, Sidonie couldn't help considering the scheme devised at Barstowe Hall feeble to the point of idiocy. If only her clamoring doubts conjured some alternative way to save her sister.

The woman still shuffled ahead. Sidonie was so rigid with cold that it was an effort forcing her legs to move. The man had offered to take neither her cloak nor bag. When she glanced back, he'd disappeared as efficiently as if he numbered among the castle's ghosts.

Sidonie and her taciturn escort approached a door in the opposite wall, as imposing as the door outside. When the woman pushed it open, it shifted smoothly on well-oiled hinges. Steeling herself, Sidonie stepped into a blaze of light and warmth.

Trembling, she stopped at one end of a refectory table extending down the room. Heavy oak chairs, dark with age, lined the table on either side. It was a room designed for an uproarious crowd, but as her gaze slowly traveled up the length of board, she realized, apart from her decrepit guide, only one other person was present.

Jonas Merrick.

Bastard offspring of scandal. Rich as Croesus. Power broker to the mighty. And the reprobate who tonight would use her body.

"Maister, the lady be here."

Without straightening from his careless slouch in the throne-like chair at the room's far end, the man raised his head.

At this, her first sight of him, the breath jammed painfully in Sidonie's throat. From nerveless fingers, her bag slid to the floor. Swiftly she looked down, hiding her shock under her hood.

Roberta had warned her. William, her brother-in-law, had been merciless in his excoriations on Merrick's character and appearance. And of course, like everyone else, Sidonie had heard the gossip.

But nothing had prepared her for that ruined face.

She bit her lip until she tasted blood and fought the urge to turn and flee into the night. She couldn't run. Too much depended upon staying. In childhood Roberta had been Sidonie's only protector. Now Sidonie had to save her sister, no matter the cost.

Hesitantly she lifted her gaze to her notorious host. Merrick wore boots, breeches, and a white shirt, open at the neck. Sidonie tore her gaze from the shadowy hint of a muscled chest and made herself look at his face. Perhaps she'd detect a chink in his determination, some trace of pity to deter him from this appalling act.

Closer inspection confirmed that hope was futile. A man ruthless enough to instigate this devil's bargain wouldn't relent now that his prize was within his grasp.

Abundant coal black hair, longer than fashion decreed, tumbled across his high forehead. Prominent cheekbones. A square jaw indicating haughty self-confidence. Deep-set eyes focused on her with a bored expression that frightened her more than eagerness would have.

He'd never have been handsome, even before some

assailant in his mysterious past had sliced his commanding blade of a nose and his lean cheek. A scar as wide as
her thumb ran from his ear to the corner of his mouth.
Another thinner scar bisected one arrogant black eyebrow.

A gesture of the graceful white hand curled around a
heavy crystal goblet. In the candlelight, the ruby signet
ring glittered malevolently. The claret and the ruby were
the color of blood, Sidonie noticed, then wished to heaven
she hadn't.

"You're late." His voice was deep and as replete with
ennui as his manner.

Sidonie had expected to be frightened. She hadn't
expected to be angry as well. This man's palpable lack of
interest in his victim stirred outrage, powerful as a cleans-
ing tide. "The journey took longer than expected." She
was so furious, her hands were steady when they slid her
hood back. "The weather disapproves of your nefarious
schemes, Mr. Merrick."

As she uncovered her features, she had the grim satisfaction of watching the boredom leach from his expression, replaced by astonished curiosity. He straightened
and glared down the table at her.

"Just who in hell are you?"

The girl, whoever the devil she was, didn't flinch at Jonas's
irascible question. Under disheveled coffee-colored hair,
her face was pale and beautiful in the heavy-lidded, voluptuous manner.

He had to give her credit. She must be scared out of her
wits, not to mention as cold as a cat locked out in a snow-
storm, yet she stood calm as a marble monument.

Not quite. If he looked closely, faint color marked her

cheeks. She was far from the indomitable creature she struggled to appear.

And she was young. Too young to tangle with a cynical, self-serving scoundrel like Jonas Merrick.

At the *bella incognita*'s side, Mrs. Bevan wrung her wrinkled hands. "Maister, 'ee said to expect a lady. When she knocked—"

"It's all right, Mrs. Bevan." Without shifting his gaze from his visitor, he waved dismissal. He should be piqued that his original prey evaded his snare, but curiosity swamped anger. Just who was this incomparable? "Leave us."

"But do 'ee expect *another* lady tonight?"

A wry smile twisted his lips. "I think not." He cast an assessing glance over the silent girl. "I'll ring when I require you, Mrs. Bevan."

Muttering displeasure under her breath, the housekeeper stumped away, leaving him alone with his guest. "I take it the delightful Roberta is otherwise occupied," he said in a silky tone.

The girl's full lips flattened. She must be repulsed by his scars—everyone was—but apart from a slight stiffening of her posture when she'd entered, her composure was remarkable. The delightful Roberta had known him for years and still reacted with trembling horror at every encounter.

Thwarted malice darkened his mood. He'd rather looked forward to teaching his cousin's wife to endure his presence without suffering the megrims. This impetuous beauty's arrival dashed those hopes. He wondered idly whether she'd offer adequate compensation for his disappointment. Hard to tell. So little of her was visible under the worn cape dripping puddles onto his floor.

"My name is Sidonie Forsythe." The girl spat out the introduction and her chin tilted insolently. He was too far away to see the color of her eyes but he knew they sparked resentment. Under delicate brows, they were large and slanted, lending her an exotic appearance. "I'm Lady Hillbrook's younger sister."

"My condolences," he said drily. Ah, he knew who she was now. He'd heard an unmarried Forsythe sister lived at Barstowe Hall, his cousin's family seat, although he'd never encountered her in person.

He sought and failed to find any resemblance to her sister. Roberta, Viscountess Hillbrook, was a celebrated beauty, but in the conventional English style. This girl with her dusky hair and air of untapped sensuality was in a different class altogether. His interest sharpened, although he made sure he sounded as if her arrival were the dullest event imaginable. "Where is Roberta on this fine night? If I haven't mistaken the date, we'd arranged to enjoy a week of each other's company."

A hint of triumph lit the girl's face, made her dark beauty blaze like a torch. "My sister is beyond your reach, Mr. Merrick."

"You're not." He flavored his smile with menace.

Her brief smugness evaporated. "No."

"I imagine you offer yourself in her place. Gallant, if a tad presumptuous to assume any random woman meets my requirements." He sipped his wine with an insouciance designed to irk this chit who'd upset his wicked plans. "I'm afraid the obligation isn't yours. Your sister incurred the gaming debt, not you. Charming as I'm sure you are."

Her slender throat moved as she swallowed. Yes, definitely jittery underneath the bravado. He wasn't a good enough man to pity this valiant girl. But for a discomfiting instant, something within him winced with fellow feeling. He'd been young and afraid in his time. He remembered how it felt to pretend courage while dread crippled the heart.

Relentlessly he mashed the unwelcome empathy down into the dank hollow where he caged all his old, evil memories.

"I'm your payment, Mr. Merrick." Her voice emerged with impressive coolness. *Brava, incognita.* "If you don't collect your winnings from me, the debt becomes moot."

"Says Roberta."

"Honor forbids—"

He released a harsh crack of laughter and saw the girl quail at last, from his mockery, not his horror of a face. "Honor holds no sway in this house, Miss Forsythe. If your sister cannot pay with her body, she must pay in the more usual way."

Her tone hardened. "You are well aware my sister cannot cover her losses."

"Your sister's dilemma."

"I suspect you knew that when you lured her into such deep play. You're using Roberta to trump Lord Hillbrook."

"Oh, cruel accusation," he said with theatrical dismay, however accurate her suspicions. He hadn't set out that night to entrap Roberta into adultery, but the occasion would have tempted a much better man than Jonas Merrick. Especially as he'd always known that Roberta's disdain for him included an unhealthy dollop of fascination. "Offering yourself as substitute is a devilish strong demonstration of sisterly devotion."

The girl didn't answer. He rose and prowled down the

room. "If I'm to accept this exchange, I should see what I'm getting. Roberta may be a henwit, but she's a deuced decorative henwit."

"She's not a henwit." Miss Forsythe edged away, then stopped to ask suspiciously, "What are you doing, Mr. Merrick?"

His advance didn't falter. "Unwrapping my gift, Miss Forsythe."

"Unwr...?" This time she didn't bother hiding her retreat. "No."

His lips curled in sardonic amusement. "You mean to wear your wet cloak all night?"

The color in her cheeks intensified. She really was pretty with her creamy skin and full-lipped mouth. Now that he was close enough to look into her eyes, he saw they were a deep, velvety brown, like pansies. Sexual interest stirred. Nothing quite so strong as arousal, but curiosity that could soon become hunger.

"Yes. I mean, no." She raised a shaking hand in its black leather glove. "You're trying to intimidate me."

He still smiled. "If I am, I'd say I'm succeeding."

She drew herself up to her full height. She was tall for a woman, but didn't come near to matching his more than six feet. "I told you why I'm here. I won't fight you. There's no need to play the villain from an opera."

"You'll endure my distasteful caresses but won't let me take your cloak? Seems a little silly."

She stopped backing away, purely because she bumped into the stone wall behind her. Her eyes flared gold with anger. "Don't mock me."

"Why not?" he asked lazily. He reached to release the ties at her throat.

She pressed into the wall in a futile attempt to escape. "I don't like it."

"You'll get used to it." His hands brushed along her shoulders, feeling trembling tension beneath the saturated wool. "Before we're done, you'll get used to a great deal."

Bleak self-awareness hardened her expression. "I imagine you're right."

The amusement left his voice. "Roberta isn't worth this, you know."

The girl—Miss Forsythe, Sidonie—stared back without shying away. "Yes, she is. You don't understand."

"I daresay I don't." If the wench was determined to rush to perdition, who was he to argue? Especially as she smelled agreeably of rain and a faint evocative hint of woman. When he slid the cape from her shoulders and let it fall in a sodden heap, he revealed a body pleasingly curved to fit his hands.

She gasped as the garment slipped, then stood quivering. Her jaw set with truculent determination. "I'm ready."

"I doubt you are, *bella*." He paid closer attention to her clothing and spoke with genuine horror. "What on earth have you got on?"

The look she shot him indicated virulent dislike. "What's wrong with it?"

He cast a disapproving glance over the ruffled white muslin, too young for her, too light for the wretched night, too unfashionable, too...everything. "Nothing, if you're dressing to play the virgin sacrifice."

"Why not?" she said with a revival of spirit. "I am a virgin."

He rolled his eyes. "Of course you are. Which begs the

question why you're presenting me with your maidenhead instead of letting your fool sister clean up her own mess."

"You're offensive, sir."

He muffled a laugh. She proved more amusing than Roberta. At the very least, Roberta would have treated him to a display of hysterics by now. He couldn't picture this grave goddess resorting to such dramatics. Perhaps this was his lucky night after all. His lurking frustration at Roberta's maneuvers, fading under the influence of this lovely girl's defiance, vanished. Trapping Roberta had been no great challenge, however satisfying the prospect of swiving his loathed cousin's wife. Seducing Sidonie Forsythe promised fine sport indeed.

"It's my best dress," Miss Forsythe said huffily.

He subjected the limp frill at her décolletage to a derisive flick. "Perhaps when you were fifteen." His gaze sharpened. "Just how old are you?"

"Twenty-four," she muttered. "How old are you?"

"Too old for you." At thirty-two, perhaps he wasn't too old in years but he was a million years too old in experience. And he hadn't spent those million years wisely.

Sudden hope lit her expression. "Does that mean you'll let me go?"

This time he laughed openly. "Not on your life."

Her spiking fear might send her scarpering. He curled one hand around her shoulder, bare under her flimsy bodice. At the contact, something inexplicable arced between them. When startled pansy eyes shot up to meet his, he tumbled headlong into soft brown. She trembled as his hold gentled to shape the graceful curve of bone and sinew.

"What are you waiting for?" she forced through stiff lips.

He should be horsewhipped for tormenting her, but still curiosity was paramount. He raised his other hand to her jaw, angling her face. This close, he could make out each individual eyelash and the gold striations in her rich irises. Her nostrils flared as though she took in his scent just as he took in hers.

Or perhaps she was so frightened, she struggled to breathe.

"The question is whether debauching my enemy's sister-in-law has quite the same cachet as debauching my enemy's wife," he murmured.

"You bastard," she hissed, her breath warm across his face.

He smiled as dread lit her eyes. "Precisely, *belladonna*."

Slowly he bent to place his mouth on hers. Her rain-fresh scent flooded his senses, made him giddy with anticipation. She didn't move away and her lips remained sealed, but the satiny warmth intoxicated him.

He slid his lips against hers in what was more the hint of a kiss than an actual kiss. Even as arousal pounded through him, insisting that he take her, that she was here to be taken, he kept the contact light, teasing. Nor did he tighten his grip on her shoulder to keep her under his mouth. The agony of suspense bordered on the delicious as he waited for her to wrench free, to curse him for a scoundrel. But she remained still as a china figurine. Except the subtle heat under his lips belonged to a woman, not unresponsive porcelain.

Before more than a second passed, he raised his head. Astounding how reluctant he was to end the unsatisfying kiss. He dragged in an unsteady breath and struggled against the powerful urge to kiss her properly. There mightn't be much cachet in fucking Lord Hillbrook's sister-in-law, but he had a grim feeling that wouldn't stop him.

Her eyes were wide and dark with shock. Because he'd kissed her? Or because for a fleeting instant, she might have enjoyed it?

"Why the hesitation?" Her tone was raw. "Get it over with."

He tapped her cheek with a chiding index finger. "I haven't had my dinner yet," he said mildly and released her.

She staggered but found her balance with impressive speed. Breath escaped her parted lips in unsteady gasps. He preferred her outrage to her vulnerability. Against his will, her vulnerability ate at his ruthlessness like rust on iron. "Won't you join me?"

She regarded him with well-deserved hatred. "I'm not hungry."

"Pity. You'll need your strength later."

He let that sink in while he sat and rang the bell. Mrs. Bevan appeared with astonishing speed. She'd probably been listening at the door. Entertainment at Castle Craven was so lacking, he hardly blamed her.

"You may serve dinner, Mrs. Bevan," he said with a cheerfulness that earned him a puzzled glance from his housekeeper.

"Aye, maister. And for yon lady?"

Miss Forsythe remained standing where she had when he'd kissed her. She was back to looking like a marble statue, but now that he'd touched her, he knew she was flesh and blood, all right.

"Two?"

The girl didn't react. Good Lord, had that kiss silenced

her clever tongue? He hoped to coax her into using it again. Not for idle conversation.

He addressed Mrs. Bevan. "No, for one. Please show the lady to her room. Mr. Bevan can serve my meal."

"Aye, maister." The woman shuffled out and after a brief hesitation, the girl collected her meager luggage and followed.

Jonas wished he could be there when Miss Forsythe discovered that in this ramshackle pile, her room also served as his.

Chapter Two

I n the elaborate four-poster bed, Sidonie huddled under the covers. Outside, the gale tore at the castle walls. Its roar made her feel even more defenseless. Fear had hounded her since Roberta had come to her at Barstowe Hall two days ago and begged for help. Fear cramped her stomach and lodged like a boulder in her throat. Fear tasted foul in her mouth.

Second thoughts came too late. Whatever Merrick did to Sidonie couldn't compare to the consequences if William discovered his wife had shared his enemy's bed. Roberta's recklessness had placed them all in jeopardy. Sidonie. Roberta. Roberta's two children, Nicholas and Thomas. But how could Sidonie maintain her anger? Roberta had been more mother than sister when the two Forsythe girls had lived under their parents' negligent regime. Then Roberta had exchanged her father's cold, sarcastic tyranny for her husband's cruelty. Over eight years of marriage, Roberta had changed from a vivacious, affectionate girl into a nervy shadow. The only time Sidonie glimpsed a trace of Roberta's former gaiety was if she won at the gaming tables.

When she was on a winning streak, Roberta was blind to all consequences. It wasn't difficult to picture Jonas Merrick luring her into deeper and deeper play. Until finally he held his enemy's wife in his power.

For pride's sake and to avoid damaging scandal, both William and Roberta kept the misery of their union a domestic secret. Jonas Merrick could have no idea of the damage he threatened to the innocent when he accepted Lady Hillbrook's vowels. Or perhaps he guessed and didn't care.

So now Sidonie waited in Jonas Merrick's bed like a sacrificial lamb. She guessed this was Merrick's room, although the only evidence of his occupancy was a set of heavy silver brushes on the dressing table, and some subtle scent lingering on the linen and in the air. When he'd kissed her downstairs, he'd imprinted himself on her senses in a way she couldn't define. And didn't like. His touch had left an invisible mark. That frightened her almost as much as what was to happen in this glittering chamber. When she pictured him crushing her into the mattress with his powerful body, a scream swelled in her constricted throat.

Her surroundings offered no reassurance. Instead, they added to mounting dread, even as they puzzled her. This was the most bizarre room she'd ever seen. Gold proliferated. On the ornate old-fashioned furniture, the sconces along the walls, the glinting metallic thread in curtains and carpets. Everywhere Sidonie saw herself reflected in battalions of mirrors. Instead of paintings, gilt mirrors

Anna Campbell

lined the walls. Cheval mirrors in each corner. A mirror above the dressing table, over the chest of drawers, between the doors of the armoire. Most surprising—and daunting—was the large oval mirror suspended from the tester above her head.

This proof of her mercurial host's vanity baffled her. His careless dress didn't indicate overweening conceit. Surely any normal man would shrink from dwelling so obsessively upon his disfigurement.

Reflected high above, she saw a pale girl lying straight and still as a cadaver under the heavy cover, gold of course. Thick brown hair was severely pulled back from her face and one fat plait snaked its way across her chest. A girl lying alone. Mr. Merrick seemed in no hurry to pursue his conquest.

At first, Sidonie had perched on a chair. When she'd started to shiver in the damp muslin, she'd changed into her night rail. As hours passed, marked by the ormolu clock on the cabinet, she'd shifted to the bed. Why draw out the preliminaries? There was no escape from the endgame.

Sourly she wondered whether Merrick would demonstrate more ardor if instead of an inexperienced stranger, her pretty sister awaited. But of course he hadn't lured Roberta here because he wanted her. He'd concocted this scheme to score points against his cousin, Lord Hillbrook. This was just the latest spiteful gambit between bitter enemies.

Tightening her grip on the covers, Sidonie struggled for fatalistic calm. But courage faltered when she imagined Merrick shoving himself inside her. Would he expect her to undress? Would she have to...touch him? Would he kiss her again? Absurdly, that seemed the greatest threat of all. His kiss left her flummoxed. It had been chaste as a child's buss upon the lips. Although the fact that Merrick was long past childhood robbed the act of genuine innocence.

She'd never been kissed before. Not by a man. Not with desire.

How sad that her first kiss occurred in such sordid circumstances. Sad and insidiously shameful. Because she hadn't hated his kiss, even though she should. Merrick's kiss had left her intrigued rather than outraged. What would it be like when he took liberties beyond mere kissing?

No, she wouldn't think about it. She wouldn't...

Easier said than done when she lay in Merrick's bed.

Although her host had long ago lost any legal right to use the Merrick name. He should by rights employ his mother's surname. Jonas Merrick was son to Anthony, the late Viscount Hillbrook, and the Spanish mistress purporting to be his wife. When the viscount's younger brother successfully challenged the supposed marriage, Jonas was declared bastard. Upon Anthony's death, his nephew William inherited the Hillbrook title and the feud between Jonas and his cousin, stemming from boyhood, had only become more vicious.

Sidonie shivered. William's reaction when he learned his bastard cousin had tumbled his wife—surely this scheme's object was that William *would* find out— was unthinkable. Remembering that Roberta's very life depended on what happened in this bed bolstered Sidonie's purpose. Until the heavy door opened and Merrick prowled into the candlelit room.

A deeply feminine fear, thick and heavy as tar, coalesced in Sidonie's stomach as she surged up against the headboard. Merrick appeared impossibly large lounging against the door, arms folded across his lean chest. Candlelight flickered over his ruined face, lending him a devilish mien.

Wearing nothing more than shirt and breeches, he should be freezing. He must have a superhuman resistance to cold. Even with the fire blazing in the grate, Sidonie was grateful to have the covers to keep her warm. And to conceal her from his gaze. Which was daft. He'd do considerably more than look at her before the night was out.

He regarded her with the same searching curiosity she'd noticed downstairs. She had no idea what went on behind those deep-set eyes. He tilted his chin toward the tray on the dressing table. "You didn't eat much."

"No." Nerves killed appetite. She hadn't eaten since breakfast, when she'd choked down a piece of toast and some tea. She swallowed to moisten a dry mouth and forced a calmness she didn't feel into her voice. "You were kind to send it up."

He shrugged as if it was nothing. During recent years Sidonie had seen little evidence of kindness and she knew to value it. He'd sent up hot water, too. After travelling all day, she'd felt tired and worn. Ridiculous how a wash restored her spirit.

"Don't interpret my remark as a complaint, but this is a nonsensical thing for you to do." He studied her as if he meant to winkle out her deepest secrets. One of those secrets gave her more power over him than he'd ever guess. Foreboding flooded her, knotted a belly already tight with fear. The knowledge she possessed was dangerous and she knew to her bones that Merrick made a bad enemy.

She pushed upright, clutching the gold covers to her chest. "By nonsensical thing, you mean sleeping with you?" she asked acidly.

A wry smile rewarded her sharpness. He had a nice mouth, expressive, generous enough to hint at sensual expertise way beyond her ken. "What happens when you marry? How will you set your lack of maidenhead right with your husband?"

Her jaw firmed and she spoke with absolute certainty. "I'll never marry." She braced for protest. Most people found it inconceivable that a woman would choose spinsterhood.

"I see." His expression remained neutral. "I imagine Roberta's experience has put you off the idea. In the interests of justice, I must point out that William is a poor example of my sex."

She raised her chin. "Most of the men I've met have been poor examples. Selfishness, arrogance, and bullying appear inalienable elements of the masculine character."

"Tut. I blush for my gender," he said lightly.

"You're hardly an exception," she said bitterly.

"Sadly true, dear lady." He straightened and strolled across to the tray. "Now what have we here?"

She frowned after him in confusion. His manner expressed no urgency. She'd been sure he'd insist upon having his wicked way the instant he arrived. That couldn't be chagrin she felt at his lack of dispatch. But there was something lowering in rendering one's virtue to an unrepentant rake, only to find him reluctant to do his worst.

Merrick wasn't living up to lurid expectations. Roberta had described a fiendish seducer, a man of surpassing hideousness. When she first saw his face, Sidonie had been appalled, mostly because such scarring could only result from excruciating injury. Now, even after their short acquaintance, she saw past the scarring to the man beneath. That man was no monster. His features intrigued more than mere handsomeness. His was an interesting face, full of vitality and intelligence. Striking.

Just as the man himself was striking.

Nervously wondering what game he played, she watched him cut a couple of slices of hard yellow cheese and place them on some crackers. For such a large man, he had surprisingly elegant hands. In the uncertain light, the ruby ring flashed sullenly like a warning. She'd expected to feel hostility and fear. And she did. But other emotions pulsing between them were less defined. Curiosity, certainly. Wary rapprochement. Something electric and unfamiliar.

The prickly interest was more disturbing than terror or dislike. She was aware of Merrick with an animal intensity she'd never felt before.

He extended the plate toward her. Without thinking, she lifted a cracker and nibbled at it as he wandered away to lean against the carved post at the base of the bed. A ghost of a smile played around his mouth. Her eyes traced the sharply defined cut of his upper lip, the full sweep of his lower one. The disturbing mixture of fear and fascination he aroused left her restless, unsettled.

"I thought you'd be—" she began, then wondered if it was wise to mention his plans to ruin her.

"I can imagine." He offered the plate again.

She took another two crackers. "Why are you here?"

"In this bedroom? Fie, Miss Forsythe, you're too coy."

She blushed with mortification. "No."

He returned the plate to the tray and poured two glasses of claret. "You mean at Castle Craven?"

"Yes." She accepted the wine and took a sip. Then another. Pleasant warmth eased alarm to a murmur. The hand gripping the sheet relaxed from white-knuckled tension. "Wouldn't it be more convenient to seduce Roberta at Ferney?"

A few years ago, Merrick had purchased Ferney, the estate adjoining Barstowe Hall's dilapidated splendor. He'd then spent a fortune creating a residence fit for a viscount. Goodness, fit for a prince. Sidonie had never ventured beyond the gates, but what she'd seen of the exterior made Chatsworth look like a shanty. The neighbors were always gossiping about the house's magnificence. Although wisely never within William's hearing. Sidonie had applauded the unknown Jonas Merrick's audacity. He made it impossible for her brother-in-law to escape the knowledge that in all ways except inheritance, he was a rank failure compared to his cousin.

Merrick's faint smile lingered as he loaded more crackers and offered them to her. "Even the most dilatory of husbands would retrieve an erring wife when he merely needs to cross his estate boundary."

She accepted the plate and propped it on upraised knees. The action meant releasing the covers. Merrick didn't seem to notice how they sagged over her bosom. "You could be right." She polished off another couple of crackers. "And naturally you enjoy the gothic drama of this setting."

"It never crossed my mind."

She sent him a skeptical glance and took more wine. The glass was half empty. How had that happened? "Are you trying to get me intoxicated?"

"No." He raised his wine in a silent toast.

"It won't work, you know."

"What won't work?"

"Trying to soften me up with liquor."

"I'm pleased to hear it. I'd hate to think you so green as to fall for that old trick." He took her now empty glass, returning it to the table along with his. "Have you finished with that plate?"

"Yes, thank you." She passed him the empty plate, which he placed on the tray. She'd expected to be cold and proud when he came to take her virginity. Instead she felt confused and surprisingly in charity toward Mr. Merrick. Not that she wanted him to do...that. But it was difficult to summon the outraged self-righteousness that had sustained her so far.

Perhaps the alcohol had done its work after all. That and his self-effacing kindness in making sure she ate something. Poor foolish Sidonie Forsythe. Forfeiting her chastity in return for a few scraps of good farm cheddar.

No, this weakness was dangerous. If she succumbed without demur, she'd never live with herself. "Stop toying with me," she demanded with sudden harshness.

With excess force, she flung away the bedcovers and lay flat, staring fixedly up at the mirror. A man who liked to watch himself with a woman deserved contempt. Heavens, he didn't even try to hide what an unregenerate voluptuary he was.

Although it was difficult to maintain a disapproving

silence when the blackguard intent on her deflowering burst into laughter. "Good Lord, Miss Forsythe, you desperately need advice on your wardrobe."

"It's only my . . . my nightdress." She refused to look at him.

Uneasiness crammed in her throat when he prowled closer. "There's room for six in there."

She shot him an annoyed glance. "Did you expect me to wear nothing at all? The night's too cold, apart from anything else."

Mr. Merrick subjected her to a thorough and searing inspection. She just knew he pictured her naked and it was her fault for mentioning the possibility. All her life, people had warned that her impulsive tongue would get her into trouble. She was most definitely in trouble. Not just because Mr. Merrick's manner had within an instant transformed from nonchalance to interest. That fleeting accounting of her body extended mere seconds, yet every inch of her skin burned. Her belly clenched with a painful mixture of shame and reluctant excitement. She met his eyes, then heartily wished she hadn't. The predatory glint was unmistakable.

"There's room for maneuver between nakedness and that tent you're wearing." His gaze sharpened. "Did you think I'd quail at all that flannel?"

"I took what defensive measures I could," she muttered, staring upward again. Although truthfully it hadn't occurred to her to pack anything other than her usual nightwear.

"You underestimate the stimulating power of imagination," he said drily. "I'm intrigued to discover the treasures beneath that billowing fabric."

In wordless horror, Sidonie turned her head to stare at him. His shell of carelessness disintegrated and she read raw hunger in his saturnine face. The air vibrated with blazing sexual awareness. In the bristling silence, the sound of rain sheeting against the windows was a jarring intrusion.

"Take it off," he said softly.

Dear Lord...

The time had come. Of course it had. She'd arrived on Merrick's doorstep inviting him to tup her. He was hardly likely to turn her away in favor of an early night with an improving book. Reluctantly, her heart thundering panic, she sat. With shaking hands, she fumbled for the night-gown's hem. Briefly her vision drowned in white flannel, then she was free. With a defiant gesture, she tossed the garment to the floor. She refused to meet Merrick's gaze just as she refused to betray her humiliation by covering herself with her hands.

Now the true wickedness of this mirror-filled room struck hard as a hammer on brass. Like endless echoes of that clanging blow, everywhere she looked, she saw her naked body. Over and over again. Pale skin. Jutting breasts. Bare legs.

Reflected a hundred times, Merrick loomed above her, tall, dominating, uncompromisingly male. In candle-light, his loose shirt glowed with supernatural whiteness. He hadn't shifted since she'd removed her nightdress, but the tension in his long body indicated any plea for mercy would go unheeded. His stance conveyed hunting readiness.

The silence stretched until she wanted to scream.

She twisted at the waist to face him. His expression

was vivid with what, even in her innocence, she recognized as arousal. In his angular face, his eyes blazed hot silver. He was no longer the languid, sardonically amused man who'd fed her a makeshift supper. This man was captive to appetite.

Dread coiled in her belly. Dread and unwilling curiosity. When she looked at Merrick, unfamiliar heat eddied through her. Since agreeing to take Roberta's place, she'd told herself her travails would be vile. Vile travails would leave her self-respect, if not her virginity, intact. Those glittering eyes hinted that self-respect would be the first casualty of this desperate bargain. She swallowed to moisten a parched mouth and her hands tangled in the sheets beneath her. She was so taut, she feared she'd snap in two if he touched her.

A muscle jerked in his cheek and his fists clenched at his sides as his leisurely investigation paused at her breasts. Seconds spun into scorching fire. To her humiliation, her nipples tightened. An aggravatingly knowing expression narrowed his eyes and a smug smile curved his lips. He knew he didn't repulse her, much as she wished he did.

His lingering attention descended to the triangle of feathery brown hair between her legs. It was as if he touched her there. Molten heat flooded her belly, made her gasp with surprise. She squeezed her thighs together and her hand whipped down to shield her sex. "Stop it," she whispered, the demand thick with tears she refused to shed.

He seemed not to hear. Instead, he stepped nearer and slid his hand behind her neck. She started, then sat unmoving. Through encroaching warmth, she felt the roughness of faint calluses on his fingers. After a charged hesitation, he ran his hand lightly down her neck to the pulse racing in her throat. Every nerve leaped and the molten sensation widened, deepened, left her unbearably agitated. Her instinct was to pull away, drag up the covers, cower.

Pride kept her still.

That searching hand dipped lower, stroked the upper slopes of her breasts. Then glanced across one beaded nipple. Unwelcome pleasure sizzled through her. In the silence, her unsteady breath was audible. Even the storm seemed to pause in anticipation. Her gaze flew to his face, where she found desire, but also something that looked like wonder. Her heart skipped a beat, then crashed painfully against her ribs.

"You're beautiful," he said hoarsely. Delicately he circled her nipple then cupped her breast in one large hand.

It was too much. She couldn't endure these lying overtures, however sweet. They lent a gloss of false tenderness to what was at its basest level a squalid business arrangement. She jerked away and slid down the bed. At last she summoned courage to look into the mirror above. She lay rigid, her body pallid against the sheets. Her face was drawn with fear and determination. Hectic color marked her cheekbones.

"Do it." She hardly recognized the strident voice. "For God's sake, don't torture me. Just...do it."

For a long time, the man reflected in the mirror didn't move. Then with a smooth swiftness that made her wanton heart kick into a gallop, he seized the heavy brocade cover.

"Your pardon, Miss Forsythe." He didn't sound at all

like the shaken, sincere man who told her she was beautiful. With a contemptuous gesture, he tossed the covers over her nakedness. Shock held her speechless as he turned on his heel and stalked toward the door. "I find tonight my taste doesn't run to martyrs."

Chapter Three

In the cavernous hall, Sidonie Forsythe stood tall and straight in a pool of pale sunshine. She wore her heavy cloak and she clutched her valise at her side.

"What the hell are you doing?" Jonas strode across the flagstones and stopped a few paces short of her. Thank God he was an early riser or he'd be too late. He'd been flicking through the prospectus for a canal scheme when Mrs. Bevan lumbered into the library to announce the young lady requested use of his carriage.

At his furious question, Miss Forsythe whipped around. She stared dismayed into his face and he knew they both revisited those blazing moments in his bed. The memory thundered through him like the blast of a thousand cannons. Her lovely eyes darkened with what he could only interpret as humiliation before anger rescued her. "Don't you ever dress like a Christian?"

Again, she surprised him. He liked that. He liked it

almost as much as he'd liked seeing her unclothed body last night. And he'd liked that very much indeed.

He released a derisive grunt of laughter. "This is my house. If I want to run around in my shirtsleeves, I will. If I tour the estate stark naked, I daresay it's my privilege."

Delicate color tinged her cheeks at the mention of nakedness. This morning she looked brighter. She must have managed some sleep after he'd stormed from her room.

He wished to Hades he had.

"It's nothing to me what you wear." Calm determination masked any disquiet. He'd lay money that composure was as false as the canal scheme's projected profits. "We'll never see each other again after all."

"I wouldn't place too much store in that particular prediction," he said drily. "It's a devilish shabby trick to sneak away without a by-your-leave."

"We have nothing to say to one another."

"You think not?" He turned to Mrs. Bevan. "Tell Hobbs the carriage isn't required."

"Mr. Merrick—" Miss Forsythe began in a repressive voice.

He'd be damned if he was squabbling with her out here while his housekeeper stood around with flapping ears. "Perhaps you'd rather continue this discussion in the library."

"I'd rather leave your house and pretend these lamentable hours never occurred."

"So vehement for daybreak." He weighted his tone with completely spurious boredom. "It's a trifle fatiguing."

"Only for a man of your advanced years," she snapped back.

Brava ancora. He could guess how awkward she felt in his presence after what had happened—and not happened—last night. Still she came back fighting. "At least let me rest my ageing bones on a cushion while you harangue me."

No answering humor. She continued to eye him warily. "I'd prefer to go."

"I'm sure you would. But I've still got Roberta's vowels. Or had you forgotten?"

Her magnificent eyes flashed hatred. "I hadn't forgotten. I paid you last night."

He gave her a nasty smile. "That's a matter of opinion." He gestured toward the library. "Miss Forsythe?"

She glowered at him, then glanced at Mrs. Bevan, who watched with avid interest. The girl's color deepened and she nodded abruptly. "Five minutes."

Jonas knew not to push his advantage. Or at least to wait until they were alone before he did. He opened the door and ushered her into the book-lined room.

Her shoulders tensed into a ruler-straight line when he lifted her cloak away. The white gown beneath was as inappropriate as ever. Although he appreciated the way it strained across her full bosom. As if once more shaping her perfect breasts, his hands curled in the cloak's rough wool. Yielding to temptation, he leaned in to catch her fresh scent. She didn't smell like rain this morning. Instead she smelled of lemon soap. Still, the commonplace fragrance stirred turbulent eddies of desire in his blood. He dropped the cloak onto a chair and stepped closer to release the ribbons on her unbecoming bonnet. Whoever chose her clothing should be drawn and quartered.

She batted his hand away and her breath accelerated—

whether with fear or excitement, he wasn't sure. Probably a mixture of the two. "Stop it."

"Just making you comfortable." The ribbons loosened and he lifted the bonnet, tossing it on top of the cloak.

"As if you care for my comfort. If you did, you'd let me go."

His lips twitched as he wandered away. "But that would have a disagreeable effect on my comfort." He gestured toward a leather chair. "Please sit down."

She remained standing uneasily in the center of the room. "No, thank you. I'll be on my way shortly."

He sauntered to the window and slouched against the frame, basking in the sun's unseasonal warmth. Last night's storm had blown itself out and the day outside was pleasant for November. Although he suspected the temperature inside the library was about to drop several degrees.

He fixed an unwavering stare upon her. "I hadn't taken you for a cheat, Miss Forsythe."

Her expression remained neutral, although she must know what he meant. "I've cheated you of nothing, Mr. Merrick."

His tone held an edge. "What would you call bilking me of your company after promising...satisfaction?"

She paled and her gloved hand tightened around the handle of her bag. "You didn't want me last night," she said flatly.

He raised his eyebrows in mocking disbelief, while burgeoning need crooned its alluring song in his ears. "You're not that innocent."

She growled softly and swung away with a flounce of filmy skirts. He caught a glimpse of two well-turned ankles. Interesting that the sight proved so arousing when he'd already seen her naked.

"You're in a humor to tease, I see."

He tilted his head back against the window frame and surveyed her down the bumpy length of his broken nose. "No, I'm in a humor to have my bargain honored."

She stopped and regarded him with a troubled light in her dark eyes. Grown men cringed from his scars. Why the hell didn't his grotesque appearance daunt this untried girl?

"I offered my ... services; you rejected them." She set down the bag and stubbornness squared her jaw. "I'm within my rights to leave unmolested."

"You're quite the lawyer, Miss Forsythe. You employed similar sophistry last night when you presented yourself in your beguiling sister's stead."

Not that he could summon one morsel of regret for the exchange. Roberta was a beautiful, if shallow, creature, and he'd have fucked her perfectly happily. Not least because every time he poked her, he'd know he cuckolded his toad of a cousin.

But Roberta's sister...

Sidonie Forsythe was a jewel such as he'd never encountered. He wasn't fool enough to leave her where he'd found her and walk away whistling.

"Surely you won't insist on full restitution." The uncertainty that had always lurked beneath her bravado became overt. "Not after—"

"Presumably you arrived expecting to repay the debt as it stands," he said coolly. He folded his arms across his chest to stop himself from reaching for her. One ridiculously chaste kiss, a brief exploration of silky skin, now the craving to touch her was a fever.

"This is insane." Like a mare scenting a stallion, she shifted nervously. "If you won't lend me your carriage, I'll walk to Sidmouth and find transport there. It's only a couple of miles." She turned and marched away.

He leaped forward and caught her arm. "Wait."

Immediately, even through her sleeve, there was that electric connection he'd felt cupping her naked breast last night. When she turned an appalled brown gaze on him, he knew she felt it, too. Much as she clearly wished she didn't. He fought the urge to sweep the girl into his arms. The brief taste of her lips had left him hungry for more. The memory of her glorious body had kept him awake most of the night. In occasional snatches of sleep, he'd dreamed of her. Naked. Willing. Sighing her pleasure as he pounded into her.

She trembled under his hand. "You don't need to manhandle me."

"I mightn't need to, but I'd certainly like to," he purred and was rewarded with another beguiling blush. Jonas couldn't recall the last time he'd consorted with a woman innocent enough to blush. The only females who took him on had become jaded with the banal charms of unmutilated men. "What about Roberta's debt?"

Miss Forsythe's self-righteousness faded. "I came to you. I—"

He struggled to ignore the fear in her face. Now wasn't the time to develop a conscience. "No matter," he said with a nonchalance he didn't feel. "Roberta can sell some jewelry to repay me."

"That's impossible." He felt her quivering resistance under his grasp. "William would find out."

Ah, at last they reached the nut of the matter. "I expect he would."

His gut twisted with reluctant remorse when tears brightened the girl's eyes. Tears she bravely blinked away. Just as she'd bravely offered herself to save her sister. Sidonie Forsythe was a remarkable woman. Which didn't make him one whit more inclined to send her away.

A strange moment to realize that he envied Roberta. It must be wonderful to know such steadfast love as Sidonie demonstrated. His father had undoubtedly loved him. But his father had been crippled by sorrow for his wife and then the ensuing scandal. Through a life of betrayal and rejection, Jonas had learned to mistrust love. Too often it masked self-serving interests. Too often it proved a fragile thread that snapped under the lightest pressure. And even if it was the powerful, overwhelming force the poets claimed, it brought destruction in its wake. Yet Sidonie loved her sister enough to sacrifice herself like this.

Bah, he became sentimental. He shook off the uncharacteristic self-pity and concentrated on the woman before him.

Her stare was bleak. "You know, don't you?"

"That William takes his temper out on his wife? Not until last night. I spent hours awake, puzzling out your behavior." And cursing like the devil that his pride exiled him to the dressing room's minuscule cot. "Your actions only make sense if the consequences of Roberta's seduction are dire indeed. And my cousin has always met disappointment with violence."

With a twist of his gut, he realized his free hand crept up to touch his disfigured cheek. Hoping Miss Forsythe hadn't noticed the betraying gesture, he forced his arm back to his side. His tone hardened. "I should have guessed."

Poor bloody Roberta. Life as William's wife must be hell on earth. Her frenetic gaiety in society made sense now—she was probably relieved that her husband wouldn't cuff her in public. Jonas could almost forgive her for the way she cringed at the merest sight of him.

Miss Forsythe looked devastated. Her voice was low and shaking. "If you know...Roberta's circumstances, chivalry insists you pardon the debt."

His lips lengthened in an unamused smile. "Like honor, chivalry isn't a rule in this game. Surely you know by now that I'm a bastard by nature just as I'm a bastard by birth."

He expected her to flinch from his plain speaking, but she confronted him squarely. "If I stay here, I'll be ruined."

With a grunt of disgust—at himself more than her—he released her arm and prowled back to the window. She came after him, standing too near for caution and staring at him as though seeking some evidence of goodness. She'd search till doomsday. The world had turned him into a monster. He'd done his best since to live up to the description.

"You must have realized that before you arrived." He forced himself to sound careless, no matter that her proximity stirred his senses so powerfully. The sun flooding through the window lit rich colors in her opulent hair. Flax. Gold. Auburn. "Presumably you've told your nearest and dearest some tale to keep them at bay over the next seven days."

"I still don't want my name sullied."

"You have my word our...liaison will remain secret." Sarcasm sharpened his voice as he continued. "Rejoice in your freedom, Miss Forsythe. This week you're at liberty."

"I'm not at liberty to become a libertine."

His lips quirked at her quick response. "Actually you are."

Sidonie Forsythe was totally unawakened—good God, how had no man seen what he had?—but she was in essence a sensual creature. He was adept enough at pleasing a woman, however grotesque his face. His deepest instincts insisted she'd relish the act once she'd conquered her qualms.

She surveyed him with unconcealed contempt. "You'd force me into your bed, knowing the only reason I'm there is to save my sister physical harm?"

"I told you—my taste doesn't run to martyrs."

Her gaze remained stony. "I'll never come to you willingly."

When he caught her hand, the jolt of heat threatened to blast his control to ashes. He drew her down beside him on the window seat. "I'd like the chance to convince you otherwise, *bella*."

When had her willingness become so important? Sometime since he'd kissed her and caught a hint of how sweet she'd be in his arms when she finally gave herself up.

She tried and failed to pull away. "Only a swaggering coxcomb would hope to change my mind in a mere week. I won't change my mind in a hundred years."

He fought another smile. Did she feel the vivid energy flickering between them? He couldn't believe he burned alone, for all she denied him with words. "You make the challenge so delicious."

"I'm not...*flirting* with you, Mr. Merrick. I'm pointing out you waste your time with this absurd scheme."

"In which case, you'll return to your sister none the worse," he said calmly, efficiently stripping her glove away. He ached to touch her skin.

The cynicism in her expression made her look older than her twenty-four years. "You don't for one moment expect to lose, do you?"

He raised her hand to his lips and pressed a fervent kiss to her soft palm. Her scent filled his head, intoxicating him like the finest wine. "I rely upon my fatal charm."

She tugged at her hand. Her cheeks were pink with outrage and what unfounded optimism read as grudging pleasure. "It would almost be worth staying to take you down a few pegs."

"I'm glad you think so." Reluctantly he released her. Touching her turned thought to chaos and he needed all his wits to gain his way. "You forget your sister's stake in our bargain."

Shock tautened her features. She *had* forgotten Roberta. "So you still compel me."

He shrugged. "Only to remain at Castle Craven as my guest. Anything further is your choice."

Straightening, she regarded him with the same chilly disdain she'd displayed last night. Would she say yes? It astounded him how eager he was for her to stay. He'd be in the devil's own thrall before the week was done. God knew how he'd keep his hands to himself until she agreed to become his lover. As surely she must.

Still his gut tightened with agonizing suspense as he awaited her assent.

She sucked in a shaky breath but spoke with impressive

firmness for a chaste woman conceding herself to a scoundrel. "Let us be clear then, Mr. Merrick."

With a mocking gesture, he bent his head. "By all means, Miss Forsythe."

Her voice turned flat as she strove for control. In her lap the ungloved hand tightened around the gloved one in silent protest at what he compelled from her. "In return for my presence in Castle Craven over the next seven days, or rather six days as I've already spent a night under your roof, you will surrender Roberta's vowels. Her debt will be fully acquitted."

"Your companionship, *bella*. Make no mistake—I want you in my bed and I'll take every opportunity to get you there. No locking yourself away in the highest tower."

"I won't cheat."

"And you won't cheat in other ways. You won't lock yourself away in your mind, either."

She flushed. "I don't know what you mean."

"Yes, you do. When I tell you of my intentions, you'll listen. When I touch you—and believe me, *tesoro*, I'll touch you over and over again, in ways you haven't imagined a man can touch you—you won't fight the pleasure."

She cast him a disgruntled glance under her lashes. "You certainly don't lack confidence, Mr. Merrick. Do I have a choice about staying?"

His smile turned sly. And triumphant. He'd prevailed. Of course he had. In this particular game, he'd always held the winning hand. He refused to acknowledge the shaming relief coiling in his belly. "Does Roberta have any jewelry William doesn't know about?"

Her lips tightened. "You really are a bastard."

"Make no mistake." This once, his cheerful self-abnegation rang hollow. She deserved better than this arrangement and they both knew it. He stretched his legs out with an appearance of insouciant superiority.

She gave a sharp nod, still with that hard light in her eyes. "You have an agreement, sir. I look forward to leaving here in a week with both pride and virtue intact."

"And I look forward to nights of untold rapture in your arms, my dear Miss Forsythe." His smile broadened as victory rang around him like a fanfare of trumpets. "May the best man win."

She subjected him to a glare of fulminating dislike, although the color lingering in her cheeks from his kiss spoiled the effect. "Make that the best *woman*, Mr. Merrick."

Chapter Four

*W*hat had she done?

Sidonie remained as trapped as she'd been since Roberta had flung herself upon her mercy two days ago. She should have known her attempt to leave after only one night would fail. While Merrick cajoled her into staying, she'd desperately struggled to avoid her fate. But the threat to her sister remained paramount. Last time William lost his temper, he'd broken Roberta's arm and two ribs. If he learned his wife betrayed him with his worst enemy, he'd kill her.

At least Sidonie had wrenched a small portion of control back, but she didn't underestimate how difficult Merrick would make it to maintain her virtue. She already found him compelling and he'd hardly exerted himself yet to suborn her. Even now, when she'd pledged her word to cooperate, her mind scurried hither and yon to find an escape. But there was nothing. Only her hollow claim that she'd cleave to her chastity, however he tempted her.

Believe me, tesoro, *I'll touch you over and over again, in ways you haven't even imagined a man can touch you.*

She hid a shiver as she recalled those low words, promising pleasures beyond her wildest dreams. A shiver of fear. Also a shiver of unwilling interest.

"Shall we shake on the deal?" He stood and extended one elegant hand in her direction.

Sidonie fought the urge to tell him he'd touched her quite enough. "Why not?"

As his hand curled firm around hers, heat tingled on her skin. Heat that had surged to flame when he kissed her palm.

As he lowered her hand, his knowing expression bolstered resistance. Privately she might admit he drew her on levels she'd never known. To his face, she meant to continue her defiance. And hope against hope a sharp tongue and prickly attitude saved her. Six days of discomfiting, unceasing awareness of her captor loomed ahead. More to the point, six nights.

She met Merrick's silvery gaze and acknowledged with a sinking feeling in her stomach that six days could be a lifetime. Only seconds into their bargain and already she recognized the dangers of allowing him to touch her when and how he liked. The memory of his fingers trailing over her naked skin blinded her to her surroundings. She shifted uncomfortably against the window seat.

He'd made no secret of his sinful plans. At least he'd been honest with her. A grim voice at the back of her mind reminded her she hadn't been honest with him. Not completely. Not about a discovery that would change his life forever. Her eyes faltered away from his as though he might read her guilty secrets in her face.

"Have you had breakfast?"

She frowned and rose, even if it meant standing far too close to him. Perching on the window seat left her feeling disagreeably like a sitting duck. "Mr. Merrick, the way to my heart isn't through my stomach."

He arched his black eyebrows. "My sights are set on parts of you other than your heart, Miss Forsythe."

"Oh." She wished desperately he wouldn't keep stealing her capacity for speech. For pity's sake, what was wrong with her? He couldn't undermine twenty-four years of rectitude with a mere kiss on the hand.

His thumb rubbed casually over the back of her hand. Except nothing he did was casual. "Given what we'll become to each other, surely we can dispense with formalities. My name is Jonas."

"I suspect it's to my advantage to preserve formalities."

"And I'm convinced of the outcome whatever we call each other, *bella*."

"Oh, very well," she said irritably. She straightened and withdrew her hand, surprised he let her go. "You may call me Sidonie."

Why not let her go? He had her exactly where he wanted. Within pouncing reach. "Excellent. The idea of whispering 'Miss Forsythe' into your ear as I slide inside you is just too arousing."

She flushed at the graphic picture he painted. "You can't say things like that."

He smiled with an annoying edge of triumph and stepped nearer, towering above her. "So early in the game, and you cry forfeit, Sidonie."

Temper came to her rescue. He might treat her ruin as an unimportant trifle, but she wasn't nearly so easy with what occurred. "I suppose I'll become accustomed to your vulgarity."

His laugh curled around her resistance like ivy clinging to a crumbling stone tower. "I'm sure you will, at that."

He strode toward the door and opened it with a flourish. "Shall we proceed to the dining room?" He surveyed her with unreadable eyes. "Then perhaps you and I can share a ride."

She blushed furiously. "Mr. Merrick—"

His smile turned wicked. "Now who's being vulgar? I need to check the property after the storm. I thought you might like some fresh air."

She marched past into the hallway. Six days. Then she'd be free, never to see the wanton and irritating Jonas Merrick again.

Those six days promised torments to shame the devil.

When Sidonie rushed into the stableyard, Jonas was talking to a small, wizened man who held the reins of two high-bred horses, a cream Arab mare and a large bay gelding. Without interrupting his discussion, her nemesis sent her a faint smile. She'd taken longer changing than arranged but he betrayed no impatience. Yet again, she contemplated the contrast between the Merrick cousins. William loathed the smallest inconvenience and lashed out if anyone delayed or obstructed him.

The last lonely years, mainly spent running Barstowe Hall, hadn't prepared her to defend herself from a dangerous roué. She supposed she must have had girlish dreams once of a fascinating man focusing his attention on her. She couldn't remember them. Once she was old enough to understand the dynamic of the marital bond, her dreams had become more prosaic: an independent, useful life where decisions were hers and no man treated her as his property.

The groom dipped his head to acknowledge her and disappeared into the stables. Merrick studied her with a glint in his eye. Part sexual interest, part approval, part something she couldn't altogether interpret. It was as though he asked a question and she said yes without knowing what she agreed to.

She shook off the disturbing sensation and lifted her chin. Her hands tightened on the elegant little crop.

"I see you found the riding habit," he said neutrally.

"I see you're prepared for all eventualities when ladies visit," she responded with a tart edge. When she'd seen the stylish black habit laid across her bed—his bed, she supposed—she'd cringed. She told herself his liaisons were none of her business, but that niggle of resentment persisted.

A deepening of the faint lines around his eyes indicated amusement. "I've never brought a mistress here, if that worries you."

"I'm not your mistress," she snapped, annoyed that he immediately attributed her ill temper to jealousy.

"Yet." He subjected her to a thorough inspection. "It fits."

"It's too tight. Mrs. Bevan had to shift the buttons. That's why I'm late."

"You're more . . . generously endowed than your sister."

She stared into his face and stupidly wondered whether he preferred a more slender woman. Compared to Roberta's willowy proportions, she was a Valkyrie. "Roberta doesn't ride," she said, telling herself she didn't care what this miscreant made of her appearance.

More hollow bravado. She was becoming quite expert in the art.

"I don't know your sister well enough to be familiar with her amusements—apart from chasing the next hand of cards."

"You judge her harshly." She bit back the impulse to tell Merrick that her sister hadn't always been the brittle, supercilious creature he knew. When they were children, Roberta's affection had been Sidonie's only refuge against their mother's indifference and their father's contempt.

He shrugged. "She was a means to an end."

Sidonie's lips tightened. "That puts me in my place."

He skimmed the back of his gloved hand under her chin. "You're in a different category altogether, *bella*."

The caress—if such fleeting contact justified the name—lasted a mere second but she felt it to her toes. This absurd physical awareness heightened rather than ebbed with familiarity. "Yes, I've agreed not to fight you," she said with a bitter edge.

"The day's too fine to quarrel," he said lightly. "Let me help you into the saddle. Kismet grows restless."

When he grabbed her around the waist, she waited for his hands to linger, to stray, but he merely tossed her into the sidesaddle with breathtaking ease. The beautiful horse sidled then settled at a reassuring word from Jonas. He had a way with females, Sidonie thought with another spike of resentment. Strange to remember Roberta describing him as so hideously ugly that he gave her nightmares. She tried to imagine what Merrick would look like without scars, but they seemed as much part of him as that sensually knowing mouth.

He stepped close enough to catch Kismet's bridle. "Still now while I adjust your stirrups."

He brushed her black skirts aside. She waited in quivering expectation for him to touch her legs but his hands were sure as they tightened the leathers. Something about the sheer competence of those strong gloved hands made her stomach jump. From Kismet's back, she had a fine view of his wild gypsy hair. It was pitch black and untidy and another indication that he insisted on the world taking him on his terms.

He shifted away and glanced up. "Are you cold?"

How she wished she could hide her reactions. "No."

She waited for some comment about her trembling, but he merely turned to collect his beaver hat from the bench behind him. Smoothly he rose into the bay's saddle and her heart slammed with admiration at his effortless strength.

Believe me, tesoro, *I'll touch you over and over again, in ways you haven't even imagined a man can touch you.*

She smothered the memory of Merrick's daunting promise and frantically sought some neutral topic of conversation as they trotted away from the castle. Difficult when every time she looked at him, she remembered him kissing her, touching her skin.

"Why do you tease me in Italian? I would have thought you'd speak—" Then she recalled that the world accounted his mother little better than a whore. The subject of Consuela Alvarez was likely off limits.

He arched a satirical eyebrow as if guessing her quandary. "You imagine I speak fluent Spanish?"

"Don't you?"

"My mother died when I was two. I don't remember her."

"Oh." She paused. "I'm sorry."

An uncomfortable silence fell. They crossed a wide green field, the cliffs to their left. The waves crashed upon the rocks below. Gulls on the wind cried like lost souls. Behind her, the bulk of Castle Craven squatted dark on the horizon. Even in sunshine, it looked a dour place.

The silence extended, became increasingly awkward. The horses' hooves landed dully on the thick grass. She was casting around wildly for something to talk about— the weather seemed too banal but a remark about the bright day hovered on her lips—before he finally spoke. "After I failed to make a success of Eton, my father took me to Venice to live."

Something in his tone indicated a complicated story behind the laconic accounting. There was so much she didn't understand, so much she wanted to know. Her feverish curiosity disturbed her. Merrick was a stranger. It would be easier if he remained so.

He went on when she didn't respond. "We rarely returned to England."

She could imagine why. She was too young to remember the original scandal of Lord Hillbrook and his imposter viscountess, but vicious gossip had persisted over the years. So much of the story remained mysterious, like how Jonas had earned the marks on his face. Sidonie was familiar with the basic facts. It was common knowledge that all his life Jonas's father, Anthony Merrick, protested the validity of his marriage. After his death, the Hillbrook title fell to William, Jonas's cousin. William, who married Roberta Forsythe for her dowry soon after inheriting.

Anthony Merrick had achieved posthumous revenge of a sort. He'd been one of the richest men in England and aside from Barstowe Hall in Wiltshire and Merrick House in London, none of that fortune was entailed. Upon Anthony's death nine years ago, Jonas Merrick had inherited vast wealth. William Merrick was left with two tumbledown houses, deliberately neglected by his uncle, and no funds to support the dignity of the Hillbrook title.

Since then, Jonas's fortune had grown exponentially. He was clever, determined, innovative, and ruthless. His wealth ensured grudging social acceptance, despite his illegitimacy. William careered from one financial disaster to another, until now he verged on bankruptcy. With every failure, his loathing for Jonas built to mania. So many times, Sidonie had heard William curse his cousin. His attacks upon Roberta became especially vicious after Jonas had bested William in some way. A reminder, if she'd needed one, of what was at stake here at Castle Craven.

Merrick veered toward the headland. Sidonie followed him down a gentle slope toward the wide sweep of beach. Despite the warm day, the waves were a gray tumult, thundering against the shore with malevolent force. Suddenly needing the release of speed, she urged Kismet to a gallop. For a sweet interval, there was only rushing, briny air and pounding hooves upon smooth sand. She heard Merrick behind her but didn't look back. For this moment, she needed the fantasy that she could outrun trouble.

A brief moment indeed.

She reached the debris-strewn end of the beach and reined Kismet to a quivering stop. She turned in the saddle to watch Merrick's thundering approach. The big bay reared to a halt behind her. Merrick's easy control over the highly strung horse shivered awareness through her. Those skillful hands that calmed a restless horse would soon touch her body.

As he leaned to pat the horse's satiny neck, he glanced up at her. A light in his silvery eyes indicated he divined the tenor of her thoughts. Of course he did.

"Feeling better?" That slight twist of his lips cut straight to her heart.

She blinked. Her heart? No, no, no. Her heart wasn't involved. She veered close enough to disaster bartering her body.

He saw her perturbation. "What's wrong?"

She bit her lip and chose dangerous honesty. "I keep forgetting you mean to destroy me."

If she hadn't watched so carefully, she might have missed the troubled frown that darkened his eyes. It struck her that, if Merrick could read her, she was learning to read him. This encroaching intimacy leached resistance, but she didn't know how to fight it.

"Nothing quite so drastic, surely," he said mildly. "This gothic setting plays with your imagination."

The gelding edged closer until Merrick's leg bumped hers. He reached to curl his hand behind her neck, tangling his fingers in the strands of hair loosened in her reckless gallop. Heat tightened her skin.

Oh, Lord...

Nervousness crashed through her like a landslide. That cursed promise to allow him access was a mistake, but it was too late to renege.

"Merrick..." She stiffened without drawing away.

"Jonas."

She narrowed her eyes. "Jonas, then. Let me go."

Holding her with gentle implacability, he loomed nearer. His answer was a whisper upon her tingling lips. "Oh, no, Sidonie. Never ask me to let you go. Not yet. Not before we've discovered paradise."

"Stop it." Her heart thumped so hard she thought it must burst.

"I would if I could."

She tensed against his grip. "Balderdash. You're just playing with me."

"Most definitely, *tesoro*. But your dilemma is your own fault. You're so irresistible and I find myself unable to... resist."

"Command your willpower, Mr. Merrick. Defeat this weakness."

"I try, dear lady. I try."

"I'll bite you," she said savagely, although she didn't move.

"I'll bite you too before I'm done." His gaze sharpened upon her lips, making her heart hammer a panicked warning. "Eat you like a ripe peach, all juice and sweetness. And lick my lips afterward."

She knew enough to recognize he meant sin. More than kissing, that was certain. For a rogue like him, kissing must be small beer indeed. "You're... you're frightening me, Mr. Merrick."

Although fear was only part of what she felt. License had never lured her. She'd never imagined she'd give her body to a man. But something about Merrick charged her blood with inchoate longing, despite what she knew of him and what he intended for her.

"Seize your courage, Miss Forsythe." He mocked her formality. Even she felt idiotic calling him Mr. Merrick when he was about to kiss her. Ruthlessness hardened his jaw. "No more preliminary skirmishes, Sidonie. Let's start the games. To the victor the spoils."

Chapter Five

Sidonie braced to revisit last night's chaste kiss. There was the same inescapable intimacy. The same reluctant delight. The same suspense, as if revelation hovered just out of reach. That had been disturbing enough. But this was...more.

The kiss was an unmistakable invitation. To what? She was too inexperienced to know. What she did know was that the slightest signal of cooperation would bring her more trouble than she could handle. As she had last night, she remained unmoving under his lips, hoping lack of encouragement would deter him.

A futile hope.

He took his time so that she moved through resistance to overwhelming awareness of physical details. The sleek texture of his lips. The soft flexing of his hand on the back of her neck. The mad race of her heart. The heat pooling in the base of her belly. This unfamiliar, unwelcome sensation lured her to sink into the kiss. Disturbed, she edged away. Kismet whickered and shifted under her.

"Shh," Merrick said softly.

"Are you talking to me or the horse?" She loathed the betraying huskiness in her voice.

He laughed softly. "What do you think?"

"I think you should stop." Her hands tightened on the reins, although she was careful not to unsettle her mount again.

"Not yet," he said mildly, even as the excitement glittering in his eyes set the blood rushing through her veins.

She gave a long-suffering sigh. "Get it over with, then."

His eyes sparked with the humor that rapidly became irresistible, curse him. "No need to beg, *tesoro*."

The grip on her neck tightened, although she'd immediately recognized the futility of running. She'd made promises to him and he still held Roberta's vowels. Kissing her stretched the boundaries of their agreement, but she'd known he plotted blatant seduction when he offered the bargain.

His lips rubbed across hers, pursed to kiss the corners, returned to suck subtly at her lower lip. More dangerously alluring pleasure blasted her. She made a muffled sound of distress, raising one hand to his chest. To push him away or draw him closer? She couldn't have said.

Her eyes fluttered shut and her senses flooded with Merrick. With his male scent, so alien yet so alluring. The emphatic beat of his heart under her palm. The firm warmth of his mouth.

When his tongue flickered out to touch where he'd kissed her, she started. What an odd thing to do. If he'd told her he meant to lick her, she would have been revolted. In practice, it was...intriguing. Another whimper escaped as her hand clutched at his loose shirt. The leashed power beneath the shirt should terrify her. Right now, that strength stirred curiosity rather than trepidation.

Already his kiss sapped common sense. She more than most women knew the cost of giving in to a man, especially a demanding, managing man. Witness her mother drifting like a ghost under her father's domination. Witness Roberta's helplessness against William. Sidonie didn't fool herself that Merrick's charm concealed anything but a will to be in charge.

She made an incoherent protest and tried to pull away, but his hold was implacable. Still he brushed his lips against hers. Pausing briefly here to taste more thoroughly. Lingering there. Without conscious volition, she pursed her lips. Just a hint of kissing him back. No more. Satisfaction rumbled deep in his throat. Her belly pitched as she realized even ceding so little, she ceded too much. Once more she tried to retreat, but it was too late. The hand at her nape flexed and brought her nearer. More heat. More gentleness. More kisses inviting her into the unknown.

By the time he raised his head, she trembled with fear, resentment, and unwilling sensual reaction. She sucked in her first breath in what felt like an hour and opened dazed eyes. He was so close, she had to lean back before his features came into focus. He watched her with an alertness that contradicted the kiss's leisurely sweetness.

"You shouldn't have done that." She wished she sounded appalled rather than beguiled.

The breeze played with her untidy hair, wafted strands across her eyes. Beneath her, Kismet was still. Merrick's bay nosed desultorily at some seaweed. A few feet away, waves crashed upon the beach. When Merrick kissed her, all she'd heard was her heart's wild dance. She'd been deaf to everything else. Including dictates of self-preservation.

With one gloved finger, he traced an invisible line down her cheek. Last night he'd touched her naked breast like this. The memory spurred the outrage she should have summoned when he started kissing her.

"Don't." She jerked away. Kismet shifted restlessly at her rider's abrupt movement.

"You've never been kissed before, have you?" Merrick didn't sound his usual mocking self. He sounded shaken. The silvery eyes were soft as autumn mist and his mouth was soft, too, full and so tempting it made her ache.

She blinked, horrified to realize she stared at him like a child entranced by Christmas candles. "What…what did you say?"

He regarded her almost tenderly. A warning clanged in her mind's distant reaches. Beware. Beware.

"You've never been kissed before."

She frowned, trying to make sense of the words. "Of course I have."

A skeptical lift of one black eyebrow. "Thousands of times, I'll warrant."

She flushed and her hands fisted on the reins as she fought the desire to slap him. "Well, once. You kissed me last night." Her voice developed an edge. "Or don't you remember?"

His hand slid under her chin and tilted her face. He

inspected her like a bizarre new species under a natural-ist's magnifying glass. "Of course I remember, *bella*. The memory haunts me. It's just that you're more . . . untouched than I'd realized."

Annoyance coiled in her belly that he dared to mock her inexperience. She tugged her chin free. "I don't make a habit of associating with unprincipled rakes. Why are you making so much of this? You know I'm a virgin."

"Oh, yes." Something flared in his deep-set silver eyes before he lowered his eyelids and studied her mouth. "But you're even more . . . virgin than I'd guessed."

"You can't be more virgin than a virgin," she snapped.

He leaned forward with unmistakable intention. She'd had enough of lying kisses and sarcastic teasing. She twisted to avoid him. Kismet snorted and sidled uneasily.

"Whoa there!" Merrick grabbed Kismet's bridle and the horse immediately settled. "Get down, Sidonie."

The brusque tone lifted every hackle that hadn't risen when he'd derided her awkwardness. "Just because I let you kiss me doesn't mean I'm about to lie down for you."

He was still laughing at her. "Even I'm not so presump-tuous, *bella*. But you're overdue for a lesson in kissing and I can't do the task justice when we're in danger of tum-bling on our arses."

If her face got any hotter, it would burst into flame. "I have no wish to suffer further tawdry pawing."

"Interest in physical pleasure is perfectly natural. Nothing to be ashamed of." He dismounted and tied the bay's reins on its neck so they didn't dangle. "There's no need to apologize."

Oh, she really wanted to slap him. Her hand curled in its glove. "I'm not apologizing."

He ignored her. "You must be burning with curiosity."

"I'm burning with the desire to box your ears."

He slapped the bay's rump so the horse trotted out of the way with a snort, then strode across to where Sidonie sat fuming on Kismet. "Repressed passion turns violent if unaddressed."

"Only if one is mentally deranged."

"I look forward to deranging you, *tesoro*. Now don't gallop away." He caught the bridle. His instincts were acute indeed. She'd been about to canter off. "Wouldn't you rather discover what you've been missing?"

"You just showed me what I've been missing. Such a lot of fuss about nothing."

"You weren't complaining a few minutes ago."

He still smiled. Blast him, he wasn't taking her seriously. Perhaps because, *blast her*, for one forbidden moment she'd been idiotic enough to kiss him back. "You caught me by surprise."

"Then this time consider yourself forewarned." He released Kismet and grabbed Sidonie's waist. She wasn't a small woman. Compared to Roberta, she was a lumbering draft horse. But Merrick easily lifted her to the ground.

"The horses will bolt," she said shakily, unaccountably wobbly on her feet with him so near. Her heart dived and swooped in her chest in a most disconcerting fashion. She was unbearably conscious of those hard, strong hands constraining her.

"If they do, they'll just go back to the stables and we'll have a walk back." As if to prove her fears groundless, Kismet sidled a few yards then stopped beside the bay.

"I'll run away," Sidonie said without shifting.

"I'll chase you."

"Why bother?"

He took her trembling hands and stupid, weak female she was, she didn't draw away. Danger clanged around her like a huge bell but she remained glued to the spot.

"Because you're quite beautiful, *dolcissima*," he said gently. "Don't you know that?"

Last night he'd told her she was beautiful. Before he'd stalked out in a huff. He sounded as sincere as he had then. Just as it had then, her heart slammed to a stop. "That's a rake's trick, to tell a girl she's beautiful."

"Is it working?" he said amiably, stripping off her gloves.

"No." She wished to heaven she meant it.

"Pity." He dropped her gloves to the ground and stripped off his own. "Damn it, you're always inconveniently overdressed."

Not always.

The thought hovered between them as if spoken aloud. She was free to run; he no longer held her. Go, go, she told her feet, but they stubbornly refused to budge. "I don't find it inconvenient at all."

"Another regrettable sign of innocence. One day you'll be grateful I showed you the ropes."

Her lips flattened in disapproval. "This is a public service?"

She wished she didn't like his laugh. Every time she heard that deep, musical rumble, another brick crumbled from her defenses. "A chap has a duty to his fellow man."

"They'll probably give you a medal," she said faintly as his hands framed her face. Sucking in a shaky breath, she exhorted herself to be strong. She strove to stiffen a backbone that showed a lamentable tendency to curve in his direction.

His palms were warm against her cheeks. "A knighthood at the very least."

"For services to womankind." She tried to sound sarcastic but the words emerged on a burst of breathless excitement.

A light flared in his gray eyes. "Oh, I intend to service you, *bella*." Before she mustered another unconvincing protest, he lowered his lips to hers.

Heat. Softness. Trembling uncertainty. A hidden longing to respond. Jonas tasted all of that when he dipped his lips to Sidonie's. He couldn't say why he was so deeply moved to be the first man to kiss her. His cock swelled to attention. Her merest presence aroused him. It had from the first. Whatever power she possessed, he was helpless against it.

Experimentally, he nibbled, licked at the seam. She was bewitching. Even now when she conceded little more than she had when he'd kissed her last night. She quivered under his hands. He still wasn't sure whether she was excited or frightened. He'd read both curiosity and dread in her pansy eyes. Her thick tortoiseshell hair tickled his fingers. After her wild ride, she looked enchantingly disheveled. It made him contemplate other wild rides he'd like to take with her.

Raising his head, he stared at her. Her eyes were shut and her lashes fluttered against flushed cheeks. His nostrils flared as he drew in the evocative scents of the sea and Sidonie.

"Open your mouth, *tesoro*." He angled her face higher. "Open your mouth for me."

At his raw demand, her eyes flared wide. For a drunken moment, he drowned in glorious brown, rich, autumnal, sensual.

"O-open...?"

He took advantage and claimed her, sliding his tongue into the interior. She made a sound of surprise and tried to back off. "No."

"*Bella,* don't be afraid."

She stopped edging away but her lips closed against him again. He returned to demanding nothing more than her stillness. She stood unresponsive, although her choppy breathing indicated she was far from unmoved. She resisted to the point where he thought he'd run mad with wanting her.

Just resistance, resistance, resistance. Endless resistance.

Then in the space between one second and the next, endless resistance dissolved. Her hand curved around his shoulder. On a sigh, she leaned into him. Warmth powerful enough to melt the chill from his obsidian heart enveloped him. The hand on his shoulder flexed into a caress. Her lips parted and at last gave up the honey within. Luxuriously he savored her mouth. She was delicious. His tongue flickered over hers and he heard a smothered protest.

If he had an ounce of charity in his soul, he'd release her. But her flavor was as addictive as gin to a toper. He'd blithely imagined he'd keep his head during this impromptu lesson. Instead she made a mockery of arrogance. She who had never kissed a man.

On a long, languid exploration, he stroked her tongue.

This time, he felt faint movement in return. He released a low growl of approval and teased her again. When she tentatively brushed her tongue against his, the surge of arousal nearly blew his head off. He, the worldly libertine, brought to his knees by an innocent's clumsy kiss. Except now she cooperated, she wasn't clumsy. She was sweet and passionate and quick to follow his lead. When his tongue danced along her lips, she copied his action. When he sucked her tongue into his mouth, she gasped with surprise then tasted him so deeply and with such unalloyed pleasure, his heart crashed against his ribs.

Even in the throes of delight, he held to strategy. His hands ached to touch her body, trace every curve and hollow. But if he pushed too far, he'd lose any advantage he'd gained. Heat rose, threatened to incinerate him. Still some distant voice in his mind reminded him this was meant as a lesson only. His arms loosened, although he couldn't summon the will to release her completely. Gradually he doused frantic passion until his mouth glanced across hers in an echo of his first kiss. Except now he knew her taste. He knew the tiny breathless sounds she made when surrendering to dark delight.

She'd be magnificent in his bed.

He chanced once last touch of his mouth to hers then drew away. She was flushed and her lips were red and moist. Her glowing beauty made his heart stumble. A man with one ounce of principle would send her on her way with Roberta's vowels safely folded in her reticule. If Sidonie stayed, Jonas would tarnish her shining goodness. He'd drag this angel down to share his hell.

"Oh, my," she whispered, staring up with eyes more gold than brown.

"Oh, my, indeed." He smiled, he feared, with drunken joy rather than the cynical amusement with which he usually confronted the world.

"If I'd known a kiss was like that—"

He loved how she didn't pretend she hadn't enjoyed the kiss, purely for pride's sake. The problem rapidly became finding something he didn't like about her. "You'd have kissed every man in your vicinity?"

A shaking hand brushed her hair from her face. He saw she gradually returned to reality and discomfiting comprehension of how thoroughly she'd succumbed to his kiss. "Well, perhaps every man under forty."

He was only human. "Shall we do it again?"

She cast him a disapproving look, marred by the tender fullness of her lips. "When you kiss me, I can't think."

"That's good."

"I need to think."

He laughed softly. "Think inside. I don't fancy a dousing. The weather's closing in."

"Oh," she said on a gasp of surprise, glancing around. Another shock of arousal jolted him as he realized she'd been so focused on him that she hadn't noticed the change from sunshine to approaching storm.

He easily caught the horses and tossed her up into the saddle. Loving the way the wind played merry hell with her chignon, he smiled at her as he mounted Casimir. "It's a pleasure to see a pretty woman sitting well on a good horse."

She blushed. How had such a gorgeous creature lived twenty-four years without becoming inured to compliments? She'd leave Castle Craven knowing how spectacular she was. He stifled a disagreeable pang at the prospect of her departure and urged Casimir to a gallop. Behind him, he heard her shout encouragement to Kismet. Ahead of a rising wind, they pelted along the beach.

Jonas had started this battle confident of victory, but he had a sinking feeling he'd end up surrendering as much to Sidonie as she surrendered to him. Damn it, he wasn't sure he could afford the sacrifice.

Chapter Six

A nother lobster patty?"

Warily Sidonie eyed the long, lean man slouched beside her on the brocade sofa, his legs stretched across a priceless oriental carpet in crimson and cobalt. Merrick hadn't done anything overtly seductive since he'd kissed her, unless one counted the lazy, heavy-lidded attention he devoted to her. Still, she didn't trust him an inch.

What she'd give for a nice straight chair, the more uncomfortable, the better. If she hadn't known Merrick would mock her mercilessly, she'd fetch an oak chair from the hall. Her back ached from the rigid posture she maintained against the temptation to sprawl. She suspected if she started lolling against the cushions, she'd end up lolling against Merrick. She knew her starchy attitude amused him. But last time she'd lowered her guard, she'd succumbed to his wiles with terrifying swiftness.

After their ride, he'd brought her to this sultan's bower of rich silks and velvets. Outside rain pounded against the mullioned windows but inside Castle Craven, everything was warmth and sybaritic comfort. Stained glass lent the light a sensuous dimness. Heated braziers scented the air with subtle perfume. This seraglio seemed incongruous inside the grim medieval fortress. Until Sidonie remembered idiosyncratic décor was the rule here. Think of the mirror-lined room upstairs.

Foreboding made her shiver. No, she didn't want to think of the bedroom. It reminded her of what Merrick meant to do to her there.

She straightened her back another degree, even as Merrick's eyelids sank lower. He looked half asleep but he remained alert to everything around him, including her increasingly frail resistance. Good heavens, he didn't have to watch her to confirm her vulnerability. Hadn't she just let him kiss her into a stupor?

He hadn't mentioned the kisses. Nor had she. But every time she met his glinting silver eyes, she remembered the shocking intimacy of his tongue in her mouth.

"You needn't keep pushing food at me," she said, even as she lifted the patty from the gilded porcelain plate. Everything delighted the senses. For a girl who had lived upon her brother-in-law's sufferance for years, and a not-too-prosperous brother-in-law at that, the luxury was overpowering.

"But it's marvelously entertaining." He smiled in a manner that made her want to upend her untouched glass of champagne over his tousled head. "You're so deliciously afraid that each morsel lures you a step nearer to ruin."

"It takes more than a few scraps to suborn me," she said stoutly. Before he could deride her unconvincing defiance, she bit into the concoction. "I see why you tolerate Mrs. Bevan's eccentric manners. What a pity she's forgotten cutlery."

Merrick sipped his golden wine. The pleasure on his face reminded her of his expression after kissing her. Devil take him, *everything* reminded her of his kisses. "What a pity," he said with spurious regret. "Eating with one's fingers is so…primitive."

She blushed. He turned the most innocent words into an invitation to wickedness.

"Speaking of eccentric manners," he said lightly, raising his glass to Sidonie in a brief toast, "you're not in a pew listening to the Sunday sermon."

"I'm perfectly comfortable, thank you," she lied.

He sank his strong white teeth into a patty. "At least take the jacket off."

She primmed her lips and wished his taste didn't linger even after the delicacies. Curse him, she'd remember kissing him until her dying day. "As a prelude to taking everything else off?"

Amusement brightened his eyes. "Should the urge strike, don't mind me."

In truth, she was overly warm. Her heavy riding jacket prickled over the muslin gown. It might be nonsensical to hide her body when he'd already seen every inch, but after those soul-awakening kisses, she desperately needed defenses. To cool the heat of the air and his gaze, she swallowed some champagne. He rose to fill a plate from the sideboard and top up his wine.

"I've had enough," she said quickly, but Merrick ignored her and filled her glass.

"Try this." He fell to his knees before her and between

thumb and forefinger lifted a small square of nuts and pastry shiny with syrup.

The couch was so low, when he kneeled in front of her they were eye to eye. She retreated against the sofa. "Move away."

"So nervous, *tesoro*." He clicked his tongue in disapproval. "And me on my best behavior. If I promise not to kiss you, will you stop worrying?"

"I—"

He smiled and pressed the pastry between her lips. She struggled to articulate a protest, then shut her eyes on a low moan of approval. "Goodness, what is that?"

"Something I discovered in Greece. I insisted Mrs. Bevan learn how to make it." Gently he tipped Sidonie's glass against her lips until she drank.

She opened her eyes. He leaned near, too near.

"Something that good must be sinful."

"Sidonie, Sidonie, such a little puritan."

Shakily she took another pastry between her fingers. Eating from his hand made her feel like his lapdog.

"You were in Greece?" She nibbled at the pastry. The spicy sweetness no longer astonished, but it was just as delicious.

"You think polite conversation will keep me in line?"

To her regret, learning about him was more tempting than any bonbon. "One lives in hope."

Slowly he drew away. "My motto."

She inhaled, filling lungs starved of air. Her relief evaporated when he lifted one of her feet across his bent knees. "What are you doing?"

His hold turned ruthless before she could jerk free. "Making you comfortable, *cara*." A few flicks of skillful fingers and he'd removed her scuffed half-boot.

"That's not a good idea," she said, even as he slid the second boot away and set it down on the carpet beside its mate.

From his kneeling position, he regarded her darned cotton stockings with unmistakable disapproval. Stupid to mind, but shame at this evidence of poverty rose like bile. With shaking hands she tugged her skirts down to cover her feet. "I suppose you're used to painted harlots flaunting themselves in silk and lace."

His lips twitched. "Painted harlots? Your imagination runs amok." He inched her skirts up past her ankles.

Lurching forward, she slammed her hand down upon his. She realized her mistake when the heat of his palm radiated over her shin. "Mr. Merrick! You have no right to undress me."

"Only your stockings, *cara*."

"Permitting the removal of my undergarments exceeds our bargain." She wriggled free and struggled to stand. The squashy sofa proved appallingly difficult to escape. When finally she rose as clumsily as a drunken bear, it did her no good. Merrick caught her hand and tugged sharply. With an undignified bounce, she collapsed back onto the cushions.

"Do you play the lawyer again, *dolcissima*?" he asked over her gasp.

"Pretty Italian blandishments don't disguise ugly intentions." She hated how priggish she sounded.

She expected more mockery but he merely leaned back on his heels and caught her foot again. He stroked her leg up to the knee and back. "Not ugly, surely."

The heat of his touch penetrated her threadbare stockings and made her toes curl. She'd never considered her feet and ankles particularly sensitive until Merrick launched his gentle exploration. Her skin burned. Her heart raced with a dizzying mixture of fear and excitement. Her hand lifted to unbutton her jacket before she recalled that he'd misinterpret any removal of clothing.

He might be on his knees on the floor, but his assessing gaze held no hint of the supplicant. Instead he challenged her to throw caution to the winds and discover what he knew and what she didn't. "Take it off."

"You move too fast, Mr. Merrick."

His fingers drew another elaborate pattern from ankle to knee. "We have a mere week, Miss Forsythe. Time's wingéd chariot and all that."

Suddenly the relentless push and pull he practiced upon her was unendurable. Merrick lured her to deny everything she believed in return for the sheer pleasure of his touch. And for the sake of that half-smile tilting his mouth. Tears sprang to her eyes. "Please stop." She hardly recognized the choked voice. "For pity's sake, please stop."

He frowned and lifted his hand. "Sidonie, I won't take it further."

"You say that but you don't mean it." Hurriedly she shoved her skirt down. "And I fall for your tricks like the veriest moonling."

In helpless frustration, Jonas stared up at Sidonie from where he kneeled. Every second in her company stoked his arousal. He wasn't fool enough to imagine the fascination one-sided. She might say no, but her cheeks flushed with excitement and he couldn't forget how only hours ago she'd kissed him. Now that her backbone lost its forbidding rigidity, she reclined against the sofa like an odalisque. An odalisque in a superfine hacking jacket.

She should look ludicrous. What she looked was irresistible.

He gritted his teeth and struggled for self-control. The urge to trail his fingers up those slender legs to the treasure at their apex beat like a tattoo. But with every step she took toward surrender, her uncertainty grew. If he pushed her too far, she'd run. Roberta or no Roberta.

The promise of the greater prize made him set her foot down. Immediately she lifted her legs and curled them under her, out of reach.

"You know I mean to seduce you."

"I know," she said in a raw voice, wiping her eyes with the backs of her hands. He tried to tell himself he was too old and cynical to find the childish gesture touching. "I've always rather despised people who allowed passion to lead them astray."

He shifted to lean against the sofa, his shoulders resting near her bent knees. "Now you find passion is a ruthless master."

Her delicate scent wafted out to torment him. He couldn't sit this close without touching her. He twisted, leaning an elbow on the couch, and caught her hand. To his surprise, she didn't jerk away.

"Fit punishment for assuming myself immune." Her voice lowered. "Every man I've known has been contemptible. My father was weak and greedy and unable to countenance a contrary opinion. He was incapable of kindness or affection. While he didn't hit my mother, his tyranny turned her into a cypher until she just faded away and died when I was twelve."

"I'm sorry." He was. The Forsythe women had appalling luck with the men in their lives. And it wasn't as if Sidonie's entanglement with Jonas Merrick would do her any good.

"My father never ceased to blame my mother for only producing two useless girl children."

The picture of an unhappy family life that she painted was vivid, if heartbreaking. "Hardly your fault."

Sidonie shrugged with a carelessness Jonas didn't believe. "The only time he ever expressed an instant of satisfaction with either of his children was when William offered for Roberta. A lord for mere Miss Forsythe? Even a shabby, slightly questionable lord counted as a triumph. Our family wasn't influential and while Roberta's portion was respectable, she was hardly an heiress."

"The uncertainty about my birth blighted William's marital prospects." Jonas didn't hide his satisfaction. After all, William had blighted most of his prospects.

"William courted Roberta as a last resort. His original ambitions were much higher. But no magnate would waste a daughter upon a man who might be disinherited any time."

"Not that he has been disinherited."

"No."

He waited for her to continue, but she remained quiet. Curious, Jonas glanced up. She stared down into her lap and her lush mouth twisted with unhappiness. He wondered why. Last night she'd been ready enough to call him a bastard to his face. This namby-pamby reaction to his scandalous origins seemed uncharacteristic. "No need to step carefully. I'm accustomed to being socially unacceptable. I've had years to come to terms with illegitimacy."

Did she guess he lied? Because of course he did. His bastardy was a wound that never healed. When she finally looked up, Sidonie's brown eyes didn't betray derision. Instead they were veiled as he'd never seen them.

"It...it can't have been easy when you were raised as the heir," she said hesitantly, and to his surprise her grip on his hand tightened as if she extended comfort.

"Ancient history, *tesoro*. What use raking up old ashes?" His gaze fastened on her lips, soft, so soft. "Are you sure you won't let me kiss you?"

"I must be wise."

"Wisdom is an overrated virtue, *amore mio*."

She cast him an unimpressed look. "You're no expert on virtue."

"Virtue is my foe. I've devoted great study to it."

He watched her struggle to summon some crushing remark and decided to rescue her. "How did you sneak away from Barstowe Hall?"

"Roberta's help."

"Even so, surely some guardian must barricade the garden gate against swains vying to glimpse the fair Sidonie."

"William has been my guardian since my father died six years ago," she said flatly.

All desire to smile left Jonas. Instead, a sickening suspicion set his gut heaving. "Good God, don't tell me the blackguard hits you, too?"

"Jonas, you're hurting my hand."

"I'm a clumsy dog," he muttered, loosening his grip. "If he hit you, I'll vivisect the worm."

"William has never hit me." She stroked his cheek, the first time she'd willingly touched him. In her eyes, he saw a softness he couldn't remember before, even when he'd kissed her.

"Why should you be safe?" Yet as he stared into the beautiful face that conveyed strength as well as allure, he guessed why. Jonas was long past crediting his foul cousin with anything like shame. But under Sidonie's clear gaze, perhaps even William retrieved some vestige of honor.

"We mostly live apart." She paused and her earlier inexplicable discomfort returned. "I run Barstowe Hall with the pittance he sends. And there's always written work for a bluestocking like me. Lately, I've catalogued William's library." She spoke reluctantly, although Jonas couldn't imagine why. The subject was hardly controversial. She was as jumpy talking about her life with William and Roberta as she was when Jonas touched her. *Almost*.

"Anything interesting?"

She avoided his eyes. "Your father took all the valuable books before his death, as you well know."

Her existence sounded like drudgery. And lonely. But he made himself smile. "So what prompted my cousin's sudden bibliophilia?"

"He's selling what's left, of course. Surely you know how close to the wind he's sailing. The last of Roberta's dowry went earlier this year in some scheme for South Seas emerald mining."

"My cousin never had the touch in business."

She cast him a disapproving look. "No need to sound so smug. You know he's reckless to compete with you."

"If he'd cut his coat to fit his cloth when he inherited, he could have lived perfectly comfortably at Barstowe Hall." Jonas was deliberately disingenuous. William was a heaving mass of jealousy, conceit, and bluster. He'd never accept life as a quiet country squire while his bastard cousin turned the world on its ear. "The man's his own worst enemy."

"I'd feel no compunction gloating over William's disasters if my sister and nephews weren't plunged into penury with him."

"What about your penury? You're damned quick to care about the fate of Roberta and her brats."

She raised her chin. "In two months, I turn twenty-five. William's guardianship ends and I'll receive an allowance from my father's will. It's not much—a plutocrat like you would scoff—but it will establish me away from my brother-in-law's tantrums. I have plans for a useful future. I intend to set up a house of my own and teach indigent girls to read so they can make their way in the world."

The idea of Sidonie slaving her life away as a spinster schoolmistress struck him as a tragic waste, but he knew better than to say so. He'd caught the militant light in her eye when she mentioned the unappealing scheme. "I'm surprised William hasn't married you off. Especially if you already have a dowry."

"I meant it when I said I'd never wed." Whatever she saw in his smile, it discomfited her enough to make her try to shift away. He didn't let her go. He began to suffer the alarming fantasy that he'd never let her go.

"Not all husbands are like William. Or like your father."

Her expression turned bleak. "It's pure luck, though, isn't it? The law gives a husband ownership of his wife. I value my judgment too dearly to sacrifice it to another's. And there's no escape—the contract binds until death. A married woman is little better than a slave."

"Not an opinion popular at Almack's."

She shrugged. "For six years, I've lived as William's pensioner and watched him brag and bully. Even though my sister's dowry was all that kept clothes on his back. Unmarried, I'm at the mercy of nobody's mistakes but my own."

"Don't you want children?"

"Not at the cost of freedom."

He frowned. "Such a solitary path you map. What about love?"

"Love?" She spat the word as though it tasted sour. "You surprise me, Merrick. I doubted you'd acknowledge the concept."

"Astonishing, isn't it?"

He waited for some derisive comment, but she remained silent. Perhaps because of that silence, he lifted the veil on the bitter truth he never mentioned. Ever. "I'm not a fool. I've seen devotion. My father loved my mother till the day he died. His heart broke when he lost her. And his heart broke anew every time the world called her 'whore'."

Damn it, he'd said too much. Revealed too much. He knew it the moment he saw Sidonie's face whiten with distress. All his life he'd survived by standing alone, relying on nobody but himself. Yet these uncharacteristic confidences placed him even further under Sidonie's spell.

He needed to remember that isolation offered safety, whatever the appeal of pansy eyes and soft female compassion.

Chapter Seven

When Sidonie entered the dining room that evening, Merrick rose from the throne-like chair at the end of the table. He sported coat and neckcloth and looked fit to grace a London drawing room, if one ignored the uncivilized marks on his face. No wonder he regarded life as his adversary. He'd paid dearly for everything he had—and still the deepest injury remained. He'd been proclaimed bastard. Nothing could change that. Nothing except the knowledge she concealed and couldn't reveal without jeopardizing the people she loved.

His bitterness when he spoke of his parents still echoed in Sidonie's mind, although he'd immediately realized he'd spoken too frankly. He'd retreated to playing the pleasant, if acerbic companion she'd occasionally glimpsed since arriving at the castle. The weather had kept them inside all afternoon and she'd enjoyed exploring his library. But one look at his face now warned her he was again the predatory man who had terrified and infuriated her last night.

She was sick to her stomach of being frightened. Tensing, she glared at him. "Don't you like my dress?" she asked sharply, lifting her chin.

"Don't you?"

"I've never had clothes like this in my life." At some point since her arrival, he'd ordered some gowns from Sidmouth. She wore a dark green dress Mrs. Bevan had altered to fit.

"You could thank me."

She surveyed him without favor. "I assume a verbal expression of gratitude will suffice."

He winced theatrically. "Why, Miss Forsythe, you suspect ulterior motives?"

"Hardly ulterior."

She stood in quivering stillness while he prowled toward her. "Turn round."

"I'm not a toy in your playbox."

His smile held a hint of wickedness. "Oh, yes, you are, *carissima.*"

"This toy has spikes," she growled, not shifting.

"I'll handle you with care." He wandered around her in a leisurely inspection that seemed to endure an hour. Devil take him, he set the very air vibrating.

"Very nice." He stepped forward to straighten the blond lace trimming the disgracefully low bodice. With mortifying swiftness her nipples hardened. She hoped to heaven he didn't notice.

"The dresses are indecent," she said stiffly, the rich silk flowing against her body like water.

"But pretty."

She shot him another fulminating glance. His eyes lit with that unholy glint she'd learned to mistrust. "Admit it. It's a gorgeous dress and you look gorgeous in it."

"It's made for a courtesan."

He snorted. "What do you know about courtesans, sweet little lamb?"

She narrowed her eyes. "Knowing about courtesans is no character recommendation."

"Cutting." His smile reeked satisfaction. "Yet still you wear the gown."

"Mrs. Bevan took away my muslin."

"She must need a dishclout."

She didn't know why she argued. Who could object to wearing something so stylish? While the silk might cling to her body, it wouldn't raise an eyebrow in any London salon. Especially on a lady no longer an ingénue. "No respectable woman would wear this dress."

He trailed one finger down her cheek, tracing a prickling path of awareness. "But, *amore mio*, you're no longer a respectable woman. You're a monster's paramour."

Heat flared in her face and she jerked away. "Not yet."

The fascinating lines around his eyes deepened with the laughter that always warmed her to her bones, in spite of everything she knew about him. "Not yet? By Jove, you offer hope."

"Arrogant pig."

He pulled a heavy oak chair from the table. Reluctantly she moved forward. He might be a somnolent tiger as he regarded her with a possessive light in his gray eyes. But she could never forget he was still a tiger. His lips twitched. "Relax, Sidonie. I promise not to accost you over the buttered parsnips."

Instead of taking the master's chair, he chose a place opposite her. He reached for the claret decanter and poured two glasses. The ruby ring glinted in the candlelight. Tonight it didn't remind her of blood. It made her think of passion. She heartily wished it didn't.

Taking a deep breath to settle the wild ballet of her nerves, she raised the glass to drink. William's cellar contained sour, young vintages. This wine tasted like everything rich and forbidden. The warmth was a frail echo of the heat stirring in her belly as she looked at Merrick, watching her, always watching her. This afternoon's confidences, however unwillingly granted, had deepened the unspoken bond between them.

She struggled to return to the prosaic world, even if a prosaic world of gourmet food and luxury and a man whose every word promised seduction. "Tell me about your travels."

Jonas gently opened the bedroom door, his hand shielding a candle.

After Sidonie had left him with his brandy, he'd lingered for hours in the library, climbing up to the balcony, as if being ten feet above ground could change his perspective on an increasingly complicated situation. Deciding to cuckold William had been the simplest of decisions. Working out how to handle Sidonie Forsythe wasn't nearly so straightforward. He'd struggled to distract himself from thoughts of her waiting upstairs, but every book he opened blurred before his eyes. All he saw was the woman.

The woman who now lay sleeping in the shadowy bed across the room.

The looking glasses reflected an endless sequence of tall, dark men in scarlet dressing gowns. His face was indistinct, but after all these years, he hardly needed reminding of his ugliness. Still he couldn't break the habit of filling his bedrooms with mirrors. He'd started as a youth when a few of his more spiteful lovers had mocked his ugliness while he'd been lost to passion. He'd sworn then that no woman would catch him so vulnerable again. Later, he'd discovered other ways of distracting his paramours, but by then he derived grim entertainment from the perpetual reminder of his deformity in comparison to the beauty of his eager bedmates.

He wondered why his scars didn't terrify Sidonie. They damn well should. People he'd known for years couldn't bear looking at him. From childhood, his scars had marked him as a pariah, something wicked and inhuman to be avoided, not approached. Odd that this untried virgin remained so sanguine.

A draft pursued him inside. Quietly he shut the door. Still Sidonie didn't stir. How surprising that she felt at ease in his bed. She slept as trusting as a child in a nursery.

He prowled across to her. The time had come to lift the stakes in their contest. After this morning's miraculous kisses, he'd retreated to allow her to catch her breath. Eventually she'd stopped jumping like a scalded cat every time he ventured near.

His chicanery had resulted in some deucedly enjoyable hours. Conversation wasn't usually what he sought from a woman. He wanted one thing and one thing only, that instant of profound self-negation when he plunged into a soft, warm body. But in this as in everything, Sidonie Forsythe confounded him.

He stared down at her curled up in his bed in her champagne-colored robe. It was a cold night, but he wasn't naïve enough to imagine that was why she retired so encumbered. No, the foolish beauty imagined mere velvet protected her. Carefully he slid his robe from his shoulders. Usually he slept naked but as concession to her modesty, he wore a shirt and silk trousers. He blew out the candle and slipped gingerly under the covers, careful not to touch her.

"Jonas?" she murmured, rolling in his direction.

His heart lurched at her ready acceptance of his presence. The sound of his name in that drowsy voice made him hard as an oak tree. Her eyes remained shut and her lush mouth curved gently. A more optimistic man might imagine she was happy he was here. At least she didn't leap up screaming.

She made another sleepy, questioning murmur and under the noise of sheeting rain outside, he heard the covers rustle as she moved. The sound was beguilingly sensual, evocative of bodies sliding together. He tensed, waiting for her to send him to the devil, but she merely drifted back into unconsciousness. Perhaps his arrival merged with her dreams. He hoped so. Even more, he hoped her dreams were pleasant.

Closing his eyes, Jonas invited sleep to descend. Last night he'd managed little rest and today's fever of thwarted desire left him jaded. Unfortunately sleep proved elusive. Sidonie's nearness tormented him. The sweet drift of scent. The hint of heat spanning the carefully calculated inches between them. The knowledge that if he moved his hand infinitesimally, he'd touch her.

His lips stretched into a wry smile as he stared into the mirror above. It was going to be a long night.

*   *   *

Sidonie reluctantly emerged from a wonderful dream of warmth and safety. God help her, she was snuggling against Merrick as if there was nowhere else in the world she'd rather be. His arm was lashed around her, holding her close. Her heart somersaulted with fear and the sleepy languor drained from her body. How had she slept with her tormentor slumbering beside her?

She should be grateful slumbering was the only thing he'd done. She was certainly grateful he wasn't naked. He lay sprawled on his back and her cheek rested on his chest, the cambric shirt a fragile barrier between his skin and hers. It wasn't long after dawn. Feeble sunshine bordered the drawn curtains with gold. The storm must have worked itself out overnight.

Her first instinct was to run, before Merrick woke and found her so conveniently placed for seduction. She tensed to rip away from his grasp. Then she caught sight of his face and curiosity, more powerful even than fear, captured her. Without dislodging his encircling arm, she slowly rose to look along his chest to his face. Observing him without his knowledge was a luxury.

She'd imagined that like most people, he'd look vulnerable in sleep.

He didn't.

The angular bones remained rough-hewn. Nobody who saw those determined features would judge the man who owned them anything but a brigand. Dark morning beard on his jaw and cheeks heightened the piratical impression.

And his scars.

This quiet morning, they struck a discordant note.

Relics of an evil Sidonie barely comprehended. It hurt to look at those marks of suffering. She'd feel for any injured creature, but with Merrick, her reaction was more personal than compassion, stronger than outrage. Gossip was silent on where the attack had happened. From what he'd said yesterday, she guessed that he'd spent his youth traveling with his scholarly father. Perhaps he'd received his injuries in some back alley in Naples or Cadiz, or in a skirmish in a wild corner of the Balkans.

In wordless comfort, she rested a hand on his chest. Under her palm, his chest was hard, rising and falling with each slow breath. Lying like this created a heady intimacy. An intimacy that sapped defenses already under siege. Unwillingly, her gaze wandered to his mouth. Relaxed, it conveyed profound sensuality. That was no surprise. From her first sight of him, lounging like a great cat against his massive chair and sipping red wine, she'd recognized a man who appreciated physical pleasure. Unfamiliar weight settled in her belly as she imagined him focusing that appreciation on her when the time came.

If the time came...

Dear God, did she already concede victory? When everything she knew insisted she couldn't give in to him. There wasn't just the danger of losing her virginity, although she couldn't welcome the chance of having her sins exposed to the world or bearing a child out of wedlock. More powerful was the unreasoning conviction that if she surrendered, he'd sap the strength that had maintained her through recent, difficult years and that would steer her into a self-sufficient, productive future.

Merrick's eyelashes fanned against his cheeks. Black like the hair tumbling across his high forehead. Sidonie resisted the urge to brush those soft strands back from his face. When he was awake, she was too busy fighting him to betray such tenderness. Now, in this peaceful dawn, she ached to show him life offered more than cruelty.

Her longing to give him respite made her pause. He worked toward her ruin. He'd plotted to trap Roberta into scandal and disgrace.

He was…

He was the most fascinating man she'd ever met. He listened to her with an attention that fed her soul. He offered glimpses of a world she'd dreamed of discovering. He made her laugh. He kissed her as if he'd die before he stopped.

This weakening against her opponent was more frightening than waking up in his arms. She shut her eyes and whispered a silent prayer against the softening of her heart.

When next she looked, Merrick's eyes slitted open and he regarded her with an intensity that made her tremble. In the strengthening light, his expression was unguarded as she'd never seen it. Fleetingly she read yearning to match hers in his eyes, misty gray as he surfaced to the day. Asleep he hadn't looked younger, but he looked years younger now. His mouth curved into a welcoming smile that pierced her heart.

Then in a flash everything changed.

The softness evaporated as if it had never existed. She read unequivocal rejection of whatever he saw in her face. She must gawk at him like an adoring puppy. What price denials now? Leaden shame crushed her.

She shrank back. His arm tightened before she escaped. At the same time, he swiftly slid sideways so the bed hangings shadowed the face he turned away. The dawn light no longer illuminated his scars. His sudden movement was violent enough to shake the bed.

Lord above...

Her confusion dissipated. Usually Merrick flaunted his scars, daring the world to pity his disfigurement. This morning he hadn't had time to don his usual armor against curiosity or disgust. With a sickening twist of her stomach, she realized that for all his defiance, he hated his scars. Hated them to the depths of his being.

He'd despise pity so she lowered her eyes. Still tears prickled. Stupid, stupid girl. She couldn't stifle the longing to take him in her arms and comfort him against a lifetime of grief. An insane, dangerous longing.

"I must be losing my touch. If I polluted the purity of your bed, I was sure you'd howl your lungs out," he said with familiar derision, at last looking at her directly. But after that revealing moment when he'd withdrawn so abruptly, she knew his careless manner was a defense mechanism.

The beautiful waking smile developed a mocking edge. She was a thousand times a fool, but she couldn't help mourning the change even as she went rigid against him. "You'll never make me scream," she said repressively, although her heart wasn't in it.

His face lit with amusement she didn't understand. "Don't be too sure, *bella*."

He talked wickedness again. At least his jibes reminded her of what she hazarded in this bed. When she'd agreed to save Roberta, she'd imagined a hundred perils. Violence. Ravishment. Cruelty. She'd never imagined that the riskiest element of her ordeal would be the wounded soul of Castle Craven's master.

"What are you doing here?" She fought to keep her voice steady.

"Not enough, obviously."

With those three words, the sweet morning turned dark and threatening. This time she made a more convincing attempt to withdraw, but Merrick pushed her onto her back with insulting ease.

"Let me go," she said through frozen lips. Her heart beat a wayward tarantella of panic and anger, largely with herself. Why hadn't she left before he stirred?

Keeping one arm firmly around her waist, he rose and slid his free hand behind her head to restrain her for a relentless survey. "Not in this lifetime."

Curse him. How she wished he wouldn't say harebrained things like that. If she'd been one whit less self-aware, she might take him seriously. Then where would she be? Fear wedged in her throat. It would be the outside of enough to leave Castle Craven not only disgraced, but burdened with a broken heart. Except she intended to leave heart-whole and scandal-free, she reminded herself stalwartly. And despairingly wished she believed that.

"This wasn't part of our bargain." She wished she could summon the will to tell him to release her in a way he'd believe. If she insisted, he'd let her be. She should be fuming at these games—she was, blast him—but still that damnable, reluctant tenderness lingered. Nothing erased the memory of his appalled reaction when he woke to find her studying him. She suspected that he tormented her now to prevent her dwelling on that stark instant.

His masculine scent assailing her, he leaned closer. She prayed for control, for common sense, for, God help the impossible wish, rescue. "There must be another bedroom."

He smiled in a way that made her wonder if he guessed how she struggled against her weaker self. "This is the only one fit for habitation. I wasn't preparing to host a house party, *tesoro*. I planned to entertain a mistress to a week of carnal bliss. Or rather I planned for that mistress to entertain me."

She stiffened as his hand slid languidly through her hair and fell to massage her nape. Sensation spread like circles on a pond. "You slept somewhere else the first night."

"The cot in the dressing room isn't designed for a man over six feet tall. I'll be damned before I let you exile me there again."

"Perhaps I could sleep there," she said with false sweetness.

To her surprise, his lips twitched. "Why do you challenge me, when you know I can't resist a challenge?"

"I hardly know you at all," she said, to remind herself as much as to put him in his place. She stifled the reckless urge to lean into his caresses.

"So why do I feel that you count every beat of my heart?"

She couldn't tell whether he was serious. If only she was so awake to his every thought as he accused. What she knew frightened as much as fascinated. What she didn't know left her floundering in an ocean of reluctant desire. "Stop playing with me, Merrick."

"You no longer want to extend the preliminaries?" He leaned over her, his big body pressing her into the mattress.

She wriggled without shifting him. "I want you to let me go."

"No, you don't," he whispered.

The problem was she didn't, not at her deepest level,

but she wasn't so lost to enchantment that she forgot what was at stake. She raised one hand to his chest to prevent him coming nearer. "Stop it, Merrick."

"Jonas."

She struggled to maintain her grip on reality. "Wicked, lying, licentious, scheming, manipulative, underhanded, wanton scoundrel."

"Say it as though you mean it." He leaned into her hand and slanted his mouth across hers. This time, surprise didn't paralyze her. Nor was she the innocent he'd kissed to daunt into incoherence. She knew the pleasure his merest touch sparked.

His hand relaxed to cradle her skull. The arm around her waist embraced rather than constrained. For one forbidden moment, she folded against him like a flower drifting across his breast. Then she broke the kiss and squirmed away until one foot touched the floor.

He caught her arm. "Don't go, Sidonie. You're safe enough. I only want to kiss you."

She cast him a skeptical look as she stood, shivering in the early morning cold. "Why don't I believe you?"

"Because you're sadly untrusting." He paused. "And because you're a clever woman."

He caressed the sensitive skin of her wrist. The leisurely stroking made her belly clench with longing, even as she recognized he sought to manipulate her back into his arms. "If I was clever, I'd have fled as soon as I saw you'd weaseled between the sheets."

He sat up, his shirt sagging to reveal the curve of one powerful shoulder. The sight of smooth tanned skin dried every drop of moisture from her mouth. Such a contrast to his marred face. She hadn't considered him handsome at first, even disregarding the scars. With every hour, his physical allure grew. Right now, she'd scorn a handsome man as banal. Idiot that she was, she'd discovered a taste for dark and dangerous and damaged.

Troubled, stirred beyond experience—and he'd hardly touched her—she wondered what had happened to the determined woman who'd arrived at Castle Craven to confront a monster. Only two days later and that woman hovered out of reach.

"Just one kiss, Sidonie. That's the price of freedom." He sounded sincere, not like the flirtatious devil whose bright silver eyes dared her.

Shock paralyzed her. It seemed too good to be true. She could depart with Roberta's vowels, almost as innocent as she'd arrived. Except that along with astonishment and relief, she experienced a twinge of invidious, unacceptable, undeniable disappointment. "You'll let me go back to Barstowe Hall?"

He scowled as he released her hand. "Are you mad? That wasn't our bargain."

"Oh, the bargain," she repeated soundlessly.

"No skimping, mind. Genuine enthusiasm."

One kiss seemed small price for escaping this room that bristled with promises of intimacy. "How do we measure your satisfaction?"

The seductive glint returned to his eyes and he reclined against the tumbled sheets with an irritating confidence. "*Bella*, I don't expect satisfaction," he purred. "Just a good-morning kiss. Nothing to scar you for life."

He used "scar" to flaunt his disfigurement. But she'd long moved past the stage where his scars struck her as anything other than tragic misfortune.

"Speak for yourself," she muttered, even as she gingerly kneeled on the bed. The mattress sagged, overbalancing her until she placed one hand on his chest. Heat sizzled from the contact, made her heart pound like a drum. His eyebrows rose in silent mockery as she snatched her hand away.

She trembled as he ran one hand down her plait. His fingers lingered tantalizingly on her breast before he withdrew. Her nipples tightened to tingling hardness.

"Good morning, Sidonie," he said with a tenderness she mistrusted.

Tenderness was the invincible enemy. The wave of feeling this morning demonstrated that inescapable truth. She could deny seduction. She couldn't deny his vulnerability. Except she couldn't deny seduction either, she admitted reluctantly, noting the slumberous light in his eyes.

He released her hair and folded his hands behind his head, tightening the lean muscles of his arms and chest. He looked like a sleepy pasha contemplating his nightly selection from the harem. For an electric moment, they stared at each other. Suspense coiled through her. He seemed content to let minutes dwindle like the bubbles in yesterday's champagne. She read expectation but nothing deeper in his eyes. He'd raised the drawbridge against incursions into his soul. The day's clear light proved less revealing than the shadows when he'd woken.

"Well?" She could no longer bear sitting like a mouse in a hollow, waiting for the hawk to swoop.

His eyes flared with unholy amusement. "Well, what?"

She clenched her teeth. "I'd like breakfast before it turns into lunch. Aren't you going to kiss me?"

Humor lines deepened around his brilliant eyes. "No."

Shock made her rock back on her upturned heels. "No?"

"You really pay no attention when you make a contract, do you, *bella*? That could get you into trouble."

At his superior expression, her hands clenched at her sides. She was in such turmoil, she wasn't sure whether she wanted to clout him or kiss him or run screaming from the room. "It's got me into trouble already. If I kiss you, can we dress and go downstairs?"

"A kiss in exchange for breakfast? How prosaic you are under that extravagant exterior, *tesoro*. Disappointing."

She ignored the compliment. She wasn't extravagant. She was perfectly ordinary. "Disappointed enough to send me away?"

"One would think you wanted to return to your humdrum life."

She frowned, again wishing she hadn't been quite so confiding in his sultan's bower. "I was safe there."

"Not if your sister's folly lands you in such straits. And with a man less…accommodating than myself."

"This is the first time she's done anything like this." Sidonie had long come to terms with her anger at Roberta. She merely needed to remember the way her sister concealed her bruises with a shame that wasn't her shame at all. She remembered William's unchecked rages. She remembered Roberta's two young sons. Sidonie had no choice about offering herself in exchange for Roberta. But Merrick was right; she was lucky. If he'd been the villain her sister described, the torments would be intolerable.

He smiled at her as though she were precious. Lying, lying smile. "You said it yourself—if *you* kiss *me*. Note the wording."

Nervousness made her stammer. "I won't. I can't. I…I don't know how."

More of that dangerous tenderness before a downward sweep of long black lashes veiled his expression. "You had several thorough lessons yesterday. I can't imagine the girl who sent me to the devil quailing at a little kiss."

She'd survived his kisses before. Scoffing laughter echoed in the recesses of her mind. Survived? Yesterday she'd positively thrived on his kisses. Meeting his gleaming silvery eyes, she shifted close enough for her leg to brush his flank. "All right."

It was just a kiss.

Chapter Eight

It was just a kiss…
Jonas struggled to maintain his careless air while his heart performed a Highland fling. However much he ached to grab Sidonie, he kept his hands by his sides as he stretched before her. If she guessed the pitch of his hunger, she'd flee the room. Hell, he wouldn't catch her before she reached Sidmouth. Deliberately he avoided dwelling upon that deplorable moment when she stared with unabashed curiosity at his nightmare of a face.

Her expression turned assessing. What the devil would she do? When she shifted again, he caught her haunting scent. She reached out and smoothed her palm down his arm. Under her tentative exploration, his muscles tightened to rock.

"You're so warm," she murmured, as if speaking to herself. "Like a furnace."

He tried to summon a reply but when she ran her hand

under his shirt and glanced across a nipple, words jammed in his throat.

"How interesting a man's body is." She combed her fingers through the hair on his chest. The friction spurred his heart to a wild gallop. "You're not at all like pictures I've seen of statues."

In spite of his extremity, a strangled laugh escaped. "Not at all."

She cast him a disapproving glance. "Pictures don't convey the size and power."

He restrained the urge to tell her about the size and power of one particular part of him. His hands clawed the sheets beneath him. "Damn you, Sidonie, put me out of my misery."

She studied him as if he presented a mathematical problem. Obscurely her calmness annoyed him. Blast her, she should be flustered. She should be all a-flutter to kiss him. "I think you should sit up," she said thoughtfully.

"At your command, my lady." He rose, piling pillows behind him.

After an infinitesimal hesitation, she pressed her hands to his cheeks. Automatically he flinched. He loathed anyone touching his scars. Hell, for her, he wished he wasn't scarred. He wished he was young and pure, gallant and worthy. When he was none of that.

She lurched forward and he drowned in womanly scent, warm and sweet with early morning. Then soft arms encircled his neck, velvet-covered breasts nudged his chest, breath drifted across his face.

Her lips met his.

Sidonie's brief confidence shriveled. Merrick's arms lay at his sides and the mouth beneath hers remained sealed.

She waited for him to seize control and sweep her into fiery heaven.

Nothing.

Trembling uncertainty built. Long enough for her to notice the smoothness of his lips. The soft hiss of his breathing. The heat of his body against her thigh. Tentatively she moved her lips, then started away at the tingling rush of pleasure. His mouth twitched at her skittishness.

"Don't you dare laugh at me," she said grimly.

"Never."

His morning beard rasped beneath her palms. She had access to a secret Merrick that the world never saw. More unwelcome intimacy. Somewhere since accepting his challenge, she'd abandoned all pretense that she did this for any reason other than the desire to kiss him.

Wicked, wicked girl.

"Blushing, Miss Forsythe?"

She refused to answer. Instead she studied his mouth. That mouth betrayed so much. Passion. Humor. A vulnerability he'd go to the gallows before admitting. She licked her lips as she remembered that mouth claiming hers yesterday.

Ah...

"You look like the cat that got the cream."

She delighted in his wary tone. "Do I?"

Without lingering on the scars, she caressed his face, then kissed each corner of his lips. He released a muffled groan. At last she seemed to be getting somewhere. Taking a lesson from him, she bit gently on his lower lip and sucked it into her mouth.

He tasted wonderful. Salty. Hot. Desperate. She traced his lips with her tongue, then lifted away to meet his silver gaze. "Damn you, Merrick, stop fighting me."

"You're not trying hard enough." He struggled for nonchalance, but his husky voice betrayed how her clumsy wooing stirred him.

"I'm just starting," she said softly.

Jonas braced for more tantalizing kisses. Containing himself when she tasted his lower lip had required every ounce of control. Blast and confound it, he'd promised to take the kiss no further. He needed to have his head examined.

She nibbled an excruciatingly pleasurable line down his neck.

"I think you're avoiding the business." Not even threat of damnation could stop his voice shaking.

She kissed his jaw. "Just preparing the ground."

This time when her mouth met his, he was incapable of denial. His lips parted and her tongue darted in to taste him. He groaned low in his throat. She tensed and withdrew. As if seeking assurance that he was a better man than she thought, she stared at him. Tragically he could offer no such confirmation. Even more tragically he wanted her so badly, he almost promised to change, to prove himself worthy.

This had started as a morning's game. Now all urge to tease vanished. And still the wordless conversation continued.

I want you.
You can't have me.
I need you.
You're not worthy of me.
That's true. Still you desire me.
Yes, still I desire you.

He heard her sharply indrawn breath. Then, slowly, oh, so slowly, she leaned in to place her mouth on his, soft as the brush of air across an angel's wing.

Jonas wasn't by nature a gentle man. Since violence had shattered his childhood, tenderness was unknown. Building his business empire had only fortified his ruthlessness. Since his father's death, he hadn't cared for anyone. He'd believed the carapace around his kinder emotions so thick, he never would. Sidonie's kiss stabbed straight to the heart he'd considered impregnable.

She flicked her tongue along his lips and this time, he let her in. On a sigh, she kissed him with unfettered pleasure. Sidonie was a quick learner. Damn him if she wasn't. Groaning, he yielded. His arms wound around her, dragging her down to sprawl across him. Until now, for all his seductive maneuvering, he'd been careful about scaring her. But she'd pushed him beyond restraint. She moaned and met his passion. He rolled her under him and hauled the covers off with a shaking hand. He couldn't remember the last time a woman had made him shake. Sidonie made him shake.

Smoothly he slid between her legs, the robe rucking up. Ruthlessly he shoved the silk nightgown aside until his hand met her thigh. He wasn't the only one shaking. In his embrace, she trembled like a leaf in a gale.

Very slowly so he didn't alarm her, he trailed his hand upward. The prospect of touching her center made him burn. His fingers curved over her mound and tangled in damp curls. He slid his hand into slippery heat, bathing his fingers in her desire. She gasped with shock and wrenched away, panting.

Damn it, too fast, too hard, too much.

"No . . . wait." Her voice was broken as he'd never heard it. She placed one hand against his chest. Under her palm, his heart flipped like a landed trout.

He placed his hand over hers. His voice was rough. "Are you content to stop there?"

She raised a troubled gaze to his face. Whatever she saw offered no consolation, he immediately recognized. His arm still encircled her. He'd need mere seconds to bring her against him. "Sidonie, give me your consent," he prompted when she stared at him as though he constituted her greatest fear—and greatest desire.

The uncertainty in her eyes intensified. "I can't."

"You want to."

A faint line appeared between her brows. "You're the voice of temptation."

He looked into her beautiful face, the heavy-lidded dark eyes, the flushed cheeks, the reddened lips he'd tasted so thoroughly. A plea surged up from his soul. "Relent, *tesoro*. Relent. And save us both from insanity."

She stiffened against his attempt to draw her closer and her stare was uncompromising. "You gave me your word the decision was mine."

He cupped her jaw. Those unwavering eyes continued to study him. *Oh, hell and damnation.* He surrendered with a sigh. "If you leave this house untouched, *amore mio,* we'll both be sorry."

The tension drained from her face and she softened in his hold until she was again the fluid, responsive woman who had kissed him within an inch of his life. This time he knew better than to restrain her when she slipped from the bed. He bit back an appeal for her to stay with him. If

his life depended on it, he couldn't say whether he wanted
her to stay an hour, a day, or forever.

Sidonie wandered along the beach, gazing out to the horizon. How could she have been so foolhardy with Merrick
that morning? She was lucky he'd kept his promise and
let her go. A man of his worldly experience must have
guessed how close she came to yielding, good sense be
hanged.

In spite of the sun, the wind was sharp. The sea was a
vista of whitecaps. Brisk afternoon breeze whipped her
hair around her face. Her half-boots crunched on the sand
as she marched away from Castle Craven. And its enigmatic owner.

Merrick hadn't joined her on her walk. In every way
that counted, he'd been absent from her all day. Since
their passionate interlude in the bedroom, he'd withdrawn, playing again the charming host, the interesting raconteur. Superficially his urbane manner remained
unchanged between today and yesterday in the library. But
she knew—*she knew*—he deliberately widened the gulf
between them. Briefly this morning, they'd shared more
than desire. Something breathtaking. Something of soul
as well as body. He'd since recoiled from all emotional
intimacy.

Discontentedly she bent to scoop up a smooth black
stone and toss it into the waves. The sea's ceaseless movement echoed her restlessness. Cursing her susceptibility
to a rake's stratagems, she collected a handful of pebbles
and pitched them one by one into the water. A stupid,
futile activity.

No more stupid and futile than knowing the damage a

man could do a woman, yet still finding herself lured to destruction.

With unwonted fervor, she hurled a silvery piece of quartz. It splashed sullenly beyond the breakers. She sighed and chewed on her lip. Her hand opened and the remaining pebbles cascaded to the yellow sand.

She had nothing to gain and everything to lose if she became Merrick's lover. Away from him, she knew that.

When she was with him…

The more he touched her, the more she wanted his touch.

Curse Merrick, he undermined everything she knew. Blinded by Roberta's tales of profligacy and ruthlessness, she'd expected Jonas Merrick to be a villain from a fairy story. Instead the man she discovered was more enchanted prince than ogre. Her heart ached for him. Even as every moment she spent with him set her conscience kicking like an angry mule.

Because with every moment, she lied. If only by omission. And the lie was a heinous one that if never exposed would shadow the rest of his life.

Sidonie could prove Jonas Merrick was the rightful Lord Hillbrook.

Cataloguing Barstowe Hall's library a few weeks ago, she'd discovered the lost marriage lines for Anthony Charles Wentworth Merrick, fifth Viscount Hillbrook, and Consuela Maria Albertina Alvarez y Diego. The document had been hidden inside a battered volume of *Don Quixote*. As Jonas's father had claimed, a traveling English clergyman attached to an Oxfordshire parish had performed the ceremony at Fuentedivallejo in Spain in 1791. The officiating parson had died before returning home. When the French sacked Fuentedivallejo in 1813, its archives burned. Sidonie had found the only proof of the wedding still extant.

Sidonie's hands fisted at her sides as she stared unseeing at the turbulent ocean. Heaven save her, she couldn't tell Merrick what she'd found. Not without abandoning any hope of rescuing Roberta from the violent hell of her life. William legally owned Roberta like he owned the sheep and cattle on his estate. If he didn't surrender his hold over his property, willingly or unwillingly, his wife was trapped forever.

Currently the marriage lines lay safe in Sidonie's London bank. She hadn't shared her discovery with Roberta— she couldn't rely on her sister keeping the secret. In a couple of months, armed with her legacy and this information, Sidonie would blackmail William into releasing his wife. Not that she trusted William to give up without fighting dirty. Sidonie's bankers had instructions to open the sealed envelope and publicize the contents if she suffered any mishap.

The day she'd found the marriage lines, she'd wanted to get Roberta away from William. But caution had swiftly prevailed. Sidonie knew enough of William's fondness for litigation to ensure the document's authenticity. Sidonie had written to the clergyman's former parish requesting confirmation of his Spanish travels and a copy of his signature for verification. No reply had arrived before Roberta played her disastrous card game with Jonas Merrick. In any case, Sidonie would still have come to Castle Craven. William's loathing for his cousin verged on mania. Even a threat as powerful as losing the title wouldn't save Roberta from her husband's retribution if he discovered she'd cuckolded him with his enemy.

Sidonie had immediately recognized that she was wrong to conceal the truth for her own purposes. Then she'd recalled William's latest attack on Roberta. She'd recalled years of abuse turning her lovely sister into someone Sidonie no longer recognized. Sidonie despised William because he was a cowardly bully, but she also loathed him because he'd stolen her beloved sister from her. Roberta, her childhood protector, had become lost in a world of her own, caring only for the turn of a card or the roll of the dice.

With the marriage lines, Sidonie could remove Roberta from William's influence and reawaken the warm, vibrant woman who must exist under the nerves and tantrums. The marriage lines would literally save her sister's life and offer a new, happier future to Roberta's children, Thomas and Nicholas.

But Sidonie hadn't yet met Jonas Merrick when she made these optimistic plans.

On that overcast afternoon at Barstowe Hall, stifling her qualms had been easy enough. As far as Sidonie knew then, maintaining the status quo harmed nobody in any material way. William had the title, much as he disgraced the family name; his cousin had the money. Any inconvenience the rightful heir suffered through losing his inheritance must have faded over time.

So Sidonie had told herself. So she'd believed.

Until she looked into Jonas Merrick's eyes and recognized how bitterly he resented his bastardy. Until her stupid, yearning heart burst to do anything within her power to ease his terrible isolation.

A few words from her and she'd change his life.

A few words from her and Roberta was condemned to lifelong misery.

A prickling behind her neck warned her she was no longer alone on the blustery beach. Slowly she turned from the wild sea. Merrick wore white shirt and breeches, but he'd made a concession to the chill by flinging a loose coat across his shoulders. He looked strong and virile. A breathtaking memory of how he'd kissed her that morning blinded her to everything but his presence.

He strode toward her, his boots striking the sand with hard purpose. "Have you been down here raining curses upon my head?"

She flinched at his question, although he'd spoken with his usual taunting humor. He was like a mistreated dog, swift to snarl to fend off a kick.

Oh, Jonas...

Her heart squeezed with agonizing compassion. He was so wounded, she wasn't sure anyone could heal him. Certainly not a chance-met girl who dallied a mere week. A girl who betrayed him with every breath. Her decisions had become so vilely complicated. The horrors she'd imagined waiting at Castle Craven paled to insignificance in comparison. She'd thought only to risk her body. Instead she risked her soul.

"Sidonie?" His eyes sharpened on her face.

"I don't need to be alone to curse you."

"I suspect not." He studied her as if guessing she hid something.

Of course she hid something. And not just that against every dictate of virtue and self-preservation, she wanted him.

As he approached, she saw that the distance remained in his eyes. She should be grateful. If he kept her out of his heart and soul, she was far less likely to make a fool of herself. That wasn't how she felt. She felt like he locked her out in the snow while inside he sat by a hearty fire drinking brandy.

He gestured along the beach. "Shall we walk?"

"Yes," she said, even as she shivered.

He noticed her discomfort. He noticed everything. "We should go inside."

Back to the house? Back to the unending, tormenting awareness that simmered between them? In a way, he was even more appealing under open sky with the wind ruffling his thick gypsy-black hair. But out here she was less oppressively conscious how every moment made surrender more inevitable.

"N . . . no." She loathed the betraying stammer.

"As you wish." He whipped off his coat. Heavy folds settled around her, swaddling her in warmth and a heady mixture of scents—horses and leather and the sea and, most intoxicating of all, Jonas Merrick. Wrapped in his coat, she felt wrapped in his arms.

She made a halfhearted attempt to return it. "Won't you be cold?"

He laughed as he strolled ahead. "The devil looks after his own."

She scurried to keep up. "I wish you wouldn't be kind," she said in a subdued voice, holding her wayward hair back from her face.

"I'm never kind."

"You never admit it at least," she muttered, guilt scourging her like a thousand flails. She had a troublesome inkling that if she weighed sin against sin, her trespasses against Jonas Merrick far outweighed his against her.

Chapter Nine

Jonas couldn't bear this. He whirled around to face Sidonie. "Don't deceive yourself that I'm a good man."

Shocked, she stared at him. Then her chin tilted at the familiar angle. "I think you're a better man than you believe."

His laugh was weighted with bitterness. "My sins condemn me."

He'd hoped to daunt her into backing down. He should have known better. "Name one. Confession is good for the soul, they say."

He bit back the retort that he didn't have a soul. Once he'd have said that was categorically true, but some rusty shreds of honor had scraped into agonizing life under Sidonie's influence. Why else would she still be virgin after nearly three days in his clutches? "*They* talk a lot of twaddle."

"You raised the subject of your wickedness. I just want to confirm how bad you really are." She paused to brush back the flyaway hair around her face. The breeze was strengthening. "Tell me just one thing you've done that puts you beyond the pale, then I'll leave you to brood romantically over your wrongdoing."

"Very droll." How he regretted challenging her. But then he remembered with repugnance the way she'd looked at him when he'd given her his coat. Strategy might insist he gull her into thinking him a decent fellow, but the prospect of her bitter and inevitable disillusionment made him cringe. Not for the first time since meeting Sidonie, he cursed that inconvenient, reluctant honor that hindered his stratagems.

"Have you killed someone?"

He could see she thought he fretted over mere trifles. "Not with my bare hands," he snapped, turning to stride down the beach.

She scuttled to keep up. "Tell me."

He wanted to consign her to Hades. Instead, he stopped and faced her. If she was so all-fired keen to count his crimes, he'd damn well tell her. But how to choose one misdeed from the hundreds to his discredit? "You want to know if I killed someone?"

She too halted, wisely keeping a distance between them. She probably guessed that he wasn't far from grabbing her slender shoulders and giving her a good shake. "Yes."

His eyes narrowed on her and his answer emerged as a supercilious drawl. "My dear, I've killed thousands."

Sidonie tangled her hands in her skirts, partly to preserve modesty against the brisk wind, partly to hide her sudden trembling. "I don't believe you."

That superior smile she'd learned to hate twisted Merrick's lips. "On my mother's grave, I swear it's true."

Swiftly shock subsided and reason kicked into life. She knew he played a game with her. A grim, grotesque game, for sure, but nonetheless there was some trick here. "How?"

His amusement evaporated and she saw he regretted revealing what little he had. "I'm not proud of this, Sidonie. Leave it."

No. No, no, no. This was the first time since this morning's kisses that she'd managed to breach the shield around his emotions. She wanted to know everything about him. Not so that she could hate him. She was tragically aware that she'd moved past the point where she could ever hate him. So much for her brave claim to despise the entire male sex.

"Jonas, tell me what you did," she said quietly, subsiding onto the sand under the headland and gesturing for him to join her. She wasn't sure he would, but after a hesitation, he sighed. He looked sad and tired. Whatever he had done—and she couldn't believe he'd really killed thousands—weighed heavily on the conscience he claimed not to possess.

He didn't answer for so long that she began to think he wouldn't. Then he sighed again and started to speak in a bleak, empty tone as if he described another man's experiences. "I've spent a lot of my life angry, Sidonie. Angry at being a bastard. Angry at the shame dogging my father, dogging me. Angry at William's blind arrogance. Angry at..." He paused and she watched his hand rise toward his scars before he lowered it again. "Well, you can imagine."

"You had reason," she whispered, but he hardly seemed to hear her.

"Even though my father was a rich man, I was avid to amass the kind of fortune that erased any stain of bastardy and scandal. I've since discovered there isn't that much money to be had. But I was young and still hopeful that if I couldn't gain respect as Lord Hillbrook's heir, I could gain it as a man who through his wealth held the fate of nations hostage. I wanted to be so rich that the world could never hurt me again."

Sidonie remained silent. The revelation that he'd defied his fate was no surprise. He was a fighter. She admired that about him but knew he was in no mood to accept praise. What he said indicated that he'd been scarred before he reached full adulthood. Curiosity about his disfigurement stirred, but she stifled questions. If she interrupted Merrick now, she'd never learn about his past.

"I wasn't too fussy about where I invested my money or where my enterprises found markets."

"You broke the law?"

He shook his head. "No, I was canny enough to stay on the right side of legality. But I transgressed a thousand moral laws."

"How?"

He shrugged. "So many ways. To give you an example, I aided the Ottomans in their oppression. They had gold. I had the materials of war. If I didn't consider consequences, the match was made in heaven. However, if I did consider consequences, the match stemmed from hell."

Profiting from the horrors of war. She could imagine how that weighed on his soul.

"What made you stop?" She didn't doubt that he *had* stopped.

"I went back to Greece after my father's death. I saw at firsthand what use my armaments were put to. When I returned to the village where I'd first tasted *baklava*, there were only ghosts to greet me. A Greek patriot had taken shelter from the authorities and the local *Sanjakbey* had executed every man, woman, and child in the place in retaliation."

How appalling. How sickening. Sidonie didn't bother pointing out that Merrick wasn't personally responsible for the bloodshed. Nor that he couldn't be sure his munitions had done the damage. That would be fatuous. "I assume you made reparations."

He stared out over the thundering sea, his eyes blind as he revisited old guilt. "You still try to see me as a better man than I am."

She realized that somewhere in his accounting, she'd reached for his hand. She tried to withdraw, but his grip closed with a firmness that belied his outward calmness. "Did you make reparations?"

His tone remained cold and detached despite the tension in his body. "What recompense can you make for a murdered family, a lost community? I stayed long enough to locate the scant survivors hiding in the hills and smuggled out those who wanted to leave. I send money to the few hardy souls who stayed. It's not enough."

"It's something. I assume you never again sold implements of war."

"I'd had graphic demonstration of the result of my rapacious greed. I decided I could live with less spectacular profits. The munitions factory in Manchester is now the world's largest fireworks producer."

Despite the seriousness of the moment, she couldn't restrain a gasp of admiring laughter. "Oh, that's wonderful, Jonas."

He stared at her with complete disgust. "Didn't you hear a word I just said?"

She frowned. "Of course."

He shook his head as if despairing of her good sense and stood, brushing the sand off with his free hand. Sidonie told herself to make some attempt to assert herself. At least pull her hand away from his. She tightened her grip. He clearly believed his confession would make her despise him, whereas so much of what she'd heard had been true to the man she knew. Right down to the final flourish of imagination in turning a factory forging tools of death into a firm producing materials of beauty and happiness.

How was she to resist him? Jonas Merrick was a man such as she'd never known.

From her place curled up on the library's window seat, Sidonie eyed Merrick where he stood before the shelves. This room was, in its way, even more seductive than yesterday's Turkish bower. Elegantly furnished as if transported whole from a gentleman's residence in London. Stacked floor to ceiling with books. Polished mahogany furniture. And circling the space high in the air, a charming balcony edged with a delicate gilt railing.

The dilemma tormenting her on the beach had given her no rest since they'd come inside an hour ago. One thing was clear. She must tell Merrick about his legitimacy. Roberta's plight was appalling but it didn't justify stealing this man's inheritance. Sidonie would have to devise some other way to save her sister. Misery weighed her down as she recalled that in Roberta's eight years with William, the marriage lines had offered the first chance of rescue. Nonetheless that wasn't Jonas's concern. By keeping the secret, Sidonie condoned William's theft of the rights and privileges of the viscountcy.

The door swung open and Mrs. Bevan stumped into the library. "'Ee has a caller, maister."

With a snap, Merrick shut the book he held. "I said nobody was to be admitted this week, Mrs. Bevan."

The woman didn't budge. "I bain't aboot to bid the Duke of Sedgemoor back on his pony."

Sidonie watched a strange expression flicker across Jonas's face. Not gratification but not precisely hostility either. "Where is His Grace?"

"Kicking his heels in the hall but he doon't look the patient type."

A grim smile flicked up the corners of Merrick's lips. "He's not."

Sidonie surged to her feet, horror and humiliation colliding in her belly. She and Merrick had been so isolated, she'd almost forgotten that she risked disgrace being here, not just for herself but for her whole family. "He can't know I'm here."

With a decisive gesture, Merrick slid the book back onto the shelf. "Hide on the balcony. I'll get rid of him as soon as I can."

As Sidonie skittered up the narrow, winding stairs to the mezzanine, Mrs. Bevan left to fetch the duke. Sidonie hardly had a chance to huddle against the balcony floor before she heard the door open again.

"Your Grace," Merrick said coldly. Something in

his voice made the hairs stand up on Sidonie's nape. He sounded like the man who had taunted her upon her arrival.

"Merrick," a deep voice replied in a neutral tone.

A barbed pause ensued. Curious, Sidonie slid forward to peep over the edge. From this angle, she had a clear view of Merrick's face. He was in one of his inscrutable humors, his expression set and the scars standing out vividly. All she saw of the other man was ruler-straight, raven hair and an impressive set of shoulders in a dark blue coat.

"To what do I owe the pleasure?" Merrick sounded like he lied about "pleasure."

"I was passing."

Merrick didn't dignify that answer with a response. Castle Craven wasn't on the way to anywhere. Sidonie knew that was why he'd chosen it for his assignation with Roberta. "I didn't hear a carriage."

"I rode up from Sidmouth. My sister Lydia has settled on an estate outside the town with her new husband."

The duke shifted and at last Sidonie saw his face. She muffled a gasp of admiration. He was breathtakingly handsome, with chiseled features, like a hero from a legend. His outer perfection threw Merrick's disheveled ugliness into stark relief. The two men were of similar height and age but there any likeness disappeared.

"So you decided to look up a fellow you haven't had a private conversation with in over twenty years?"

"Richard suggested I come."

"Oh, well, that explains it."

After the sarcastic rejoinder, another of those electric silences descended. Sidonie couldn't define the relationship between the two men. It was more complex than mere dislike or a meeting between incompatible acquaintances.

"Devil take your overweening pride, Merrick. I'd have left you to rot, but Richard insisted that I warn you about Hillbrook's threats."

This time Sidonie's soft gasp of dismay was clearly audible. Dear Lord, what on earth was wrong with her? Her heart thudding triple time, she cowered against the balcony floor. She prayed she'd ducked before the duke caught sight of her.

"What the deuce was that?" the duke asked sharply. She couldn't see whether he glanced up at her hiding place. "Have you got a woman here, Merrick? Is that the reason for sequestering yourself in this damned inaccessible ruin? When I went to your offices, it took forever to wheedle your whereabouts out of your head clerk."

"No woman worth her salt would endure Devon in November." Jonas sounded careless. Sidonie hoped his tone proved more convincing to the duke than to her. "Your imagination plays tricks on you, old man. Mice infest these old houses. Any rustles or bumps are purely down to rodents in the wainscoting."

The duke's lack of response indicated skepticism. Sidonie's heart raced at a dizzying speed as she waited for him to inquire further. Although surely that would be a breach of manners for the famous Duke of Sedgemoor. Even she, in her isolation, had heard His Grace was a paragon of decorum and virtue. He seemed an unlikely associate for the disreputable Jonas Merrick. But they must share some link of amity or commerce or why else was the duke here?

Merrick's voice developed an edge of impatience. "What's William saying?"

"He's threatening you with death and ruin, claiming he'll report you for sharp practices over that lunatic emerald scheme. He loathes you."

"That's hardly news."

"Are you saying you didn't bend the rules in dismantling the company?"

"Nothing likely to bring the law down on my head. Did I have a word in certain ears about the mines? Perhaps. But the enterprise was doomed to founder well before I shot holes in it."

Panic jammed in Sidonie's throat, choking her. Was William even now taking his frustrations out on his defenseless wife? She'd never been able to save Roberta from William's violence before, often as she'd tried, but it was torture to be so far away and not know what was happening to her sister.

"You're a dashed cold fish, Merrick." Sidonie raised her head in time to see the duke's expression harden into disdain. At least his attention was now on Merrick and not on any possible eavesdroppers. "I knew coming here was a waste of time. I've delivered the warning as I promised Richard. I'll see myself out."

Merrick sighed audibly. The belligerence seeped from his stance and he gestured to a chair. "Sit down, for God's sake, and take a glass before you go. It will be dark by the time you're back in civilization."

"Don't inconvenience yourself." But the duke subsided into one of the leather chairs and watched with a discontented air as Merrick filled two glasses from the decanter.

"Your health," Merrick said drily, raising his brandy to

his guest and leaning with apparent indolence against the massive desk.

"Your continuing health is the reason I'm here," His Grace said after a sip.

"My cousin has never hidden his wish to expunge the bastard filth from the family escutcheon."

"Richard saw him at White's last week. The man seems to be undergoing some kind of collapse."

"A financial one, anyway. He borrowed heavily to buy shares in the mines. My information is he has nothing left to repay his debts."

"He blames you for that."

"So he damn well should. My whole life I've done my best to ruin him."

"Which is no more than he deserves, whatever opinion I harbor of your methods." The Duke paused. "I can't help feeling sorry for Hillbrook's wife and children, though. They haven't wronged you."

Jonas shrugged. "It can't be helped. At least they won't starve on the streets like many another who made the mistake of investing in William's ramshackle projects."

Sidonie's hands tightened into fists. How could he speak so heartlessly of Roberta's sufferings and the fate of her children? After all, much as Jonas might hate William, Roberta's sons were blood kin to him. This afternoon he'd spoken with more compassion about Greek villagers who were strangers. The impulse to tell Merrick of his birth receded under a wave of sick anger. He sounded so smug as he spoke of William's ruin and Roberta's looming destitution.

"You mightn't be quite so sanguine if you heard the man."

"He's sworn to destroy me before." Merrick took an unhurried sip of brandy. "And as you see, often as he's tried, I'm still here."

"Richard seemed to think he was close enough to complete breakdown that the threat was worth heeding."

Dread oozed down Sidonie's spine. Dear God, let Roberta be all right. At least the boys were in school and out of their father's immediate reach.

"You and Richard might have saved my bacon in the past. It doesn't mean that as a result you owe me a lifetime's protection."

"I came here in good faith." His Grace passed Jonas his empty glass.

Merrick straightened in obvious dismissal of his guest. "And I assert my right to disregard your warning. I appreciate your concern, but I can protect myself against William's pathetic plots."

The duke rose and surveyed Merrick with frustration. "God forbid the great isolated monument to his own self-importance, Jonas Merrick, should accept aid."

A strange expression that might almost be shame or remorse flickered over Merrick's face. Yet again Sidonie realized that, despite the confidences she'd forced out of him over the last days, she understood very little about her mercurial host. "Through bitter experience, I've learned that I'm better fighting my own battles."

"Not always."

A silence fell, heavy with unspoken words that Sidonie could only guess at. "No, not always. But at least now if I fail, I go down alone."

To Sidonie's surprise, a short laugh escaped the duke. "Well, you've always been ready to beat your own path to hell. Who am I to offer you a rope to climb out of the pit you've dug yourself?"

"A damned presumptuous busybody," Jonas said without a trace of warmth to rob the insult of its sting. "Does it look as if William is taking his anger out on his wife?"

Furious denial made Sidonie clench her fists against the tiles. Surely Merrick wouldn't make her family's humiliations public. The duke looked surprised. "I didn't know he did."

Merrick shook his head. "I wondered if he sought other targets, seeing I'm presently out of reach."

"Richard said he could only rant about you being Satan's spawn and how he'd laid evidence with the magistrates. Apparently Hillbrook hadn't been home in three days when they encountered one another. He seemed to be hitting the brandy hard. Richard seemed to think..."

"Richard's an old woman."

The duke's expression hardened into hauteur. Even Sidonie's brief observation indicated that he was a remarkably self-contained man. Despite Merrick doing his best to taunt him, he'd maintained his equilibrium. "You're a dashed ungrateful sod, Merrick. But then you always were."

Merrick performed a mocking bow. "What do you want, Your Grace? Paeans of gratitude?"

"I told Richard you'd pay us no notice. You've paid us no notice since Eton. My conscience is clear. You, my dear childhood companion, can go to the devil under your own auspices." The duke turned on his heel and stalked from the room without a backward glance.

Merrick remained where he was, staring thoughtfully

at the closed door. Then he raised his head to Sidonie, unerringly finding her. "Was that edifying?"

"No," she said in an arctic tone, standing and negotiating the steps until she stood facing him. "You really don't give a farthing about what William might do to Roberta, do you?"

"Oh, I care very much what William does, *bella*."

She turned toward the door, too angry to bandy words. "I have to go to her."

He leaned away from the desk and caught her arm. "No, you don't."

"If he's losing his mind—and it sounds like he is—she's in more danger than ever."

"Last night, Lady Hillbrook was hearty and hale and enjoying herself prodigiously at the Nash ball. With her husband nowhere in evidence, you'll be pleased to learn."

Sidonie was too surprised to draw away. "How do you know?"

Merrick looked bored, but she'd discovered he assumed that expression as a way of concealing his thoughts. "I set a man to watching her after you told me William beats her. If anything untoward happens to Roberta, I'll know."

Sidonie hissed with scornful dismissal. "Don't lie. We're in Devon. Roberta's in London, miles away."

"I have a network of couriers and carrier pigeons all over England. News takes mere hours to reach me, wherever I am. Mr. Bevan runs a complex for the birds in the east tower. I can show you if you like."

"Oh." Sidonie's anger evaporated and she sagged in his hold as her knees gave way with relief to hear Roberta was safe. Again he left her utterly bewildered. But the duke's visit had firmed her intentions. She had no choice but to delay informing Merrick about his inheritance. She'd need the marriage lines to control William's behavior, now he faced bankruptcy. They were her only leverage against his temper. "Why would you bother? You don't like Roberta."

He shrugged. "It pleased me."

"So you already knew William intended to report you to the magistrates."

"Yes."

"But his behavior is erratic enough to send your friend down here."

Jonas's laugh was bitter. "Sedgemoor's not my friend."

"He obviously remembers you fondly if he's willing to brave the road to Castle Craven."

A spark of grim amusement lit Merrick's eyes. "We share a similar plight." He released her and subsided into the chair the duke had vacated. He gestured to the chair's twin at his side. "I take it you've never heard the gossip."

As she sat, Sidonie almost found it in her to smile. For a man without a legal name, he could be astonishingly lordly. "You know I don't get out into society."

"Even so, you knew all the stories about me."

"You're family."

"At Eton, Cam Rothermere, the man you saw today, Richard Harmsworth, who sent Cam on his futile mission of mercy, and I were collectively known as the bunch of bastards."

This didn't make sense. "But he's a duke."

"I'm the only one of the three officially declared a bastard. The other two are merely the result of questionable unions that have kept tongues wagging for years. Because their fathers acknowledged them, Cam and Richard

retained their rights and privileges. Cam's mother overflowed with such family feeling, she shared her favors
equally with the late duke and his younger brother. Nobody,
apparently including the duchess, knows who fathered
Cam, although at least his blood is unquestionably Rothermere. It's a complete mystery who sired Richard Harmsworth. His mother never admitted who shared her bed, but
when she produced Richard sixteen months after her husband left for St. Petersburg, her adultery was revealed. The
late Sir Lester Harmsworth recognized the child as his in
the absence of another heir, but there's never been much
doubt that he was absent at Richard's conception."

The anger she'd felt over Jonas's indifference toward
Roberta stirred anew. She surged to her feet and glared
at him. "I would have thought you'd be the last person to
crow over another man's illegitimacy."

He shrugged without rising. "Perhaps I appreciate having such exalted company on my dunghill."

"That's horrible. And mean-spirited."

"You sound disappointed, *bella*." His tone was snide.

She blinked away tears. She knew it wasn't the right
time to challenge him. Whatever his feelings about his old
schoolfellow—she still couldn't decide whether they were
cohorts or opponents—the duke's visit had left Merrick in
a prickly humor. "I thought you were a better man."

He laughed without amusement. "I told you I have no
scruples. Dark deeds built my empire, *tesoro*. If the dark
deeds harmed my cousin's prospects at the same time, all
the better."

"I'm sure it can't be helped," she said sarcastically.

"Ah." He surveyed her out of unreadable steel gray
eyes. "So that's what's got you all het up."

"I can probably blame you for each of Roberta's bruises," she said, not trying to spare his feelings. "The mention of your name turns William into a maddened bull."

If Merrick were a cat, his tail would lash in warning. "Do you hope for some expression of regret?"

She should step away and wait until they were both calmer. But some imp pushed her to needle him. "I'd like a return of the sister I remember, not the wreck she's become after eight years as William's wife."

He sighed and turned to stare out the windows at the encroaching night. His tone became less confrontational. "If it's any consolation, I suspect William would have beaten his wife, whether I'd existed as a thorn in his side or not. He's a born bully. Even before he officially became the Hillbrook heir, he was cruel to animals and smaller children. My father banned him from the house before he was seven for torturing a tenant's son with a branding iron."

Sidonie was angry enough to ask the question that had troubled her since her first night at Castle Craven. "How did you get your scars, Jonas?"

He glanced back at her, his features a mask of inscrutability. "The results of a misspent youth. I was attacked before I knew how to defend myself from those seeking my destruction. I've learned better since."

And those defenses were well and truly raised against her right now; she knew without him having to tell her. It must be as she suspected. He'd been scarred somewhere on the Continent when he traveled with his father. "Is that all you have to say?"

His stern expression didn't ease. "Yes, I think it is."

She marched toward the door with a dismissive flick of

her skirts. "Then I can only echo His Grace's sentiments. May you and your secrets go to the devil."

The beautiful, mobile lips twitched as he stepped forward to open the door for her. "I've been the devil's minion for years, *carissima*. Never deceive yourself on that count."

Chapter Ten

Sidonie's eyelids drooped with weariness by the time Merrick joined her upstairs. It was past midnight, and she still wore the blue dress she'd put on earlier. She sat up in one of the gilded chairs by the blazing fire, determined to stay awake. Never again would he catch her unawares as he had last night. She'd wanted to stay angry with him after the way he'd rebuffed her in the library but he'd been such an urbane companion over dinner, her barbs had found no purchase against his smooth facade. It was difficult to keep sniping at someone who returned no reaction to one's resentment.

Ostensibly she'd been reading for hours, but emotional turmoil scattered concentration. So much had happened today, her mind buzzed with questions and anxiety. Kisses, deepening attraction, confessions, the duke's visit, William's threats. And uncertainty about what would happen tonight. How could the rather insipid Edward Waverley hold her attention when fascinating Jonas Merrick might arrive any moment to share her bed?

After leaving the dining room, she'd made a half-hearted attempt to find somewhere else to sleep. But Merrick hadn't exaggerated when he'd described most of the castle as uninhabitable. Since their picnic, the Turkish bower had been cleared of furniture and there was no fire in the dressing room with its much-maligned cot. Even so, she'd briefly considered taking some blankets from the bedroom and sleeping there, until she realized it was the first place Merrick would seek her. Hiding only put off the inevitable. And she'd promised to remain available to him, curse him.

She heard the door snick open. Nerves jumping like grasshoppers, she raised her head from the book she wasn't reading. In his red robe, Merrick looked the soul of decadence. One hand curled around a half-full decanter of brandy and two crystal glasses dangled from the other. As he stepped into the room, the ruby ring flashed in the candlelight.

Insidious attraction rippled through her and her nipples tightened against her silky shift. "I hope you're not naked under that," she said before she could remind herself that his state of undress wasn't the wisest choice of topic.

The erratic humor that always caught at her heart lit his face to brilliance. As he smiled, his white teeth were startling against his dark features. For a breathtaking interval, she didn't see the scarring; she just saw a dazzlingly handsome man.

"Miss Forsythe, again you put me to the blush."

She prayed he didn't guess how her body hummed with awareness. She was appallingly vulnerable to him, especially at times like this when he wasn't acting the rake but was purely his provoking, intriguing self.

"I don't want you sleeping here." With effort she kept her voice even, although her hands were unsteady as she shut the morocco-bound volume and placed it on the mahogany table at her elbow.

Merrick wandered across the room with a casual air she knew to mistrust. He set the glasses on the dressing table and filled them. "Don't you?" he asked idly, approaching to pass her a brandy.

"No," she said with lamentable lack of force. She'd expected more reaction to her statement. Raising her chin with a defiance that felt utterly manufactured, she accepted the glass. "No, I don't."

The only sounds were the fire's crackle and the rain slamming against the curtained windows. The weather reminded her of the night she'd arrived, when she offered herself to degradation. Instead she'd found . . . what? She wasn't sure she knew.

With the same unhurried air, he chose the chair on the opposite side of the marble hearth and sat with a flourish of red silk. She noticed as his robe parted that he wore loose gray trousers beneath. Relief tinged her next breath.

"Very well," he said, still in that suspiciously mild voice.

This was all too easy. She drank to fortify failing courage, the brandy burning her throat. "So you'll leave me alone?"

A smile teased his lips as he raised his glass in a toast. She tried not to watch the working of his strong throat as he drank. She sucked in a breath, but still her chest felt constricted. Air suddenly seemed in short supply.

"Of course not. You'd be disappointed if I did." Laughter added such warmth to his words that she longed to extend her hands toward the heat.

Stop it, Sidonie.

"I'd live," she said drily. "You said you'd cooperate."

"No, I merely acknowledged your wishes."

"You'd make a wonderful politician," she said caustically.

"Come, *tesoro*. You know I won't leave you alone tonight. This morning I woke in your arms. It's a privilege I won't willingly forgo."

For one treacherous moment, she remembered how cherished and safe she'd felt lying next to him. When the last place she was safe was in bed with Merrick. Bracing her shoulders against the chair, she stared him down. She hoped he couldn't see past her stalwart exterior to her susceptible heart. This new uninvolved Merrick left her drowning in a morass of confusion. She'd lay money he wasn't nearly as tranquil as he pretended. When she met his silvery eyes, she saw the distance had returned. It made her want to scratch and kick at him until he returned to her.

Which was absurd. He'd never been with her. Not in any meaningful sense.

This was the third night from the mere week Sidonie had granted. Impatience tightened Jonas's gut. Cam's unwelcome visit had reminded him that he had only this short interval before the outside world shattered their isolation. Confound him for an arrogant dog, but he'd imagined she'd be under him by now. He had no difficulty reading the expressions flickering across her lovely face. Bewilderment. Irritation. Determination boding ill for his nefarious plans.

None the reaction he wanted.

He wanted melting surrender.

"You imagine you've got me where you want," she said sharply.

"You can trust my honor," he said, meaning it although he wished it wasn't so. This awkward chivalry worked against all his predatory intentions. "Until you say yes, you're safe enough."

After a revealing pause, she spoke. "I won't say yes." She sounded sure, but he noted how her hand clenched in her blue skirts.

The fire blazing at his back was damned hot, no matter that it was cold as an ice storm in hell outside. Or perhaps he should blame the heat on his rampant lust. Jonas slouched in his chair and released the shoulder fastening on his robe.

"A gentleman would—" Any stricture faded and her gaze seared the triangle of skin under his open robe. She looked at him as she'd look at her first meal after a month of starvation. She looked at him as though he were a clear pool of water in the Sahara. It was like she touched him, although she remained decorously across the hearth.

Oh, Sidonie, stop torturing yourself. Stop torturing me. What use virtue if it smothers all passion?

She blinked as if returning to the real world and he saw the effort she made to wrench her attention from his chest. She lifted her gaze to his face, but he knew she didn't really see him. His heart pounded like a drum and his grip on his glass threatened its destruction. If he'd guessed his nakedness would conjure this incendiary effect, he'd have run around bare-arsed the past three days. No matter that it was November and the wind off the sea cut like a saber.

He lurched forward to correct the slant of her glass. She seemed unaware of anything beyond the sexual energy blazing between them.

She blushed at his action and straightened against the

gold upholstery. He was a cad to delight in her confusion, but she had him in such a maelstrom, he was devilish tickled not to suffer alone. Her eyes were glazed, her cheeks flushed. She licked her lips, leaving them glistening and, oh, so kissable.

Her voice was husky. "Sir, I…"

Damn this. He stood and prowled across to retrieve her glass before she spilled brandy over her pretty dress. Her fingers trembled as she pulled free.

"Shh." He placed the glass on the side table. Ignoring her discouraging posture, he started to take down her hair.

She batted at his hands. "Merrick! Stop it."

"Calm, *bella*." He stood before her, blocking any escape.

"I won't be calm," she snapped, trying ineffectually to stop him spreading the mane of hair over her shoulders. It crinkled after its confinement and caught the firelight, shining gold and brown and red, the rich colors of autumn.

"Sir? Merrick?" he chided gently, reluctantly raising his attention from her cleavage and reaching for her hand. He felt the soft quiver of uncertainty undercutting her outrage. "You know my name."

Her voice resonated with wariness. "What are you up to?"

He urged her to stand. As expected, she pulled back against the chair. "Preparing to kiss you goodnight, *bella*."

She cast him a look of smoldering dislike, which did nothing to hide the hunger darkening her eyes to starlit black. "Please leave this room."

"Harsh, Miss Forsythe, harsh. Exiling me to a cold and

lonely chamber on a night that would freeze the balls off a marble statue."

She blushed at his profanity. "Mrs. Bevan will lay you a fire."

"Cruel as well as harsh. I'd lack the soul of charity to disturb her slumbers."

"You haven't got a soul."

He bit back the admission that if he had a soul, it had migrated into Sidonie's keeping. Tomorrow surely, with Lucifer's blessing, he'd return to his cynical, selfish, solitary self. He gave her hand a more determined tug and she rose, trembling. "Such pretty lips to say such nasty things."

Before she mustered a reply, he kissed her.

She stood stiffly in his arms, beautiful, slender, discouraging. Except in the last days he'd learned to read her responses. She'd tasted delight and the experience left her dangerously open to his caresses.

"Give yourself up, Sidonie," he crooned against her lips.

Still she stood silent and cold under his kisses. He stroked her hair, neck, shoulders, arms, deliberately avoiding her breasts. At last a soft whimper escaped. She shuddered deeply as the stiffness leached from her body. He'd prepared for more of a fight, but her arms circled his neck and she sagged against him with a sigh.

Triumph surged. Without giving her chance to protest, he swung her up and carried her the few steps to the bed. Carefully he laid her on the silk covers and came down over her, his legs bracketing hers.

Sidonie plucked discontentedly at his robe and he slid it off as he kept kissing her. Lips, cheeks, nose, breasts, neck. She made a sensual sound deep in her throat as her hands encountered bare skin. She stroked his back, up and down, up and down. The ache to bury himself between her thighs drove him to madness. Impatiently he reared up and wrenched at her dress. With shocking ease, the gown tore to the waist. The half corset and transparent chemise did little to hide her.

He nipped at her lips to keep her distracted. And because he couldn't get enough of her taste. Urgency whipped him onward. He didn't pause to savor, to enjoy. Although pleasure flooded him at every brush of her skin, every broken moan of surrender.

Jonas trailed kisses down her throat while his fingers drifted lower. Still he paused before touching her breast. Every second of this encounter was weighted with importance. He couldn't describe the feeling even if he wanted to. She curved her hands around his buttocks, digging her fingers into the thin trousers. He shut his eyes, prayed for control, prayed for skill to give her pleasure, prayed he'd survive the next hour.

When at last his palm covered her breast, she whimpered against his lips. Gently he rolled her nipple. She bucked and the pressure against his cock blinded him with scarlet need. She moaned his name, the sound lovelier than music.

He took her other nipple between his lips. Immediately his senses drowned in Sidonie's sweetness. She sobbed and arched. His hand meandered down to the soft curls covering her sex. Victory thundered in his heart. Vision faded to fiery darkness. Then fiery darkness exploded into light as he slipped his fingers between her legs. He groaned appreciation into the warm skin of her shoulder.

Carefully he slid one finger inside her. She was slick

and hot, but not yet ready, in spite of the ragged saw of her breath and the way her arms tightened around him as he invaded her body. He slid in a second finger, moving in and out. He kissed her again, tasting desperation, and brushed his thumb against her center.

She jerked and cried out. Holy Hades, she was sensitive. She approached her peak and he'd hardly started. He kissed her harder while his thumb circled and tormented. She tensed and heat welled over his fingers. For what seemed an eternity, she convulsed against his hand.

He'd never forget watching Sidonie cross the threshold of pleasure for the first time. Except for two flags of color along her cheekbones, she was pale. Her lips were red and full. Her voluptuous breasts trembled, the nipples beaded. When he was old and sad, he'd smile to remember that once he'd held Sidonie Forsythe and shown her the path to bliss.

He wanted to quote poetry to her. He wanted to tell her what this moment meant. He wanted...

But he was merely human and what emerged sounded like a rake's meaningless flattery, although he meant every word from the bottom of his worthless heart. "You're so beautiful."

His words shattered the spell of intimacy. Horror banished delight from her expression and her body straightened into rigidity. "Let me go," she said in a raw voice, pushing uselessly against his bare shoulders.

"Sidonie..."

She was past heeding him. Her efforts to shove him away became more frantic. "Let me go. Now."

He heard the seeds of hysteria and immediately shifted to the side, even as she continued to batter his shoulders. "It's not—"

He stopped, not sure what to say. It wasn't important? The problem was it was important. More important than anything in his entire misbegotten life.

Clumsily she squirmed away, bringing her knees high and cowering against the headboard as if she expected him to leap on her. With shaking hands, she wrenched her dress together.

"You took advantage." She sounded as if she loathed him. Even on the first night, she'd never spoken to him with such rancor.

"Sidonie, please..." All gifts of eloquence had abandoned him. Rolling out of the bed, hoping some physical distance would soothe her, he reached for her. She flinched away as though avoiding a blow.

"I'm so stupid," she said in a broken voice, then set a great crack in his heart when she wiped her eyes with shaking hands. Sod it to hell and back. She was crying. He felt like the lowest worm ever to crawl upon this foul earth.

"You're not," he said, even as his belly cramped with sick shame and misery. In an attempt to ease her grief, he dared to touch her arm.

That was a mistake, too.

She recoiled and scrambled from the bed. Panting as if she'd run a mile, she stood in the center of the room. She looked young and afraid and heartbreakingly vulnerable. Not at all like the siren who had measured the heights of pleasure only seconds before. The mirrors reflected a woman with eyes huge and dark as bruises. A woman who stood proudly even as her mouth twisted in humiliation.

"*Bella*." He stepped nearer even as reason told him she'd interpret any approach as threat.

"Don't *bella* me."

"I didn't mean to upset you." He was a blundering clod-pole with no idea what damage he did. Why couldn't she be an easy woman? Except if she was, she wouldn't be Sidonie Forsythe and he'd rapidly reached the conclusion that Sidonie Forsythe was the only woman he wanted.

"No, you meant to seduce me before I realized what you were up to," she said sourly.

He bit back another protesting Italian endearment. They both knew she'd fathomed his scheme.

She didn't wait for his reply. She cast him a hate-filled glare. "The pity is I always succumb. You touch me and my mind turns to custard. I don't know how you manage it, but it's jolly clever."

Her knuckles shone white as she clutched her bedrag-gled dress and backed toward the door. His great seduc-tion had disintegrated into complete disaster. She blasted all stratagems to dust.

"*Tesoro*..." Then he remembered she didn't want his endearments.

"Don't try and bamboozle me with cheap flattery."

How to make her believe that calling her his beauty and his treasure was the truth? "Where are you going?"

She inched toward the door. "Away from you."

"It's the middle of the night. This is the only warm room in the house."

Her jaw hardened with purpose and she regarded him as if he were a snake. Frankly he didn't feel much above one. "I don't care."

"Sidonie," he said as evenly as he could. "I swear I won't touch you."

"After tonight, I don't believe your word." She was almost at the door.

He stifled the urge to excuse himself. He'd promised to await consent before he took her. He hadn't really infringed the agreement. Except excuses were dry legalities. Ruthlessly he'd sought to quash her resistance.

"I'll go," he said grimly. Dear God, another night on the cot in the dressing room. He'd limp like an arthritic octogenarian tomorrow.

"No." She tugged on the door until it slammed open against the wall, making the mirrors rattle. Her repeated image wavered around them.

"Don't be silly."

Her glare should have blasted him to ashes. "I'm not being silly."

"You can have the bedroom," he said, then made the ultimate mistake.

A few steps to reach her and he caught her shoulder. He felt the fine bones beneath his hand and the soft brush of her hair across his knuckles. He also felt endless, unshakable rejection. He'd made a right shambles of this, bugger him for a benighted fool.

With a violence that shocked him, she struck his hand away. "Don't touch me."

She took a pace back, another, then whirled to dash headlong into the corridor beyond.

Chapter Eleven

Sidonie ran blindly, stumbling in frantic haste. Anything to escape Merrick and terrible, dangerous temptation. Reason disintegrated. There was only primitive instinct. All she knew was the need to separate herself from what he'd done to her in that elaborate bed.

Through the hallway, carpet brushing bare feet. Down the staircase, over the chill of stone. To the cavernous great hall with its ghosts and faded tapestries. Like a hunted animal, she darted through dark rooms, thankfully empty and easy to navigate. The main door was locked every night at sunset and was too heavy for her, but she could reach the grounds through the rear of the castle.

"Sidonie!"

From upstairs she heard Merrick calling. Part of her knew she acted like a madwoman and she should end her lunatic dash. If she said no and meant it, he'd leave her alone. She trusted him that far.

It was herself she didn't trust.

Not after those astonishing moments in his arms. He'd made her his creature and she couldn't bear it. She'd spent her life swearing she'd never become some man's slave. Yet she verged on infatuation with Jonas Merrick. A devilish, vengeful, damaged man. She needed to regain the woman she'd been before she arrived, and banish the wanton creature who moaned and writhed under Merrick's skillful ministrations.

She tore at the wrought-iron handle on the terrace doors. She struggled for breath. "Open, curse you, open," she sobbed, fingernails breaking as she scrabbled at the latch.

A flash of lightning revealed the key in the lock. Of course. With a shaking hand, she turned the key, shoved the glass door open, and dashed into the storm. Immediately, the wind barreled into her like a charging elephant.

"Sidonie, for God's sake, come back!"

Merrick's voice was nearer. She guessed he was in the hall.

"Sidonie, where are you? For heaven's sake, there's no need for this."

She couldn't look into Merrick's eyes and remember him doing...that. With a strangled sob, she banged the door shut behind her and stumbled into rain-swept darkness.

Damn it, where in Hades had she got to?

Jonas heard the door crash from the back of the house and his heart dived into his gut. Bloody, bloody hell—if Sidonie ran outside, she was in danger. More danger than he presented. Horrific images flooded his mind of her lying lifeless under the cliffs.

He grabbed a lantern from the hall. His hands shook as he lit it. Every second seemed an hour. He snatched up the greatcoat he'd left draped over a worn oak chair. Roughly he tugged it on as he rushed across the flagstones on bare feet.

Praying Sidonie hadn't got far on such a wild night, he dashed through the house and burst out into the storm. Freezing wind and rain pummeled him. He staggered and wondered how a woman, even one as stalwart as Sidonie, had made headway.

"Sidonie!" The howling wind whipped his words back into his teeth. He struggled to raise the lantern, to locate her. But the light offered feeble defense against inky darkness.

Hell, hell, hell.

Where the devil was she? She could have run in any direction. But he had a bleak premonition she'd head for the cliffs. Cursing, he slipped and slid across the lawn, hoping she'd gone this way, hoping she hadn't. Progress was slow and he fell on his arse more than once.

"Sidonie!" Good God, surely she must know he wouldn't hurt her.

But then she'd trusted him not to force her and he'd come damned near. For one breathless moment while she'd quivered under him in a climax sweeter than any he'd ever witnessed, he'd poised to plunge between her thighs. He was a savage. Guilt strangled his gut.

He should have left her alone.

The rain drenching his hair and pouring down his neck, the stabbing cold, all seemed inadequate punishment for the evil he'd done. It was too late to change what had happened. He hoped it wasn't too late altogether. "Sidonie!"

If she didn't make it back safely…

He refused to complete the thought. He'd find her. Or die trying.

When he lifted the lantern, he saw no sign of her. The gardens were large and overgrown. She could be anywhere. He shouted her name again. Nothing. The storm made such an almighty noise, perhaps she didn't hear him. Or perhaps she was too frightened to answer.

Christ Jesus, this was such a bloody mess.

Should he fetch the Bevans? But if she'd run ahead, any delay could mean she stumbled over the cliffs. He tasted sour bile. Surely any fall would be accidental. Surely he hadn't driven her to preferring a watery grave over facing him.

Sidonie was strong. She wouldn't be at Castle Craven if she wasn't. She wasn't the type to sacrifice life before virtue.

Was she?

Oh, dear God, what had he done?

Panic was a foreign emotion, at least in adulthood. But the idea of Sidonie harming herself made him crazy with dread, flooded his mouth with acrid fear.

"Sidonie!" he called again, but she wasn't here. He'd *know* if she was near.

Lightning transformed the landscape into a nightmare of silver and black. Staggering, calling, he battled through overgrown shrubbery toward the sea. Its roar rose over rain and wind.

Surely Sidonie would hear it too and stop.

Branches whipped and scratched him. He hardly noticed the stings. The greatcoat offered scant protection but he didn't care. He was big and strong. Sidonie was terrifyingly fragile against this weather.

Panting, Jonas broke onto the grassy area above the thrashing waves. He raised the lantern but the light penetrated only a few feet.

Jagged lightning split the sky again before he saw Sidonie standing a few yards away. In the white flash, he read the tension in her body. Thank God and all his angels, she wasn't near the edge, although she stared over the stormy sea as if awaiting a lover's return.

He sucked in his first full breath since she'd disappeared into the night. Relief made him lightheaded. She was alive.

She was alive.

Only now did he acknowledge how the idea of losing her to the rocks below had gashed his heart with grief. He'd sacrifice everything, even the hope of touching her again—and touching her was as close to heaven as he'd get—to keep her in this world. She didn't even need to be in *his* world.

He didn't bother calling again. If she'd heard him before—even over the storm, she must have—she hadn't answered.

Slowly, partly because of the gale blasting off the ocean and partly because he didn't want to scare her, he approached. The last time he'd scared her, he'd sent her careering into danger. He'd cut his throat before he did that again. "Sidonie?" he asked when close enough for her to hear.

She turned, her dark eyes glittering with what looked like hatred. She was pale and her hair clung like wet black satin. "Leave me alone," she said in a voice that cut through the lashing wind.

His belly clenched as she backed toward the cliff. Now

that he'd found her, his fears about her flinging herself into the sea seemed ludicrous. But the cliffs were treacherous and if she lost her footing, she could still come to disaster.

He started to reach for her before remembering the last thing she'd want was his touch. His hand fell to his side and he spoke with what calm authority he could muster in the middle of a thunderstorm. "Sidonie, come inside. It's not safe here."

At least she stopped edging away. The wind tore at her ragged clothing and she twined her arms around her chest. In a less watery setting, the glance she shot him would have incinerated him. "It's not safe inside."

He didn't contradict her. She wished him to perdition, but he couldn't leave her out in this tempest. He set down the lantern and tugged the greatcoat from his shoulders, swearing when the wet wool stuck to his arms. The wind caught the heavy garment and threatened to rip it from his grasp.

"Here." He struggled close enough to drop the coat over her quaking shoulders. It provided precious little protection against the howling gale, but it was something. She wore only her ruined gown. Torn to shreds, thanks to his vile impatience.

"You'll get cold," she said in that emotionless voice.

He managed a smile, although he didn't feel like smiling. He felt like shooting himself for a lumbering dunderhead. "I'll survive." Taking a risk, he extended his hand. "Come inside. Please."

She stared at his hand as if it offered hemlock. "I don't trust you."

Icy rain slammed into his body like bullets. "At least hate me inside where it's warm."

She straightened with difficulty against the wind and wrapped his coat more securely around herself. He expected a blistering response, but she remained silent. Then his heart cracked as she turned and picked her way over the sodden grass. She headed doggedly toward the break in the shrubbery where he'd forced his way through. He caught the pale flash of bare feet as she struggled for balance and another stab of guilt pierced him. She hadn't asked for any of this. She wasn't even here because of her own debt but because of her cackle-brained sister, who was probably tucked up safe and warm in bed. If not gambling with money she didn't have in some hell.

Jonas caught Sidonie as she staggered under a vicious blast of wind. In his grip, the sleeve of the greatcoat was soaked. He wouldn't send a dog into this weather. She jerked away. "I told you to leave me alone."

He tightened his hold and waited for her to regain her footing, even though she bristled with resentment. Only then did he release her.

He'd dismissed the greatcoat as poor protection, but wearing nothing but silk trousers, he endured the weather's full force. What bloody imbecile chose Devon in November for a tryst?

They staggered onto the lawn. The power of the wind caught Jonas unawares. Struggling to stay upright, he heard Sidonie cry out. He turned, the rain so thick it distorted vision. Through the downpour, he saw Sidonie crouched on the sodden grass, rain pounding down on her bare head. He'd reached the limit of his strength. Sidonie must be past exhaustion.

"Hell's bells." He set down the lantern and strode to where she huddled, her body forming a defeated curve.

This madness had continued too long. Whatever he did, she couldn't hate him more than she did at this moment. He braced against the wind and bent to scoop her into his arms.

"Don't touch me." She began to struggle but was too weary to make much impression.

"I've had enough of this," he snapped, firming his grip. "You can't make it back to the house on your own two feet."

"I can," she protested, but the memory of her fall was too fresh for defiance to gull him.

"I'm not standing here freezing while we quarrel."

"You're such a bully."

He sighed. "Give it up, Sidonie. I know I'm the big bad wolf and you wish me to Timbuctoo, but bear with the touch of my foul hands until I get you inside."

Jonas waited for argument, but she'd reached the end of her strength. His heart gave a great thud of victory as her cold hand curved behind his neck. Juggling wet coat and wet Sidonie, he collected the lantern. "Take this."

Without speaking, she held the lantern as steady as she could while he battled forward. She wasn't a feather-weight and with the wind and the saturated greatcoat, he struggled to advance.

The terrace doors banged in the wind as he shouldered his way inside. Sidonie reached past him to tug them shut behind them. Even though the storm lashed windows and rattled doors, the silence in comparison to outside was shocking. A silence heavy with a thousand things unspoken.

"You can put me down now," she said shakily, wriggling.

"Be still." His shoulders ached and his legs felt fit to

collapse, but he wasn't letting her go. He strode through the hall to the staircase, leaving a string of puddles behind.

"I can walk," she insisted.

He wanted to disagree. Then recalled how his recklessness had driven her outside. Feeling sick to his gut at his arrogance, he stopped and carefully placed her on her feet. Only to watch good intentions disintegrate.

She wavered, her eyes fixed on his face. He wished she wouldn't look at him like that. As though she expected him to fix everything. He couldn't fix a damned thing.

"Oh," she said on a soft gasp. Her frightened gaze clung to his as she crumpled with an oddly graceful movement.

"God give me forbearance." He grabbed her before she hit the ground. He lifted her again, his grip slipping on wet skin. "Don't argue."

"I wasn't going to," she said in a muffled voice.

His movements were clumsy with exhaustion. But he wouldn't relinquish her under threat of torture. Devil take her, she belonged in his arms, even if this was the last time he ever held her.

When Jonas entered the bedroom, he felt her stiffen. "No…"

She didn't trust him. He couldn't blame her.

Very gently he settled her on a chair near the fire. "*Bella,* you have no reason to believe me, but I swear on my mother's grave that I'll let you sleep in peace after I've got you dry and warm. Right now, you're freezing and wet as a herring."

She stared at him. He had no idea what went on behind that glazed brown gaze. Finally she gave an abrupt nod. Her teeth were chattering and blue tinged her lips. "Very well."

He helped her out of the greatcoat. Her hands were white with cold and her movements uncoordinated. Manfully he kept his eyes on her face, not the curves beneath her shredded clothing.

He crossed the room to grab a pile of towels from the washstand. He flung one around his neck and gently began to dry Sidonie with another. Apart from her shivering, she remained still as a doll. The first towel was soon saturated and he reached for a replacement.

When he'd mopped up most of the rain, he dropped the waterlogged towels on the floor and turned to the dressing table. Trying to appear avuncular and harmless, he poured her a brandy. He held it as she sipped, waiting until her hand steadied enough to keep the glass level. Then after roughly wiping the worst of the water off himself, he fed the fire until it blazed.

Slowly Sidonie came back to life from the silent creature he'd hauled upstairs. Color seeped into her face under the influence of liquor and heat. He knew he had no right, he'd promised to act the gentleman, but he couldn't help staring. An uninvolved bystander would probably say Sidonie looked a complete wreck. Her thick hair hung in lank black rats' tails. Under her tattered hem, her slender feet were scratched and filthy.

To Jonas she remained inexpressibly lovely.

She was always lovely to him. Despite valiant efforts to keep his emotions uninvolved, he'd become disastrously and irrevocably besotted with Sidonie Forsythe.

And it was too bloody late to do anything about it.

Too bloody, sodding, fucking late.

Chapter Twelve

Through a haze of physical misery, Sidonie watched Jonas rip a blanket from the bed. He held it out as he approached. "You need to get rid of those wet clothes."

She wouldn't have thought her blood had defrosted enough for blushing. But blush she did. To the roots of her sopping hair. How could she sit before him wearing hardly a stitch of clothing? She tugged uselessly at her torn dress, spilling her brandy in her clumsiness.

He rescued her glass and placed it on the side table. "It's all right, *bella*."

"I can't—" she said brokenly. Humiliating tears flowed down her cheeks. She huddled against the chair to hide her appalling loss of control.

"I'll turn around," he said gently. He untangled one of her hands from her rags and drew her to her feet.

"You're being very gentleman-like," she said on a dark tide of suspicion, although a hiccup spoiled the admonitory effect.

Instead of proclaiming good intentions, he passed her the blanket and turned his back. "Undress and wrap that around yourself."

In spite of her exhaustion, she couldn't help staring at his body. He might as well be naked. The silk trousers clung to taut buttocks and outlined powerful thighs and calves. He was so strong and alive, he set the very air around him singing. She dearly wanted to hate him, if only to displace the shame coagulating in her stomach, but it was impossible. He'd carried her so gallantly out of the rain and his care now filled her with warmth that contrasted with still freezing extremities. She shivered and curled her toes under her feet, rubbing them against the thick Turkey carpet to restore circulation.

Her clothes were in such a state that after a few quick movements, they slipped to the floor. As she gathered the blanket she cast Jonas a wary glance, but he wasn't watching.

Then she looked past him to the mirror.

She was about to curse him for a cheat when she saw his face reflected in the glass. Chilled as she was, eager as she was to preserve what remained of modesty, the blanket drooped unheeded from icy fingers.

Jonas's eyes were squeezed shut and he looked in excruciating pain.

Of course he must be perishing with cold. But this seemed like...more. This agony stemmed from something more momentous than mere bodily discomfort. He looked like all his dearest hopes came to dust.

The urgent need to comfort him lodged in her tight throat. She lifted her hand toward him.

She bit her lip and told herself she was absurd. Just

because she felt torn to ribbons after tonight's events didn't mean he was equally affected. Her imagination ran away with her. Still she studied the harsh, wretched lines of his face and couldn't help thinking that this man desperately needed succor, softness . . . love.

Love . . .

The word startled her from paralysis. Hurriedly she bundled the blanket around her shaking body. "You can turn around," she said dully.

When he did, the mask was in place. The kind, concerned mask he'd worn since bringing her inside. "For God's sake, sit down, Sidonie." He sounded as deathly tired as she felt. "You look about to collapse."

He prowled across to the washstand and dashed water into the basin with such impatience that it overflowed. As she slumped into her chair, he returned to kneel at her feet.

"What are you doing?" She remained mortifyingly aware of her nakedness beneath the insecure covering.

"You can't go to bed like this." He lifted her filthy right foot and began to wash it in lukewarm water. Curse him. He hid behind this gentleness. She'd caught a glimpse of his true feelings when he'd turned away. This act of playing nursemaid was false, false, false.

"Stop it, Merrick." She tugged her foot away.

He jerked his head up to stare at her in shock. "Dear God, Sidonie, can't I touch you even this far?"

His beautiful mouth twisted into a bitter line. His unhappiness shouldn't have such power to wound her, not after only a few days. But it did.

"I swear I mean no harm." His voice was hoarse with sincerity. He prepared to stand. "If you won't accept help from me, I'll wake Mrs. Bevan."

It seemed capricious to ask him to stay. Jonas was dangerous. To escape him, she'd fled into the downpour like the host of hell pursued her. She touched Jonas's hand before she remembered she meant to keep her distance, hoping to make him keep his. "No."

He frowned but didn't withdraw. She couldn't fault him for finding her behavior puzzling. After tonight, he must think her demented. Perhaps the rain had rusted her brain. She couldn't conceive of another reason for her shilly-shallying. "I don't want you acting my servant."

"Too bad." His smile lacked genuine amusement. "It's either me or Mrs. Bevan."

She extended her leg toward him. After a pause, as if confirming her cooperation, he returned his attention to her feet.

Finally Jonas dropped the cloth into the bowl and rose to carry it to the washstand. He returned with the last of the towels and began to rub her hair.

"Merrick!" she protested.

The friction sparked a heat in her blood that didn't entirely result from returning circulation. When he lifted the towel and she could see, his face was set in unyielding lines. He didn't look like the man who had laughed with her and kissed her. Or who had shown her ecstasy. She shouldn't want that man back. He threatened more than virtue. He threatened everything she valued.

She loathed the distance he set between them. In spite of the way he abased himself in unspoken apology. Because that's what he did, however he derided himself as a man without conscience. While she hadn't understood every emotion when she'd watched him unobserved, she'd recognized remorse. She cursed herself for a hysterical ninny, running away as though a mere "no" wouldn't stop Jonas.

"No" was something she was lamentably slow to say.

The blanket slipped, revealing the upper slope of her breast. Hurriedly she hitched the covering higher. He didn't seem to notice. She should be thankful he treated her with respect instead of like a sugarplum ripe for his devouring. Contrary creature she was, she felt piqued.

An hour ago he'd wanted her. Surely desire couldn't die so fast. She didn't know. She wasn't familiar enough with desire to judge.

Glancing at the mirror across the room, she stifled a dismayed cry at the witch staring back. No wonder Jonas wasn't interested. Her hair was matted, her face was a wan oval, and her eyes stood out like dark pools.

"Have you finished?" she asked, disgruntled with herself, with Jonas, with the whole world.

"Soon." He refilled her brandy and passed it across. "If I leave you for a moment, will you promise not to hare off?"

A flush heated her cheeks as she accepted the glass. She couldn't blame him for treating her like an ill-disciplined child. "I've run enough."

"Good to hear." He bowed his head in acknowledgment then left.

When he returned he'd dressed in shirt and breeches. His ministrations had definitely returned her to warmth and life. She even spent a moment regretting that he was no longer nearly naked.

Wicked girl.

He laid another shirt across the foot of the bed.

"What's that?" she asked suspiciously.

"I don't know where Mrs. Bevan put your nightdress," he said mildly.

"Oh." She was obscurely disappointed at his thoughtfulness. Of course she didn't want to sleep beside him naked. Except he'd promised she'd sleep alone, hadn't he?

Another pang of insidious disappointment.

He'd combed his unruly hair and it gleamed like black satin against his head. He reached for her hairbrush, set out on the dressing table as though this were her room. Whereas she was only a transient occupant.

She needed to remember that.

He stepped nearer and lifted the brush to her tangled hair.

"No." She jerked away. She didn't want more spurious consideration. She wanted the real man.

"Hush." He pressed his palm to her cheek, holding her as he carefully worked the brush through the snarls in her hair.

The room fell silent. The crackle of the fire. The soft whisper of the brush. Rain falling against the windows. The storm outside, like the storm between her and Jonas, calmed.

He brushed her hair until it was nearly dry. He had to reach forward to catch the brandy glass. Lazy delight swirled through her at the glance of his hand over hers. Each stroke of the brush leached away another layer of resistance. After all the fear and anger, she slid into a fog of languorous docility. Perhaps soon he'd take her to bed. Surely he hadn't meant it when he said she'd sleep alone.

He set the brush aside and lifted her into his arms. She murmured sleepily and nestled into his chest. She was warm. He was warm. Everything was delicious warmth. She smothered a yawn and shut her eyes.

Jonas . . .

She might have spoken his name aloud. She nuzzled his chest, drawing in more rain-fresh scent. She thought he growled softly in his throat. She wasn't sure. She was so tired, she wasn't sure about much.

He set her down on the bed, the mattress sagging beneath her, and pulled up the covers. His arms slipped away with what felt like reluctance and the loss pierced her drowsiness. She whimpered in protest and waited for him to slide in beside her.

She kept her eyes shut. Looking at him veered too near to admitting she'd stopped fighting. She heard him sigh. His clean scent flooded her senses when he pressed his lips to her forehead then briefly kissed her mouth.

She waited for him to join her in the bed.

And waited.

Struggling free of exhaustion, she opened her eyes to see Jonas methodically snuffing each candle until only firelight remained. In the flickering light, his expression was somber. He looked older than she'd ever seen him look before. She was so weary, it was difficult to summon real panic but she recognized something was wrong.

"J-Jonas?"

Without glancing at her, he trudged toward the door. "Goodnight, Sidonie."

Alarm shattered her lethargy. "What—"

Even as she struggled to stand, to follow him, he left her alone, the door sighing shut behind him.

The rattle of curtains woke Sidonie. Last night's storm had cleared to sunshine. She was by herself.

She'd only slept a few hours. Jonas's erratic behavior had vanquished exhaustion. When he didn't return, she'd gone looking for him. Eventually cold and lack of success forced her back to the bedroom.

"There be tea on the table." Mrs. Bevan shuffled around the room collecting last night's detritus. Damp, crumpled towels, the discarded blanket, ruined clothing. Sidonie blushed when the woman gathered the remnants of her extravagant gown, but Mrs. Bevan spared it hardly a glance.

"And good morning to you," Sidonie muttered. She sat, piling pillows behind her. She shoved the sleeves of Jonas's shirt up her arms.

"Maister said order the carriage when 'ee's ready." The woman still fussed around the room.

What?

"I...I don't understand," Sidonie said in a suddenly shaky voice that reflected her suddenly shaky heart. "Why would I want the carriage?"

Mrs. Bevan's shrug was remarkably expressive for such a taciturn woman.

Because she wasn't sure what else to do, Sidonie turned to the tea on the nightstand. Only after she'd filled the delicate china cup did she notice the bundle of papers tied with a blue silk ribbon on the tray.

Foreboding curdled in her belly. "What's this?"

Mrs. Bevan cast her a disinterested glance. "Maister said give en 'ee."

Sidonie's hand hovered over the packet as though it might bite. "Where is mais...Mr. Merrick?"

"Aboot." With that uninformative answer, Mrs. Bevan left the room.

Whatever was in those papers wouldn't give Sidonie what she wanted. She knew that to her bones.

She snatched the bundle. The papers were ragged and of irregular size. Frowning bewilderment, she ripped away the ribbon and unfolded the top document. She recognized Roberta's round girlish hand. All the messages were simple. And listed increasingly large sums of money owed to J. Merrick above Roberta's signature.

Her sister had lied to her.

Back at Barstowe Hall, the amount she claimed to have lost to Jonas had been appalling. The total of these promissory notes was astronomical. Beyond anything her sister could hope to repay. Beyond the value of everything William owned, even if he honored his wife's reckless gambling.

"Oh, Roberta..."

Then like a hammer striking, the full significance of the packet became clear.

Jonas had set Sidonie free.

Chapter Thirteen

Sidonie had always claimed she stayed only to retrieve Roberta's vowels. Jonas, with a magnanimity that should surprise her but didn't, returned the vowels unconditionally.

Go. Run. Flee.

Her practical self insisted she seize this chance. She'd got what she came for. She was free. More to the point, Roberta was free. Sidonie could return to her real life, set plans in train for Roberta's rescue and a new independent life for both Forsythe sisters. An independent life that unaccountably began to sound like bleak loneliness.

Nothing held Sidonie at Castle Craven. Nothing except the fleeting expression in a man's eyes when he believed himself unobserved. Nothing except shared laughter, the sizzle of a man's touch, and surcease from solitude that she only now realized had burdened her heart like shackles.

Nothing...

Perhaps nothing was what Jonas felt now.

Stubbornly she refused to accept that was true.

After a long, frustrating day, she feared she must accept it was true. By late afternoon, she recognized Jonas had no wish to be found. At least not by his houseguest.

Sidonie finally returned utterly discouraged to the comfortless great hall, wondering whether she'd neglected somewhere obvious in her search. In a shadowy corner, Mrs. Bevan swung a broom. Flying motes of dust caught the light through the narrow windows high above.

"'Ee may as well be gone," Mrs. Bevan said with what Sidonie interpreted as satisfaction.

"No," Sidonie said, even as she was tempted to preserve what remained of her pride and leave. After all, Jonas's absence made his rejection clear, didn't it? A sensible woman would read the writing on the wall and return to safety and the comforts of the familiar.

But she didn't want the comforts of the familiar. The tragic fact was that she wanted Jonas. She wanted Jonas with every beat of her heart. By returning Roberta's vowels, he'd changed everything between them.

She'd spent her life swearing that she'd never place herself in a man's power. After witnessing the way masculine dominance destroyed both her mother and sister, she'd vowed never to surrender body or will to male tyranny. But somewhere in the last days, she'd recognized Jonas as the one man in a million who wasn't a tyrant. She'd teetered on the brink of yielding for the last couple of days. His care and remorse last night had shifted the balance forever. And now that he'd granted her freedom by returning Roberta's vowels, she was impatient to rip away all barriers between them.

Native caution derided her as just another fool woman,

telling herself this time, this place, this man were different from other times, places, men. She ignored native caution. For once she intended to follow her heart rather than her head. She meant to become Jonas Merrick's mistress with a wholehearted joy that would have astonished the girl who arrived at Castle Craven.

She might be too late to tell Jonas what she wanted.

Or for him to muster a shred of interest in her confession.

"If 'ee wants to reach Sidmouth afore dark, 'ee must leave soon."

"I'm sleeping here," Sidonie responded with an obstinacy that didn't reflect the nerves bouncing around her belly.

"Please 'eeself. But maister said the young miss'd be away first thing."

"Maister doesn't know everything," Sidonie snapped, perching on one of the oak chairs lining the walls.

"Maister be riding. Set off afore cock crow. Oft he be away days." Mrs. Bevan delivered the overdue information, then paused in her housewifery to rake Sidonie with a disapproving scrutiny. "'Ee could sit till doomsday and he woan show to do eer bidding."

"I don't care," Sidonie said, her heart sinking. What if Jonas was gone for days? She couldn't linger as an interloper forever.

She'd worry about that when she had to.

Jonas thought she'd rush off the instant she got Roberta's vowels. Why would he imagine anything else? But as she read uncharacteristic pity in Mrs. Bevan's faded eyes, Sidonie couldn't dismiss the depressing knowledge that she was making a complete fool of herself.

Again.

*   *   *

"Be 'ee still here, miss?"

At Mrs. Bevan's question, Sidonie stirred from where she'd slumped in the hard chair. She stretched and winced as muscles complained after extended immobility against unforgiving surfaces. "What time is it?"

Mrs. Bevan's lantern made the shadows loom darker. "Near eight. Be 'ee wanting supper?"

Sidonie had hardly eaten all day but her stomach churned at the prospect of food. "No, thank you."

"I brung 'ee this."

Shocked, Sidonie noticed that Mrs. Bevan extended a cup of tea in her direction. "Th-thank you."

"Why don't 'ee go up to bed? 'Ee can't bide here all night. Maister may be away a week."

"I don't care."

"'Ee be a stubborn wench."

Definitely.

"If 'ee be set on waiting maister out, why not bide in the book room? It be warmer and I'll set 'ee a fire."

Some superstitious corner of Sidonie's mind insisted that she must catch Jonas the moment he came inside or she'd miss her chance and find herself on her way to Barstowe Hall after all. She couldn't explain this to Mrs. Bevan. Even to herself, it sounded irrational. "I'm fine here."

The woman's dismissive sniff indicated her opinion of that remark. "'Ee be mad as maister."

Probably.

Sidonie lifted the teacup and took a sip. The warmth was welcome. With nightfall, the temperature had dropped uncomfortably low. She waited for Mrs. Bevan to return belowstairs but she continued to stare at Sidonie as if she gawked at an exhibit at a fair. Or more likely Bedlam, Sidonie thought with a grim spurt of amusement.

"'Ee mightn't credit this but maister was the sweetest lad I ever beheld."

Not just a cup of tea, but confidences. What was the world coming to? Still, Sidonie couldn't pretend she wasn't interested. "Have you been with the family so long?"

"Mr. Bevan and I joined the late viscount's service just afore his wife passed. Sad days.

"The lad, maister he now be, were only two then. His old lordship were lost in a world of his own aften her ladyship went. Out of his head with grief, he were. Raising the lad fell to me and Bevan. O' course, we bided at Barstowe Hall then. His lordship were always one for flitting hither and yon. Chasing dusty old books. Couldn't see use of it meself. Mostly young maister bided home without his father, such a loving, sunny bairn he were."

Sidonie had difficulty imagining dark, complicated Jonas Merrick as a sunny child. Especially as the picture Mrs. Bevan painted of his childhood was a lonely one.

"Then the lad were called baseborn and the bad times started. The world be cruel to bastards. There bain't much sunshine in Jonas Merrick's life since he were eight year old."

"Did you go with the family to Venice?"

"Aye. Though I've no truck with furriners."

Mrs. Bevan must know how Jonas had been scarred. Sidonie bit down the urge to ask. He'd hate to think she'd gone behind his back to find out. "Were you in Italy long?"

"Till his old lordship passed on, must have been '17. Horrible smelly place Venice were. Water e'en where streets should be. Though I were right glad to be there when his lordship left for eastern parts afore young mais- ter's scars could heal. I wouldn't trust furrin servants with the lad's care. Doon' like to speak ill of the dead but that were ill done of his lordship, to up and go like that. His lordship should have bided at least till the lad weren't at death's door no more, but after his wife passed on, he never could bear one place long."

Horrified, disbelieving, Sidonie stiffened against her chair. She hardly believed it, especially after the loving way Jonas spoke of the late viscount. Had Jonas's father left him to the care of servants after the attack? It seemed selfish to the point of devilry. And Jonas had been young when he was injured, she'd gathered from the few hints he dropped, no older than an adolescent. Hardly surprising Jonas was so determined to rely on nobody but himself, so sure that the world was likely to kick him in the teeth before it offered a greeting.

"Why are you telling me this?"

Mrs. Bevan shrugged and reached for the empty tea- cup. "Had an inkling 'ee might be interested. Had an inkling 'ee might have ideas of brightening maister's life. Now, be 'ee off to sleep like a Christian?"

Sidonie refused to be drawn on the subject of brighten- ing Jonas's life. Mrs. Bevan was a cunning old vixen. She'd seen more than Sidonie had realized. "No, I'll wait here."

"Suit 'eeself." Mrs. Bevan shuffled away after pausing to light a lamp on one of the wooden chests. "I bid 'ee good e'en."

Sightlessly Sidonie stared into the darkness, her mind whirling with what she'd learned. She'd always known Jonas had led a difficult life. For heaven's sake, one only had to glimpse his face to know that. But hearing he'd been set to grow up a completely different man made her heart contract with pity. Even more as she knew that the boy's generous, affectionate spirit still lived inside him, much as he struggled against acknowledging its existence. She'd seen flashes of it, most recently last night after her wild dash into the storm.

She admired that even a trace of the loving, sweet child remained. His life had been nothing but betrayal, from the moment he was declared bastard. Even earlier than that, when his mother died and his father descended into a chasm of sorrow.

She couldn't continue to betray him.

Once she returned to Barstowe Hall, she'd make sure Roberta was hidden out of William's reach, even if it meant her sister was forced to live as a fugitive. Then she'd write to Jonas with the truth about his legitimacy. She probably should tell him immediately, but she couldn't forget the way he'd spoken to the duke, dismissing Roberta's claims on his compassion in favor of his quest for revenge against his cousin. Once Roberta was safe, Jonas Merrick was welcome to take back his inheritance.

Stiff and tired, Jonas eased himself off Casimir's back in the stables. Instead of removing the horse's tack, he leaned against the beast's heaving, sweaty sides. It was late, nearly midnight. And cold as a witch's tit. He'd been out since before dawn after days of interrupted sleep and no sleep at all last night. Leaving Sidonie, he'd fled the house—and temptation—to one of the dilapidated follies that punctuated the overgrown garden.

Casimir whickered and turned his head to bump his

master in wordless comfort. The horse's company was about all he could bear today.

Although encroaching company wasn't exactly a pressing concern. The vast house awaiting him was empty of the one person who'd given it life. Since boyhood, he'd felt alone and despised, but he'd never before sunk so low. He felt like a mongrel cur booted to the gutter. He felt like shit stuck to his worst enemy's shoe.

He felt remarkably sorry for himself.

Impossible to summon the joyless, dogged determination that had always kept him going through life's vicissitudes. All he could manage was the gloomy premonition that he'd be lonely as long as he lived.

He'd done the right thing this morning. Sending Sidonie Forsythe back to her family as innocent as the day she'd arrived put him on the side of the angels.

Almost as innocent.

No, he refused to recall her pleasure. Or her kisses. That way lay only misery. His father always said doing the right thing was its own reward. Just now Jonas would dearly love to take issue with that opinion.

He didn't know how long he huddled against Casimir. He appreciated the horse's uncomplaining placidity. But a man couldn't spend his life skulking in a stable, however much he might wish to. Still, he wondered why he bothered to go through the motions as he settled Casimir, then plodded through the freezing, starry night to the castle. His candle lit the way through the silent, cold house. He'd got used to it as silent and cold before Sidonie arrived. He'd get used to it again.

The assurance rang as hollow as his footsteps on the flagstones.

He could sleep in his own bed tonight. But how could he endure lying in sheets that smelled of Sidonie? Until he arranged for another room prepared to his standards, he was consigned to the dressing room.

Not that he cared. He wasn't likely to sleep.

Right now, even though his eyes were gritty and every muscle ached after hard riding, he doubted he'd ever sleep again. Castle Craven was rumored to be haunted. For him it was. Sidonie's memory would linger forever.

With his wicked plan in ashes, he could leave. The problem was, unless Sidonie waited at the end of his journey, he had no interest in going elsewhere. If he could gather the energy, he should get a gun and put himself out of everyone's misery.

Inured to its atmosphere of ancient malevolence, he stepped into the hall. Nothing, not even the threat of spiteful ghosts, competed with the chill inside him. He would come back to life again. Eventually. People did unless fate took a drastic hand, he supposed.

Jonas was so sunk in gloom, he was halfway across the cavernous room before he noticed a light against the far wall. It was unlike Mrs. Bevan to leave a lamp for him after he'd been carousing. Not that he'd had the stomach for drinking. One day he might find fleeting solace in the bottom of a tankard. Tonight his sorrow extended beyond alcohol's reach.

He trudged forward to blow out the lamp. And stopped as if he'd crashed into a wall of glass, astonished to realize why it was there.

"Sidonie?" he whispered, afraid if he spoke too loudly she'd disappear. His heart thudded so violently, he was surprised the sound didn't wake her.

If he'd been drinking, he'd doubt the evidence of his eyes. Unless he'd gone mad indeed since this morning, Sidonie Forsythe hadn't left at her first chance. Instead she stretched across two of the hellishly uncomfortable chairs that formed the hall's principal furnishing.

She stirred at the sound of her name, but didn't wake. With an unsteady hand, he raised his candle to study her. Her cheek upon her hand, she'd curled up like a cat under one of his old coats. Thick lashes resting on pale cheeks lent an impression of innocence. He felt like a satyr for what he wanted from her. This was why he'd lurked in a dank stone pagoda all night, cursing unruly desire and virtuous women and his inconvenient conscience.

Damn it, he should have left a note telling her she was free to go. During the short hours remaining of last night, in his head he'd written thousands of words to her. Because he couldn't say enough, he'd said nothing. He'd assumed she'd immediately understand that he relinquished all hold over her.

Why the deuce hadn't she gone?

The world accounted him a brave man. He wasn't sure he was brave enough to send Sidonie away when she hovered within reach. Such a coward was the infamous Jonas Merrick. After all his weaselly avoidances, now he still had to say good-bye to her face. The prospect of putting a bullet in his brain became more appealing by the minute.

"Sidonie," he repeated more insistently.

Her eyes cracked open and stared at him groggily. For a dazzled interval, he swam in endless brown and felt so damned happy to see her, devil take the rest of the world.

*   *   *

Sidonie wasn't sure where she was. Except she'd heard
Jonas speak her name. Just the sound of his voice filled
her with elation.

She stared at him, transfixed by the unabashed delight
in his face. Then he straightened and stepped back. A
chill dropped over his expression so he looked stern and
not at all like the man who had smiled at her as though
she was his dearest treasure.

Oh, how she wished she was his dearest treasure.

"What are you doing here?" he asked sharply.

Disoriented and stiff from her makeshift bed, she
struggled to sit. Mrs. Bevan must have dropped a coat over
her at some stage. Even so, she was frozen. She clutched
the thick folds to her and remembered Jonas giving her
his coat last night to keep her from the storm.

"Is it late?" Her voice emerged as a croak.

"After midnight." His scowl didn't lighten. "Answer me."

It didn't occur to her to lie to save her pride. What
was the point? He'd discover soon enough she'd flattened
every defense. She brushed back the strands of hair tick-
ling her face. She must look a complete disaster. "I'm
waiting for you."

He made an impatient gesture. The ruby glittered
evilly in the candlelight. "No, I mean what are you doing
still at the castle? I thought you'd be long gone."

She flinched. He sounded irritated. The tiny kernel of
certainty that he couldn't turn from her so abruptly shriveled. She'd never been fool enough to expect a declaration
of undying devotion, but this irascible stranger made her
cringe. "I thought—"

He silenced her with another angry wave of his hand.

"This is madness. You've got Roberta's vowels. I didn't expect a good-bye. I expected you to take your precious chastity and run."

She flushed as the last mists of sleep faded. God help her, she'd made a terrible mistake. "I thought—" Her voice cracked and she started again. "I thought you surrendered Roberta's vowels to leave me free to choose what happened between us."

His mouth tightened. "That's why I gave them to you. So you were free to bring this disaster to an end."

He was blunt to the point of spite. She'd only known him a few days. He shouldn't be able to carve her heart into bloody strips with a few words. She'd derided pride as a useless luxury when she decided to challenge her dismissal. Now pride insisted she couldn't cry before him.

"I should go," she said shakily.

"Exactly." He stepped back as if her presence offended him. "But it's too late tonight."

She rose on unsteady legs, feeling sick, wishing herself anywhere but here, wishing she'd taken the powerful hint and left this morning. "I'm sorry."

He scowled at her. Had she imagined that smile when he first saw her? "What are you sorry for?" He sounded bitter although she had no idea why. "All blame in this mess is mine."

"I acted like an idiot last night."

"Leave it, Sidonie." He sounded tired. Tired and disgusted with everything. "Go to bed."

Still she didn't move. She wasn't sure why. Actually she knew why. It was because of a smile. And because she had a sudden piercing memory of his expression in the mirror after he believed he'd put her in danger.

He did a fine job now of pretending indifference. Last night he hadn't been indifferent. She refused to believe he was shallow enough to change in a few hours. She drew herself up and stared directly at him. "Why did you give me Roberta's vowels?"

An intensely masculine growl of frustration. She wondered why she wasn't even a little afraid of his temper. "For God's sake, Sidonie!"

"Jonas..."

She faltered into silence as he grabbed her hand and hauled her out of the hall and into the library. Thank goodness this room had a fire. The hall provided a frigid setting and she'd imagined a thousand ghosts eavesdropping on their argument. He released her the instant they were inside. Like a naughty schoolgirl, she stood trembling on the Turkey carpet before the desk.

She raised her chin. He might want her gone. He might find her person distasteful. If either of those were true, she'd make...*damned* sure he told her so. "Why did you give me Roberta's vowels?" she asked again in an uncompromising tone.

"So you'd leave." He sounded equally uncompromising. His fists opened and closed at his sides, indicating his resentment.

She stiffened her backbone. She already knew this wouldn't be easy. "Why do you want me to leave?"

"Why do you want to stay? You were desperate to get away last night."

She flushed. "You know why I ran away."

He sighed and turned, but not before she caught a flash of desolation in his face. No, he wasn't nearly the furious monolith he wanted her to believe. A fragile tendril of hope unfurled toward the light and stopped her retreating.

"I know I pushed so far that you were desperate to escape."

Guilt weighted her belly. Why, oh, why, had she been such a henwit? "I wasn't running from you."

He cast her a disbelieving glance. "Looked that way."

"What happened . . . frightened me. I was running from myself."

She waited for some hint of understanding. Instead he strode across to the window and rattled the curtains wide to reveal the starlit cliffs. "It makes no difference."

"Yes, it does."

"Sidonie, listen to me." He was back to sounding tired and sad and dauntingly immovable. "Go to bed. In the morning, take my carriage and go wherever you will. Hades, for all I care. I don't know what you hope to achieve by this confrontation, but whatever we shared is over."

Right now she was glad he didn't look at her. She suspected her face betrayed her despair. The question she forced through her tight throat emerged husky and uneven. "How can it be over when it hasn't started?"

Jonas stared out at the cold world and wondered just what hell he'd wandered into. How strange that tonight all was calm beauty outside when his inner landscape was a blasted wilderness. He should have kept riding and never come back.

"What do you want, *bella*?" he asked with an idleness he didn't feel. "Blood?"

He heard her step nearer. Her hand curled around his arm. She rarely touched him—unless he tricked her into it. Now when it could lead nowhere, confound her, she lost her shyness.

"I want...honesty."

He fought the urge to shake her off. Even through his coat sleeve, her touch burned. He yearned to sink into the numbness that had possessed him before her advent into his existence. What he wanted didn't matter. Long ago he'd learned that lesson. He resisted the impulse to touch his scars.

"Why?" he asked despairingly, his hand clenching in the gold velvet curtains.

"Jonas, talk to me. Yesterday you wanted me. Is that no longer true?"

She did want blood, it seemed. Reluctantly he turned to her. "I'm sending you away for your own good."

"Does that mean you still want me?"

What to say? He could lie but he had a nasty feeling she'd never believe him. "I don't want to want you."

She stepped so close that her haunting fragrance teased his senses. Her face was pale and intense. "I don't want to want you either."

This time Jonas managed to shake off her hand and step away, telling himself he controlled this encounter. When he knew he was at her mercy.

How ruthless a sweet woman could be.

She still wore his greatcoat. It lent her appearance an incongruously stately air. Her hair was rumpled and tendrils curled around her beautiful face. The sight was powerfully sexual, as though she started to undress for a lover.

He stifled a groan. Exactly what he needed to think about when he tried so desperately to be noble. All his animal instincts shrieked that Sidonie was here; for once she didn't appear unwilling, and the carpet was soft enough for what he had in mind. "I'll destroy you," he said bleakly.

"You might prove my salvation."

His lips twisted in an unamused smile. "I'm nobody's salvation, least of all yours." He knew it was unwise to prolong this encounter, but he couldn't let it go. "Last night you were convinced I was the devil incarnate. What's provoked this self-sacrifice?"

"It's not self-sacrifice." The look she shot him contrasted with the innocence of her pink cheeks. "If you touch me, I promise not to run."

Dear God...

The impulse to accept her invitation at face value and roll her under him was overwhelming. But he'd learned self-control in a hard school. "I intend your ruin."

An uncharacteristically cynical expression crossed her face. "Today I thought you'd lost interest in ruining me."

"Oh, hell, Sidonie..." He swung away and slumped onto the window seat, staring down at his hands linked between his knees. If he kept looking at her, he'd touch her. If he touched her, all good intentions were dust.

After a pause, she sat beside him. Reckless chit. Didn't she perceive the risk? He clutched his hands so tightly together that the knuckles shone white.

"You'll think I'm disgustingly forward," she said in a subdued voice.

Jonas didn't dare look at her. "Go away, Sidonie."

She didn't heed his gravelly plea. "I've decided I'd rather like...to be ruined."

Her voice trailed away so he needed a moment to

realize what she'd said. His head jerked up so fast, he hurt his neck. He stared at her in disbelief. "What the hell?"

She raised her chin and met his eyes. He read uncertainty and hard-won courage in her face. "I said—"

He leaped to his feet as though he were the offended virgin and she the pursuing rake. "You're out of your mind."

Sidonie remained seated, watching him as though she gradually made sense of his behavior. He wished he could say the same.

"You had a week to seduce me, Jonas." She had the temerity to smile at him. "Congratulations. You've succeeded."

Chapter Fourteen

If she'd felt less on edge, Sidonie would have smiled at his shocked reaction. Her surrender flummoxed this notorious man of the world. Her surrender left her flummoxed, too, but the last few minutes had answered some urgent questions, however uncommunicative Jonas proved.

He went against his strongest inclinations when he sent her away. He still wanted her. That clarified the most important issues. The rest she'd work out.

When she sat beside him, she hadn't mistaken how he'd trembled, a slow combing wave that ran through his body. Over the last days, she'd learned so much about this man and his reactions. Thrilling to imagine what remained to learn. She was apprehensive and excited. If she relinquished this chance to explore the passion flaring between them, she'd regret it all her life.

He scowled at her. "You don't mean it."

She stood as he backed away. "Of course I do."

His jaw set hard as stone. "I won't do it."

"Heaven help us, Merrick. You're suffering a temporary surfeit of honor. You'll get over it."

He glowered at her. "The promptings of my conscience aren't a minor illness. I'm trying to do the right thing, *tesoro*."

"I know." She hesitated, seeking words to explain her capitulation. "When you returned Roberta's vowels, I realized I didn't want to leave you."

If she expected her bald confession to crack his resistance, she was disappointed. His expression remained austere, his slashing eyebrows lowering over his eyes. "I've set you free."

"Free to give myself to you."

Still he didn't relent. "Why?"

He was so suspicious. Life hadn't dealt him an easy hand and he'd learned to be wary of happiness or love or kindness. Her heart ached for him. She wanted him with her body, but more than that, she longed to offer him rest from his demons. Because for all his strength and determination, demons tormented him. She'd known that from the first time she saw that bizarre mirror-filled room upstairs.

She licked lips dry with nervousness and twisted her hands in her skirts. "Because I want to."

"Not good enough."

She stepped closer, her heart racing. He'd come direct from the stables. Odors of horse, leather, and the outdoors melded into a surprisingly pleasant fragrance. "Seems good enough to me."

He retreated, keeping the distance between them. "You're suddenly very certain of yourself."

She dared another step. He tensed as though scenting

danger. Wise man. She meant to be dangerous. She meant to crush his fragile scruples and take him as her lover. Her skin tightened with wanton anticipation.

A huff of amusement escaped. "For heaven's sake, Merrick! You're jumpy as a cat in a thunderstorm."

He didn't smile. "This is no laughing matter."

"Actually it is. Ever since I arrived, I couldn't turn around without you breathing down my neck. Now you act like a vicar with a wayward parishioner."

He turned away and she strained to hear him. "When you ran away last night—"

She grabbed his arm. She braced for rejection, but he remained still, his muscles taut under her touch. "I was a stupid little girl, frightened by what I didn't understand. Jonas, you told me this week offered me a freedom I'd never know again. It's taken me too long to see how right you are. Until now, my life has been barren. Don't send me back into the cold, not without the memory of joy to keep me warm."

Where on earth did she find the courage to say these things? She'd never spoken like this to anyone. She'd been so busy bolstering her defenses, she hadn't let Jonas glimpse her soul. Right now, she'd serve up her soul on a platter if he asked. He wasn't asking and she served up her soul anyway. Her voice thickened with tears. "Don't make me beg, Jonas."

He sighed heavily and when he turned toward her this time, she realized something had changed. But still she didn't see the eagerness she wanted. His face appeared, if anything, sterner. "What if I get you pregnant?"

Her hand tightened on his arm and she resisted the impulse to stamp her foot. What in heaven's name was wrong with the man? "You weren't worried about that last night."

For the first time, she caught a glimmer of rueful humor in his expression. "Last night hunger for your exquisite body turned thought to mush. Right now, I'm still moderately sane. Tell me, beautiful Sidonie, what if you have a child?"

Devil take him. He was a tougher opponent than she'd expected. Tough and smart. If she hoped to prevail, she'd need to be tougher and smarter.

"Roberta and I discussed that," she said through stiff lips. The Forsythes weren't a prolific family. Sidonie's mother produced two daughters from her long marriage. In eight years, Roberta bore only two sons. Odds were if Sidonie submitted to Jonas, she wouldn't conceive.

Which she knew pinned her hopes to a mere prayer.

He looked unimpressed. "And concocted some hare-brained scheme, worthy of your sister."

"You're cruel," she said hoarsely, dropping her hand from his arm and stepping away.

He shook his head. "No, I'm trying to make you see reality, not some addled romantic notion. You were wiser yesterday, *amore mio*, when you ran away."

An angry sound emerged from her throat. "If you're so keen to keep me away, why call me such names?"

His mouth relaxed slightly. "You're right. It's not fair. My conversion to man of principle isn't complete, *bella*. I'm doing my best."

Her stare was unflinching. "I liked you better as an unrepentant rake."

"No, you didn't. Tell me what you and Roberta cooked up."

"I'll live on my legacy somewhere obscure and pose as a widow. It's the obvious solution if I...if you get me with child." Her eyes sharpened on his unconcealed disapproval, although she admitted the plan sounded flimsy. "Roberta says there are ways to prevent conception."

"Does she indeed?"

Her cheeks heated. "Are there?"

"Nothing totally reliable."

She sucked in an unsteady breath. This was more like haggling over the price of a loaf than entering into four days of sensual abandon. "You needn't worry."

He took her hand. It was the first time tonight he'd touched her. Perhaps she made progress after all.

"I'm not worried." He sounded different, like the man who brought her to shuddering release. The abrupt change left her reeling and not a little wary.

"You're not?" She sucked in a shaky breath and curled her fingers around his. Now that he'd touched her, she wasn't letting go until she had to.

"If I get you with child, I want your word you'll tell me."

"I don't think—"

"I want your word you'll tell me and we'll marry."

Shock slammed through her and she tried to jerk away. "Marry? You?"

His lips lengthened in a wry smile. "Please don't spare my feelings."

She stiffened, horrified where her recklessness had led. It had taken her painful soul-searching to reach a point where she was willing to trust her body to Jonas. The idea of trusting the rest of her life to him pushed against barriers she'd spent years fortifying. "You know I have no wish to marry."

All humor fled his face. "No child of mine will be born a bastard."

"You don't want to marry me."

His eyebrows arched. "I can think of worse fates."

Astonishment made her words sound like flat denial. "Well, I don't want to marry you."

"Clearly, but that's my offer."

She drew herself up and this time he released her. "After all the flirtation and...kissing and promises of seduction, you'll send me away if I won't agree to this one thing?"

His jaw set in an implacable line, although she read regret in his eyes. "Ridiculous, isn't it?"

"You didn't say this last night."

"Yes, well, last night proved a salutary lesson in the consequences of the selfish quest for pleasure."

"You never thought about pregnancy? That's too disingenuous."

"It seemed counterproductive to raise this subject too early."

She glowered. Why, oh, why was he doing this? Why wasn't he catching her up in his arms and kissing her into a wild heaven? "It's counterproductive to raise it now."

A faint grimness shadowed his features. "I know I'm nobody's idea of husband material, Sidonie."

"No man is husband material," she said sourly, challenging what she hoped was mere bluff. "Perhaps I should go back to Barstowe Hall after all."

Before he spoke, she knew he wouldn't relent. Of course he wouldn't. He understood the stigma of illegitimacy too well. "You're free."

Free to return to her dull life at Barstowe Hall. Free to

forgo her only chance at forbidden pleasure. Free never to see Jonas Merrick again. The thought chilled her like the wind against the cliffs last night.

She was free but she cursed her freedom.

"I don't want to leave you." Her gaze clung to his face as she frantically sought some hint of concession.

For a moment, she thought she might have won. He made a convulsive movement toward her and raised his hand to touch her.

He stopped before making contact. Strain tightened the skin over his angular features. "I don't want you to go, *bella*."

"Marriage is such a—" Her voice petered away.

Jonas surveyed her with a perceptive light in his eyes, as if he guessed her turbulent thoughts. "Serious step."

The thought of marriage made her feel choked and trapped. More trapped than she'd felt offering herself to save Roberta. That was for a night, at most a week. Marriage was a lifetime of servitude. Rationally she recognized Jonas wasn't William. It didn't matter. The long-standing fear of male oppression born in childhood remained. She'd never deliver herself into a man's power the way a wife delivered herself to a husband. The way Roberta had delivered herself to William. The way her mother had delivered herself to her father. "Perhaps the need won't arise."

"Perhaps not." His beautiful voice flattened, always a sign that he struggled for control. "Contingencies must be considered."

"I'd expected a passionate lover, not a quibbling lawyer."

"Sorry to disappoint, *tesoro*." To her regret, he turned

on his heel and stalked toward the door. "Sleep on it. The carriage remains at your disposal."

"I don't want you to be a good man," she said in a muffled voice, frustration and chagrin swirling in her belly.

He frowned as he looked back. "I'm not good. I'm a beast and a brute. Didn't Roberta tell you?"

She swallowed piercing compassion. "My sister was mistaken."

Sadness tinged his smile. "No, *bella*, she wasn't."

He left her alone in the shadowy library.

The rewards of virtue were sparse indeed.

Jonas surveyed the mean little bed in his dressing room and couldn't help thinking of the feather mattress he might be sharing right now. Soft, warm, roomy. And filled with the charms of Sidonie Forsythe. For all that, he couldn't be sorry he'd made the ultimatum.

Sighing, he slumped onto the bed to tug off his boots. At least Mrs. Bevan had lit a fire so the room wasn't the usual icy hellhole. Any chill emanated entirely from his yearning heart.

He caught himself staring into space with one boot in his hand and the other still on his foot. How elated he'd been to discover Sidonie downstairs. Briefly everything had turned right in his world. He was in such a pathetically bad way, seeing her when he'd thought never to set eyes on her again had seemed a blessing.

Whereas it was a curse.

The sooner she left his life, as she inevitably would, the sooner he'd forget her.

No point saying he'd never forget her.

Sidonie was just another woman. The conviction that

he'd see her face when he shut his eyes the last time, probably as a bitter, bereft old man, was mere fancy. Nobody could mark his heart that deeply in four days. He might feel like she had, but good sense would prevail. One day.

He set down his boot and tugged off the second one. Every moment had a horrible pointlessness. Another moment would follow, then another. All the way to the end. Not one scrap of light or love or laughter in any of it.

Feeling like that old man, he rose and shucked his shirt. He splashed water into a bowl and sponged the day's dirt away. The water was warm but felt cold. Everything felt cold. His life was immutable winter.

Ah, Sidonie, if only you knew what pain you cause.

He turned to grab a towel and something, perhaps a stray eddy of air, made him glance up. Sidonie, her hair flowing around her like shot silk, hovered in the doorway.

Jonas bit back a groan. How much more could he take before he broke? Midnight encounters with his only desire tested resolve beyond measure. Especially when his only desire wore nothing but his sheer white shirt extending to mid-thigh.

The towel slipped from his hand as droplets of water trickled down his naked torso. "What is it, *tesoro*? Is something wrong?"

Her face was pale and set and her tension was visible even from several feet away. When she didn't immediately answer, concern made him step forward. "Are you ill?"

She shook her head. Her great dark eyes fixed upon him as though she drowned and he offered her only hope of reaching shore.

"Sidonie?" he asked, seriously worried now. "What's wrong?"

"Don't," she croaked, and her delicate throat moved as she swallowed. He couldn't help remembering how fine and fragrant the skin there was. She'd given him more than she should. Damn it, she hadn't given him nearly enough.

"Don't what?"

"Don't . . . say anything."

What the hell? None of this made sense. Before he could inquire further, she launched at him with a rush of bare feet.

Automatically he caught her. His mind had a confused moment to register warmth and softness. His heart had a gratified moment to bask in touching her. Only a moment . . .

With trembling hands, she grabbed his head and dragged him down to press her mouth to his.

He'd been so busy inuring himself to never kissing her again, this onslaught left him bewildered. Her scent flooded his senses, mingling with the lemon soap he'd used for his wash. Teeth clashed as she clumsily forced her mouth against his. There was no sweetness. Just blind, angry determination to prevail.

After mere seconds, she pulled away to stare into his face with heart-stopping focus. She looked near to tears and her breath emerged in choked gasps as if she struggled against lancing pain. "Kiss me, curse you."

"Sidonie . . ."

"Kiss me," she grated out. In a frantic rhythm, her hands opened and closed on his bare arms.

"Gently, *tesoro*, gently." He pressed his palms to her cheeks to hold her still. His heart crashed against his ribs when he noticed blood on her lower lip where he must have nicked her with his teeth.

"No," she moaned, pitching forward to kiss him again, still with that agonized violence. Her breasts mashed against his chest. She might as well have been naked. The pearls of her nipples tormented him through the thin linen. For all his misgivings, her unbridled assault had him hard as a pikestaff. He staggered under the enthusiasm, although he tasted more anguish than delight in her kiss.

No, he couldn't do this. It wasn't right. He ripped his mouth away from hers and resisted the fretful tug of her hands to bring him near. "Sidonie, what the hell is this?"

"I'm seducing you," she said jerkily, stretching to run her mouth over his jaw. Sharp little nips lit a chain of explosions through his mind and made his cock throb with need. Devil take her, she drove him mad.

"This isn't how it should be," he said in a raw voice, his hands tangling in the back of her shirt. He told himself to push her away, but some things exceeded mortal will.

"It's how it must be."

So warm, so soft, so bloody eternally desirable, she slid against his body. He squeezed his eyes shut and prayed for control. What on earth was wrong with her? He feared she was here against her will, although he couldn't guess why. He no longer held any power to compel her.

She wriggled in his arms, hooking a leg behind his knee and clawing at his shoulders. It made him hotter than Hades, blazing to have her, but still he struggled to keep his head. His hands lost purchase on her loose shirt and slipped to the lush curve of her bottom.

As his palms encountered satiny skin, astonishment jammed the breath in his throat. Under his shirt she was naked. "Good God..."

He told himself to make her slow down. To check this was what she wanted. Confirm she'd marry him if he got her with child. Except when she touched him, she made mockery of resolution. Still he could stop if he had to. He wasn't an animal. He was a rational man, not a mere toy in her pale, slim hands. He told himself a thousand things as his touch became caress, exploration, enticement. He traced the smooth arch of her arse, gradually dipping lower.

As he touched the secret parts of her, she jerked. "Shh," he soothed.

She was gloriously wet. He groaned and hid his face in her shoulder, bared under the loose collar. The darkness behind his eyes flared into flame as he stroked her. The craving to plunge into her became a storm to rival last night's wild weather.

"Don't let me go," she begged, sagging against him.

"I don't think I can," he said in despair. He wrenched away long enough to extinguish the candles, sinking the room into firelit shadow. He'd prefer full darkness, but this dimness would have to serve. Rationally he knew that Sidonie had long ceased to shrink from his scars, but his vulnerable heart couldn't bear for her to come so close to surrender only to realize she lay in a monster's arms.

She was panting when he caught her up against him. More kissing. More fevered caresses. When he swung her toward the narrow bed, he fell first so his weight didn't crush her. She crawled up his body and kissed him. Physical urgency overwhelmed caution. He opened his mouth, ravishing her with lips and tongue and teeth.

He rolled her onto her back, rising over her. "I'll rip this shirt to shreds."

"Let me take it off," she said breathlessly through a tangle of dusky hair. Her lips were swollen and her eyelids drooped over glittering eyes. She shifted and a drift of her arousal intoxicated him. He straddled her legs. The shirt hitched, revealing dark curls at the apex of her thighs. Lord above, she was beautiful. Everywhere.

She watched him as though she wanted to devour him. He'd remember that hungry expression as long as he lived. And count himself privileged, even if he had no more of Sidonie than tonight.

"Don't look at me like that," he groaned.

Her smile made his heart cartwheel. "I like looking at you."

Her confession slammed through him like a gunshot. Damn it, she sounded like she meant it. He should remind her he was hideous inside and out. Warn her she risked destruction giving herself so wholeheartedly.

His protest died unspoken when she tugged the shirt open to reveal her breasts. Round. Perfect. He kissed one beaded raspberry nipple and she arched on a whimper of pleasure. Such a sensual creature. Such a shining soul.

He loved her shining soul.

Tragically, he loved more than that.

The idea slithered through his fuddled mind like a snake. Then Sidonie sighed and conscious thought abandoned him. All that remained was the thirst to possess. He parted her legs and slid between her thighs. She sighed again. These sweet little sighs would have him losing himself before he was inside her. He explored her satiny cleft, brushing the center. Once. Twice. A third time. She made a strangled sound and surged against his hand.

The urge to have her beat a pounding march in his

head. Still, her virginity tempered recklessness. With a gentleness that made him shake, he slid one finger into her. Slick heat made his cock swell with eagerness. She clenched in welcome. He withdrew, feeling each clinging inch, then penetrated her with two fingers.

Blast and damnation, she was tight. She'd feel like heaven when he thrust into her, but he dreaded hurting her. Her breath escaped in jagged rhythm to match his stroking. The broken exhalations were astonishingly arousing. Hell, right now, everything about her was arousing. She could recite irregular Latin verbs and it would make him crazy.

God help him, he knew he should wait, but he couldn't. Drawing back, he met dark brown eyes. Fathomless. Rich as coffee. Sparking with uncertainty and desire.

His hand shook as he ripped at his breeches. "Sidonie, forgive me," he said on the last gasp of a drowning man.

Chapter Fifteen

Sidonie's mist of pleasure receded as she felt hard pressure between her legs. She whimpered at the discomfort and dug her fingernails into Jonas's bare shoulders. Immediately he stopped. He bent his head into her neck, long shudders running through him. There was something poignant about this strong, experienced man shaking with need in her arms.

She shifted to ease the sensation between her legs. This far, the act was disagreeable but not painful. She wriggled again and felt as much as heard him groan into her skin, his breath warm and damp.

"Sidonie, if you do that, I won't be able to stop."

"Don't stop." She'd ventured so far. She couldn't retreat now.

He rested his weight on his arms but even so, his body crushed her against the hard, narrow bed and restricted breathing. Or perhaps that was the rush of her heart. The intimacy of this connection went beyond anything she'd imagined. She hadn't seen that part of him before he pressed it into her. It felt the size of a brick. And twice as hard.

When she'd decided to batter down his reluctance and make him take her, she hadn't counted on how profound the experience might prove. It was terrifying how dominated she felt. If it had been any man other than Jonas, she'd struggle to break free. She lay quiescent, while her pulse galloped not just with fading arousal but also with long-held fear of masculine oppression.

This is Jonas. This is Jonas. He won't hurt you.

She inhaled and her muscles loosened a fraction. He inched farther with a smoothness that surprised her. A whimper escaped her at the unaccustomed fullness and he stopped again. His heart thundered against her chest and under her hands; his back was slick with sweat. The pleasure she'd always found in his arms ebbed beyond reach. This was sticky, awkward, and starkly physical. It wasn't at all how she'd felt when he kissed her. She loved his kisses. She didn't love this.

Although for all the discomfort, the union held a grim fascination. She'd never felt so close to another human being. It was like she breathed for both of them.

"Don't fight me, Sidonie." Jonas sounded like he too teetered over a chasm. "You'll shatter like glass if you do."

She shut her eyes and grabbed another shallow breath. "I don't know what to do," she said helplessly, her fingers digging into his damp skin.

He released a harsh breath that could have held a laugh. She felt the muscles of his back flex and release. "It's all right, *tesoro*. I'll keep you safe. Trust me."

Her embrace tightened even as the impulse to shove

him away gathered like a scream. Right now he was everything she wanted and everything she didn't want. His lips grazed her neck and found a place where she was all sensitivity. To her astonishment, fleeting excitement shimmered through her. When she'd thought any possibility of pleasure had fled.

His back tightened and he moved more purposefully. This time when he thrust, her world exploded into scarlet pain.

For what felt like forever, Sidonie's cry resonated around the room. The pain was excruciating, as though Jonas tore her in half. He'd turned terrifyingly still, although his chest rose and fell roughly over hers. It was frightening to be so aware of his every breath, his slightest shift. Why on earth did women do this? She bit back a demand for him to get off her.

Jonas kissed her neck again, as if in apology, and through fading agony, she experienced a tiny frisson. The pleasure countered the pulsing incursion. She shivered, overwhelmed by conflicting sensations. His musky scent. The hard reality of his body. The stinging pressure between her legs where she was a maid no more.

He scraped his teeth across coiled nerves in the hollow between her neck and shoulder. This time she didn't inhale through a red haze of pain. Infinitesimally he moved. She was so attuned to him that the tiny slide felt like an earthquake. He cupped her breast, tweaking the peak to an aching point. More pleasure to color discomfort.

He squeezed her nipple and it was as if a heated wire ran to where his body joined hers. She sighed and this time, the sound conveyed more than protest. With a soft groan, Jonas slid carefully from her body. She experienced a faint quiver at the friction, then nothing.

She opened dry eyes and stared at the beams on the ceiling. Merrick's face was still buried in her shoulder. Now that he'd withdrawn, she should be relieved. Instead she was irritable and disappointed.

Was that it?

Before she voiced any reaction, he slowly thrust inside. This time, her body stretched to receive him. After brief resistance, he planted himself deep with a long, satiny glide.

Deeper than before. So deep he touched her heart.

She braced for pain. There was discomfort but nothing to compare to the thrills juddering through her. He claimed her in a way he hadn't claimed her when he'd taken her virginity. Her muscles unfolded like a bird taking flight or a flower blooming. The effect was extraordinary. She hadn't cried before, but this beautiful wholeness brought stinging tears to her eyes.

"Oh, Jonas," she whispered. "I didn't know."

"There's more." He rose on his arms to stare into her face. What had been cruel invasion now felt hot, hard, and fulfilling.

He looked younger, kinder, a brighter image of the man she knew. A man life hadn't mistreated or betrayed. Whatever the pain of this union, she loved that she gave him this momentary peace. This encounter lurched from the physical onto a different plane. A plane revealing a new emotional landscape. She felt lightheaded, lost.

She blinked back more foolish tears and brushed away a lock of hair that tumbled over his forehead. Tenderness lit her from within. As though this man were her other half. As though they were meant to be together forever.

Stupid.

"I hurt you."

She found it in her to smile. "Not now."

"I'm glad." He tilted his head to move into her caress like a cat.

Carefully, so she relished each inch, he slid free of her body. She shut her eyes on the loss, although his retreat awakened a thousand new sensations.

"Prepare to be surprised, *il mio cuore*." He dropped a fleeting kiss to her shoulder. The salute's reverence moved her as deeply as anything else in this painful, astonishing encounter.

"Show me, Jonas," she murmured, surprised at how readily she entrusted herself to wherever he wanted to take her. Right now if he asked her to fly to the moon, she'd grab his hand and ask which way to leap.

"With pleasure."

He thrust again. Under them, the bed creaked loudly. Her hands curled into his shoulders and she tilted her hips. The change in angle launched a volley of pleasure. An incandescent web of delight tangled around her.

He groaned with audible approval and pressed a fevered kiss to her lips. All became biting, eager passion. He surged in and out of her as endlessly as the ocean surged against the cliffs. Tenderness dissolved into hunger, although its memory lingered like the echo of distant music and lent a glow to rising excitement.

Jonas drove her higher and higher. She stretched beneath him as he pounded into her. She opened dazed eyes. Tendons stood out in his neck and his mouth thinned over his teeth. He looked savage. He looked desperate. He looked like a man she trusted with her life.

For a blinding moment, she poised on the edge of something beyond comprehension. Something wild, free, and true. Then the tension spiraled and shattered, and she tumbled into a dazzling hail of fire. Flame assailed her from every direction. The astonishing pleasure took her where she'd never been before. Into the stormy ocean. Up with the whirlwind. One with the lightning.

From a distance, she heard a guttural groan, then Jonas tensed and liquid heat gushed inside her. He moved once, twice, three times, then collapsed upon her with another groan.

Sidonie lay on her back, gasping and staring upward. Jonas's body pinned her to the mattress. Jonas's arms held her against the night. Jonas's seed pooled inside her. He'd taken her on an incendiary journey to ecstasy. Now she floated back to earth with every preconception in tatters.

As rapture slowly ebbed, she reluctantly returned to the real world, even if that world was forever changed. Beneath the lingering pleasure, disquiet stirred. She almost wished Jonas had left her in ignorance of this radiant joy.

Because having tasted such joy, how could she live without it?

Through the golden haze, Jonas recognized a growing imperative to move. He must be heavy as the devil, crushing Sidonie into this rock-hard mattress.

He wasn't eager to shift. Superstitiously he feared if he broke the physical connection between them, some awful fate would befall. He didn't trust happiness. He'd experienced so little since his father's disgrace. Making love to Sidonie Forsythe—he wanted to call it fucking but to his dismay the crudity felt blasphemous—was as close to paradise as he'd ever get.

One minute more. Surely his allotment of bliss could encompass another minute. Was that too much to ask?

Now that he resumed something approximating thought, he was aware his knees ached from digging into the unforgiving cot. Otherwise he was in heaven. His nose was buried in Sidonie's shoulder and her scent surrounded him. Lemon. Female. A trace of sweat after he'd used her well, for all that she'd been a virgin.

He should be ashamed. He'd hated himself when she'd screamed. Then she'd started to purr and the world turned to fire.

Her arms circled his back and her hair clung like silk to the side of his face. He loved her hair. Hell, right now, he couldn't think of one damned thing about her he didn't love. He tried to blame his well-being on the awe-inspiring sex. Good sex always left a man in a fine mood. This was the best sex he'd ever had, in spite of Sidonie's inexperience. In spite of that gut-wrenching moment when she'd cried out because he hurt her.

He'd almost stopped then.

Thank holy heaven she'd got into the business quickly after that. His heart leaped in delight as he recalled her squeezing him at the height of pleasure. A memory to illuminate an entire life.

She made a soft sound, perhaps of discomfort. Perhaps of exhaustion. He really should move. He tightened his arms, daring fate to steal her away. He didn't trust fate. Fate and he had long shared an uneasy relationship.

She shifted. The glide of her body teased his cock and

he hardened. He wasn't a savage. He couldn't tumble her again straightaway. Nor could he spend the night pinioning her to this bed because he feared losing her. Still it was only with utmost reluctance that he separated his body from hers and rolled aside.

He'd forgotten how narrow the bed was. "Hell's bells!"

He only just saved himself from a humiliating slide to the floor. As he gingerly found his balance on the mattress edge, the impossibility of his situation struck with the force of thunder. He'd ruined her and relished every moment. He could well have made her pregnant. She intended to leave him in four days.

Breaking through the fog of self-disgust, he heard a sweet sound that returned him to the sunlit world he'd briefly inhabited. He glanced at Sidonie and amazement almost made him tumble from the bed again.

The woman whose maidenhead he'd just stolen was smiling. No, she was giggling. He'd expected tears and recriminations.

The shirt drooped from her shoulders as she leaned against the pillows. She looked ravishing. And ravished. His beard had chafed the delicate skin of her face and neck. The primitive within rejoiced to see her wearing his mark. Her hair was a wild mane about her shoulders. Candlelight illuminated a hundred colors in its darkness.

She'd raised the sheet over her lush breasts. Her modesty reminded him she was new to this. Unwelcome tenderness flooded his heart.

"This cot isn't big enough for two, is it?" Amusement laced her voice like brandy laced a mug of coffee on a cold night.

"Are you laughing at me, baggage?"

Hitching the sheet, she settled against the wall behind the cot. "Yes."

"What possessed you to seduce me here when there's a perfectly comfortable bed down the hall?"

Pink touched her cheeks. It charmed him that she could still blush. Her innocence reflected the purity of her soul. He didn't believe in much, but he'd come to believe in Sidonie's goodness. Her enchanting smile faded and she cast him an uncertain glance. "I don't like the mirrors."

She must believe him the vainest dog in Christendom. He supposed he should explain the décor, but why spoil these luminous hours? He propped himself on one elbow, keeping a careful eye on the edge of the bed, and took her hand. "Are you all right?"

After a hesitation, she nodded. "Yes."

He waited for more but she remained silent. For a woman, she was deucedly closemouthed. How he wished she'd confide in him, trust him.

Why should she?

Except she'd trusted him with her body. He didn't underestimate what that meant. He wanted to thank her. He wanted to beg her to stay. He wanted to tell her she was the most marvelous being in creation. Emotion silenced him, made it impossible to express what lay in his heart. He raised her hand to his lips and kissed her palm with a veneration that sprang from his soul.

He wasn't good enough for her. But by God, he meant to make her happy while he had her.

Chapter Sixteen

As Jonas whirled her into the bedroom from the corridor, Sidonie hid her face against his shoulder. Her belly twitched with nerves. Last night she hadn't had to endure the mirrors. "Can we sleep in the other room?" she muttered into his shirt.

His laugh was a soft rumble under her ear and his arms tightened around her. "Courage, *bella*."

"I can't watch myself doing...that."

All day, he'd kissed her and touched her but had taken the caresses no further. She supposed he was being considerate, letting her recover from last night, but she was past appreciating his thoughtfulness. Frustration had come near to driving her mad.

"Trust me." He swung her up with an ease that made her breath catch. Curse her longing heart, she swallowed her protest and curled her arms around his neck. She should insist on walking, if only to confirm that his merest glance didn't turn her knees to water.

As he gently settled her on the bed, she met her gaze in the oval mirror above. She sprawled across the sheets in her ruby silk dress. Under the glass's stare, the connection between the man and woman was palpable. Jonas leaned over her with unmistakable intent, but an air of protectiveness for all that. Sidonie's eyes glowed with uncontrollable excitement.

"You turn me into a sybarite."

"A man lives in hope," he said softly, drawing a sparkling pin from her hair. He dropped it onto the nightstand and sat on the bed beside her, his hip nudging hers.

She slid up to lean against the headboard, watching Jonas with a hunger she didn't try to hide. His angular features showed the strain of long hours of self-denial. She hadn't mistaken the urgency with which he'd rushed her away from dinner. "I didn't thank you for my present."

This evening when Sidonie came upstairs to change, the jeweler's box had been waiting on the bed. She'd cringed to think Jonas proclaimed his conquest with some garish bauble. But as always, he was a man of surpassing subtlety. Inside the box, a dozen sparkling hairpins lay on white silk. Exquisite sprays of ferns and flowers. She'd never owned anything so pretty.

"I look forward to your gratitude," he said as more pins joined their fellows on the nightstand.

"I'm sure." She supposed she should be ashamed of what she meant to do with this man in this bed tonight. In spite of a lifetime of unsullied virtue, she couldn't conjure a shred of compunction. Instead she felt...free.

Jonas removed the last pin, brushed aside her loosened hair, and kissed her neck. That same sensitive spot he'd found last night when he'd been inside her. A thrill rippled through her, spiced with memory and anticipation.

She curled a hand around one powerful arm. "I thought…I thought you might humiliate me with diamonds," she said unsteadily as he nipped his way to the curve of shoulder uncovered by the scandalously low-cut gown.

She felt him smile against her. "Diamonds a humiliation, *amore mio*? Clearly I know the wrong women."

"Clearly," she said sourly, not wanting to think about his other lovers. Before or after her. Other lovers would feel him shaking with desire in their arms. Other lovers would hear that deep growl when he found release. Other lovers would lie in blessed satisfaction after he'd shown them paradise.

He raised his head and stared at her with a warmth that radiated to her toes. His arms loosely circled her waist. "Jealous, *tesoro*?"

"Madly," she said sarcastically, hating those faceless women. She wanted to scratch out their eyes and pull their hair and warn them to stay away from what was hers. It would be amusing if it wasn't tragic. Beyond the next few days Jonas wasn't hers, no matter what fancies addled her mind.

His expression alerted her to a private joke. "What is it?" She paused and her grip on his sleeve tightened. "Oh, no. You didn't. They *are* diamonds, aren't they?"

"Only small ones, *tesoro*," he said apologetically. His eyes glittered with what she tried not to interpret as delight.

"I suppose that's all right, then."

"Will you thank me with a kiss?"

"Should I? After all, they're only *small* diamonds." She couldn't resist running her hand down his unscarred cheek. Beneath her palm, his skin was firm and smooth. He must have shaved before dinner. She drew him down to her. Above her in the mirror, the man sank toward the sitting woman. Under the white lawn shirt, his back moved subtly as he kissed her.

"You're not getting into the spirit," he complained against her lips.

She shifted. "It's the mirror."

"I'll make it right." He leaned down to open the nightstand and drew something out, then kissed her tenderly.

Too quickly the kiss ended. She grumbled incoherently and followed him, holding his shoulder and pressing her mouth to his. His tongue flickered out to meet hers. Triumph flooded her. But he withdrew after a mortifyingly brief taste. "Shut your eyes."

"Merrick..." She reached a point where his teasing grated rather than amused. He watched with the half-smile that had her heart performing acrobatics.

"Shut your eyes. Please, Sidonie."

The "please" was meant to disarm. Confound him, it disarmed. She bent forward from the headboard and shut her eyes. It was a relief not seeing a hundred Sidonies.

"And my name is Jonas," he said softly. "Surely after last night, you can bring yourself to use my Christian name."

She knew she was ridiculous. Calling him Merrick helped maintain the illusion that she wasn't tumbling headlong into enchantment.

Merrick teased and taunted, and schemed to dishonor Roberta. Merrick was sarcastic and powerful. Merrick, no matter how appealing, she could resist.

Jonas...

Jonas was someone else entirely. Jonas hid a breath-taking generosity of spirit from all the world except her. Jonas had struggled to the point of pain last night to save her hurt. Jonas was so lonely and damaged, she'd sell her soul to heal him. Jonas called to her heart as nobody had before.

Jonas threatened her in ways that became clearer with each minute. And in ways that would leave her ruined indeed, well beyond the physical, when she returned to Barstowe Hall.

"Jonas." She wanted to sound short and snappy. Instead his name emerged as a sigh of concession.

"That's better."

She didn't need to open her eyes to confirm that his expression reeked satisfaction. "Can I look now?"

"Not yet."

Her hands clenched in the sheets. Denying sight sharpened her remaining senses but she couldn't help feeling defenseless. She smelled lemon soap overlying his individual scent. The bed was soft beneath her. Her hair lay heavy around her shoulders, sliding against her skin as she moved.

The mattress shifted as Jonas stood. She heard his boots brushing across the carpet. Every hair on her body lifted as he stopped beside her. He didn't touch her but she was so aware of him, he might as well. On a whisper of material, something smooth and cool covered her eyes.

"What are you doing?" she asked sharply, starting as his hands moved deftly behind her head. She opened her eyes to darkness. She lifted one hand to rip off the blindfold.

Jonas caught her. "No mirrors."

"They're still there." She gave a halfhearted tug. Uncertainty lent her tone a raw edge. "I don't like these games."

"Ten minutes, *tesoro*. That's all I ask. After that, if you don't like it, we'll play something else."

She exhaled with annoyance. "You think just because you ask nicely, you'll get your way."

"Manners maketh the man, *amore mio*."

"Do you always blindfold your lovers?"

"Often." She could tell he meant *always*. She shivered, not sure whether she was appalled or curious. She suddenly remembered how he'd snuffed the candles last night before tumbling her.

"You're a manipulative devil, Merrick." Her tone was edged.

"Jonas."

She sighed. "Merrick for the next ten minutes."

Her answer was grudging permission to continue. He released her and she heard him shift again. Dear God, she was painfully conscious of him when she could see him. Plotting his movements through sound alone threatened sanity. Thought dissolved when he dropped a kiss on her lips. Her hands curled in her skirts as she fought the urge to grab him by the ears and make him kiss her properly.

"Thank you," he whispered.

"Ten minutes." She had a sinking feeling each minute would last an hour.

"I'm counting, *tesoro*."

Trying to track him, she turned her head. She jerked when he caught her hand and kissed the pulse at her wrist. Without benefit of sight, her skin felt unnaturally sensitive.

She bit her lip then jumped when he pressed a finger into the cushiony flesh. His touch felt like a kiss. She felt the air shift, then his mouth covered hers. He sucked her poor gnawed lip into his mouth. Her heart set out on a frenetic gallop. Before she could deepen the kiss, he withdrew. Frustration coiled in her belly. Clumsily she reached to catch him but he avoided her.

Confounded blindfold.

She supposed she could take it off. She wasn't a prisoner. Something made her leave it in place. But, oh, how it smarted, waiting for those glancing caresses from every direction.

"You're playing with me." She hated how breathless she sounded. She fumbled after him and caught his arm to keep him still.

"Oh, yes."

This time she had warning. His breath was warm on her neck, raising a legion of goose bumps. His mouth traced a tendon until she trembled.

"Have we had ten minutes?" she asked in a ragged tone.

"Not yet," he said casually, nibbling a hot line along her jaw. "You're the most delicious dish in creation, *dolcissima*."

He kissed the corners of her lips and she whimpered. He smiled against her cheek. For all that she missed her vision, there was something breathtakingly seductive about feeling his expressions rather than seeing them. What he did to her felt forbidden, like a wicked sensual adventure.

Her fingers dug into the muscles of his arm. "At this rate, I'll be ninety before you do anything about it."

He shook off her hold. "Patience."

She felt the mattress dip as he kneeled behind her. It shouldn't make any difference where he was. She couldn't see him anyway. But having him at her back put her on edge.

All capacity for speech fled when he tugged on her gown. As the dress sagged open, she felt the drift of air on her bare back. The sharp nip of his teeth on her earlobe set off another cannonade of response. A pulse began to pound, heavy and hard, between her legs. She gulped in a mouthful of air. She kept forgetting to breathe.

"You make me wanton." Resentment pricked under growing arousal.

"A wonderful wanton." Silk glided over her skin when he lowered the gown from her shoulders.

"That's a devilish provocative corset," he said after a pause that made her skin tingle.

Her cheeks heated. She wore the most revealing of her new underclothes. A shift so fine, it was almost nothing. A corset lifting her breasts high for a man's hands. For Jonas's hands, she'd thought with a surreptitious thrill when Mrs. Bevan had laced her. Roses and lilies snaked across the corset, stirring brazen thoughts of limbs twined in lovemaking.

"It's sinful," she whispered, fighting the urge to cover her bosom with her hands.

"Exactly, *bella*." She heard his amusement. The blindfold made her hearing so acute, she was alert to every shade of emotion in his voice. That beautiful baritone wrapped around her like a thick blanket on a wintry night.

Suddenly she needed her eyes. To check whether he was predatory or triumphant. Or perhaps worse, whether he regarded her like the one perfect rose in his garden. When she fought so hard to resist his power over emotions as well as senses, that was the most terrifying option of all. She rose onto her knees. Her hands shook as she lifted them to the blindfold.

"No, Sidonie." He caught her hands.

"Take the blindfold off, Merrick," she demanded.

That low laugh stroked her nerve endings like thick velvet. Good God, his voice had her panting. How helpless would she be when he touched her in earnest?

"Not yet." He brought her hands higher and glanced a kiss across each set of knuckles. A caress fleeting as a puff of summer wind. Her belly tightened with arousal. She inhaled, striving for clarity. If she insisted, he'd remove the blindfold. But he'd asked her to trust him. Even while she hated how the request twisted her into knots, she couldn't deny him.

Poor Sidonie. Soon she'd be unable to deny him anything.

He still held her hands. Stupid girl, she drew strength from that clasp. She stiffened her backbone, feeling her breasts rise against the shift.

"Sidonie?" he asked softly, letting her hands fall into her lap where they opened and closed nervously in the crumpled skirt.

If he pushed or insisted or bullied, she'd withstand him. But he made her name an invitation to discover marvelous secrets.

After a pause, she reluctantly nodded. "Very well."

Chapter Seventeen

Jonas released his breath and strove against identifying his reaction as knee-trembling relief. How he wished he could paint Sidonie now, kneeling in front of him, her lavish body draped in a whisper of silk. He wanted to keep her like this forever so he could relive this moment on cold, lonely nights.

What artist could recreate Sidonie's sensuous beauty? No mere dauber could capture the feminine musk on the air. Or depict the soft, uneven pattern of her breathing. Her skin was flushed. A pulse fluttered in the hollow of her throat. Her lips were full and dark, although he'd hardly kissed her.

Over and over in the mirrors, she emerged from the loosened gown like a water lily from a lake. He loomed over her like a nightmare. Usually he derived twisted satisfaction from the contrast between a beautiful woman in his bed and his physical hideousness. He brushed aside one of the pink ribbons supporting the chemise. She jumped with nerves.

"Don't be afraid, Sidonie," he crooned, shaping his hand to her shoulder. She felt so fragile, yet she was stronger than the thick stone walls surrounding them.

"I'm not afraid." Clearly a lie. He knew she was unsure, even afraid. The blindfold must strike her as strange and wicked. Her courage scoured his heart. She'd face down Satan himself with that arrogantly tilted chin.

"You've done this before, you know," he said with a hint of teasing laughter.

"I could see you then," she responded tartly.

Brava, bella. Don't stop fighting. "Without sight, other senses take over."

"You make me shy," she said so quietly, he bent nearer to hear. He caught the haunting fragrance that was Sidonie's alone. Shutting his eyes, he drew that essence into his lungs.

The need to be inside her crashed like rolling thunder. Still, he kept his touch light as he traced a path down one white breast to the lacy edge of her shift. If he kept her in his bed the next three days, if he drank her kisses until he was intoxicated, if he explored every mystery of her exquisite body, surely he'd be sated. Except he already knew his appetite would merely feed on its desire. He'd never have enough of her.

Gently he lowered the silk to reveal one hard pink nipple. Startled, she jerked back on her knees. When he cupped her breast, her breath escaped in a whimper. With unsteady fingers, he unlaced her corset and drew it away. Dear God, she was lovely. He could worship her body for a lifetime and still feel he hadn't done her justice.

Careful not to dislodge the blindfold, he drew the red dress, then the shift, over her head. He extended her long legs, tugging her slippers off and rolling stockings over elegant ankles and feet. He dropped the scraps of silk to the floor and trailed his hands slowly up satiny skin, pausing just below her sex. "It's a sin against nature to cover a woman so glorious. I decree you stay naked."

Her laugh was husky as she leaned back on her hands for balance. "I'd shock Mrs. Bevan."

Jonas's hands ran along her thighs, feeling her muscles lengthen. Her position made her lush breasts jut. When he drew her nipple into his mouth, she trembled. She trembled more powerfully when he shifted his attentions to her other breast.

Her fingers wove through his hair, holding him nearer. "I'm guessing you're still dressed," she said drily.

He lifted his head. "How do you know?"

"Merrick, your tone is too superior for it to be otherwise."

Seconds ago, she had him wanting to fall to his knees in veneration. Now she made him want to laugh. What a bewitching mixture she was. "Jonas."

"Blasted, importuning, lecherous, deceiving snake Jonas," she said with saccharine sweetness.

He tumbled her onto her back in a tangle of slender limbs and floating hair. "You say the nicest things."

Her hands clenched in his shirt when he came down over her. "I knew you hadn't undressed."

"In good time, *la mia vita*." He braced himself on his arms to stare at her. Stretched out under him, she looked like a sulky goddess. "What's your hurry?"

"Dawn rushes upon us."

"Dawn doesn't mean an end to pleasure," he said silkily.

His sulky goddess blushed so furiously that the color seeped below the blindfold. What a darling she was. More luscious than Mrs. Bevan's *baklava*. A hint of the exotic. Spice and honey that lingered on the tongue and made a man crave more. Made a man want to gorge.

Lurching to his knees, he reefed the shirt over his head, tossing it disregarded into the corner. Once more he lowered himself over her. Her soft sigh of pleasure at the brush of his naked chest against her breasts resonated through his bones. He drew away until mere inches separated them. Her strong, graceful hands were frantic as they explored his chest and grazed his hard belly. Her quick, glancing touches made more than his belly hard. His cock ached so painfully, his whole body throbbed. She skimmed a nipple and he stifled an agonized groan.

He battled for restraint. He hadn't lingered over her last night. Tonight he meant to make up for that. Very gently he parted her legs. Candlelight flickered on glistening pink folds. He caught her heady scent.

She tried to cover herself. Her voice shook with nervousness. "You're looking at me, aren't you?"

"You're beautiful."

When she started to draw her legs together, he placed one hand on her thigh. He exerted no pressure, but his heart somersaulted when she immediately lay still. Her hand dropped away from her sex.

Inhaling a breath redolent of aroused woman, he knew himself in Elysium. He kissed her with unfettered need. She opened immediately. He sucked her tongue into his mouth, feasting on her. Trailing kisses down her slender body, he became so lost in delight, he almost abandoned his goal. She moved restlessly and her legs spread wider. She couldn't know his intention but her body instinctively prepared itself.

*   *   *

Sidonie's every muscle tightened as Jonas's mouth settled against her most private place. "Wh...what are you doing?"

She tried to scramble up the bed. When he raised his head, she inhaled with shaky relief. She tried to close her legs, but he lay between them.

"Be adventurous, *bella*." She heard his smile.

She fumbled at his shoulders, but he was immovable as a mountain. "You can't possibly want to put your mouth...there."

He laughed softly. "*Tesoro,* you taste sweeter than wine."

Embarrassment threatened to incinerate her. She could remove the blindfold, but, curse him, she didn't want to see his face. Jonas had looked at parts of her she'd never expected anyone to see, parts she couldn't even name.

"I don't—" Words wedged in her throat. She dug her hand into his thick hair, holding him still between her thighs. "Please, Jonas. Don't make me do this."

The silence lengthened. The sea's distant thunder played counterpoint to her wayward heartbeat. A night bird called forlornly outside, lost on the ocean.

"The last thing I want is to frighten you." His voice was as serious as she'd ever heard it. He shifted up, his body sliding along hers. He placed a nipping kiss on each breast.

Her tension eased as she realized he wouldn't force this disturbing intimacy. Kissing her between the legs seemed outlandish to the point of perversity. "Th-thank you," she murmured and ran her hand through his hair in gratitude.

Groaning appreciation, he rubbed against her, pressing

her into the mattress. Last night, she'd been too over-whelmed to explore his body. Curiosity swelled, sharp, hungry. She possessed senses other than sight. Hearing. Smell. Taste. *Touch.*

Her hands slid up his chest to his shoulders. Measured by touch, he seemed larger, more formidable. Daringly she reached down to stroke him there, where he was a man. He tensed and she wondered whether he liked what she did. Then he pushed himself into her hand with an urgency that fueled arousal. She squirmed against the sheets to relieve the swelling heat between her thighs.

"Hell, Sidonie," he groaned, and she heard his tormented pleasure.

She did nothing more than cup him, unsure what was permissible, what gave delight. He felt vibrantly alive. And impressively big. Difficult to believe he'd pushed that rigid weight inside her last night.

In her ear, his breath was an unsteady rattle. Astonishing that she'd so swiftly brought this worldly man to the brink. She bit her lip, summoned courage, and curled her fingers. He shuddered and lowered his head to her shoulder to mutter profanities that sounded like prayers. The sensuous softness of his hair brushing her cheek contrasted pleasurably with the virile power in her grasp.

Discovering his body through touch alone was fascinating. He'd explored her with the attention a mapmaker devoted to an unknown coastline. Whereas he remained *terra incognita.*

Not after tonight.

Feeling like the bravest woman in Creation, she fumbled with his breeches.

"*Bella . . .*"

"Roll onto your back." Much as she resented its presence, the blindfold lent courage she doubted she'd muster under his knowing silver gaze.

She waited for Jonas to mock her boldness, but the mattress dipped as he shifted. Sidonie kneeled above him to stroke his rod through the opening of his breeches. She tightened and released her grip in a primeval rhythm.

"Damn it." He sounded in pain.

"Should I stop?"

"Good God, no." He demonstrated his sincerity by raising his hips. "How the hell do you know to do that?"

"I want to please you." Changing the pressure, she drew upward to the tip. Her thumb smeared a drop of moisture across the head.

"Holy merciful God." He slid away, breaking her hold.

An incoherent complaint escaped her. "What are you doing?"

"Undressing," he muttered.

Quivering with impatience, she waited. "Can I take off the blindfold?"

"No." He leaned over her, pressing her onto her back.

When he scraped his teeth over her nipple, she jumped at the sharp pleasure. She wriggled and bent her knees to frame his hips. When she reached down to continue her intriguing experiments, he grabbed her hand. "No, Sidonie."

Chagrin flooded her. "You said you liked it."

His laugh was rueful. "If you touch me, I'll explode."

"I've never—" She drew a shaky breath. "A man's body is a mystery."

"My apologies for curtailing your investigation."

Odd how humor stoked desire. Last night, giving

herself had been such a desperate matter. Now laughter lent spice to passion. "I'll further my inquiries later."

He gave an exaggerated groan. "If I survive that long."

She loved his laughter. She loved that he faced the world with a reckless smile on his scarred face. Her heart crashed against her chest. A revelation descended. A revelation unrelated to the desire heating her blood.

She didn't just want Jonas Merrick. She didn't just find him fascinating. She *liked* the reprobate. She liked him more than she'd liked anyone. When she left, longing for the lover would burn like acid. But the true tragedy was she'd miss Jonas himself. Nothing would fill the gap he left in her life.

He ran his hand down her body to her mound. She felt another of those surges of wet heat then forgot self-consciousness when he kissed her with ravenous hunger. Still kissing her, he stroked along the sleek folds. He found a particularly sensitive place and circled his finger until she whimpered and dug her fingers into his shoulders. He slid one long finger into her and worked it in and out. A powerful pulse beat in her belly and her breath emerged in broken sobs. He pushed her higher, but every time she came close to breaking through into that bright world, he'd stop, only to build response again.

"You devil." She shifted restlessly. Lights flickered behind her eyes. His fingers curled against a spot inside her that vibrated with delight. She felt herself beginning to fall, to melt, to yield. He pulled away again.

"Stop tormenting me." She was a tortured mass of nerve endings. Pleasure hovered out of reach, more agony than delight.

"Not yet."

Another of those fiendish strokes. Another flash of response that pushed her to the edge but didn't tumble her over into relief. Every muscle was on fire and only Jonas had access to lakes of cool water to ease her fever.

"You leave me no pride." She stretched up in an instinctive attempt to snatch her bliss.

"I want your hunger." For the first time, through the thunder in her head, she heard the strain in his voice. This long seduction wore him down, too. He wasn't far from losing control.

"I hunger," she admitted, hardly aware what she said.

"Not enough."

"Will you tease me until I cede everything?" she grated, flattening her heels on the bed to change the angle of those satanically tormenting caresses.

"Hell, yes." He bent to her nipple.

The rough friction of his tongue made her jerk against his stroking hand. She raised her hand to his head. This time when he thrust his fingers into her then retreated, she tugged sharply at his hair, eliciting a grunt of discomfort.

"You're a beast."

"Do you want me, Sidonie?" Demand throbbed in his voice.

He kissed her breast with such tenderness that it blasted a chasm in her heart. A chasm she suspected might never knit. He was a devil indeed.

And she was damned alongside him.

He kissed her other nipple with the same breathtaking tenderness. The hand in his hair relaxed into caress. Her pride seemed a paltry thing compared to this need. The desire. The admiration. The... affinity which she refused to dignify with a more potent name.

"Curse you, Jonas, of course I want you," she admitted on a rush.

Finally he touched her where she needed him and release crashed down over her in a headlong torrent of rapture.

Chapter Eighteen

Jonas gave Sidonie no chance to recover from her climax. He inched inside her, feeling tantalizing resistance. Her hands clenched against his shoulders and she bowed up on a moan to take him deeper.

"Are you all right?" he asked roughly, holding still so she grew accustomed to his size. He'd hurt her last night. He couldn't bear to hurt her again. The delay before she replied extended for a millennium. He prepared to withdraw, although stopping would break him. Then miraculously her body flowered around his and she inhaled on a shaky breath.

"Sidonie?" he prompted, although he felt how perfectly they fit.

"I'm fine." Her choked laughter vibrated through him and almost made him spill himself. "More than fine."

Thank God.

He buried his face in her shoulder, his senses replete with Sidonie. Her musky scent, her choppy gasps for air, the softness of her skin, the burnished flow of her hair. He shut his eyes and basked in the knowledge that in this instant she was unequivocally his. Their communication was silent and complete. They existed in a radiant world separate from harsh reality.

If only this connection could last forever.

Her hands relaxed against his shoulders. He relished the play of muscles around his cock as she caressed him from the inside. He'd never felt so cherished. He tightened his buttocks and pressed farther. She made a sound low in her throat.

"You're...smiling," she said breathily, stroking his arms down to his hands.

"How do you know?" He linked his fingers with hers, leaning his weight on his elbows. The union, body to body, hand to hand, mind to mind, was unearthly. She touched every atom of his being.

"I can feel it against my skin," she said huskily. "It's... nice."

"What about this?" he asked gruffly, lifting his hips.

Again she met him. She gave another of those intriguing murmurs of pleasure. A man could become addicted to those murmurs the way an opium eater turned slave to his drug.

Very slowly he withdrew, relishing the way she released him inch by inch. She exhaled on a shivery sigh then sighed again when he thrust. Immediately there was that ineffable heat. How would he live without this? He'd been cold all his life. She made him feel alive.

Her hands curled around his and she arched. A vermillion wave of need overwhelmed him and he began to pound into her, going deep and hard. But even in his extremity, he still felt the link between their straining bodies, between their clinging hands.

She rushed toward her peak. He braced above her and accelerated the cadence. The searing friction drove him to the brink. He thought his jaw must crack with his efforts to rein himself in.

At last, at last, she released a hoarse cry and her hands clenched on his. Passion blazed through him like wildfire. He shuddered over her, pouring his life into her. When at last he slumped exhausted in her arms, he knew he'd never be the same again. Sidonie had carved her name on his soul.

Sidonie woke to darkness. Not the darkness of night, but of the blindfold. Jonas's hands were running in long caresses down her naked body from breasts to hips.

Automatically she shifted to remove the cloth around her eyes, but he caught her hand. "No."

"Jonas, I want to see you." He'd made love to her three times last night and each time, she'd been blindfolded.

He kissed the hand he held. "It's better this way."

She fought the weakling urge to let him have his way as long as he kept touching her. "Better for me or for you?"

"For both of us."

"Liar." She wrenched away and this time managed to rip the blindfold off. As she'd thought, it was morning. Jonas had opened the curtains and sunlight poured into the room, turning the mirrors into dazzling reflections. Jonas lay beside her, his head propped on one bent arm, the blankets drawn up to his waist.

He turned away from her regard. "Don't."

"I know what you look like," she said steadily, tugging

the sheet over her breasts. Something about the brightness, the mirrors, and the blindfold made her self-conscious
as she hadn't been self-conscious during the tumultuous
night.

His voice turned harsh in such contrast to the husky
praise he'd heaped upon her last night. "And so do I."

She frowned. "Do you think I'm going to start screaming because I've realized my lover is scarred?"

"I'd rather not remind you that you're in bed with a
monster."

"I'm not in bed with a monster. I'm in bed with Jonas
Merrick, the most breathtakingly exciting man I've ever
known." She drew a deep breath and prayed for patience.
"Don't you trust my desire, Jonas? After last night?"

"Don't you trust me if you can't see me?"

"Don't you trust me if you *can* see me?"

The blindfold wasn't just about trust, although she recognized that was a large part of it. It was also about the
emotional distance that, in spite of the blazing physical
satisfaction they'd shared, he still struggled to maintain.
When she'd seduced him in the dressing room, he hadn't
had a chance to raise any barriers. For all the heady bliss
she'd experienced last night, she'd known that he'd fought
to establish a breath of space between them. An infinitesimal gap between the breathtaking lover who transported
her to ecstasy and the real man. Even as his body pounded
into hers, a hidden corner of his soul remained separate.

Was she greedy to want that hidden corner to become
hers, too?

"Your scars don't matter."

Temper flared in his eyes, turned them molten silver.
"Of course they fucking matter."

"Oh, my dear…" she whispered. He was so hurt. She couldn't bear it. "Forget what you look like. The total of what you are is so much greater than what you see reflected in all these mirrors."

His voice was toneless and the stare he turned on her was stony. "The women I've bedded find my scars offer a piquant thrill. A titillating glimpse of gothic horrors."

"You underestimate yourself." She knew even as she spoke that his self-hatred was so deeply seated, he wouldn't heed her. How she loathed those unknown women who had convinced him he was less than other men.

"When I was younger and not quite so arrogant, I may even have noted an element of compassion in a lover. Gruesome adventure for a bored widow or charity case? I find either option distasteful. The blindfold ensures equality. The mirrors remind me that only blindness can perpetuate that equality."

Yet again, her heart broke for him. The world had bruised his noble spirit, until he started to beat his enemies at their own game. Knowing him as she did, she could imagine he delighted in turning women who had scorned him into slaves to pleasure. Was that what he felt when he took her? She couldn't bear to countenance the idea. "You know I want you."

"That's no mystery. You're an innocent who's discovered bed sport. A man with my disadvantages quickly learns how to give a woman pleasure."

His cruel response made her stomach churn with sick anger. Even after the night they'd just passed, he couldn't bring himself to trust her. Every day she spent with him gave him greater capacity to hurt her. She'd always sworn she'd never put herself at a man's mercy. It seemed by giving herself to Jonas, she'd opened herself up to a world of pain. She'd been right to be wary. But it was too late to protect herself. "Don't insult both of us."

He sighed and raised himself against the headboard. "*Bella,* let's not fight. Having you in my arms is such a joy. Don't spoil it."

"You don't need to blindfold me to find joy, Jonas," she snapped, wanting to hammer the truth into his stubborn head.

His eyes were bleak as they settled upon her. "Let me play my games, Sidonie. They harm nobody."

Frustration coiled in her belly. He wouldn't admit that she was different from those other women who had scarred his soul as deeply as some assailant had scarred his face. "We made love without the blindfold the first time."

A grim smile flitted across his lips. "You assaulted me before I made my usual preparations."

"You didn't offer much resistance."

"I thought you'd left me forever. I wasn't myself."

Ah, at last. An admission of need, even if he didn't recognize it as such. It gave Sidonie hope that perhaps before the week was done, he'd surrender his whole self to her. "And you're yourself when you blindfold me?"

"Precisely." He picked up the blindfold and extended it. He'd retreated from harrowing honesty. She could see his defenses go up against her as clearly as if he erected a physical wall between them. "It's my eccentricity, but I hate the idea of anyone watching me when I'm with a woman."

"You hate the idea of losing control," she said shortly.

The smile built. "That, too." He paused. "Are you complaining?"

She sighed. Curse her soft heart. He needed her and if the only gift he'd accept was sexual pleasure, she'd live with that. For now.

"No." She reached out and snatched the blindfold. "I'll give you your way."

"I'll make sure you don't regret it." He waited for her to cover her eyes, then lunged forward to kiss her with a passion that incinerated lingering doubts.

The next two days whirled by in a daze of sensuality. Sidonie existed on a plane that retained no link to her life before Jonas Merrick took her to his bed. She should be ashamed of the wanton she'd become. Instead for the first time she felt utterly true to herself. But for all the joy she found in Jonas's arms, she was poignantly aware that each hour together was measured.

Inevitably, remorselessly, their last afternoon arrived. Neither mentioned the fact, but mutual awareness of approaching separation weighted the air like a miasma. Sidonie watched Jonas now across the library, memorizing every detail, because soon memories of him would be all she had.

Can I bear to leave tomorrow?

An hour ago they'd ventured downstairs. The bedroom had become a private universe that neither was eager to escape. But Jonas had mentioned something in a book, the route of a yacht trip he'd taken with his father down the Greek coast. He lounged on the window seat, a large atlas open on his lap.

Since she'd become Jonas's lover, golden hours of physical pleasure had spun into eternity. The prospect of relinquishing this rich, vibrant connection so soon after discovering it made Sidonie want to weep. Although she hadn't cried. Not once. She'd have ample time to cry once she left.

"What is it?" Jonas turned a page of the atlas before looking up.

"I'm wondering what's for dinner." She perched on the desk, flaunting herself. She wore the red dress and her hair tumbled in disarray down her back.

A smile lit his eyes. "Is that so?"

She cast him a look under her lashes that she'd learned drove him wild. "All right, should I tell you what I'm really thinking?"

"If you must." Light through the tall windows gleamed on his overlong black hair. He wore breeches and a loose shirt open at the neck. How could she resist touching him? Although delay built potent suspense.

"I must." She smiled and swung her bare feet in a consciously provocative action. "I was thinking if I'd known what fun debauchery was, I'd have chased the gardeners years ago."

Jonas slammed the book shut, surged to his feet, and covered the distance between them in three strides. "Stay away from the gardeners, madam."

"They wouldn't mind." Goodness, when had she become this flirtatious trollop? She shouldn't enjoy his blatant jealousy quite so much.

"I'm sure they wouldn't." He placed his hands flat on either side of her, hemming her in. He didn't touch her but his big, powerful body was near enough for her to feel his heat. "But they're off limits. As are footmen and postboys and cowherds—and butchers, bakers, and candlestick makers."

She drew Jonas's scent deep into her lungs. Even trembling with desire, she fought to maintain her light tone. She liked teasing him. Over the last few days, she'd discovered teasing him had one certain outcome.

She liked that outcome even better than teasing.

Slowly she tilted back on her hands until her bosom tested the gown's décolletage. On first wearing, she'd considered this dress indecent. After two days mostly naked, wearing clothes at all felt like a major concession to decorum. "How appallingly dull."

"Exactly." His gaze dropped to her cleavage, shamelessly displayed, and his nostrils flared. She'd always considered herself ridiculously over-endowed, but she'd quickly discovered Jonas liked her generous breasts.

"And unfair."

"It seems perfectly fair to me." He leaned in until only an inch separated them. The yen to bridge the gap pulsed pleasurably in her blood. "You're too dangerous a weapon to fall into careless hands. You should be locked away where you'll do no harm. With me."

"How would we pass the time?" She adopted an air of boredom. Her heart pounded so hard, surely he must hear it. She arched her neck so her hair cascaded across the blotter behind her.

"Let me demonstrate." His laugh trickled down her backbone like perfumed oil. "Brace yourself."

"Well, that's romantic. The chambermaids must swoon at your slightest word."

"They collapse at the mere mention of my name. I'm always tripping over insensible domestics. It's devilish tiresome."

"I'm sure." She hardly knew what she said. God help

her when he finally laid those clever hands on her. "Shall we go upstairs?"

"Yes."

She began to slide off the desk but he caught her waist, keeping her in place. Even through her dress, the shock of contact made her stomach lurch. Startled, she looked up. "Jonas?"

"Later." From the adamant line of his jaw, she guessed he intended to use her here in the library.

"We can't." Her insouciance dissolved into fluster. "What if Mrs. Bevan comes in?"

He shot her a mocking look. "You don't sound nearly as bold as you did a few minutes ago."

She blushed. And cursed that she did. "Well, what if she does?"

"Believe me, Mrs. Bevan knows to wait for a summons." To her surprise, he kissed her, a desperate ravishment that left her breathless. His voice lowered to a seductive murmur. "I love that I can still make you blush."

"I still have a few morals left."

"We'll have those out of you in no time. Prepare yourself, *bella*. Your education continues."

Ruthlessly he turned her so she bent across the desk with her feet resting on the floor between his. She placed her hands flat on the blotter to save herself from falling. He brushed aside the soft weight of her hair and pressed a sucking kiss into her nape. She trembled and her knees turned to water.

When he lifted her skirts above her waist, exposing her, she couldn't restrain a nervous whimper. "What are you doing?"

"You'll see."

Actually she probably wouldn't. She wasn't blind-folded as she'd been every time he'd tumbled her in the bed upstairs, but he still turned her away from his face. How she longed to look into his eyes when they made love. Every time he denied her that privilege, her yearning became stronger.

"Let's go upstairs." She edged away. She guessed he meant to mount her like an animal. His earthy crudeness should disgust her. Instead her heart slammed against her ribs with flaring excitement.

"Not yet," he said mildly, placing a commanding hand on her back as he gently but inexorably pushed her down. She trembled as air brushed her private places. She knew Jonas watched her ... there. She was caught between piercing curiosity and the modesty she thought she'd abandoned with her virginity.

"How convenient that you're not wearing drawers, *la mia vita*." His voice vibrated with approval. And need.

"If you tell me to trust you, I'll clout you with the ink-well," she muttered, her hands fisting against the desk.

He laughed softly. "Have I led you astray yet?"

"You've done nothing but lead me astray," she said drily, wondering how he expected her to string more than two words together.

"You'll need something to hold onto." His voice deepened to a growl.

"You?"

Another laugh. His hands shaped her hips and stroked her bottom. Under his caresses, she shifted restlessly. "Later."

She stretched to curl her hands over the desk's edge. As she rested her forehead on the blotter, her bottom tilted higher. "I feel ridiculous."

"You have a beautiful arse, *tesoro*." He bit one buttock and she started, even as heat pooled in her sex. She made an inarticulate protest and tried to sidle out of reach, but he slid one leg between hers, trapping her.

"Ah, Sidonie, Sidonie, Sidonie," he sighed, the repetition of her name a paean of praise.

The slow glide of silk skirts higher up her back heightened response. This position was frightening and bordered on uncomfortable, but it was wildly stimulating to wait for Jonas to use her like a stallion used a mare. She pressed her face against her extended forearm, muffling a whimper.

When she felt his mouth against her leg, she jerked. Before he reached the top of her thigh, she was shaking as if she had a fever. He couldn't kiss her there, not when she'd forbidden him, her horrified mind insisted.

He released her. The abrupt cessation of sensation left her wallowing. And feeling more than a little silly with her bare rump hitched under his nose.

"Do it," she demanded, past pride.

"You'll give me my way?" His voice was raw.

"As if you ever take anything else." Her blood roiled with need, her pulse pounded like a thousand drums. If he didn't touch her soon, she'd shatter into red-hot shards like overheated glass.

Those hard, ruthless hands ran up her legs with a sureness that made her burn. She heard him fall to his knees behind her. When he parted her, her belly knotted with agonizing anticipation. This was sinful, so sinful.

When he put his mouth between her legs, pleasure crashed through her. Before she came to terms with what happened, his tongue moved along her cleft.

"Jonas, that's so wicked." She slumped against the desk as her knees finally gave way.

His teeth grazed her and the pleasure focused. He explored her with his mouth, sucking, nipping, licking until she was dizzy. His tongue penetrated her in a slide of thick, wet heat. Through the storm, she heard a woman's broken cry. Everything became blazing sensation. Her bones melted to hot honey.

It could have been terrifying careering along the edges of the sky. Except firm hands kept her anchored and a man's whispered praise played bass counterpoint to the brazen tattoo of her heartbeat.

Chapter Nineteen

Jonas held Sidonie's hips as she shuddered with pleasure.

Damn it, he should feel triumphant. She'd shattered as delightfully as he'd imagined she would. Instead he felt he should stay on his knees and say a prayer of thanks to a God he wasn't sure he believed in. He placed a reverent kiss on each lush buttock.

He was damned glad she couldn't see him. If she caught his expression, she might guess the unwelcome profundity of his reaction. Even as his mouth possessed her, she'd possessed him. He had a powerful premonition she'd possessed him for all time.

Sidonie started to straighten. She must think they'd finished here.

Not nearly.

"Don't move." Surprising how difficult it was to speak.

"I won't." The swift obedience was another sign of how high he'd taken her.

He drew a choked breath and rose on humiliatingly wobbly legs. He was hard as granite. Fumbling, he released himself from his breeches.

"Spread your legs," he said brusquely. Gentleness was beyond him. Hunger pummeled him like one of the wild coastal squalls.

She didn't seem to mind his gruffness. As she opened, her musky fragrance flooded his senses. He gripped his cock and tilted his hips until the thick head teased her glistening sex. She gave another of those luscious whimpers that always made him crazy to be inside her. She nudged back in encouragement. The slide of her cleft threatened to unman him. He bit back a curse.

Listening to her unsteady panting, he pressed forward. She was tight, wonderfully tight, swollen after her climax. Her whimper this time conveyed a trace of protest. He stopped, dragging in breath after breath as he strove for control. The urge to claim her tightened his balls and hollowed his gut.

She inched back and took him farther inside. The clench of her passage blasted him with heat. He was a barbarian to enjoy this so much when she wasn't ready. Except the hot moisture bathing him told him she wanted him. When she bumped against him in unmistakable demand, he couldn't resist. On a long groan, he buried himself deep. He resisted the impulse to move. He wanted to savor this perfection. The world that always seemed so discordant, so unwelcoming, turned right when he was inside Sidonie. He bent over her, his belly crushing her arse. She stretched under him with a soft moan and the change of position spurred him on.

He started slowly, withdrawing luxuriantly. But soon

madness set upon him. His balls had ached like the devil since he'd angled her over the desk an excruciating eon ago. He dipped one hand beneath her bodice and found one beaded nipple. He heard her breath change. He released her breast and grabbed her hips, slamming deeper and higher. Through the whirlpool in his blood, he felt her brace against the desk and push back.

His shaking hand found her beneath the froth of skirts. She jerked and released a hoarse exclamation. His world dissolved into delight.

After what felt like years wandering among the stars, Sidonie returned to find her cheek pressed against the blotter, the rim of the desk jabbing her belly, and Jonas's body pinning her down. His face was buried in her hair. He sprawled across her, cutting circulation to one arm. She flexed her fingers to relieve pins and needles and bit back a grunt of discomfort. With a reluctance she could feel, he tensed before moving away.

"Not yet," she protested sleepily, even though he was heavy and the blotter provided an unforgiving pillow.

"I must be squashing you." His hoarse voice hinted the encounter had been earth-shattering for him, too.

"You are, but I like it."

"You're insane."

She loved it when he lit her world with ecstasy. Perhaps more, she loved these quiet moments when she rejoiced in a closeness she'd never felt with anyone else. At such times, even the slight distance he maintained became almost transparent, so she could imagine more existed between them than just physical passion.

Jonas Merrick was unique. As a man. In her life.

There would be no other.

Her heart faltered. Her happiness rested on the frailest of foundations. Reality's slightest breath would scatter it to the four winds.

The memory of that incendiary moment when he took Sidonie from behind clouded Jonas's mind as he followed her upstairs after dinner. So clouded that he only caught her calculating expression after he'd removed his shirt.

His attention sharpened on the way she leaned with apparent artlessness against a gilt bedpost. Accidental or not, the effect was spectacular. Sidonie with tumbling dusky hair and wearing, or half-wearing, red silk.

Now that he thought about it, she'd been unusually quiet all evening. As if hatching some plot. Sexual satisfaction made him dozy. Not that right now he felt particularly satisfied. Hunger for her gnawed at him, hunger fueled by the grim knowledge that this was their last night.

Their last night...

Around him, the mirrors reflected a hundred Sidonies. One caused enough trouble. Which didn't mean he was in a rush to say good-bye. He already knew her departure, damn it to hell and back, would feel like someone removed his liver slowly with a blunt spoon.

"What are you conniving?" he asked warily, standing in the middle of the room with his shirt bundled in one hand.

"I have no idea what you're talking about." She tried to look innocent. A few days ago, she wouldn't have had to try. He'd loved her innocence, but even more he loved the richness of this woman she'd become. God help him, he'd never believed such a woman existed in this tired, bad old world.

At last at a visceral level, he understood his father's outrage when he heard his beloved wife derided as a whore. Jonas had always believed himself incapable of experiencing the enduring love his father had felt for his mother. Because his life was bereft of close friends or lovers, he'd assumed he was a shallower, less steadfast man than the late viscount.

This past week made him wonder if perhaps he could want one woman alone. If she was the right woman.

Jonas struggled to banish the disturbing reflections. "Doing it too brown, *amore mio*. You're scheming something."

"Not I, sir," she said without great force. A half-smile hovered around her lush red lips. Damn it, he didn't trust that smile. Her gaze flickered to where his interest was visible and the smile intensified.

"I hope your evil plan involves two of us in that bed before much longer," he grated out.

Her smile faded and she shot him a surprisingly searching look under long lashes. He was astonished to realize that beneath her teasing, she was nervous. *Why the hell should she be nervous?*

Before he could ask, she burst into speech. "Please take off your clothes and lie on the bed."

Alertness tightened every muscle. Why should a request likely to elicit immediate cooperation make her skittish? He kept his voice neutral. Whatever this was about, he realized it was important. He needed to keep his wits about him. Difficult at the best of times with Sidonie.

"Let me blindfold you first."

Her jaw firmed. "No."

Ah. It seemed she finally rebelled. He should have

expected this earlier. He wondered why he didn't insist on his way as he had every other time she'd objected to the blindfold. Perhaps because his skin tightened with excitement at the prospect of temporarily surrendering control on this, their last night together. Perhaps because she'd demonstrated that she trusted him so many times, he owed her a return of the favor. His stomach curdled at the idea of making love to her face to face with no hindrances, but he stifled his qualms.

With any woman but Sidonie, he'd insist on his will prevailing. With Sidonie, he was willing to allow her some leeway. He wouldn't let her go too far.

"As you wish." Without shifting his attention from her, he dropped the shirt to the floor.

She sucked in a jagged breath and watched with blatant fascination as he shucked off his breeches. "Goodness me, you're so big."

Her unabashed admiration made him laugh. "You know just the right thing to say, *tesoro*."

She blushed but didn't look away. Her boldness sent heat spooling through him. "You haven't let me see you before."

"Eyes are overrated," he said, lying through his teeth. Reflections of Sidonie proved sight a priceless gift. Fate could mete out no worse punishment than denying him sight of Sidonie after tomorrow.

Her mouth adopted a wry line at his asinine remark. When she folded her arms, her extravagant bosom plumped above her bodice. He muffled a groan of frustration. "You're wearing too many clothes."

"Later. Now I want you to lie down."

Heaven help him, he was already hot as the sun and

he hadn't even touched her. Who knew a bossy woman would put him in such a lather? "Are you going to kiss me all over?"

"Possibly." The spark in her eyes contradicted her primness.

His nerves jumping, Jonas padded toward the bed and stretched out upon the crisp white sheets. Sidonie hesitated before following. Sensual curiosity thundered in his head. What was her game?

"Thank you." She leaned down, offering him a breath-taking view of her breasts under that deucedly loose bodice, and slanted her lips over his. The kiss ended swiftly, but even that fleeting contact made him swell hard and thick. Glancing at his cock with another of those secretive smiles, she lifted his arm and reached toward the headboard.

He tilted his head to watch her. Suspicion tempered his pounding need. "What are you doing, *bella*?"

She bit her lip. The way her small white teeth dug into that full pink flesh was always damnably arousing. "Don't fight me."

"Why would I fight?"

Quickly she slipped a cord from under the pillow and lashed his wrist to the bedpost. Damn his complacency. At this rate, he mightn't have the chance to pull her back into line. Shocked, he jerked against the tie and started to sit up. "What the hell?"

"Don't." She placed one hand flat on his bare chest.

She didn't exert much pressure. Even if she did, he was strong enough to throw her off. But the warmth of her palm on his skin made him stop as though turned to stone. He poised, balancing on the arm she hadn't tied—

the kingdom's biggest blockhead could guess her intentions now—and regarded her with baffled anger.

"This is risky play, *amore mio*," he said soberly.

He tugged on the cord, expecting it to loosen, but Sidonie tied an efficient knot. He shouldn't be surprised. She was efficient with most things. He admired that—except when she turned that damned efficiency against him.

The color deepened in her cheeks. "Humor me."

Glancing past her, he saw them reflected over and over. Tethered naked like a beast, he looked confoundedly defenseless. Standing over him, Sidonie appeared distant, queenly, omnipotent. He loathed what he saw.

She shifted to the other side of the bed. "Give me your hand."

"No." He reached to undo the cord.

She caught his hand. "Please."

Her request didn't mollify him. Anger rose, a potent brew with ever-present desire. "We haven't been at this long enough for you to tire of the usual variations," he said snidely and suffered a stab of remorse when her eyes darkened with hurt.

"I'm too inexperienced to know the *usual variations*." She lent the last two words scathing emphasis.

With her watching him with that plea in her gaze, he couldn't quite bring himself to untie the cord. "Believe me, *tesoro*, what you're doing now exceeds boundaries most wives permit."

"I'm not a wife." Her spirit revived. "I'm your mistress."

His heart kicked in protest. A mistress implied a woman of impermanent status passed from keeper to keeper. He didn't feel that way about Sidonie. "You hate the mirrors," he said flatly, hoping to coax her back into cooperating with him.

"I hate the blindfold more."

The telltale flicker in Jonas's cheek told Sidonie that she pushed him to the edge. Her belly knotted with trepidation, but she couldn't give up now. She hovered so close to shattering the final barriers between them. Their first night together had left her with a confusion of vivid impressions. Since then, Jonas had blindfolded her. This was her last chance to watch his expression as his body united with hers. She wanted to cherish that memory against the future. She meant Jonas to look into her eyes as he took her, so she didn't remain some faceless, blindfolded woman he pleasured, but Sidonie, Sidonie, Sidonie. And that recognition would blast to ashes the tiny but distinct separation he maintained between them, even now.

She was such a savage. She meant to carve her name on his heart in bloody letters that scarred him more deeply than the wounds on his face. She meant to be unforgettable.

At least that was the plan.

"Devil take you, Sidonie." The aching despair in his low baritone made her heart cramp with anguish. She waited for him to say more but he remained silent. He glowered at her as if he hated her. Right now he probably did. Even sitting taut and naked with one hand fastened to the bedpost, he looked formidable enough to make her quail if she wasn't quite so determined.

"Don't refuse me, Jonas," she said softly, laying her hand over his racing heart. His hunted expression told her he felt under attack.

He raised his free hand to his face before he realized how the gesture betrayed him. Dear God, she'd seen that gesture before. What a slow-top she was, not to realize its significance. A world of pain lay buried inside this man. She'd always known it. But sometimes, like now, his suffering made her so furious, she wanted to squall like a banshee.

He tugged at the cord. "You breach our arrangement, madam."

Not *bella,* not *tesoro,* not *amore mio,* or any other extravagant Italian endearment. *Madam.*

If she'd needed proof how her siege angered him, she had it. Still she stood her ground, trying to ignore the apprehension kicking in her stomach. "You released me from that arrangement," she said through stiff lips.

Restlessly he rolled over to concentrate on undoing the cord. "I've had enough."

"Don't," she said, her voice choked.

His fingers paused in their work and he shot her a coruscating glare. Astounding how those silvery eyes incinerated bravery to ashes. If she faltered now, she'd never have another chance to challenge him.

Of course you won't. Tomorrow you're heading back to Barstowe Hall.

She strove to ignore the taunting voice in her head. Tears stung her eyes. "It's my turn to ask you to trust me."

Like his voice, his smile held more regret than rage. "The road to hell is paved with good intentions, *bella.*"

To her astonishment, after a tense silence, he lay flat on his back and extended his free hand above his head. Compassion scored her heart as she recognized what the concession cost him.

His attention didn't waver as she tied his wrist to the other bedpost. Quickly she circled the bed to tighten the first bond. Deliberately she didn't look at the magnificent body arrayed against the sheets. Her hands were unsteady enough.

She moved to secure his feet. She felt vibrating tension as she lifted lean ankles. He was far from easy with what she did. That still he submitted made her belly clench with gratitude.

"Will you blindfold me?" She heard how he struggled for an offhand tone. His strained expression made the scars stand out white and shocking against his face. His Adam's apple bobbed as he swallowed. He was naturally a dominant male. Even if she hadn't long ago guessed that most of his games stemmed from self-consciousness about his injuries, she knew he'd hate the way she seized control.

Although there were definite benefits in what she did. She couldn't help the way her gaze lingered as it traveled up his body to his face. "Do you want me to blindfold you?"

"What I want doesn't count."

Her lips twitched. "You sound like you're five years old."

To her relief, he laughed, the sound reluctant and rusty. "Easy to mock when you have me where you want."

This time, her eyes swept him with deliberate languor, lingering on the virility that rose hard and demanding between his thighs. "I definitely want you."

His eyes narrowed until silver glinted between sooty lashes. "Show me."

Chapter Twenty

Jonas stretched on an excruciating rack of desire and shame. Stoically he stared into the mirror above, but the view offered no reassurance. A big ugly man lay naked and spread-eagled on a wide bed. His cock stood at attention and his eyes glittered with panic.

He was hers to do with as she willed. The thought was loathsome, even as his rational mind reminded him this was Sidonie who had never treated him as less than a man. But old wounds of mockery and disgust barely healed. He just had to look at his scars to know that some old wounds didn't heal at all. This vulnerability was why he never surrendered control when he took a woman.

When Sidonie placed her hand flat on his abdomen, he jerked at the radiating heat. His belly tautened until it was hard as stone. His cock throbbed like the very devil. And she hadn't even started her seduction.

She moved her hand in tantalizing circles. His heart

thumped fit to burst and his breath kept jamming in his throat. "You didn't need to bind me."

"Yes, I did."

Yes, she probably did. They both knew he liked to command. That was one of the rewards of his games with blindfolds and mirrors. He had a grim feeling his ascendancy ended tonight.

"Where did you get the cords?" Not that he cared. All he cared about was that she moved her hand and touched him where he burned. Arousal built to such a pitch, it almost swamped shame.

"The curtains." She perched on the bed and the soft curve of her hip warmed his flank through her skirts. His heart thundered as he recalled she wore nothing underneath the dress. As if he touched her, his hands opened and closed in their bonds.

"You've cheated me," she said thoughtfully.

In its erratic travels, her hand swept lower and for one flaring moment she skimmed the hair at the base of his erection. He groaned with frustration and felt himself thicken. "How?" he croaked.

She leaned down and her hair fell forward, catching the glow of candlelight, brushing the over-sensitized skin of his belly. He sucked in a painful breath as hunger blazed through him. Automatically he reached to touch her hair, only to come up short against the cord. Damn it.

She ran her hands along his ribs. He thought she'd forgotten his question. Hell, he was close to forgetting his name. He couldn't condemn her distraction. She pressed her mouth to the center of his chest.

"You've been hiding your magnificence." She nipped at one pectoral even as he jerked in protest.

"Don't ridicule me."

He regretted his response when compassion darkened her eyes, deepening them to velvet. She cupped his face. He tried to evade her but she had him trapped. "Oh, Jonas..."

The murmur echoed in the heart he struggled to barricade against her. It felt like she held his brittle soul in the palm of her hand. Would she crush it to dust? His experience of the world said yes. His experience of Sidonie made him long to entrust her with everything he was.

"I love your body," she said softly. "It's so beautiful."

He felt as though a knot of tarred rope stuck in his gullet. He couldn't have spoken even if he could think of something to say. Nobody ever called him beautiful.

"You're breathtakingly exciting. You've turned my nights to fire. You've lit my whole world with flame."

"Sidonie..." No other woman struck him dumb. Blast her, she did it all the time without trying.

"Hush." Her fingers traced the marks on his face.

Hell. He didn't want her dwelling on his hideous face. He tried to wrench away. If he wasn't tied down, he'd run from the room like the coward he was.

Damn her. Damn her to Hades. Why did she do this?

"Don't," he forced out.

"Hush," she said again and placed her lips on the thick scar bisecting his eyebrow.

"No," he choked, but she didn't seem to hear. Instead she shifted her attentions to the long slash dividing his cheek. He squeezed his eyes shut and wished she'd tied the blindfold over his face.

He hated this. *Hated it*.

"You're shaking." She spoke against his temple, her breath feathering his hair.

"Stop it." His hands fisted in their bonds.

"Oh, my love," she murmured with gentle chastisement.

The endearment cut straight through him. Even as he loathed her pity, he yearned for her tenderness. No woman had shared this sweet softness with him. It made him feel weak, needy, but he couldn't prevent his heart opening to her. When she kissed his broken nose, tears burned behind his eyes. Hell, no. He refused to weep like some puling milksop. But the angry words demanding she desist died unspoken when she pressed her mouth to his.

Jonas was so proud. Too proud.

Even now when Sidonie offered comfort for his sufferings, he fought to rise above human weaknesses like pain and loneliness. He was so used to battling the world alone, he didn't realize she was on his side.

He shook violently, as though he were trapped naked in an ice cave. She wanted to warm him, bring him next to the fire so he wouldn't be cold anymore.

His lips parted and she tasted a tenderness that made her heart constrict with longing. The kiss exploded into fierceness. He ravaged her mouth as if to punish her for pushing past desire into the dangerous world of emotion.

Breathlessly Sidonie raised her head and stared at him. He focused on her face, then lower to where her bodice gaped. Heat surged, left her giddy. Blind instinct made her kneel over him. Discovering with her lips the sinewy shoulders. The hard line of his collarbone. The racing pulse in his throat. She heard excitement in his groan when she nipped his neck.

She licked her lips. His salty taste lingered. She wanted more.

He tugged at the cords. "I have to touch you."

She shook her head.

His voice lowered to persuasion. "Sidonie, untie me."

"No." If she released him, he'd take over. All she'd prove was that she couldn't resist him. He already knew that. Her hand curled around his rod. Tonight was her last chance to touch, taste, torment him as she willed. Fair revenge after he'd tormented her so often. Watching his reaction to her caresses conjured new magic.

She slid lower. Paused. Then gathered courage to proceed. Delicately she licked the flushed head. His taste overwhelmed her senses, more pungent than his skin. Even as he growled protest, she drew him into her mouth.

Jonas released pent-up breath as Sidonie's mouth closed over his cock. He hardly believed she did this. His skin felt so hot, smoke should rise from his body. He struggled not to thrust upward. He didn't want to scare her into withdrawing. Not now. Not when she promised to transport him to paradise.

He needed to bury his hands in that mane of hair. Only when he tried to lower his arms did he remember she'd bound him. The sensation of her soft, wet mouth on him banished everything else from his mind.

Her tongue flickered, then she lifted away and stared at him with a question in her eyes. He had no right to beg her to continue. To do...more. Still the plea trembled on his lips. Only with the greatest difficulty did he bite the words back.

Then incredibly she tightened her hold and took him into her mouth once more. Tentatively she sucked. He bucked against the cords around his ankles and released a strangled curse.

On a shocked gasp, she withdrew.

Dear God, Sidonie, don't stop. Don't stop now.

"Don't you like it?" she asked unsteadily.

He fought to clear his vision. Even her tentative experiments left him reeling, as if she flung him into an abyss from a mountaintop. "Of course I like it," he snarled.

Her cheeks were flushed and her lips were damp and red. He wanted that mouth on him more than he wanted to live. A troubled frown crossed her face. "You don't sound very comfortable. Am I not doing it right?"

"You don't have to do this." He couldn't believe he'd said it. Where the hell had this sodding knight in shining armor come from?

"I want to." She licked her lips as though she relished his taste.

His balls tightened until he feared they'd explode. He stared at her, vainly seeking some sign of disgust or hesitation. "Dear Lord, Sidonie, you shouldn't have even thought of this."

To his surprise, her lips quirked. "I have an active imagination."

His brain started to work despite the fog of thwarted desire. He was such a fool. This was no milk-and-water miss. This was the shameless hussy who had tied him to his bed. This was the gallant woman who never quailed from his scarred face. "Good God, you really *do* want this."

"Yes."

He glared at the bonds. "Untie me and I'll show you what to do."

"Don't spoil my fun. I'd rather discover on my own."

"I mightn't survive the experience."

"Big, brave Jonas Merrick?"

"I'm only flesh and blood."

Her smile became pure seduction. "Yes, you're that."

Any response evaporated in a searing burst as she firmed her grip and moved her hand up and down. Every muscle cramped with sensation. A drop of pearly liquid leaked onto the tip. He gritted his teeth and told himself he wouldn't spill into her hand.

A strange expression crossed Sidonie's face.

Please don't let it be revulsion.

Before Jonas could muster protest or plea, she bent and deliberately licked away the evidence of excitement. The abrasion of her tongue made him clench his hands. Much more and he'd incinerate the damned cords. Then at least he'd be free to show her what he wanted.

She raised her head. His heart slammed against his chest as her slender throat moved. He sucked in a ragged breath. She had him in such a fever, he kept forgetting to breathe. He knew it would never happen, not with a woman like Sidonie, but the prospect of flooding her mouth with his seed then watching her swallow made him insane with yearning. Time slowed. Through narrowed eyes, he watched her lower her head.

If she stopped, she'd kill him.

Surely she'd stop.

He bit back a long groan as she took him deeper. His sight faded to black.

Her shyness melted away. Instead there was hot, wet suction as she drew hard. In his wildest dreams, he'd never imagined she'd do this. Not of her free will. She was a little clumsy. Strangely her lack of familiarity with the act reinforced pleasure. And touched his heart, much as he cursed his heart's involvement.

She bobbed her head until she took most of him. He groaned again and his hips surged. "Sidonie, *bella*..."

She increased the pressure and he squeezed his eyes shut, battling to hold back. Devil take these ties. He couldn't roll her onto her back and plunge into her as he longed to do. Not that he'd last more than a few seconds.

"Sidonie, stop." His voice sounded raw.

Slowly she lifted her mouth, the slide excruciating. Hell, she'd have him whimpering like a baby.

"I want to keep going." Her voice was deep and husky as he'd never heard it. The woman who licked her lips savoring his taste knew she possessed him.

Of course she did.

"I want to be inside you." Faint vestiges of the man he'd once been winced to hear him beg. "Untie me."

"Oh, no." Her smile was provoking. Where had she learned to smile like that? The woman who arrived at his castle wouldn't smile like that. She'd been a furled rosebud, fragrant with potential. This Sidonie was a full-blown flower, sweet-scented and luscious. "Not now I have you where I want."

"Have pity, *anima mia*." He'd never called her that before, although it was true. She was his soul. When she left tomorrow, she'd carry his soul with her. God help him.

Straddling him, she hovered over where he needed her. She hitched her skirts around her hips, giving him a breathtaking glimpse of dark curls hiding her sex. The knowledge of what she was about to do—surely she meant to ride him, although it was a position she hadn't yet tried—crashed through him like an ax. All moisture dried from his mouth. His head swam.

No wonder. Every drop of blood had rushed to his cock.

Her musky scent goaded him. Although he hadn't touched her, she was aroused. She placed one hand on his chest then slowly, oh, so slowly, lowered her hips, using her other hand to guide him into her body. Delicately she took the tip and he groaned long and hard when she stopped there. He waited for her to cover him. Instead she rose, her sleek cleft teasing the swollen head.

The witch had teased him all night. He couldn't endure much more. She was inhuman. He feared he was far too human. The humiliating likelihood of losing himself on the sheets loomed.

"Sidonie." Her name was a strangled protest. He writhed against his bonds, clumsily lifting his hips. He was past finesse. Good God, he was past thought. Perhaps it was a good thing that she still wore the red dress. If she was naked, he'd have lost his mind hours ago.

Still she held herself apart, the wicked girl. Once, twice, he lurched upward and each time she poised far enough away for him to feel her heat. She laughed, a low sound of excitement. Her eyes were opaque and dilated. These games had an incendiary effect on her, too.

"Damn you, Sidonie," he choked out. "You're enjoying this."

"Oh, yes." She dropped perilously close.

This time she luxuriantly moved her hips, bathing him in liquid heat. Over his galloping heart, he heard her whimper. Her hand curled in his chest hair. Her grip tightened and she sank over him more fully. In shaking suspense, he waited for her to pull away.

On a deep breath, she slid down. A long keening sound of pleasure escaped her.

"Jove and all his angels," he grated as glorious warmth enclosed him.

The sensation exceeded all experience. The delay had built him to a pitch that he no longer felt connected to earth. She claimed his whole body. This act pleasured him from the soles of his feet to the tips of his hair. She'd marked him forever. More deeply than the scars disfiguring his face. Every cell sang her name.

Just as he reached the limits of restraint, so did she. She rippled around him, shooting wild shocks through him with each exquisite fraction of withdrawal. She lowered once more and clasped his length. He gasped and the slight shift set off new quakes. She sighed with voluptuous enjoyment. His vision cleared. The beautiful face, the abandoned expression, the flushed lips and cheeks. His fear had deprived him of so much. The blindfold had denied him this. He hadn't known what he'd been missing.

Her nipples pressed wantonly against her bodice. His hands curled uselessly above his head. Hell, she must untie him. He couldn't bear not touching her. Before he could articulate this demand through the jumble in his mind, she reared, with less control this time. On a choked cry, she came down hard and the world ignited.

Chapter Twenty-One

When Sidonie returned to earth after that astonishing climax, she was boneless with exhaustion, as if she'd built a mountain single-handed with a spade. She mustered energy to untie Jonas and tug the crumpled silk dress over her head. Then she curled up in his arms and sought oblivion.

Now as she stirred from sleep, she felt warm and sated and safe. Making Jonas wait had nearly killed her, but it had been worth it. He'd become completely hers in a way he never had before. And she knew at the height of his pleasure, his ever-present awareness of the scars separating him from other men had faded to blind rapture. She'd longed to give him surcease from his torments. Watching his eyes as he lost himself to her, she knew she'd succeeded.

She didn't move, afraid to disturb him. Then realized that much of her current contentment radiated from his lazy caresses across her back. He stroked her like a cat.

Like a cat, she stretched and purred delight, loving the way her skin slid against his.

"Did I sleep long?" Her voice sounded rusty, as though she hadn't used it for a long time. Or she'd screamed at the peak of pleasure.

"Not long." His voice was a deep rumble under her ear.

Tonight was too short to waste in sleep. She rubbed her cheek against the soft hair on his chest. Impossible to believe that in the morning she'd dress in old clothes and step into Jonas's carriage to leave. She'd imagined this last night would prove a melancholy experience. Instead they'd fortified their bond rather than spoken a last good-bye.

As she rose on one elbow, the candlelit mirrors reflected a brazen woman, draped naked across her lover. Meeting her eyes in the mirror, she drew courage from the level gaze. No mistake that she'd need courage for what she intended now. More courage than she'd needed to tie Jonas to the bed and have her wicked way with him.

She thought he might draw her down for a kiss, but he stared up at her as though memorizing every pore of her skin. He skimmed his hand across her features. Forehead. Eyes fluttering under his touch. Nose. Cheeks. Chin. Lips.

"How adventurous you've become, *bella*." He sounded drowsy and reflective. In the flickering candlelight, the gray eyes were soft like morning mist.

She smiled under his fingers. "You forgive me for binding you?"

"If I can return the favor."

"Of course." She shivered with anticipation, then unhappy awareness punctured her excitement as she realized their time together was now measured in hours. She slanted her lips across his in a kiss that she hoped conveyed everything she'd felt during the last miraculous days. The kiss was also a silent apology. She didn't fool herself that he'd appreciate what she meant to do.

He intensified the kiss, shifted it into passion.

So tempting to cede. But she couldn't. Slowly, she lifted her head and brushed his black hair back from his angular face. She'd come to know him so well. More compelling than her curiosity, compelling as that was, was the desperate need she sensed in him to unburden his lonely soul. She longed above all to give him peace.

As if he guessed her intentions, his relaxed expression leached away. She paused to repent the loss of his contentment. *Courage, Sidonie.*

She sucked in a breath. "Jonas, how did you get your scars?"

Jonas's gut lurched with horrified denial. Hell, he should have expected this. Which didn't make Sidonie's question any more welcome. Once she'd asked him and he'd rebuffed her, but after tonight, they'd reached a point where he could no longer deny her the truth.

Unable to hold her searching, compassionate gaze, he rolled away to sit on the edge of the bed with his back to her. In the mirrors, he watched her rise to her knees behind him. He knew that stubborn expression too well to imagine he'd avoid interrogation.

Unfortunately for his efforts to keep her out of his head and heart, determination wasn't the only emotion she displayed. Worse than stubbornness was vulnerability in the downturned corners of her lush mouth, and uncertainty in her deep brown eyes. Eyes that expressed no judgment, merely a profound concern for him, concern that a more sentimental man than Jonas Merrick might describe as loving.

"I don't want to talk about this," he said grimly, burying his face in his hands so he didn't have to see his hideous reflection.

"I know you don't." Her voice ached with sadness.

He raised his head. "It's our last night, *carissima*. We should be lost in pleasure."

"Tell me, Jonas." She sucked in a shaky breath, then her hands snaked around him. He stiffened even as he yearned to accept her embrace. Her hold felt protective, as if she defended him from unknown terrors. The sensation of someone watching out for him was unfamiliar and fiendishly alluring.

He flinched when she laid her cheek against his back, pressed her breasts against him. Her skin felt silky and warm. Odd how affecting these gestures of comfort were. Jonas strove to insist her gentleness meant nothing, but not even he believed that. It was a sobering reflection upon his life that he couldn't remember anyone else offering him open affection. His father had loved him, but he'd been an Englishman with an Englishman's inhibitions. A handshake or an arm flung around his son's shoulders tested the heights of demonstrativeness. And his father's affection for his son had always been a pallid emotion compared to his grief for his wife.

Sidonie's silence and undemanding embrace wore down defenses fortified over more than twenty years. He linked his hands over hers. "It's not a pretty story," he said gruffly.

*   *   *

Sidonie hadn't been sure Jonas would tell her. There was no real reason he should. She felt his shuddering tension. She'd known almost from the first that his scars were a forbidden area for curiosity and now she forced him to confront the events that left him so horribly marked. Dredging up words to describe past horrors would hurt him.

Heavens, it would hurt her.

Just before she relinquished hope of anything further, he spoke. "It happened when I was ten. At Eton."

Her arms tightened. She verged so near this ultimate mystery. If he denied her now, she couldn't bear it.

"Some older boys took exception to the baseborn mongrel in their midst and expressed their opinion with their fists."

Horror jammed her throat. "They deliberately tortured you?"

"Boys are little barbarians, *amore mio.*"

"You didn't deserve this." Despite her best efforts to remain calm, her voice cracked with emotion.

He turned and twined his arms around her. She no longer provided comfort; he did. He dashed away the tear that trickled down her cheek. "Don't cry, *tesoro*. It was a long time ago."

And every day he relived it as if it happened anew. She knew enough about him to dismiss his stoic reassurance as a lie. "That's not the point. It was wrong."

A strange expression crossed his face, a wryness she couldn't interpret. "It proved a salutary experience. A lesson in not getting above myself. A bastard shouldn't put on airs appropriate to his legitimate brethren."

His cutting words sounded eerily familiar. Suddenly

like a fist smashing into her belly, Sidonie understood everything. And wished to heaven she didn't. Probably nobody else would recognize that clipped, dismissive intonation. But she'd lived with William six years. She'd heard him rage against Jonas. Bemoaning his cousin's success, he'd used those exact words.

"William cut you." It wasn't a question.

The silvery eyes were guarded. "That's a wild guess."

"But accurate."

Expecting Jonas to pull away, she raised one hand to his scarred cheek. He remained unmoving, then with a low sound of acceptance, pressed his face into her palm. "How clever of you to realize."

"I should have realized earlier." Her voice shook. Curse her blindness. The clues were there in Jonas's pursuit of revenge against a man unworthy of his time. The words telling him he was Viscount Hillbrook surged up but she bit them back. She already knew that in his vendetta against William, Roberta and her children were of little importance to him. Better she settled Roberta somewhere safe, then sent Jonas the marriage lines.

"William rallied half a dozen bully boys and they waylaid me behind the chapel."

"That's unfair. You aren't responsible for your parents' sins."

His smile was unamused. "Perhaps not. But that's the cruelty of children, isn't it?"

Blind indeed. Before coming to Castle Craven, she'd been so hopelessly shallow to imagine Jonas's bastardy wouldn't affect him. Whereas the more she discovered about him, the more she realized his disinheritance was his life's besetting tragedy. "I'm so sorry, Jonas."

"I didn't guess they intended more than the usual beating until William pulled out a carving knife. He said the world needed to know I was beyond the pale."

Sidonie shuddered and choked down rising nausea. The whole incident reeked of William. The braggadocio, the cruelty, the cowardice of attacking his enemy after mustering superior forces. Jonas would have fought like a demon. But one small boy, no matter how valiant, had no chance against a gang of older thugs. Her hand curled around his neck. "You're lucky he didn't kill you."

Jonas's grunt wasn't exactly a laugh. "He damned near did. Thank God, two of my schoolfellows rescued me."

"Only two?"

"They made so much noise, William and his cohorts fled. The masters might despise a bastard, but they couldn't countenance murder on school grounds."

"The duke was one of the boys." So much of that prickly conversation in the library with His Grace, the Duke of Sedgemoor, became clear.

"Richard Harmsworth and Camden Rothermere. Bonny fighters, although Richard looked like he'd blow away in a slight breeze and Cam always toed the straight and narrow. A brawl wasn't his style at all."

She discerned an unlikely trace of affection in his voice. She was so glad Jonas hadn't always been a lone wolf. It seemed sad that the friendship had faded over the years, although she knew better than to say so. From what the duke had said, Jonas had deliberately distanced himself from his rescuers. "I'm glad you had friends."

"I'm not sure you'd call us friends. More like orphans in the storm, sticking together for protection. Eton wasn't kind to boys of questionable birth."

"School must have been a nightmare for all of you."

"Richard made a great show of caring for nothing, which lent him cachet with the brutes. Gossip about his parentage shadowed Cam but, his father's son or not, he was heir to a dukedom so people were less eager to offend him than a mere peasant like me. He was only twelve then, but he was damned ducal ordering those mongrels away."

"I'm surprised you stayed conscious." She flinched to imagine the scene, shouting boys, fists thudding into flesh, blood. Was Jonas screaming? He was only a child and terrified for his life through agonizing pain.

His grip tightened around her waist. "I wasn't for long."

Still something puzzled her. "Why didn't you and the other boys stay friends?"

His expression hardened. "That was hardly a shining moment for me. I doubt any of us wanted to be reminded of it, even if my abasement was etched on my face forever."

Again she'd been blind. Shame lay at the basis of so many of Jonas's actions. Shame made him stand alone against the world. Shame made him reject any hand of friendship. He'd interpret kindness or goodwill as a sign of condescension. However illogical it was, she understood why he considered his scars relics of humiliating defeat at his cousin's hands. Jonas's pride had helped him survive in a hostile world but it hadn't made life easier for him. "Even your father abandoned you."

She felt him stiffen. More shame. She should have realized long ago that at least some of his defensiveness stemmed from humiliations too painful to be borne. "How do you know that?"

"I wheedled it out of Mrs. Bevan."

He sighed. "My father was a broken man. He never got over losing my mother and when the marriage was declared invalid, his spirit shriveled to nothing. He loved me, but scholarly research filled his life. After he took me to Venice, a colleague discovered a Roman encampment in Wallachia. He left me with our staff there to see if the find supported his pet theories."

Yet again she recognized Jonas's reasons for mistrusting personal relations. "That's terrible."

Jonas's careless response didn't convince. "He wasn't likely to hover by my bedside and at least he stayed until I wasn't likely to die."

Her stomach churned with anger. "Very generous."

"You didn't know him." Jonas's voice warmed. "He was a marvelous man, clever, physically fearless, far-thinking. He taught me to stand on my own two feet. That was a lesson I needed to learn."

It was yet another sign of his generosity of heart that he'd continued to idolize his father, who sounded to her like a fatally selfish man. "I didn't hear that William was expelled."

"He wasn't. He was the future Viscount Hillbrook when all was said and done. And boys will be boys."

Sidonie flinched at Jonas's cynical tone. Although who could fault his anger? He'd found no help from those charged with his care.

Jonas was still speaking. "My cousin was caned and sent home for the term. As far as I know, he was accepted back into school the next year under promise of good behavior."

"That's disgusting."

"Yes, it is, rather." His gaze was lightless as his inner

vision dwelled upon events so long ago. "The worst of it is he showed no jot of remorse. He laughed as he sliced my face, joked with his loutish chums about his artful carving."

Another shudder ran under Sidonie's skin. She could so easily picture William's enjoyment as he disfigured the cousin who excelled him in every way except birth. Jonas spoke so prosaically, but she couldn't help picturing the gory details of his ordeal. He'd been a child. An innocent.

Inhaling on a sob, she kissed his scars. He trembled but didn't withdraw. Tears burned her eyes but she blinked them away. If she cried, he'd think she pitied him and he'd abhor that. She didn't pity him. She admired him more than she'd ever admired anybody.

"I'm glad you didn't die." She cursed the inadequacy of words.

He turned his face until his lips met hers. "Right now, *bella*, so am I."

"I hate that you went through this. I hate it." Outrage vibrated in her voice. She couldn't banish the image of William crowing in triumph over his fallen cousin.

Jonas smoothed her hair away from her face with a tenderness that seared her heart. "I hate that William won."

She grabbed his wrist hard. "You were a child fighting odds you couldn't hope to match. You bear no blame. It's all William. And the cowardly dogs who held you down." Her tone lowered to throbbing sincerity. "I'm glad you've beaten him at everything since. I'm glad your success makes him feel half a man. Because that's what he is. He's less than half a man. He's no man at all."

This time his smile wasn't as strained. "So fierce, *tesoro*."

She recoiled, but his arms stopped her getting far. "Don't mock me."

He sounded sheepish. "I'm actually taken aback that you're so firmly on my side."

She stared at him, wishing she could make him see himself as she did. "I'm always on your side."

She twined her arms around Jonas and brought him close to her body. For once the contact wasn't sexual, but purely human comfort. She'd nurtured and protected people before. Roberta. Roberta's sons. But the profundity of what she felt as she embraced Jonas surpassed previous experience.

I'm always on your side.

No one had ever spoken those words to Jonas. Gently she held him to her breast on the tumbled bed. Her scent surrounded him, rich with the musk of satisfied woman. By God, he'd never have these sheets washed. He wanted Sidonie's fragrance surrounding him forever.

When Sidonie herself was gone.

He lashed his arms around her as if daring the world to rip her away. Devil take it, she was crying. His story had distressed her. He wished he hadn't told her, no matter what relief he'd found in sharing the horror. "*Bella*, I'm sorry."

"No, I'm sorry." Tears thickened her voice.

He kissed the soft hair on her crown, which was all of her he could reach. She seemed determined to hide against him. When she kissed his chest, his cock predictably stirred. He didn't do anything about it. Instead he curled around her, holding her safe. Just as she'd held him safe when he'd exposed his childhood humiliations.

Usually he felt at odds with the world but right now, everything was perfect. He was warm, he was physically sated, and the woman he wanted more than any other lay in his arms.

Time unwound like a shining skein of gold and despite his intention not to lose a second of this night, he sank into sleep.

Sidonie slowly emerged from sleep to darkness and shimmering pleasure. The candles had burned out and the fire was a dull glow in the hearth. Jonas kissed his way over her belly then rose to join his body to hers. In this hazy space between slumber and waking, his commanding possession felt like a declaration of love.

Jonas moved incessant as the tide, thrusting deep and lingering at the peak of each stroke. The sensation was astonishing. Gentle but ruthless. He surrounded her with strength, passion, care. His breath sawed in and out of his parted lips. The scent of arousal and clean male sweat intoxicated her.

Still not fully awake, she sighed, low and sensual. Her bones felt like water and she flowed against Jonas as naturally as silk. He stopped moving, just filled her so completely that he touched her heart.

The connection was perfect, soul and body.

Slowly—everything about this astonishing union was slow, as if they stretched every second to eternity and beyond—she arched to press her breasts against his chest. She felt no need for speech. Nor apparently did he. There was just the smooth slide of bodies, the ragged susurration of breath.

She stroked his back, feeling the muscles flex. Her

hands curved over firm buttocks, digging into the flesh, pushing him deeper inside. He groaned. His next thrust was more emphatic, although radiant tenderness lingered like sunset on the horizon.

She raised her knees, changing the angle. Coherent thought fled. He accelerated, drawing her climax closer. The bed creaked and she moaned. Need gripped like talons. She tightened her thighs around his hips, urging him to continue.

By the time his unearthly control frayed, she was sobbing. His thrusts weren't as measured; the skin beneath her hands was slick with sweat. She tensed around him. He groaned like a man tested to the limit, shifted once more, and light exploded behind her eyes. Vaguely she felt Jonas go deep as he gave up his seed.

She opened dazzled eyes to gray light. The new day arrived. Jonas had made love to her for the last time, transporting her to a paradise beyond the realms of imagination. She blinked back tears even as pleasure inundated her.

The good-bye was spectacular. It was still good-bye.

Reluctantly, Jonas rolled off Sidonie to lie panting at her side. The separation cut like a knife, hinted at the separation soon to come. He was exhausted. He'd given her everything he had. He'd never felt so consumed. The night had been astonishing, unforgettable.

Now the night was over.

He glanced across at Sidonie's face, clear in the advancing light. She was crying. How he loathed her tears. They made him feel like someone scraped out his guts with a rake. He struggled for comforting words, but what they'd just done robbed him of speech. Since they'd made love, she hadn't looked at him. He stared into the mirror above. She sprawled beside him. Her tears conveyed misery beyond speech, more agonizing for their silence.

She took his hand, lacing her fingers between his with a sweetness that made his heart cramp. She drew his hand to her lips and kissed his knuckles with reverence and gratitude.

And love?

Hell, he didn't know. But as he stared up at the mirror, he felt a sting behind his eyes at her gesture's unconstrained poignancy. He swallowed again and tightened his grip so even if she wanted to leave, she couldn't. It astonished him how difficult it was to find the one word he needed after these exquisite days. The one word he had no right to say.

He forced the forbidden syllable from his tight throat.

"Stay."

Chapter Twenty-Two

Jonas felt the sinuous softness drain from Sidonie's body. She tried to tug her hand away but he held on. He meant to hold on to more than her hand, damn it.

He knew what she'd say before she spoke.

"Jonas, I can't." Her voice was husky with tears. She made a less emphatic and equally futile attempt to break free.

"Of course you can." She wasn't eager to leave him. He couldn't have mistaken the situation so badly. For God's sake, she'd just been crying as if her heart broke. He reared up on one elbow to study her. The weak daylight filtering into the room illuminated her face. She looked sad and defeated.

She turned to him and once more he tumbled into fathoms of brown. Nobody looked at him the way Sidonie did. Thank God she'd dragged him kicking and screaming to abandon the blindfold. His heart constricted as he recalled staring into her eyes when he moved inside her.

He'd floated in eternity. It was unbearable to think he'd never again experience that ineffable connection.

"You said it yourself. I have a mere week of freedom. If I'm late back, I'll be found out."

He frowned and brought their linked hands to his lips. He kissed the erratic pulse at her wrist. "Would that be so bad?"

"I don't want people calling me a whore." Her slender throat moved as she swallowed. "I won't miss you less for the sake of another day in your arms."

With her departure breathing down his neck, the confession didn't mollify. He leaned over her as if sheer physical presence could change her mind. His voice emerged as a growl. "I'm not talking about one more day, Sidonie."

Her mouth constricted with unhappiness as she touched his scarred cheek with one of those caresses that always pierced his heart. "Another two days. Three. A week. It's only putting off the inevitable."

Jonas sucked in a breath, knowing how recklessly he was about to dare fate. "You could stay forever."

She flinched as if he'd hit her. "Jonas…" She lowered her hand and clenched it against the sheets. "It's impossible."

"Why?"

Her lips twisted in a bitter smile. "I'm at heart a conventional creature. Think of the scandal if the world discovered you kept Lady Hillbrook's sister as your mistress."

He sucked in another breath and steeled himself to say what he should have said first. "Then, hell, marry me."

Shock flooded Sidonie. Shock, dismay, denial, and a lurking, unforgivable gratification. She stared into Jonas's face, wondering if he'd run mad. "M-marry you? But you don't know if I'm going to have a baby yet."

"That's not why I'm asking you." He shifted up against the headboard and stared down at her with a light in his eyes she'd never seen before. "Think about it, Sidonie. Why shouldn't we marry?"

"Because—" Her voice faded. At last she wrenched her hand free. And immediately missed the connection.

His mouth quirked with derision. "That's a good reason."

She rose to her knees so their eyes were level. She was achingly conscious of their nakedness, but it seemed too missish to raise the sheet, given the night just passed. "You can't be serious."

A muscle flickered in his cheek, proof that this astonishing conversation wasn't a momentary whim. "I'm unencumbered with a wife. You're unencumbered with a husband. There's no legal impediment."

Her lips flattened in distress. "There's more than legalities to consider and you know it."

"On your admission, you're not happy with Roberta and William." He paused while a discomfited expression darkened his face. "I'm one of the richest men in the kingdom. Perhaps that compensates for my personal deficiencies."

His self-denigration hurt her. She didn't care about his money. She only cared about him. Much good it did her.

"Don't be a fool. You know I—"

Even as they demanded to be spoken, she bit back words that committed her to a lifetime with him. She was astonished that her first reaction to his proposal wasn't a categorical refusal. The plan never to marry had been one of the pillars of her existence for as long as she'd comprehended the unequal relations between husbands and wives. Jonas had taken a mere week—admittedly a passionate, emotional, life-changing week—to bring her to a point where the idea of marriage was no longer anathema. Of all the changes he'd wrought in her, coaxing her from innocent girl to sensual woman, making her see the world in much wider terms than she ever had before, this was the greatest.

But marriage still meant voluntarily placing herself in someone else's power for the rest of her life. Even as the desire to accept his proposal bubbled up inside her, she adjured caution. She'd known him a mere week. She needed to solve Roberta's dilemma before she revealed the truth of his origins to Jonas and perhaps, *perhaps,* agreed to become his wife. Not to mention the possibility that when he realized she'd been hiding such significant information, he mightn't want to marry her anymore.

Nerves made her voice shake. "You know I want you. Any woman would be lucky to have you."

The disbelieving look he cast her struck her bruised heart like a blow. "Any woman who could stomach a troll."

Anger spurred courage. She straightened and took his face firmly between her palms. "You're the best man I know."

He responded with a laugh so poisoned with cynicism, it made her belly twist with pity. "Which is why you're floundering to find a way to say no."

She kissed him hard before she released him. "You're a fool, Jonas Merrick."

His jaw firmed and his expression didn't lighten. Her

stomach sank as she realized he remained convinced of his essential unworthiness. "Does that mean you'll stay? I doubt it."

"Jonas, I always swore I'd never marry," she said gravely.

He reared up from the pillows and curled one powerful hand behind her head, his fingers tangling in her disheveled hair. "I'm not William."

"Of course not. But I'd still be your property."

His hand tightened at her nape. "I'll sign anything. Give you money, rights, land, houses."

"I'd still be your wife."

"That's not a death sentence."

"I'm sorry," she said helplessly. "If I were to marry any man, it would be you. I don't expect you to understand."

She hardly believed that the sarcastic, disdainful scoundrel she'd met a week ago would forsake pride to propose. She hardly believed that in spite of everything she knew about marriage and everything still to be resolved between them, she considered his offer.

"Do you really think life alone is better than life as my wife?" He released her, his silvery gaze unwavering. "You speak of what you'll lose if you marry. What about what you'll gain? Don't you want children? Wouldn't you like someone to turn to when you're troubled? Can you live without a man's touch?"

The question wasn't whether she could live without a man's touch but whether she could live without Jonas's touch. She extended her hand in a silent plea for forgiveness. Even as part of her wondered if she'd be so very wrong to say yes. "Jonas, I don't make my choice lightly."

He ignored her gesture and desolation edged his voice.

"I hardly blame you for refusing. I'm no great prize, after all."

Her lips tightened. "Stop feeling sorry for yourself."

He looked startled. "It's true."

"You're the cleverest man I know." She wondered why she argued when he seemed prepared to accept refusal. Still she persisted. He must see he was remarkable. Her hands fisted against her thighs. "You're considerate and funny and you're a lover out of my dreams. Should I develop a taste for luxuries—which I may well do after this week—you're so plump in the pocket, you wouldn't notice if I started buying gold-plated underthings."

His smile was uncertain, nonetheless it was a smile. Her churning misery eased a fraction. "I'd notice anything you did with your undergarments, *amore mio*."

She blushed and the urgency faded from her voice. "You underestimate your appeal, Jonas. How long before you talked me into bed? Three days? Four? And I was a woman of unquestionable virtue."

His smile developed an acerbic tinge. "Careful. At this rate, you'll consent to be my wife."

"It's been a week." If only he knew how near she verged to relenting and consigning everything else to the devil. But even now when she longed to fling herself into Jonas's arms and dare the world to snatch her away, she couldn't forget William's last assault on Roberta or her fear when she heard that he became increasingly divorced from reality. First she must settle Roberta somewhere safe, then she'd tell Jonas about his birth. Only after that could she decide whether her future lay with him.

"I make my mind up quickly, *bella*." He paused. "I suspect you do, too."

"You hardly know me."

"Don't be a silly widgeon, Sidonie." This time his smile held no shadows, only endless tenderness. For one crazy moment, she stared into his intense features and every obstacle dissolved like mist in the sun. A lifetime with this fascinating man seemed promise of heaven.

"I'm flattered by your offer, Jonas. But I...can't."

The glow seeped from his eyes and he shifted to the edge of the bed. "That's your prerogative."

He sounded cold, composed. Beneath the chill, she heard turbulent grief. He shouldn't sound like that. Not after only a week. She reached for him but stopped short of making contact. "I'm sorry."

He shrugged. Once his indifference might have convinced. After all, the man she'd met a week ago had seemed nothing but power games and spite. Now she knew better.

"You made no promises."

Except she had. With her heart. With her body. With a thousand sighs of surrender. Did she underestimate him? Was it possible that if she admitted what she knew, Jonas would devise some solution to Roberta's dilemma? He was daring and resourceful and his fortune gave him a power in the world she couldn't hope to match.

Then like an echo she heard him saying to the Duke of Sedgemoor, *"It can't be helped."*

Roberta's safety was too important to risk on a man Sidonie had known a mere week. Shocking enough that Sidonie would commit herself without hesitation, but she couldn't forget her responsibility to her sister.

She stared directly at this man who had given her such transcendent joy and took the coward's way out. "Jonas, I need to think."

When he faced her, he didn't look any happier. He was wise enough to guess she'd more than half-decided against marrying him. "I have a feeling if you go away, I'll never see you again."

"Give me a month. Everything has happened so fast."

"A week."

Surprisingly, given how difficult the discussion, she laughed. "You're so demanding. A woman would need to be sure of herself to take you on."

His silvery eyes glittered. "You're up to my weight, *carissima*."

The tragedy was she believed she was, too. She bent her head. Her voice was a mere thread of sound. "A week."

Chapter Twenty-Three

Jonas eyed Sidonie where she sat beside him in the swaying carriage. Unwillingly he'd conceded the wisdom of abandoning her new clothes, but he couldn't like seeing the shabby white muslin. He should have told Mrs. Bevan to burn the rag instead of merely laundering it. When Sidonie returned to him, as surely she must, he'd drape her in silks and diamonds.

And, by God, he'd burn that eyesore of a cloak.

Her posture was straight and self-contained, gloved hands linked in her lap and attention fixed on the passing countryside. For most of the journey, she'd dozed fitfully with her head on his shoulder. He'd stared into her lovely face and noted marks of weariness and care—and the indefinable air of a woman who had recently enjoyed sensual fulfillment.

She'd been unusually quiet all the way from Devon. In fact, she'd been unusually quiet since his impulsive proposal, apart from the inevitable argument after he insisted on accompanying her home. Much as he loathed referring to his swine of a cousin's house as Sidonie's home.

It was now late afternoon and they approached Ferney, the mansion he'd bought to put his cousin's nose out of joint. How astonishing the difference a week made. Or a week such as the one he'd spent with Sidonie. He'd gloated, raising that gaudy monument to his worldly success at William's front gates. Jonas had intended it as a permanent reminder that while he might be a bastard, he was a damned rich bastard.

Now his quest for revenge seemed infantile.

Jonas's time with Sidonie sucked the infection from old wounds. Perhaps it was the beginning of wisdom that he at last relinquished his cousin's chastisement to heaven. He cringed to recall how he'd used Sidonie's sister in his machinations. Roberta had invited trouble, but he'd been a blackguard taking advantage. Sidonie had been too quick to forgive him for that. His intentions had been rotten to the extreme.

More important than revenge was the need to convince Sidonie to marry him. His proposal had been impulsive but the instant he spoke, he recognized their affair could have no other outcome. She was a woman a man wanted for life. Sidonie Forsythe was a creature of fire and light. He craved that heat like he craved air. When she was with him, he rejoined the great tide of humanity. He felt like a man a woman might even come to...love.

He contemplated Sidonie's slender form in the shadowy interior. Had he planted a child in her womb? He was a cad to trap her so dishonorably, but the prospect of Sidonie growing round and lazy was breathtakingly appealing.

She turned her head to study him. He hoped to hell she didn't guess his thoughts. "You can't come to Barstowe Hall. If William finds out I've been with you, there will be the devil to pay."

"Hobbs has orders to head for Ferney, then I'll walk you across the park. I'll keep your reputation safe, *bella*." He wanted to keep more than her reputation safe. He wanted her to confide her whole life to him.

Slowly, Jonas, slowly. Patience reaps its own rewards.

"You needn't come. I doubt brigands will leap on me in deepest Wiltshire."

"You'd deprive me of the last of your company, *dolcissima*?"

"You think this is easy?" she asked dully. "To leave you after what we've shared?"

He seized her hand. Immediately the storm in his blood quieted. Her merest touch set the world spinning in the right direction. He waited for her to withdraw. Apart from those sweet moments curled against him in sleep, she'd hardly touched him all this long day. His proposal had destroyed their physical ease with each other.

Until now.

She gripped his hand hard and he felt her desperation, even through two layers of leather. Perhaps the week apart would work to his advantage. She'd have time to realize she missed a man in her bed. Except, curse him for a sentimental fool, he wanted more from her than physical desire. He wanted the generous heart that led her to offer herself to a monster's embrace in her sister's place. He sounded petty and jealous and needy, but he wanted her to love him the way she loved Roberta. With that same unconditional devotion, that same clear-eyed appreciation. Sod it, selfish it might be, but he wanted her to love him *more* than she loved Roberta.

"You needn't go, *tesoro*," he said gently. "I can turn the carriage around and we'll be back in Devon tomorrow. Or we'll stay at Ferney. I won't cavil at offering you a bedroom. Preferably mine."

"Don't tempt me." Compared to her usual smiles, this one was a caricature. As if to soothe a headache, her free hand rubbed her brow. Guilt stabbed him. He had no right to torment her. She sighed, the sound inexpressibly sad. "You make everything sound so sensible when we both know it's wrong."

His voice shook with sincerity. "What care I for scandal? What care you? Where has toeing the line got you? A damned thankless position as William's drudge and Roberta's cat's paw. I've lived with scandal since my father's marriage was declared invalid. Confront it with your head high and it cowers away."

Her hand tightened. "You promised a week before I have to make up my mind."

"You can do that at Ferney."

"You drive coherent thought to the wind."

Did that mean she'd stay? One glance at her determined expression confirmed his doubts.

The coach rolled to a gentle stop before the ostentatious house. After Jonas grabbed Sidonie's bag and helped her out, Hobbs continued to the stables. A footman opened Ferney's tall doors with a flourish, but Jonas waved him inside.

For the first time today, he read genuine amusement in Sidonie's eyes when she surveyed the ornate Portland stone façade with its balustrades and pediments and columns. "You know, I've longed to see inside Ferney. The neighbors are agog at the extravagance. I was so disappointed when your hall at Castle Craven contained hardly a stick of furniture."

Without pleasure, he glanced at the house's pillared portico and grand double staircase. "Buying it was childish."

She made no attempt to pull her hand from his. "Oh, I don't know. It upset William mightily. I consider the money well spent."

Hell, he couldn't let her go. Not yet. "Why not stay an hour? I'll show you the house. The servants won't gossip. They're far too well paid to risk their positions."

She shook her head, lowering it so the ugly bonnet hid her face. When he burned the blasted cloak, he'd toss that straw contraption on the pyre as kindling.

"Jonas, you don't understand." Her voice was subdued. He realized her composure was entirely superficial. Beneath the apparent acceptance, she was unhappy and unsure. "If I don't go now, I fear I won't go at all."

He gripped her hand as if he never meant to release her. "Then don't go."

She raised her head and stared at him. Her eyes were dull and her face was pale. "You needed a week to seduce me into a state of insanity where I'm considering marriage. Give me a week to decide whether to change a lifetime's intentions."

It sounded reasonable. Damn it, it *was* reasonable. "I'll stay at Ferney. You merely need to cross the boundary."

She stroked his jaw in a tender gesture that recalled a hundred other tender gestures. He stifled the urge to bully her. She wouldn't bend. His woman was strong and resolute. If she embarked on life with him, she'd have to be.

Still she stared at him as though she'd die if she looked anywhere else. Did she know how close he was to sweeping her into his arms and racing her away?

"Thank you," she said softly.

She touched his lips in a gesture of farewell and he caught a glimmer of tears. Trapped in her fathomless brown gaze, he felt the fatal declaration rise. He beat it back, although she must know he loved her. Every action betrayed his feelings, however risky the words. "Sidonie..."

"Oh, my dear..." Her voice cracked and she sagged, her strength failing. His arm circled her waist even as she straightened and focused upon him. "Don't make this more difficult."

"At least eat something before you go."

Her smile was shaky. "You're still trying to feed me."

"Something to restore you after the journey." His pride revolted at how he begged another minute, another hour, but he was beyond caring.

She shook her head. "No, Jonas."

" 'No, Jonas' is all you ever say," he responded with a hint of savagery. He knew he was unfair, but he was just so damned miserable.

Her smile wavered into a warmth that calmed his anger. "Not always."

He shut his eyes as the memory of wild nights overpowered him. Good God, at this rate, he'd be bawling like a motherless calf.

She touched his scarred cheek again. "Just kiss...kiss me good-bye."

He told himself she'd be back in a week. Surely she'd see sense once she faced lonely reality. Surely she'd miss him the way he'd miss her. But that wasn't how it felt. It felt like she forsook him forever.

He drew her into the shadow of the staircase to shield her from anyone in the house. Slowly he twined his arms around her, relishing how perfectly she fit his body. Her hands slid up his chest, trailing fire even through his clothing, and linked behind his neck. He stared down at her, memorizing each feature. The wide, shining eyes; the marked brows; the pointed, determined chin indicating stubbornness under the sweetness. Didn't he know that to his bones? If she wasn't stubborn, she'd still be in his bed. If she wasn't stubborn, he wouldn't love her so much, confound her.

His head inched down. Her lush lips parted and passion surged, as it always did when they kissed. The world flared into heat and demand. He thrust his tongue into her mouth, staking the claim she denied with words but affirmed with every caress. She moaned and kissed him back voraciously, as though struggling to jam a lifetime into one embrace.

All too soon, the kiss changed, its fire retreated until only banked embers remained. The recognition that this was farewell threatened to rip his aching heart in two. She whimpered at the back of her throat and slowly, reluctantly drew away.

He let her go. What choice had he? He'd promised her freedom if she married him. If he compelled her now, he'd prove himself the tyrant she feared in a husband.

Very slowly, she lowered her arms as if she hated relinquishing the contact. Tears glinted in her dark eyes, but her head was high and she stood straight. "Take me back to Barstowe Hall, Jonas."

*   *   *

Sidonie needed her key to slip into Barstowe Hall through the kitchens. At this hour, the small staff usually gathered there for tea. To her surprise, the cavernous, underground room was empty. She'd prepared tales about her visit to London, but nobody was present to hear. Nor did she need to make excuses about one of Roberta's town friends dropping her off at the gates on an urgent errand elsewhere.

Nor did she encounter any servants as she made her way through the house. The silence was uncanny, eerie. A shiver chilled her skin. The rooms were cold and shadowy as wintry evening closed in.

"Hello?"

The only response was the echo of her voice. What on earth had happened in her absence? Had William turned off the staff? She knew things were bad with her brother-in-law, but she hadn't realized his finances reached quite that pass.

She was walking toward her bedroom along the second-floor corridor when she heard a muffled bang from the schoolrooms above. Fear tightened her skin. Had a robber broken in? There wasn't much to take. William had sold anything valuable. Whatever little remained after Jonas's father had ransacked the house before his death.

Quietly, she set her bag down and lifted a chipped earthenware vase from a side table. If it had been whole, William would have sold it long ago.

She crept up the next flight of stairs. Carefully she inched the nursery door open and raised the vase above her head. Only to drop it in shock.

"Roberta?" she asked over the crash of pottery on bare floorboards.

Her sister whirled around from clearing the crammed and dusty shelves along one wall. At her feet sat two gaping valises. One overflowed with toys. The other was empty.

"Goodness gracious, you frightened the life out of me." Roberta rushed forward through the pottery shards to hug Sidonie. "Are you all right? I've been so worried about you."

Sidonie returned the hug, feeling Roberta's trembling tension. Her sister's manner was always brittle but this surpassed her usual nervousness. Something was seriously wrong. "I'm fine."

Robert drew back and surveyed her with a frown. "That's a little pat for a woman who's just returned from the monster's lair."

"He's not a monster."

"He didn't hurt you?"

What to say? "No."

"I'm so glad. Although I can hardly believe it. I must hear everything, but not now. Now you have to help me." Roberta turned to grab another handful of toys from the shelves and stashed them into the empty bag.

Apprehension stabbed Sidonie between the temples as she finally saw her sister properly. Roberta looked dreadful. Distraught and untidy, when Lady Hillbrook always appeared in public *comme il faut*. Dust hemmed her green muslin dress, grime smudged an alabaster cheek and her coiffure wasn't far from collapse.

"What in the world are you doing? Where are the servants?"

With unsteady hands, Roberta pitched a cracked slate into the empty bag. "I sent them off for the afternoon. They're all sneaks and spies."

From habit, Sidonie checked her sister for signs of violence, but she seemed unharmed. "Are you all right?"

Roberta avoided her eyes and grabbed a worn set of lead soldiers that the boys hadn't touched for years. She struggled to stuff them into the bag. "Of course I'm all right. Oh, for pity's sake, why can't these things fit?"

Sidonie surged forward and grabbed her sister's busy hands, holding them until she caught Roberta's undivided attention. This close, she saw the blind panic that underlay Roberta's confusion. Only one person terrified Roberta like this. "What's wrong, Roberta? What has William done?"

What in heaven's name was going on? Had William found out about the losses to Jonas? Had the mental instability the duke mentioned at Castle Craven burgeoned into full-grown madness?

Sidonie could see Roberta was too distracted to think beyond the present moment. Even the peril she'd sent Sidonie into didn't really register beyond her current fear.

"We can't talk now." Roberta flung off her sister's grip and turned to snatch another handful of toys. "We have to go before William arrives."

"Are you leaving him?"

Roberta dropped the toys willy-nilly. A cricket ball with a split seam missed the bag and rolled across the floor. "Yes."

Sidonie wasn't sorry to hear the news, although she wondered just how she and her sister would survive until the legacy came into effect in January. "But why?"

"The man's a pig."

"He's been a pig your whole married life. Why leave now?"

"There's no time to explain." Roberta's eyes glittered with spiraling dread. "For pity's sake, help me pack."

Sidonie's tone firmed in an attempt to calm her sister. In eight turbulent years of marriage, she'd never seen Roberta like this. "Just tell me what's going on."

Nervously Roberta checked over Sidonie's shoulder as if expecting William to appear like a bugaboo from a children's story, rising to devour his victim. "Sidonie, don't push."

"This behavior seems lunatic. And what do you want with the boys' toys?"

Roberta cast a fleeting glance at the overflowing bags. "Don't be a slow-top, Sidonie. I'll need money. Curse that blackguard for stripping the house of everything worth selling." Her expression brightened. "Did you find anything valuable in the library?"

Sidonie shook her head. "It's all rubbish. What's made you leave William?"

Roberta finally stopped flinging toys about and looked at her, twisting her hands in painful distress. "I lost at cards."

Sidonie, still reeling from parting with Jonas, staggered back. Horror made her light-headed. Hardly believing what she heard, she pressed a shaking hand to her sinking heart. She was too appalled to be angry, although she'd be angry soon enough. "Roberta, you didn't. After losing that fortune to Mr. Merrick?"

Roberta had the grace to look abashed, but she rushed on before Sidonie mustered further censure. "A mere trifle. Two hundred guineas at piquet to Lord Maskell. The scoundrel pressed for payment, then threatened to tell William."

Oh, Roberta, no…

The scale of this disaster beggared imagination. Sidonie had assumed her sister would be so chastened after skirting disgrace with Jonas that she'd change her ways. What a naïve fool she'd been. Roberta would never change. She was addicted to gaming the way a toper was addicted to brandy.

"Roberta, how could you keep gambling after what happened with Mr. Merrick?" she asked through stiff lips.

Roberta's shrug was unconvincing. She'd known what she risked, but she'd gone ahead and gambled anyway. "I had a run of luck. Only a ninnyhammer leaves the table when the cards are kind."

"Until you lost two hundred guineas," Sidonie said bitterly. Acrid rage curdled her stomach as she battled the impulse to wring her sister's delicate neck. "Where do you intend to go?"

Oh, Jonas, I wish I'd stayed with you. I wish I'd never left Castle Craven and your arms.

"I thought Brighton or Harrogate. Somewhere amusing."

Sidonie's lips tightened, but she resisted screaming. It would do no good. "Haven't you had enough amusement?"

Roberta's lips started to tremble. "Don't be cross."

"I can't help it." Sidonie sucked in a deep breath and sought some solution to this catastrophe. The clamor of competing obligations made her dizzy. The marriage lines gave her some pull over William, but that meant never telling Jonas about his legitimacy. And if Roberta hurt William's pride, it was possible that out of spite, he'd insist on her continuing to live with him, title or no title. Sidonie also needed time to arrange for William to release guardianship of his sons. Roberta's hysterical escape would make William so angry, he'd never negotiate. Sidonie knew from experience how unreasonable he was when taunted.

She struggled to speak calmly. "William will find you in a fashionable town. You need to disappear. At least until my legacy comes due. Even then, William mustn't know where you are. He has the law on his side if he wants you back."

The frenzy drained from Roberta's eyes and briefly she became again the older sister Sidonie had always loved. "You know what my life has been. You of all people should support my bid for freedom."

"You haven't thought about this." Sidonie stifled the urge to say more.

"I'll think once I'm away." With renewed agitation, Roberta reached for a set of spillikins high on the shelf beside her. "We must go. He'll know I came here. It's the first place he'll look."

Through the red haze of anger, she saw Roberta's expression change. Her sister went white as new snow, the dirt on her face standing out like a scar against her ashen complexion. As she faltered back, spillikins tumbled from her grip to clatter onto the floor.

Like a deadly miasma, William's oily tones oozed through the fraught atmosphere. "So gratifying you know me so well after eight years of wedded bliss, my dear."

Chapter Twenty-Four

I ce thickened Sidonie's blood. "William..."

He slammed her against the wall when he shoved past, forcing the air from her lungs in a painful *whoosh*. As he strode toward Roberta, his boots crunched on broken pottery. Using his bulk to intimidate, he loomed over his cowering wife. "Tried to scarper, did you, bitch?"

"I...I'm sure I don't know what you mean, dear heart," Roberta stammered, edging away until she bumped into the empty shelves behind her.

Dread tangled Sidonie's belly into painful knots. One look at William's slitted eyes and swelling cheeks, and she knew the moment she'd fought so long and hard to avoid rushed toward them. William was about to kill Roberta.

On trembling legs, Sidonie surged forward to force herself between Roberta and William. "Don't you touch her!"

"Get out of my bloody way, you useless slut!" Keep-

ing his gaze on his wife, William grabbed Sidonie's arm
with bruising force and flung her to the floor. As she went
down, she banged her head. Agony overwhelmed her and
briefly her world turned black. Frantically she fought
to clear the fog of pain from her vision. Voices echoed
weirdly as she sprawled at William's feet, words only
gradually making sense through the ringing in her ears.

"Don't hurt my sister!" Roberta cried, flinging herself
in front of Sidonie.

"Shut up, you useless cow." Hazily Sidonie watched
William seize Roberta by the hair and force her to her
knees. He tugged roughly until her neck strained at an
awkward angle, forcing her to meet his eyes.

"William, please, I beg of you!" Tears cascaded down
Roberta's ashen cheeks.

William's face was scarlet and spittle collected at the
corners of his mouth. He raised one beefy fist over his
wife. Sidonie's belly lurched with sick horror. "Maskell
told me what you'd been up to."

"Please don't hit me!" Roberta struggled to break free
but came up short when William savagely wrenched at
her disheveled chignon.

"Let her go!" Sidonie screamed.

Clumsily Sidonie staggered to her feet and threw herself at William. Hissing, she dug her fingernails into the
hand gripping her sister, deep enough to draw blood. For
a few blind seconds, she wasn't attacking Roberta's violent husband but the jackal who had disfigured Jonas and
laughed while he did it.

"Fucking hell! You little cat!" With a wild swerve,
William released Roberta, who subsided gasping to the
floor and turned on Sidonie.

William was heavy with fat, but he was still a big, powerful man and more than a match for a woman Sidonie's size. Ruthlessly he pried her fingernails off him then cuffed her. Pain exploded through her body as she smashed again onto the bare floorboards amid broken pottery and scattered toys. Her hands clasped over her head, she curled into a ball to protect herself. Fighting unconsciousness, she braced for William to kick her. Behind her, she heard Roberta edging across the littered floor away from her husband.

"What—" she heard Roberta say in choked astonishment, then there was a thunder of boots and a resounding crash.

"Touch her again and you're a dead man."

Astonishment kept Sidonie huddled against the floor. Her ears must be playing tricks. She was sure that was Jonas's voice. But it couldn't be. She'd left Jonas at Ferney.

Gingerly she lowered her arms. Hands fisted at his sides, Jonas stood gasping over William, who lay splayed upon the floor.

"Jonas—" she croaked, her relief more dizzying than William's blows. On a surge of hope, she tried to stand, but she couldn't yet coordinate her limbs.

"Get up, you devil, so I can knock you down again," Jonas hissed through his teeth to William. His angular face was stark with abhorrence and rage.

Shaking his head to clear it after what must have been a powerful blow, William struggled to sit. One plate-like hand nursed his jaw and his eyes focused on Jonas with a poisonous loathing that made Sidonie shiver. "Get off my property, you bastard scum."

"Jonas, what are you doing here?" Sidonie asked.

Without shifting his attention from his cousin, Jonas stepped back to offer his hand. "Are you all right?"

"Yes...yes." His hand was strong and warm and shored failing courage. Rising set her head swimming and she clung to him until she found balance.

"What the hell is this?" William lunged to his feet with renewed temper. Sidonie shrank toward Jonas as fear slithered down her backbone. "You call this blackguard by his Christian name? Have you lifted your skirts for this muck, you little trull?"

"Shut your foul mouth." Jonas wrenched away from Sidonie and reached William in one bound.

William surged forward to hurl Jonas against the shelves. He landed with a deafening thud, dislodging what toys remained. Through the clatter, Jonas's agonized grunt made Sidonie's belly clench with horror.

"You fucking bastard, how dare you set foot in my house?" William gasped, pulling back to slam a punch into Jonas's face. Jonas straightened against his pain and with a groan, heaved his cousin away. As William staggered, Jonas's fist connected with William's chin so hard that the man's head jerked back.

William stumbled but landed a savage blow to Jonas's belly that had him bending and gagging. Taking advantage, William stepped in and pummeled Jonas in the kidneys. Jonas's breath emerged in agonized gasps as he sank beneath William's fists. Sidonie's heart cramped with terror; she waited for William to land the killing blow. But unbelievably Jonas recovered to strike at William. Blood burst from the older man's nose and sprayed everywhere.

Sidonie scuttled out of the way, casting a glance to

where Roberta crouched beneath the window. She realized she was praying in idiot fragments. Over and over. *Let Jonas win. Let Jonas win. Let Jonas win.*

For what felt like forever, the two big men grappled with each other. Stumbling on debris. Dodging punches. Occasionally striking vulnerable flesh. There was little science and no civilization in the combat. It was like watching wild animals fight to the death.

Sidonie swallowed her gorge and checked Roberta, who watched the vicious struggle with wide, frightened eyes. For the moment, she was safe enough. Sidonie looked away, desperate to find a weapon just in case, God forbid, William prevailed. She snatched two skittles from the top of a bag. Sidonie straightened, her sweaty palms slick on the wooden clubs, to see Jonas break free of William's assault and at last begin to press his cousin. The sickening thud of fist against muscle and bone set Sidonie's belly roiling. The concentrated hatred on each man's face promised murder. She didn't want to watch, but she couldn't stop.

William was hulking and powerful, but Jonas was younger and fitter. Sidonie sucked in her first full breath in what felt like hours when she noticed the bigger man tiring. His blows came less swiftly and often went wild. Sidonie drew another shuddering breath and tightened her grip on the skittles, wanting to attack William but fearing she'd fatally distract Jonas if she entered the fray.

Inch by inch, William retreated under the barrage of punches. His defense was increasingly ineffectual and his eyes were glazed. He lumbered over the floor, smashing against walls and shelves, drunk on hatred and pain. Jonas's face hardened until he was a stranger. His very lack of expression as he beat his cousin into a bloody mess terrified Sidonie more than mere rage could.

William fell into a corner, trapped under his cousin's attack. Jonas shot a sharp upper cut to William's chin and he went down in a confusion of arms and legs. The impact of his landing shook the floor. Jonas stepped forward to stand over his fallen enemy, his shoulders heaving, a trickle of blood marking one temple. Faint bruising shadowed one cheekbone.

"Get up," he gasped. "Get up, you scurvy maggot, so I can finish the job."

On a sob, Sidonie dropped the skittles and rushed forward to grab the bruised hand Jonas opened and shut at his side. His muscles were hard as rock and he vibrated with fury that had festered, she knew, for years.

"Jonas, don't," she said unsteadily.

Jonas didn't look at her. His focus was all on William, who groggily propped himself against the shelf behind him. One of William's eyes was swollen shut and gore smeared his face. "I want to kill the toad."

"I know, but you can't." She had no great wish to extend William's miserable life, but she couldn't let Jonas murder him. "He's not worth it. Even after what he did to you all those years ago."

"Hell, I don't care about that." At last he glanced at her, his eyes flaring with barely contained aggression. "Nobody hits you while I've got breath in my body."

Shock sent her heart crashing against her ribs. Jonas had fought William not because of what happened at Eton but because he wouldn't see her hurt. He'd been her champion, not avenger of his own wrongs. An astonishing surge of emotion that extended far beyond mere gratitude left her reeling. Roberta had been her protector when she'd been a little girl but since then, she'd fought every battle alone.

"Thank you," she whispered, the words utterly inadequate. Briefly forgetting their audience, she lifted his fist and pressed a reverent kiss to his broken knuckles. "But you can't kill him."

With her kiss, the inhuman chill slowly drained from Jonas's expression. Thank heaven. Once more he looked like the man she knew. He sucked in a choked breath and she felt his coiled tension ease. "As you wish."

Her stomach dipped with giddy relief. With a shaking hand, she reached up to dab the thin ribbon of blood from his face. Then reluctantly she drew away and limped to where Roberta huddled under the window, quietly sobbing. She crouched at her sister's side and put an arm around her heaving shoulders. "It will be all right, Roberta."

Jonas addressed William in an authoritative tone. "I want you to leave this house—"

William scowled up at Jonas and released a scornful bark of laughter. Roughly he rubbed his sleeve over his face to soak up the welling blood. "It's my house, you little shit. Much as you wish it otherwise."

Jonas's beautiful mouth stretched into a wolfish smile conveying equal measures dismissal and contempt. "You're welcome to your gewgaws, cuz. With creditors howling on your tail, you won't keep them long. You won't lose the houses—they're entailed as we both know. But you'll lose everything else, including Lady Hillbrook."

"Like hell I will!" William struggled to his feet, using the shelves to haul his bulk upright. He glowered at Jonas and his hands curled at his sides in futile rage. "Roberta's my bloody wife."

"Bloody is the accurate description, I gather." Jonas's voice was frigid.

"You're very brave with a gun in your hand, my bully boy," William sneered. Only then did Sidonie notice that Jonas now held a small pearl-handled pistol.

"No braver than you with an army of thugs to back you against a ten-year-old boy. Hardly surprising you've progressed to terrifying women. You always chose opponents who couldn't fight back." He looked past William to where Roberta and Sidonie clung together. "Lady Hillbrook, will you come with me? I'm taking Miss Forsythe to Ferney."

"If you go with this swine, you're never welcome in this house again, you filthy whore," William snarled at Sidonie.

"Keep a civil tongue in your head." Jonas lifted the pistol with a deadly grace that made Sidonie's heart stutter with alarm. Icy foreboding flooded her when she recalled the rage in Jonas's eyes as he stood over William. It would take little encouragement to make Jonas pull the trigger.

Keeping the pistol aimed at William, he stepped toward Roberta and extended his hand. "Lady Hillbrook?"

Roberta gained her feet with Jonas's help before snatching her hand away. Eyes huge and glistening with panic, she watched William like a mouse watched a snake. Dear God, had William cowed Roberta to a point where she wouldn't seize this opportunity to escape, even now? Sidonie's irritation with her sister faded, as so often, to helpless pity.

Jonas held out his hand to Sidonie. "Miss Forsythe?"

"We can't leave her." Sidonie rose with his aid and angled her head in Roberta's direction. "He'll kill her."

"I want you off this estate, you baseborn mongrel," William insisted from the other side of the room.

"By all means show us out," Jonas said.

William's lip curled with futile derision. "I'll show you to hell first."

"For shame, cuz, there are ladies present." Jonas gestured toward the door with the gun. "Step ahead, if you please."

William's face flushed so red, an apoplexy looked likely. A purple vein throbbed in his temple and his uninjured, pig-like eye narrowed with hatred. Grudgingly he limped toward the door.

"Come, sister," Sidonie said softly. "You'll be safe with us."

"I'm not sure." Roberta's glassy gaze fixed on her husband's broad back as he crossed the threshold.

Sidonie left Jonas's side to take Roberta's trembling hand. "You can't stay. You know what he'll do."

Her sister stared at her as if the words made no sense. Then she nodded and followed docilely as they left the nursery. Down two flights of stairs to the landing above the flagstoned hall.

At the top of the last flight of stairs, William turned with a superior grin on his bruised face. As the beating's effects ebbed, his native arrogance revived. "Enjoy your moment in the sun, bastard. You're welcome to the slut, but no court in the land will keep my wife from me. Even better, when I reveal poor dear Lady Hillbrook's addiction to the card tables, I'll have cause for locking her up as a lunatic."

Horror made Sidonie falter. Every time she thought

she'd measured the depths of William's villainy, he plumbed a lower level. He spoke of condemning Roberta to a living death in the same tone as she'd heard him order an unwanted litter of puppies drowned in the brook.

"We'll see who wins that particular battle," Jonas said grimly, his gun raised in unconcealed threat. "Overconfidence was always your failing."

"What a fitting end to the beautiful Forsythe sisters." William's eyes glittered with spite as his gaze swept Roberta and Sidonie. "One a bastard's whore, the other raving in her own filth in Bedlam."

White-faced, Roberta snatched her hand from Sidonie's and stood quivering under her husband's jibes. Sidonie turned to speak to her in a low, steady voice. How she hated to see the coward eight years as William's wife had made her sister. "He can't do it, Roberta. He only wants to score points against you, against Jonas. He's a toothless tiger."

William laughed, rocking on his heels in a threatening manner. "A toothless tiger, am I? We'll see. We'll see."

"I'm not mad," Roberta insisted in a shrill voice, wrapping her arms around herself. Her gaze remained fixed on William. "You can't lock me up."

"Yes, I can, my greedy little dove."

"Lady Hillbrook, don't listen. He knows he's lost," Jonas said gently. Sidonie cast him a grateful glance, but Roberta didn't seem to hear.

"Lost, have I?" William blustered, edging away from Jonas's gun. He rested his hands on his hips in a domineering manner.

"I won't let you lock me up," Roberta said more strongly, daring a step toward her husband. Her fists clenched at her sides and her chin lifted with a defiance Sidonie hadn't seen in her for years.

William's lips curved in a smile of such patronizing sweetness that it made Sidonie's stomach heave. On his bloodstained face, the expression was ghoulish. "You'll have no choice, my darling."

Roberta took another uncertain step closer. "Yes, I will, you foul bully."

William laughed again, the braying sound harsh. "Good God, does the worm turn? Who would have thought? Mind you, if my viper of a cousin wasn't sporting a pistol, you wouldn't be so brave, would you, my beauty?"

The reckless light in Roberta's eyes made Sidonie tense with apprehension. If she ventured too near, would her husband hit her? "I haven't been brave, William," Roberta admitted in a reedy voice, her cheeks flushing with humiliation. "I was once but you beat it out of me."

"You were more fun to clout than to poke. Which isn't saying much. What a pity you still lack discipline. When I get you back, we'll remedy that. Before I shut you away forever."

Roberta inhaled on an audible gasp. Then quick as lightning, she rushed ahead and shoved William square in his chest. "Roast in hell forever!"

"You little bitch . . ." William flailed to catch his wife as he teetered on the lip of the stair. He'd backed recklessly close to the edge. He snatched at her filmy skirts, tearing the fine muslin.

Roberta jerked away from his clawing hands. For a sickening second, William tottered between safety and disaster. His hands slid uselessly, seeking purchase against the banister.

Horror kept Sidonie frozen. Even as Jonas dove to prevent the unfolding disaster, a feline sound of fury escaped Roberta and she pushed William again.

This time, her husband lost his footing on an ungainly stumble. With a choked scream, he tumbled backward down the stairs.

Chapter Twenty-Five

For what felt like forever, Sidonie listened to the horrible *thud, thud, thud* of William's cumbersome body slamming against every step. When he finally crashed to the base of the staircase, the sound echoed like a scream.

Jonas dashed downstairs several at a time, shoving the gun into his pocket. He bent over his cousin, checking the man's throat for a pulse. Roberta hovered on the landing, her gaze glued to the man sprawled below.

"Jonas?" Sidonie called over the balustrade.

Jonas looked up, his face austere. The light from the tall windows lay stark on his scars. "He's dead."

Sidonie had known William was dead from the moment she saw the unnatural angle of his neck. The fall needn't have killed him, but he'd gone down awkwardly. The impact of his weight must have crushed the fragile bones at the top of his spine. Jonas's enemy was no more. William would never again strike Roberta or terrify his sons into sobbing night terrors. Surely Sidonie should feel more than numbness. But staring down at William's motionless body, she felt nothing. Apart from a bleak premonition that their troubles had just started.

Sidonie wrenched herself from shocked paralysis to realize her sister was shaking like a sapling in a high wind and just might throw herself after William. "No, Roberta," she gasped, darting forward and gripping her sister's arms from behind.

"What have I done?" Roberta turned to stare helplessly at Sidonie. "Oh, dear Lord, what have I done?"

All trace had vanished of the harpy who flung herself at her tormentor. She looked lost, small, and vulnerable. Tears flooded her large blue eyes as she trusted in Sidonie to solve this dilemma as she'd solved so many before.

Jonas ascended the steps toward the two women. "We have to make it look like an accident or, at worst, suicide."

"But William—" Sidonie began.

Jonas's mouth curved in a grim smile. "Was too egotistical to do away with himself? Hopefully the world didn't know him as we did. We must divert all suspicion from Lady Hillbrook."

Again, Sidonie's heart surged with admiration. A lesser man would gloat at his enemy's demise, but Jonas's sole concern was Roberta's well-being.

Roberta collapsed sobbing against Sidonie, hiding from the sight of William's body. Sidonie's arms encircled her sister as she glanced at Jonas. What on earth could they do to save Roberta? She didn't deserve to hang for putting an end to the man who had abused her.

"Roberta," Sidonie said, fear sharpening her tone. "Stand up straight and think. Unless you want to face a murder charge." Even if Roberta claimed her life was at risk, chances were a legal system unsympathetic to rebellious wives would hound her.

The word "murder" made Roberta stiffen and pull away slightly. "He was a brute," she said shakily.

"Undoubtedly." Jonas looked stern and purposeful. "But hardly the point. Where are the servants?"

Roberta sucked in a breath and the blankness faded from her eyes. Her voice emerged high and thready. "I sent them to the fair in the next village."

"They're coming back tonight?" he asked.

"Of course."

"They'll return soon." With difficulty, Sidonie untangled herself from Roberta and nervously checked the window at the top of the stairs. The drive, thank heaven, remained empty in spite of the lengthening shadows. "Jonas, you must go. If anyone discovers you were here, it will be disastrous. Suspicion will immediately fall on you."

"I know. My feud with William is too infamous for my presence to be construed as innocent. But I hate to leave you alone to deal with this shambles."

Sidonie was so used to managing on her own, struggling to chart a course through impossible situations. This time she could rely on Jonas. She'd already trusted him with her body. But now she trusted him with her life. More, she trusted him with her sister's life.

An extraordinary moment to realize how profoundly she'd fallen in love with him.

For days she'd struggled against this revelation. Now that she at last acknowledged the truth, deep peace settled in her heart. She'd resisted falling in love with Jonas, terrified he'd turn her into a weakling, incapable of living without him. But as she accepted what she felt, what she'd felt almost from the start, strength and power filled her. It was as though she tapped into some mysterious source of energy pulsing through the world.

I love Jonas. I love Jonas.

"Does Lady Hillbrook take laudanum?" he asked.

Her sister never traveled without a supply of the drug. There were days when laudanum offered Roberta her only escape from horror. Roberta shot Jonas a frightened glance. "You're not suggesting I kill myself, are you?"

Jonas's lips quirked at her dramatic tone. "No."

"Then what?"

"Take a dose and go to bed."

"I couldn't sleep. Not after this." Her sister's gaze slid from Jonas's face as though his scars offended her. Even here where he did his best to save her, Roberta couldn't look him in the face and say thank you.

Oh, my love, no wonder you've learned to mistrust the world.

"Listen to him, Roberta," Sidonie said urgently. "He's your only hope of avoiding the noose."

Roberta's eyes widened in fear. "Surely it won't come to that."

"Surely it will." Sidonie tried to shock her into understanding their dire situation. She looked at Jonas. "What do you want us to do?"

His gaze met hers. The panic thundering in her chest quieted under the glow of approval in his gray eyes.

"Lady Hillbrook, I want you to take enough laudanum to put you to sleep. When the servants return, they'll discover you unconscious in your room. If anyone asks, you slept all afternoon and had no idea your husband arrived. His death comes as unexpected news."

"Yes." Roberta sounded stronger. "Yes, I can do that."

"Sidonie, we need to clean up the nursery, then you need to leave the house until the servants return. You'll walk back across the park and enter the house to discover William's body. When the authorities arrive, you'll say you came down from London with Roberta, then took a stroll while your sister recovered from the journey. We need to establish that the house contained only two people, a sleeping Roberta and William, who faced irretrievable financial ruin. He either fell or in a fit of despair threw himself down the stairs."

Frail hope stirred. "You know, it just might work."

Roberta shot Jonas a suspicious glance. "You're very cozy with my sister, Mr. Merrick."

Jonas's mouth flattened with impatience. "We'll talk about that when you're not facing arrest for murder, Lady Hillbrook. Now we must act."

Roberta frowned, but even she realized there was no time for an inquisition. "If I must."

Sidonie released a relieved sigh. "Roberta, go and lie down. I'll help Jonas then come and mix your laudanum."

Roberta clasped Sidonie's forearm with a shaking hand. "I can't believe it's come to this."

"Courage." She embraced Roberta.

Roberta drew away and nodded slowly. She turned toward her room but hesitated and her voice rose with hysteria. "I...I can't. I can't walk away when he's lying there dead. It's too horrid."

"Shut your eyes, Lady Hillbrook." Jonas stepped closer and swung Roberta into his arms. Roberta squeaked with shock, but after a delay that pierced Sidonie's heart, she twined her arms around Jonas's powerful neck.

"I assume she uses the viscountess's apartments," he said over his shoulder to Sidonie.

"Yes. They're along—"

"I know."

Of course he knew. He'd grown up in this house.

Left alone, Sidonie's strongest instinct was to avoid looking at William, but macabre curiosity won out. In death her brother-in-law seemed shrunken, the shock and rage of his last moments distorting his face. His dull eyes glared past her and his body twisted grotesquely against the flagstones. The effects of his fight with Jonas were obvious. She hoped to heaven nobody attributed the bruises and abrasions to anything except the fall.

She still didn't feel anything. Relief or grief or regret. It disturbed her to be so cold. She should feel something when a man whose life she'd shared for six years, however unwillingly, lay dead in front of her. Her only real reaction was a vengeful wish that William roasted in hell for eternity.

When Jonas approached, she glanced up. He'd retrieved a bottle of brandy from Roberta's supply for mixing with her laudanum. Sidonie's expression must have betrayed her troubled thoughts because he sent her a reassuring smile. "We'll come through this, *tesoro*. Have faith."

She believed him. Such power he held over her. With a naturalness she thought abandoned in Devon, she reached for him. "Thank you."

He caught her against him for a brief kiss. She shut her eyes as his lips moved against hers. The sweet contact ended too soon.

Jonas drew away to uncork the brandy and splash it across William's body. The scent of liquor sharpened the air. Then with sudden violence he flung the bottle onto the flagstones to shatter.

"That was clever." She reached for his hand. "I still don't understand why you came here this afternoon."

"I wanted to make sure you got home safely. I meant only to watch you go inside, but the house looked deserted."

"I'm so glad you checked. William was ready to kill Roberta."

"Now he'll never threaten her again."

Sidonie shivered as if William's ghost breathed cold air against her nape. "I'll clean up the nursery and look after Roberta. You must go, Jonas."

She tasted his reluctance to abandon her in his swift kiss. As she watched him stride away with his usual purpose, she blinked back tears. It seemed wrong that they should be apart. Such a difference a week had made to proud, solitary Sidonie Forsythe.

Jonas's plan to save Roberta worked more smoothly than Sidonie could have expected, even in her most optimistic moments.

She entered the house from the terrace just as the aged butler, who to her knowledge hadn't been paid in six months, started lighting the lamps. Thus he discovered William's body and fetched Sidonie from the terrace. After the wrench of parting from Jonas, she didn't need to feign distress. Recovering from a hefty dose of laudanum, Roberta was quiet and dozy and hardly aware of events when she woke to news of her husband's demise.

Sir John Phillips, the local magistrate, arrived that night to complete the formalities. He accepted Sidonie's tale of being away from the house all afternoon. During a short interview, Sidonie hinted at William's financial woes and his increasing reliance on alcohol. Sir John, an elderly gentleman of sedentary habits, showed no interest in pursuing William's death as other than accidental. To Sidonie's relief, Jonas's name was never mentioned.

Beneath her surface calmness, Sidonie was worried sick about Roberta. She couldn't forget that terrifying instant when her sister seemed likely to throw herself after her foul husband.

The next morning, she carried a breakfast tray up to Roberta's room. After depositing the tray on a table, she pushed the curtains apart and opened the window so fresh air dissipated the sickly scent of laudanum and the heavy perfumes Roberta favored. Roberta's only response to these activities was a pained groan. "For pity's sake, Sidonie, my head aches like the devil."

Well, that answered any questions about how Roberta was feeling. Sidonie took pity on her sister to pull the curtains half closed so brightness filtered into the untidy, overcrowded chamber. "Sir John is content to rule William's death an accident."

"Good." With another groan, Roberta pushed herself up in the bed, slumping against the headboard. In the daylight, she looked ten years older than she was. Sidonie's rankling irritation with her sister for continuing to gamble drowned under a wave of helpless love. When they were small, Roberta had seemed so strong and clever. Now she was lost and defenseless, a mirror image of their sweet, sad, ineffectual mother.

Forcing the painful memories away, Sidonie poured Roberta a cup of tea. "We're lucky he's so lazy."

Roberta grunted as she sipped her tea. Weariness, distress, and the aftereffects of the drug shadowed her blue eyes. Sidonie began to tidy the room, collecting scattered clothes and shoes and jewelry. Silence reigned until suddenly Roberta started to shake so violently that the cup rattled against its saucer.

"Sidonie, what are we to do?" Tears poured down Roberta's cheeks and a strangled sob escaped her.

"Oh, darling. Roberta..." Sidonie dropped the handful of silk scarves she collected and rushed to rescue the cup. She sat on the edge of the bed and curled her arms around her distraught sister. "It's all right. Don't cry. You're free. He'll never hit you again."

"William's gone. I can hardly believe it." She buried her head in Sidonie's shoulder until finally broken howls subsided to soft mewling. Finally she drew away to wipe her eyes and sniff. "I hardly know what to think."

"We'll come through this, Roberta." Sidonie echoed Jonas's words from yesterday as she reached into the nightstand drawer for a handkerchief.

Roberta wiped her eyes and blew her nose. "I loathe how we had to rely on that odious man." Roberta's eyes sharpened and with a sinking feeling, Sidonie realized her sister's immediate concern had shifted from her husband's death. "What happened in Devon? You and that Merrick creature seemed great chums yesterday. I imagined after your ordeal that you'd abhor the very mention of his name."

God give her strength. Sidonie wasn't sure she was up to this discussion, although she'd known it was inevitable. She still wasn't sure what she wanted to tell Roberta. Not the full story, that was for sure. "He was kind to me."

"That doesn't sound like the ruthless devil I know. Merciful heavens, Sidonie, the scoundrel compelled you into his bed. He's little better than a thug." The opium's effects well and truly ebbed. Roberta's gaze focused in a way Sidonie found discomfiting. "Or did you somehow talk him into letting you keep your maidenhead?"

"I told you yesterday that he didn't hurt me." If she blushed any hotter, she'd self-combust.

Sidonie dreaded more questions, but even worse than an inquisition was the way Roberta's face tightened with remorse. Roberta grabbed Sidonie's hands, wringing them in her distress. "Oh, my dear sister, I'm so sorry. You've gone and fallen in love with the villain. I thought you'd be safe. He's so hideous and rough. But of course, you're so inexperienced with men. I should never have let you go. How can I forgive myself?"

Sidonie tore free of Roberta's clinging hold and rose to stand trembling by the bed. "He didn't force me although he could have. I thought you'd be pleased about that."

"Except the cur was too clever for both of us. He was wicked enough to seduce you into cooperating in your ruin and now you'll break your heart over him." Roberta scowled at her. "It's part of his revenge on our family. He hates me. You know that."

"He hated William."

"Any strike at me was a strike at William. And he struck at me through you."

Sidonie stepped back to distance herself from Roberta's horrible, maniac insinuations. Nobody could be so Machiavellian as Roberta painted Jonas. "He helped you yesterday."

"Only because he's plotting something. You'll see."

Roberta rose on shaky legs, clinging to a bedpost for balance. Her cream lace nightdress flowed around her, adding to the dramatic effect. "Wake up, girl. He's over at that ridiculous house right now, sniggering at your foolishness."

"He's not like that. If you knew him as I do..."

"Listen to yourself! You sound so inane. Jonas Merrick set himself to ruining William and everyone associated with him. Confound him, he's succeeded. William's dead after seeing every enterprise ruined. I'm so debt-ridden, I'll never hold my head up in public again. And he's convinced you that he's some kind of knight in shining armor. Fit revenge on all of us, wouldn't you say?"

Sidonie wouldn't listen to this calumny against the man she loved. "He had every right to hate William. William scarred him."

Even before she spoke, Roberta's calmness indicated that this was no revelation. "I know. Which gives him every reason to destroy any connection of William's."

Sidonie felt sick and faint. She loved her sister but sometimes the changes wrought in her over the last years left her staggering in horror. Roberta hardly seemed to care that her husband had disfigured a younger boy from sheer spite. "You never told me about Jonas's scars."

"It's hardly something one boasts of." Roberta paused. "And it's all so long ago, isn't it?"

Except it wasn't. Jonas had suffered all his life for what his cousin had done. Roberta sighed with impatience. "I suppose you think his scars are romantic. You spend too much time with your nose buried in a book. Honestly, Sidonie, I thought you of all women would have more sense. The man is incapable of finer feeling. After all, he set out to seduce me and then had no compunction in depriving you of your virginity."

The gorge rose in Sidonie's throat. Hearing Roberta speak was like viewing the week at Castle Craven through a distorting mirror. Sidonie refused to listen to her poisonous insinuations. Roberta was wrong. Sidonie knew Jonas. She knew the attraction flaring between them had ambushed him, too. Hadn't he asked her to marry him? The feelings between them were strong and genuine. She must believe that. If she loved him, she had to trust him.

Which meant, astonishingly, she'd decided to accept his proposal.

Heavens, what a change in a woman once determined to lead her life alone and independent. Sidonie Forsythe was about to do the unthinkable and surrender herself to a man in matrimony.

Roberta surveyed her with a troubled scowl. "What is it, Sidonie? You have the most bizarre look on your face."

Sidonie shook her head. This morning, she'd hoped to tell Roberta that Jonas was the rightful Viscount, warn her before Jonas used the marriage lines to claim the title. Roberta's difficult humor discouraged sharing such unwelcome news. How she wished she'd told Jonas yesterday, but in the confusion and panic after William's fall, she'd thought only of concealing Roberta's crime.

She hoped that when she revealed everything to Jonas, he wasn't so angry that he withdrew his proposal. She could write to him, she supposed, but that seemed a cowardly method of handling this last secret dividing them. It was only a couple of days' delay, after all. Once William was buried, she'd go to Jonas as she'd gone to him at Castle Craven. She'd give him the marriage lines, then tell

him that she loved him and wanted to be his wife. Surely
he'd know that her acceptance was unrelated to his new
status. Good God, she loved Jonas Merrick so much, she'd
marry him if he came to her a pauper.

The next days passed in a flurry of activity as Sidonie
handled funeral arrangements, the estate, her sister, and
her nephews, who arrived home from school. Neither boy
seemed overly upset to hear of their father's end. Roberta
remained of little assistance. She mainly stayed in her
room wallowing in a fog of laudanum. Her complete
collapse fortified the impression that she was a grieving
widow. After their acrimonious encounter the morning
after William's death, Sidonie was grateful that her sister
remained largely uninvolved in practical matters at Barstowe Hall.

Soon the story Jonas concocted was so widely accepted
that Sidonie almost believed William had jumped to his
death to avoid the shame of bankruptcy. Sidonie's ever-
present fear of her sister's arrest subsided to a distant
hum. It appeared Jonas was right and they would make it
through. Those nightmarish seconds when Roberta shoved
her husband down the stairs might never have occurred.

Sidonie had originally hoped to escape to tell Jonas
about the marriage lines. But she'd quickly realized that
to avoid suspicion falling on him, it was better to have
no open contact between Ferney and Barstowe Hall for
the present.

Sidonie supported Roberta's faltering progress down the
aisle of the village church after William's funeral service. The sickly scent of lilies procured at great expense

from London had her head aching—or perhaps she had a headache because of Roberta's generous hand with attar of roses.

She blinked eyes scratchy with exhaustion. No matter how weary she was when she collapsed into bed, she couldn't sleep. It was odd; she'd slept alone for twenty-four years and only shared Jonas Merrick's bed for a matter of days. But it seemed wrong not to lie in his arms at night and wake to his presence in the morning.

The church was crowded with local gentry, tenants, and a few of William's London acquaintances. Nobody seemed particularly cast down. But then William had devoted most of his tenure as viscount to quarreling with his neighbors and embroiling them in pointless legal disputes. Not one soul genuinely regretted his absence. What a sad epitaph, Sidonie couldn't help thinking, much as she'd loathed her brother-in-law.

She turned to check on her nephews trailing behind their mother. Seven-year-old Nicholas had handled his role in his father's rites with a stoic courage that had brought tears to Sidonie's eyes. Young Thomas at five had become restless during the service, but settled upon his brother's hissed reprimand.

Ahead six brawny tenants carried the coffin, piled with more lilies, through the double doors. The villagers despised William as a man who brought ruin to the estate and who blustered to hide his complete ignorance about farming. Sidonie gathered from the servants that the local tavern had resounded with toasts to William's long sojourn in hell.

Unsuitable thoughts for church. Her grip tightened on Roberta's slender arm. "Are you all right?"

"Yes." Her sister's fading tones reflected extended laudanum use rather than sorrow, although today she'd done
a marvelous job of playing the shocked, bereaved wife.
"I'm glad *that* man didn't have the gall to come."

Sidonie didn't need to ask who that man was. Jonas's
gallantry in coming to Roberta's rescue hadn't softened
her attitude. "You're cursed ungrateful," Sidonie hissed,
then forced her expression into neutrality as she nodded at
a neighbor who was casting them a curious glance.

Roberta didn't hear. Deliberately, Sidonie suspected.

Jonas's absence stabbed her like a knife. She'd hoped
to encounter him today, if only as a silent presence at
the back of the church, but he'd stayed away. He was no
hypocrite. He wouldn't pay public respects to a man he
despised.

Mercifully over the past days, Roberta's brief surge of
concern for her sister had subsided. She'd been in no state
to inquire too carefully into what had happened in Devon.
Anyway, what could Sidonie say? *I thought to give myself
to a monster but instead lost my heart to an enchanted
prince?*

An enchanted prince who was unquestionably the new
Viscount Hillbrook. The letter confirming the identity
of the clergyman officiating at his parents' wedding had
arrived while she was at Castle Craven.

Outside the church, sunlight dazzled Sidonie. As her
vision cleared, she noted a strange hush in the crowd, different from the respectful silence appropriate to a funeral.
Puzzled, she saw a commanding man in black march-
ing with unhesitating purpose toward Roberta. She had
no idea who he was but immediately recognized his aura
of power. It was a quality Jonas shared. With a sudden

lurch of fear, she ushered the boys toward Barstowe Hall's housekeeper.

"Lady Hillbrook?" The stranger performed a cursory bow. "I am Sir Pelham George from London. May I have a private word? I apologize for intruding upon this sad day, but my time in Wiltshire is limited."

Perhaps he was a creditor. Sidonie was surprised William's debtors hadn't already descended like vultures. This man didn't look like a creditor. He looked like someone who ruled a small kingdom by personal edict.

"I'm not myself, Sir Pelham," Roberta said in the breathy tone she'd adopted since William's death. Raising her veils, she fixed her tragic blue gaze upon the gentleman. "I beg your indulgence. Please call at Barstowe Hall tomorrow when I may feel stronger."

Sidonie shouldn't resent her sister's dramatics. After all, she'd convinced everyone that she genuinely mourned her husband, making her an unlikely murderer. Sidonie waited for this stranger to fall victim to Roberta's blond beauty. Instead his expression remained stern as he extended his arm. "My lady?"

The crowd's avid curiosity buzzed around them. Dread coiled inside Sidonie. Dear God, was Sir Pelham here to arrest Roberta? But his manner was solicitous rather than threatening—and nobody but Roberta, Sidonie, and Jonas knew the truth behind William's death.

"If you insist." Sulkiness pierced Roberta's pretense at the pliable, pitiable widow. Her lips thinned as she accepted his escort. "My sister will accompany us."

Without speaking, Sir Pelham bowed to Sidonie. He drew Roberta aside while Sidonie followed. "My lady, this news may prove distressing."

Cold sweat prickled across Sidonie's skin as she frantically wondered what she'd do if this stranger took Roberta into custody. Roberta's eyes widened with immediate panic and her delicate throat moved as she swallowed. "Sir, I cannot imagine what more could distress me, given I've just lost my husband."

The man's expression became impossibly severe. Something in Sidonie guessed what he planned to say before he spoke. Heaven lend her strength, she'd feared for the wrong person. Roberta wasn't under threat.

Across a long distance, she heard the deep rumble of Sir Pelham George's voice, every word clear as a bell. "After evidence laid with the local magistrate, Jonas Merrick has been arrested for the murder of his cousin, Viscount Hillbrook."

Chapter Twenty-Six

Sidonie clutched her shabby brown cloak around her and shifted on the wooden chair to relieve her numb backside. The fear that beat like a drum beneath every breath almost distracted her from her discomfort. Around her, austere Roman faces glowered down as if to insist that she had no right to be here, in the foyer of Rothermere House, the Duke of Sedgemoor's extravagant London mansion.

The statues looked sterner by the minute. But even supercilious marble patricians couldn't match the disapproval expressed by the duke's butler when opening the door to such a badly dressed woman. A woman purporting to be sister-in-law to the insolvent, now deceased Lord Hillbrook. A woman claiming no acquaintance with His Grace but who insisted upon seeing him on behalf of a man awaiting trial for murder.

The butler had several times indicated that His Grace wasn't at home. Sidonie had several times indicated with all the frosty hauteur she could muster that she'd wait. For Jonas's sake, Sidonie endured the servant's rudeness, just as she endured this long delay. Grim determination had got her from Barstowe Hall to London after the funeral two days ago and to Newgate Prison yesterday. Grim determination had kept her at Rothermere House all day. Tonight she'd sleep at Merrick House, William's London property, under the careless eye of its scant staff. Tomorrow grim determination would spur her to pursue her quest to clear Jonas's name.

Knowing it was pointless expecting a nobleman to receive her earlier, she'd arrived at the duke's house midmorning. Now long beams of light through the fanlight above the door showed afternoon advanced toward evening.

She still hadn't advanced beyond the entrance hall.

Other people had come and gone, she assumed to see His Grace. She was familiar enough with aristocratic ways to know that "not at home" meant not at home to petitioners who arrived without appointment and with a barely concealed air of desperation. The parade of approved callers had ended about an hour ago. Bleakly Sidonie was aware that the butler would soon throw her out. She was tired, she was disheartened, she was stiff with sitting so long, and she was so thirsty she could drink the Thames dry. Unwelcome petitioners didn't rate tea or even a glass of water.

Her belly cramped with hunger but she disregarded it. She hadn't eaten since last night, when she'd choked down some bread and cheese after a fruitless day fighting to convince Jonas's jailers to allow her to see him. Naïvely she'd imagined she merely needed to request an interview with a prisoner and it would be granted. But no amount of pleading had got her beyond the gates.

When she'd first glimpsed the prison's dark, sinister bulk, she'd felt sick with fear and outrage. The very stones of Newgate seeped misery. Jonas didn't belong there. Jonas belonged with her. She'd save him from hanging if it killed her.

Biting her lip, she curled her fingers into her white muslin skirts. How Jonas would despise seeing her dressed this way. Clearly an opinion the churlish butler shared. She'd thought to borrow one of Roberta's dresses, but her sister's fashionable figure meant everything Sidonie tried strained across overflowing curves. Sidonie had hoped it wouldn't matter what she wore. She'd mention Jonas's name and the duke would see her. After all, hadn't Camden Rothermere saved Jonas at Eton? Hadn't he come to Castle Craven to warn Jonas of William's erratic behavior? Her experience in the increasingly chilly hall indicated that Jonas's churlishness to the duke in Devon had snapped any boyhood bonds between the men.

Where did that leave her?

Her hands clenched so hard in her meager skirts that the knuckles shone bloodless. Fierce demons of despair had snapped at her heels since she'd learned of Jonas's arrest. She hadn't even waited to learn what evidence had been laid against him before she'd set off for London. Anyway, she could guess. The feud was common knowledge and the duke had said at Castle Craven that William sought legal redress for the failed emerald scheme. It would take little for suspicions to focus on William's cousin if the authorities decided to treat Lord Hillbrook's death as other than accidental.

She was going to save Jonas. She wouldn't fail. She was his only hope.

Perhaps she should try Jonas's other Eton friend, Richard Harmsworth. She'd assumed a duke would make an ideal champion, but today's ordeal indicated the duke might remain beyond reach unless she waylaid him away from his watchdogs. Except her knowledge of the habits of London gentlemen was close to nonexistent. The butler was right to treat her as a country mouse. She didn't know enough of this sophisticated world to plan an effective campaign.

Well, you can learn.

Perhaps she should leave and smarten her appearance. The problem was she was woefully short of money. And time. She needed to get Jonas out of Newgate, where they kept him pending his trial. She didn't have the luxury to wait for a modiste to fashion a stylish gown. Even if she could afford such a thing. Sidonie only had what little she'd saved from Barstowe Hall's miserly housekeeping. And the proceeds of selling her hairpins.

The diamond pins had been a precious memento. She'd expected to mourn their loss. But what were pretty chips of polished stone compared to this threat to the man she loved? She'd relinquished them with no twinge of regret. What she'd regretted was how little she'd received in exchange.

A clatter of hooves outside interrupted her gloomy meditations. The door opened wide with welcome. On a blast of cold air that sent her huddling into her cloak, a tall man swept into the hall.

The superior butler could raise a smile. Who knew? Sourly she watched footmen dash forward to take the newcomer's cape, gloves, hat, and cane and whisk them away.

Sidonie had never seen a man so beautifully turned out. His garments fit like a second skin. She slid her slippered feet beneath the chair. In spite of her efforts last night, she was humiliatingly aware dirt from the streets around Newgate soiled her shoes and her hem was black with grime.

"Sir Richard!" The warmth in the butler's voice was in marked contrast to his greeting to Sidonie.

Her heart kicked into a gallop. Sir Richard? Could this be Jonas's rescuer? The man who had asked the duke to call at Castle Craven? She heard a sharp yip from outside and the elegant gentleman turned to pat a shaggy mongrel that trotted in after him. Sidonie waited for the starchy butler to expel the dog, but he merely smirked indulgently.

"Water for Sirius, Carruthers."

"At once, Sir Richard." The butler shot a peremptory glance at a footman, who disappeared in search of the hound's refreshment. The hound clearly rated above Sidonie.

Sirius was astoundingly ugly. Part lurcher, part whippet, part any number of breeds Sidonie couldn't place. He was a medium-sized dog with a brindle coat and a curved, feathery tail. He made an incongruous companion for the exquisite Sir Richard. As if aware of her curiosity, the dog turned his bright black eyes in her direction and wandered across to investigate, claws clicking on the marble floor.

"Hello, Sirius," Sidonie said softly, standing and extending a hand for him to sniff.

"He won't bite," Sir Richard said, and she realized he too had strolled closer.

"I'm not afraid." She scratched the animal behind his ears. His eyes shut with bliss. "I like dogs."

"He's an unregenerate flirt. No pretty lady escapes his notice."

"Sir Richard, His Grace awaits." Behind them, the butler sniffed with disapproval.

"A little patience will do his ducal soul good." Sir Richard's blue eyes didn't waver from Sidonie's face.

Sidonie mightn't be familiar with London gentlemen, but she recognized an out-and-out rake when she met one. Sir Richard was accustomed to charming women into doing exactly what he wanted. Up close, he was as handsome as his dog was ugly. Perhaps that's why he kept the beast, to emphasize the contrast.

"Are you waiting to see Cam?"

Sidonie couldn't imagine why he wasted his considerable address on her, but if there was a chance this man—whether the Sir Richard she sought or not—could get her in to see the Duke of Sedgemoor, she wouldn't discourage him. "Yes."

"Miss Forsythe arrived without appointment or introduction," the butler said frostily.

"I need the duke's help," she said, still fondling Sirius's ears. The dog's tail waved back and forth with lazy enjoyment.

The man's gaze ran over her, as if assessing her intentions. Perhaps he feared she was a discarded mistress, except surely no duke's ladybird worth her salt would sport such a dreary outfit. "I'll help if I can. What is your name?"

"Sidonie Forsythe. My sister Roberta is . . . was married to Viscount Hillbrook."

Loathing swiftly darkened the man's face under his thick golden hair before urbanity descended once more. Sidonie's instincts, already aroused, screamed this must be the Richard Harmsworth who had saved Jonas. Hope surged, dousing the exhaustion of this long, frustrating day.

"My condolences for your loss, Miss Forsythe."

Her hands fisted in Sirius's wiry coat. Dear God, let her be right. Let this man be Jonas's childhood ally. "Thank you. I'm here about Jonas Merrick."

"Jonas?" The man looked surprised. "I hear he's been accused of Hillbrook's murder."

Sidonie stared straight at him as the dog, sensing her tension, butted her skirts. "He's innocent."

"You seem sure."

"I am."

"He's an obvious suspect. The long-running animosity between the two men means—"

"He didn't kill Lord Hillbrook," she interrupted, eliciting a soft whine from Sirius. She laid her hand on his head to soothe him.

Her vehemence intrigued the man as, she could see, did her immediate defense of a man who was her brother-in-law's enemy. Sir Richard's jaw firmed in a way that made her wonder if he was quite the louche dandy he appeared. He extended his arm. "Miss Forsythe, I find you of interest. I'm sure Sedgemoor will as well. Would you care to accompany me into the duke's library?"

"Sir Richard, this lady is unknown to His Grace," Carruthers bleated behind them.

"She is, however, a great friend of mine. Pray announce us, my man."

"His Grace specifically said he'd see no unscheduled callers."

"He'll see me. And Miss Forsythe is with me." He paused. "And, Carruthers, take the lady's cape. I'm surprised you've let her wait without the basic courtesies."

Sidonie's lips twitched when ten minutes ago, she'd thought she'd never smile again. Fate had granted her a chance to save Jonas. What she made of it was up to her.

"Sir Richard Harmsworth, Your Grace, and Miss Sidonie Forsythe," Carruthers intoned, standing back as Sidonie and her escort entered the duke's luxurious library. When she heard her champion's name, fledgling hope spread its wings and prepared to soar.

From behind a massive Boulle desk, the familiar dark-haired man rose with his hand outstretched, then paused with a frown when his attention fell upon her. His bone structure was so hard and pure, it seemed carved from the same marble as the statues outside. The assessing green eyes held no welcome. Sidonie shivered and her optimism faltered.

With obvious familiarity, Sirius trotted to the rug before the roaring fire. He stretched out and rested his nose on his front paws.

"Miss Forsythe, to what do I owe the pleasure?" The duke's voice was cool but, thank goodness, not hostile.

Sidonie curtsied and reminded herself someone with his commanding presence was exactly who she needed. Mustering courage, she raised her chin and returned his direct stare. "Your Grace, I request your aid for Jonas Merrick, wrongfully charged with the murder of my brother-in-law, Lord Hillbrook."

Comprehension entered the duke's eyes, but didn't warm his expression a single degree. "I see. I should have realized when Carruthers said Forsythe. You're Lady Hillbrook's sister. I don't believe we've been introduced, although I see you know Richard."

She saw no point in deception. "I met Sir Richard in your hall where I've waited all day. He helped me barge in upon you," she said crisply. "I'm sorry for intruding, but I believe you and Mr. Merrick were once friends."

The duke's eyebrows arched with a hauteur that would have daunted her had she been one whit less desperate. "Merrick and I were schoolfellows. We haven't exactly been bosom-bows since."

Beside her, Sir Richard made a dismissive gesture with one elegant hand. "Oh, dash it, Cam, Jonas has hoed his own row since his parents' marriage was declared invalid. You know he's always been a proud devil, even as a boy. He's too stiff-necked to admit he might need friends."

Oh, my love, you've been so lonely. The reminder that she was most likely Jonas's only ally bolstered Sidonie's purpose. "He needs friends now."

"Is that what he told you?" The duke sounded bored as he gestured for her to sit.

"He hasn't told me anything." As she subsided into a chair facing the desk, she swallowed to moisten her dry throat. "They won't let me see him."

The duke sat and regarded her over steepled fingers. "The question arises why you want to see him at all. It's public knowledge Hillbrook and Merrick loathed each other. Which I suspect is why he was arrested. One would assume family loyalty places you in Hillbrook's camp."

Sidonie's color rose and her eyelashes flickered with

322 Anna Campbell

embarrassment. These men must guess her interest was more intense than a woman seeking justice for a stranger. "It's all a terrible mistake. Lord Hillbrook committed suicide. Mr. Merrick is innocent."

"So why do you need to see him?"

Because without him, I'm an empty husk. Because I need to touch him more than I need the air I breathe. "I can prove his innocence."

"Egad, that's a strong claim, Miss Forsythe." Sir Richard wandered to the sideboard and helped himself to a generous brandy.

The duke wasn't so impressed. Another supercilious arch of dark eyebrows. This man had the aristocratic mien down to a T. "I'm sure Mr. Merrick has engaged competent solicitors. You should take your proof, whatever it is, to them."

She could hear he doubted the existence of any proof. "I don't know who they are."

"Would you like me to find out?"

"No, thank you, Your Grace. The information is . . . private to Mr. Merrick. He needs to know the details before I pursue the matter."

Over tapping fingers, the duke contemplated her for a bristling interval. Her stomach knotted as she prayed he wouldn't dismiss her. If he did, she'd turn to Sir Richard. If he wouldn't help, she'd track down Jonas's solicitors, although right now she had no idea how to do that. Perhaps someone at Newgate might know. She'd already tried Jonas's offices in the city, but they'd turned her away. Tomorrow she'd go back and stage a more determined siege. She wasn't giving up.

"Miss Forsythe?"

She turned at Sir Richard's voice and realized he extended a glass of water toward her. She smiled gratefully. "Thank you."

"Perhaps we should order tea?"

"N...no, thank you," she said shakily after taking a sip. "I...just need to see Mr. Merrick. His release is all that matters."

The duke's gaze sharpened and she flushed, knowing she confirmed her personal interest. Shakily she placed the glass on the desk in front of her.

"That's a devilish queer expression, Cam old fellow," Sir Richard said suspiciously. "What are you thinking about?"

The duke's lips relaxed almost into a smile and he didn't shift his regard from Sidonie. "Mice."

Sidonie flushed to her hairline and gulped some more water to hide her embarrassment. Surely he hadn't guessed that she'd been at Castle Craven when he warned Jonas about William's mental instability.

"Sirius likes her," Sir Richard said in what seemed a non sequitur. At the sound of his name, the dog raised his head and surveyed the room's occupants.

The duke cast Sir Richard an impatient glance. "Unlike you, I don't base my whole acquaintance on a mongrel's good opinion."

"Harsh words, sirrah." Sir Richard dropped into the leather chair beside Sidonie's and slouched picturesquely. "You should, you know. The dog's a confounded genius."

"He's brighter than his owner, I'll give him that," the duke muttered, and Sidonie caught an unexpected glimmer of humor on that austere face.

"No brains, no brains at all. Never claimed to have a

thought past dinner. You're the one with the head on his shoulders, Cam. Always have been. That's why you and Jonas were such chums at school."

Sidonie suspected Sir Richard wasn't the fribble he purported. So far, he'd done a remarkable job of getting everybody to jump to his wishes and with little apparent effort. She couldn't forget that moment he'd decided to help her. The gaze that swept her had been sharply perceptive.

"That's not entirely why," the duke said, no hint of a smile remaining.

The ebullient Sir Richard briefly sobered. Again, the change was so fleeting that Sidonie would have missed it if she hadn't watched him closely. She recalled Jonas's tale of scandal shadowing each man's birth. "No, not entirely."

The duke sighed and leaned back in his chair. Her heart sinking, Sidonie wondered if she'd imagined his fleeting lightness. His features were all severity now. "I suppose Sirius, confound him, wants me to haul Merrick out of jail."

Sir Richard shrugged. "You can do it. Wave that blue-blooded hand and Merrick's a free man before breakfast."

The duke's mouth flattened. "I'm not sure about that. Pelham George is on the case, I hear."

Sir Richard clicked his fingers to indicate dismissal. "You run rings around that George fellow. Dash it, Cam, you run rings around everybody I know—and not just because you're a duke."

"I can certainly arrange for Miss Forsythe to see Merrick. I'm just not sure I should."

"I mean to help Mr. Merrick." Her hands clenched in her skirts.

"I'm sure, dear lady. But these are matters for men of the world. Would you tell me the nature of the proof or, even better, show it to me? I promise on my honor, I'll take the matter as far as I can."

Sidonie's jaw tightened at his patronizing tone but she kept her voice even. "I'm sorry, Your Grace. I can't do that."

"At the risk of leaving Mr. Merrick languishing in prison?"

She raised her chin. "I need to see Mr. Merrick. It's of the utmost urgency. If you can't arrange a visit, I'll find someone who will."

The duke's chilly green gaze focused on her as if she were a rare scientific specimen on a glass slide. He didn't answer her.

"Come, Cam. Get the girl in to see the chap. We can take it from there. You know you're going to help," Sir Richard drawled, raising his glass so the brandy caught the light. "I only had an evening at Crockford's ahead. I'd wager more than I meant to lose there that you planned to bury your head in blasted paperwork. Wouldn't you rather assist a valiant lady in a mission of mercy?"

"You make me sound poor spirited if I say no." The duke's deep voice was neutral. Sidonie couldn't guess his intentions. Her heart raced with dizzying suspense as she waited for him to offer support or send her away.

Dear God, don't let him send her away.

"Well, confound it, you are." Sir Richard drank his brandy as nonchalantly as though a man's life didn't hinge on the decision.

Sirius rose with a yawn and padded across to lay his head on Sidonie's lap. Absently, she scratched his ears while watching the duke. Would Sedgemoor come down on her side? Would his loyalty to Jonas endure? Or would he decide that he owed Jonas nothing and that Sidonie was merely an inconvenient petitioner?

The pause extended. In the silence, the fire crackled and popped. Under her ministrations, Sirius gave a canine groan of pleasure.

The duke sighed heavily and stood. He didn't smile as he stared down at her. "Very well. Miss Forsythe, Sirius has his way. You and I are off to Newgate."

"No such luck, Cam, m'dear." Sir Richard rose, disturbing Sirius, who turned to watch his master. "I'm in on this reunion."

Chapter Twenty-Seven

J onas lay reading *The Essays of Elia* on the luxurious bed brought, like all the furnishings in his prison cell, from his London house. When he heard keys rattle at his door, he set the book aside with a sigh of irritation.

What the hell did his jailer want at this late hour? After three days in prison, Jonas knew the routine. And the routine was that mostly he was left to himself, unless he was discussing the conduct of his trial with the ruinously expensive solicitors he'd employed. The turnkey was paid well to stay away and keep the curious, who were legion, at bay.

Sitting up, Jonas ran his hands through his untidy hair. The door swung wide to admit his jailer. Behind him was a woman. Not just any woman. The woman who haunted his dreams. The woman he'd missed like the very devil in the week since he'd seen her.

"Sidonie..." he breathed, wondering if he'd gone mad. Surely he hadn't. Everything in his cell was how it always was. Her presence alone transformed it into paradise. His heart somersaulted with sudden, unexpected happiness.

"Half an hour, miss."

She pushed back the hood of her hideous cloak and cast a nervous glance at the jailer. "Thank you."

"I take it you're happy for the lady to stay, Mr. Merrick?" The man's expression was blatantly salacious.

"Mind your manners, Sykes," Jonas said in a dangerous tone. "The lady is a member of my family."

"Aye, sir." The man's head bobbed and he scuttled away, locking the door behind him.

"What the hell are you doing here?" Jonas strode across the Turkish rug to clasp her hands. Seeing her was like standing in sunlight after a long, hard winter, but he couldn't be easy meeting her in such surroundings.

"Oh, Jonas," she said in a broken voice and started to cry.

"*Tesoro* . . . sweetheart . . . my love," he choked out, cradling her in his arms. "Don't cry. Please don't cry."

So many times since his arrest, he'd remembered holding her. So many times since his arrest, he wondered if he'd survive this latest crisis and hold her again. The reality of having her here surpassed all fantasy. He drank in every detail. Her warmth. The scent of her hair and skin. The way her hands curled around his arms to keep him close. In his lowest hours, he'd wondered if he imagined the passion and joy of those days at Castle Craven. They were so divorced from current bleak reality.

"I've been so afraid," she muttered into his shoulder, sliding her arms around his waist.

He kissed wherever he could reach. Her hair. The side of her face. Her shoulder. Her neck. All the while the litany of endearments flowed. He was helpless to resist calling her every sweet name he knew.

After too short an interval, she sucked in an unsteady breath and started to withdraw. He tightened his hold. "Not yet."

When she raised her face, her eyes were swollen with crying and her cheeks were flushed. She was the most beautiful thing he'd ever seen. "Jonas, we haven't got long. We must talk."

"I'd rather touch you." He held her slender shoulders and feasted his eyes on her. She caressed his scarred cheek. He no longer minded her touching his scars, so much had he changed.

"Are you all right?"

"Yes." He pressed his face into her hand. She was here. She was here. He hardly believed it. "Now I am."

She glanced around the extravagantly furnished room. "I'd imagined—"

He found it in himself to be wryly amused as he took her hand and drew her toward the bed. He'd never imagined he'd laugh in this bleak prison where every stone whispered that his luck had run out and he wouldn't escape execution.

"I know. Manacles. Racks. Fetid water seeping from bare stone walls. There are advantages to being a rich man, *carissima*. This cell costs a fortune, but I won't be here long. The evidence is circumstantial at best. I'm paying through the nose for my lawyers. They'd better damn well earn their keep." He hoped his completely false optimism convinced her. He couldn't bear to think his fate troubled her.

They sat on the bed facing each other, holding hands. "What happened? Everything was going so smoothly."

"Don't you know? I thought the gossip would be all over Barstowe."

"I left as soon as I heard of your arrest. Luckily Roberta had her carriage at Barstowe Hall. I tried all day yesterday to see you but they wouldn't let me."

"Bless you." Her loyalty touched him. He didn't underestimate her difficulties getting to London. She had no funds, rushing away would make her a target of local talk, and he couldn't picture Roberta supporting Sidonie's efforts to reach him.

"Why did they even think to arrest you?"

"A combination of old scandal and bad luck. A neighbor riding along the back lane saw me crossing Barstowe Hall's grounds the day William died. Then one of the maids at Ferney got hysterical under questioning and started blabbing about me coming home bruised and disheveled the day of the murder. William's latest legal case against me about the emerald mine didn't help either. Seemed to give me a fresh motive for wanting the miscreant dead."

"That all seems...flimsy."

"It is." He refrained from saying how old, public enmity might still condemn him. Pelham George was no fool and he'd only prosecute if he thought he had a good case to send Jonas to the gallows.

Sidonie's eyes were somber in the lamplight. "Jonas, I can save you."

"I doubt it." His voice deepened into irony. "Unless Roberta signed a confession."

Sidonie's grip firmed. "Roberta was...against me coming to London."

Roberta was afraid suspicion might shift from Jonas to her. "I'm sure."

"You could have turned her in."

He laughed humorlessly. "Nobody would credit any accusation against her." He paused. "She doesn't deserve to die for what she did. And there are her sons to consider."

Her hands clenched hard around his. "You could hang."

"We're not at *point non plus*."

Although in his heart he acknowledged he was far from innocent. He hadn't shoved the blackguard down the stairs, but he'd frequently wished William dead. Not just because of the attack at Eton. He'd wanted William dead for stealing the heritage Jonas had always believed was his.

Now Jonas rotted in jail and nobody lifted a finger to help. He'd always known society tolerated rather than liked him. His bastardy stuck in people's craw, even those eager to take advantage of his financial acumen. Still, to have it confirmed so categorically that, for all his wealth, he remained *persona non grata* was a salutary lesson. He'd assumed some business associate might offer aid, but nobody had stepped forward. So much for his youthful dreams of having so much money, he was invulnerable. Money hadn't saved him from the humiliation of prison. Money hadn't rallied hordes to his support.

Everyone abandoned him to his fate.

Except gallant Sidonie.

"Jonas, please listen to me. Please."

Something in her frantic plea pricked his instincts. "What is it, *bella*? Some rash plan? A scramble down the walls at dead of night? A tunnel to the street? A pistol concealed under that atrocity of a cloak?"

To his regret, she tugged her hands free, then, even worse, she rose to stand a few feet away. He leaned back on his elbows, his gaze unwavering. Even if he couldn't touch her, watching her was manna to a man locked away from her for days.

Her angry gesture dismissed his lightness. "Don't joke."

What the hell was going on? All desire to tease vanished. Her agitation reeked of fear. And wretchedness. Apprehension tightening his gut, he sat up and looked directly at her. "You're making me nervous, Sidonie."

She fumbled with the shabby reticule he hadn't noticed tied to her wrist. He'd only seen her. He'd only ever seen her.

"Here." She thrust something at him.

He ignored her gesture. Instead he watched her face. Her expression made him devilish uneasy.

"Jonas, look," she said abruptly.

He glanced down to a yellowing paper in her shaking hand. Automatically he reached to take it. It took a few moments to realize what he held. His head whipped up and he stared at Sidonie in disbelief. "Is this real?"

She shrank under his shock, although he was too astonished to be angry. "Yes."

Anger stirred. "How long have you known?"

That was all he cared about now, although he knew he'd care about much more once his mind came to terms with what she'd presented to him. He immediately dismissed any possibility that she'd found this document in the last day or so. She looked too guilty for that to be true.

"I . . . I discovered it in Barstowe Hall's library a couple of weeks ago. It was . . . it was folded inside the back cover of the second volume of *Don Quixote*."

"Of course you immediately recognized the document's significance." His tone was flat. He should be overjoyed. He held his parents' marriage lines. All his childhood dreams came true.

Under the bite of his voice, she seemed small and vulnerable. Just at the moment, he couldn't find it in himself to pity her.

"Of course."

"It didn't occur to you to tell me?"

She didn't cringe, but nor was she the brave, defiant woman he knew. Except everything he knew about her turned out to be false. In a petty, mendacious world, he'd believed she was the one pure, shining beacon. How tragically wrong he'd been.

He rose on legs that felt shamingly unsteady and stepped toward her. She flinched away. His laugh was bitter. "Just because I'm now Lord Hillbrook, it doesn't mean I've turned into William. I won't hit you."

When she bit her lip, it usually touched his heart. Damn her, it still did. She wasn't what he'd thought she was. She was a liar. The woman he'd called his life and his soul and his beauty was a gorgeous shell over a pit of foul deceit.

"I...I had my reasons for keeping it from you," she whispered.

His smile felt like a rictus grin. "I'm sure."

She spoke in a rush. "You don't understand what it was like living with William and Roberta. How...how terrifying it was when he beat her. Finding the marriage lines seemed like a gift from heaven. I...I planned to use them to blackmail William into letting Roberta go. They were the only power I had against him."

"While the world continued to believe my father was

at best a fool and at worst a liar. That my mother—" He paused and sucked in a shuddering breath. "That my mother was a whore."

She paled and twisted her hands together. "I know... I know I was wrong to hide the discovery, but you and your parents were unknown to me. William went near to killing Roberta last time he beat her. Her need... her need seemed greater than yours."

"And justice go hang," he said sourly. He tried to make himself view her as a stranger. Because a stranger was just what she was. What a fool he'd been. What a pathetic, needy, gullible fool.

He could almost understand what she'd done. After all, her sister's life had been at risk and nobody knew better than he just how destructive William's temper was. He just couldn't forgive the decisions she'd made. He couldn't forgive that she'd made him believe she was honest to her soul when she wasn't honest at all. Above all, he couldn't forgive that by making him believe in her, she'd made him as vulnerable as that boy screaming under his cousin's knife.

With a faint revival of spirit, she straightened. "You're a grown man. I didn't know... I didn't know then how you'd suffered, how illegitimacy ruined your life."

He made a dismissive sound in his throat even as his pride cringed to remember what he'd confided in her during those sweet nights in Devon. He'd trusted her with so much that he'd never shared with anyone else. And all the time when she'd pretended to care, she'd nursed this betrayal.

"No, you'd rather William retained the title he disgraced. If he hadn't died, would you ever have told me?"

Her voice was low and her gaze flickered away from his. "I needed to work out what to do. That week...that week with you shook my certainties. But then the duke told you about William's rampage. I'd hoped to settle Roberta somewhere safe, then tell you, but I had to see whether she was in danger first."

"It didn't occur to you to tell me the truth and let me look after Roberta?" That was a huge part of her treason, that she'd given him no chance to decide his future or find some solution that protected Roberta and her sons.

"I—"

"Of course it didn't. I might have unfettered access to your body, but you trusted me with little else."

"Don't." She shut her eyes as if she couldn't bear looking into his face. She was as white as paper. Jonas told himself he wouldn't take pity on her. He wouldn't. But her misery still tore raw strips off his heart.

"I find myself bewildered that you gave yourself to me at all." Damn it all, he should shut up. Now. Berating her only confirmed what a gullible idiot he'd been. After all these years of trusting nobody, he'd trusted Sidonie. And she'd played him for a dimwit. "I suppose you were curious. Or perhaps you felt you owed me some recompense for stealing my inheritance."

She sucked in a breath that sounded like a sob, but to her credit, she didn't retreat. "Please, Jonas, you know that's not how it was."

He gave another of those unamused laughs. God help him, he could either laugh or cry and he'd humiliated himself quite enough. "It turns out I know nothing about you." His voice lowered to acrid self-castigation. "I thought you were the only true thing in my misbegotten life. I discover you're nothing but a pretty parcel of lies, base metal not gold."

"You're . . . you're not fair." She raised her head and stared at him with a spark of defiance. "Roberta is my sister. I knew you a week. A mere week. Once I discovered what your illegitimacy cost you, I agonized over whether I was doing the right thing. I agonized the whole time."

He stepped away, partly to break the physical pull she exerted, no matter what he'd discovered about her. "Not enough to tell me the truth."

"I told you the truth in everything apart from this," Sidonie whispered, twining her arms around herself in a defensive gesture that shouldn't stab his conscience.

"This turns everything else into lies," he said wearily. He was angry, but anger was merely thin defense against the devastation hovering to crush him. If he didn't love her so much, she couldn't wound him like this.

"You—" She swallowed, the movement of her slender throat vulnerable.

He fought the traitorous urge to take her in his arms and tell her everything was forgiven. Because, hell and damnation, he couldn't forgive her. Not when he remembered his father dying a broken man, far from home, mocked by the world that once revered him. Not when he remembered schoolboy taunts about his dago slut of a mother. Not when he remembered the blazing agony of William's knife carving his face, marking him forever outcast.

Sidonie watched him and if he didn't mistrust every perception about this woman, he'd say his rage broke her heart. "You hate me now. I . . . I can't blame you. It's too late to make amends. You're right. I should have trusted you. Even if I didn't trust you, I should have told you. Every day William held the title after I found the marriage lines, I abetted his theft."

She sounded so reasonable. He couldn't bear it. He lashed out, just wanting her to go away and leave him to drown in his wretchedness. "Do you hope to wheedle a pardon?"

"No." After a fraught pause, her voice emerged more strongly. She looked as severe as a stone angel. Whereas there was nothing angelic about her at all, God help him. "Jonas, hating me isn't what's important now. What's important is what use you make of this information. If you tell people that you found the marriage lines before you visited Barstowe Hall and that's why you went to see William, you'll convince the authorities that you had no motive for murder. Faced with losing the title, William had stronger reason than mounting debts to kill himself."

"It sounds like a fairy tale," he said sarcastically. He fought the urge to crumple the marriage lines and pitch them at her.

"Except it explains so much. I imagine once you're Viscount Hillbrook, the world will be happy to hear protestations of innocence." She plunged a shaking hand into the pocket of her shabby cape and produced another paper. "This confirms Reverend Trask was in Spain when your parents married and there's a letter with his signature for matching with the marriage lines."

Looking at her stung him, stung like hell. His embarrassing, sentimental hopes for a life with her scattered like ashes. He hated her. He hated her almost as much as he loved her. He longed to destroy the love. He had a bleak feeling that the love would destroy him. "You've delivered your news. I don't want you here."

She paled even further and he muffled another unwelcome pang of guilt. She deserved to suffer. She'd cut his heart into mincemeat. Worse, she'd fleetingly and cruelly made him imagine that someone might love a monster like him. That was her real crime. He'd never forgive her.

She was ashen and unshed tears brimmed in her eyes, but she wouldn't back down, no matter how beastly he was. Hesitantly she stepped forward and placed the letter on the table against the wall. "Please listen, Jonas. This is your key to freedom. If you say you went to Barstowe Hall to tell William that you're legitimate, people will know you didn't kill him. If anything, he had motive to kill you."

"Why haven't I mentioned this until now?" he asked, then descended to more sarcasm, hating himself, hating her, hating every damn thing in the world. "Did it slip my mind?"

She flinched at his tone and he felt mean and small for baiting her. He was so livid, he wanted to smash everything to Hades. But needling her made him feel like he tortured a kitten. Not that Sidonie was so defenseless. Or so innocent.

"You have—" She sucked in an unsteady breath. "You have every right to be angry. But please listen. If you say you waited to tell William's family, and my visit here confirms that, people will believe you're a hero rather than a villain. A man who, at risk to his life, considered the feelings of a suicide's grieving widow and orphaned children."

She sighed and brushed her hair back from her face. It was considerably untidier than when she'd arrived. He remembered as if it had happened to someone else how he'd dragged her against his body and how his heart leaped at the sight of her. When she came in, he'd felt complete. He'd never feel complete again.

"What a touching story. Unrelated to anything like reality."

Her lips tightened. "Don't let self-destructive rage win, Jonas. Once you think about this, you'll realize that this piece of paper, however tardily delivered, gives you a future. And a name. And a way out of this murder charge."

"Very bracing, my darling," he said drily. "I find myself quite roused to action."

She drew herself up and stared at him. The blank despair in her eyes mirrored the agony in his heart. He tried to tell himself that her anguish was more deception, but he couldn't quite believe it. "Don't let this chance pass you by because you loathe me. You believe I wronged you. I did. I had good reason, but that reason doesn't justify my actions."

"Get out of my sight." He couldn't bear to look at her. He couldn't bear to remember everything she'd made him feel and know none of it was real.

She whitened and staggered before he watched her gather faltering courage and stand her ground. Shaking hands drew her hood over her rich brown hair. "I ... I wish you well, Jonas," she whispered and turned away.

Damn her, however angry he was, he couldn't let her go like this. He didn't even know if she came alone or with a maid. Newgate was in a dangerous quarter of London and it was the middle of the night. "Sidonie..."

"Yes?"

He couldn't see her face but her rigid shoulders spoke of control barely maintained. "Do you have someone with you? I'll pay Sykes to escort you home if not."

She didn't face him. "What do you care?"

The bitter, unacceptable truth was that he cared enormously. "I don't wish ill upon you."

"That's big of you," she muttered and rapped hard at the door.

"Sidonie, I want you safe," he said helplessly as she swept past the turnkey toward the shadowy hall. "I want you to be...happy."

She'd gone and didn't hear.

With a groan, he slumped onto the bed and buried his face in his hands. How sodding wonderful. At last he could vindicate his parents and restore his birthright. He should be cheering his bloody head off.

He didn't give a rat's arse whether he lived or died.

"Merrick? Merrick, what the devil's got into you?"

Dazedly Jonas raised his head. Two tall, well-dressed men crowded into his cell. It took him a few moments to recognize the Duke of Sedgemoor and Richard Harmsworth. Men who had once saved his life. Men who he'd avoided for years because every time he saw them he relived the vile shame of his scarring.

"Where's Sidonie?" He surged to his feet and thrust past them, but the corridor outside was empty.

"I sent Miss Forsythe home in my carriage," Sedgemoor said with a hint of disapproval. More guilt. Jonas guessed she'd been unable to hide her distress.

Sedgemoor continued. "Before she left, she asked us to offer our services."

Brava, bella. He had no idea how she'd managed it, but with the assistance of these two darlings of the *ton*, he was sure to evade the hangman. He wished he cared.

"The lady says she has proof of your innocence."

"Yes, yes, she does."

So the dance began. He drew an unsteady breath and realized Sidonie was right. While he might resent accepting her advice, he wasn't stupid. He had to prove his innocence and the story she'd concocted would serve as well as another. Once free, he'd assess what remained from his ruined life. And whether he could be bothered to fix any of it.

He studied these men who had come to his rescue long ago and who came to his rescue again. Sedgemoor and Harmsworth had never scorned him for his bastardy. Both, in spite of their scandalous backgrounds, were known as men of their word. If they pledged themselves to help, they would indeed help. He straightened his shoulders and struggled to sound purposeful. He couldn't fail now. He owed his parents justice. "I have my father's marriage lines."

"Good God," Harmsworth breathed. "You're Viscount Hillbrook. That sets the cat among the pigeons."

"Indeed." It was too late to revenge himself on William by taking what he'd valued most. It wasn't too late for Jonas to restore his parents' good names. "Now I've received blessing from my cousin's family to make circumstances public, I intend to claim my inheritance."

Chapter Twenty-Eight

"Mrs. Merrick requests an interview, my lord."

At the stentorian tones of the butler he'd employed to run his London home, Jonas laid down his pen and rubbed tired eyes. "Here at the house?" he asked, astonished.

For three months, he'd been officially acknowledged as Viscount Hillbrook and he'd only started to make headway through the tangle William had left of the estate. He'd started on the current batch of paperwork before breakfast. It was early afternoon and he couldn't see himself getting away before dinner.

Now Roberta wanted to see him. He hadn't spoken to either Forsythe sister since that bitter encounter in Newgate when he'd turned, hurt and angry, on Sidonie. Three months was time enough to repent his temper but did nothing to soothe the ache in his heart. Yearning for her stopped him sleeping. If he occasionally dropped into a restless doze, harrowing dreams tormented him.

He was in a damned bad way.

Such a bad way, he occasionally wondered if he could overcome pride to crawl back to Sidonie in forlorn hope of a kind word. After the way he'd lashed out at her, he didn't expect forgiveness. She'd saved him and he'd reacted not with gratitude but with rage. But then prudence would demand he let well enough alone. Leave her free to pursue the future she had no intention of sharing with Jonas Merrick.

She'd made that more than clear.

When he'd settled an allowance on Roberta and accepted financial responsibility for William's sons, he'd offered Sidonie a stipend, too. At the time, he'd still felt bruised that she'd put her sister before him—how lowering to recognize jealousy was at least partly to blame for his outburst. But even in his anger, he couldn't bear to think of her scratching out a meager living. He wanted her to be able to buy a pretty dress or a new bonnet.

Some City lawyer had replied on her behalf, rejecting any assistance from the Hillbrook estate. She'd made no acknowledgment of the gift as a personal matter. Her chilly refusal left Jonas feeling like she'd sliced open a barely healed wound. Common sense and self-preservation insisted he leave their dealings there. Common sense proved a deucedly cold bedfellow on a winter night and he was near to consigning it to the devil. If he chased Sidonie, he risked humiliation. Humiliation seemed a luxury compared to this endless, gnawing yearning.

In Devon, Sidonie had wanted him. He'd been wrong about so much, but surely he wasn't wrong about that. Perhaps if he groveled low enough, she'd deign to bestow her favor again. So pathetic he'd become in his loneliness.

All his life he'd imagined that if he claimed his heritage, wiped the stain of dishonor from his parents' memories, acquitted that brute William for his spite, he'd be happy. He couldn't remember a time when he'd been unhappier.

As he said, pathetic.

Even he was sick of how he moped around Merrick House. He needed a good kick up the arse.

"My lord?" the butler prompted, extending the silver salver with Roberta's card once more.

Jonas realized he'd drifted off again. His continual distraction was another thing to blame on Sidonie. He'd been hailed as the most incisive financial mind of his generation. Nobody would say that these days.

Roberta was here at Merrick House. Probably to cavil about her allowance—Jonas had hedged the payment with strict conditions to curtail her gambling and extravagance. To hear news of Sidonie, it might be worth enduring a tirade about his stinginess.

His pride really was in tatters.

He glanced at the butler. "Show Mrs. Merrick in and have tea brought, Jenkins. Inform the stables that I require Casimir saddled once my guest has left."

Roberta must want something—she never came near him unless she did. This time, he wanted something from her in return.

Sidonie let herself out of the tall white house in Paddington and sucked in a breath of fresh morning air. Well, fresh as London air got. Late February offered scant promise of spring, although yesterday in Hyde Park, she'd noticed a few brave snowdrops. This year winter lasted forever.

Or perhaps she carried winter with her.

Shivering, she shrank inside her brown cape. Since arriving in town two months ago, she'd bought a couple of secondhand dresses, but she couldn't summon interest in ordering a wardrobe befitting her new independence. She barely summoned interest to struggle out of bed each day.

The morning was advanced but hadn't warmed much from frosty beginnings. As a woman past first youth lodging in an irretrievably middle-class neighborhood, she at least could wander abroad unchaperoned. She was later than usual. It had been especially difficult to rise and dress today.

As always lately, the need to make permanent arrangements for her future nagged at her. For weeks, she'd battled the lethargy that had gripped her since visiting Jonas in Newgate. At first she'd been too heartsick to care where she went, so she'd returned in a fog of despair to Barstowe Hall. But Roberta's caprices soon grated and Sidonie couldn't forget how her sister had blithely abandoned Jonas to face accusations of murder.

Life in Wiltshire became increasingly disagreeable as Roberta whined about Jonas Merrick stealing her place in the world—however many times Sidonie explained that if anyone was a thief, it was William and by association, William's family. Inevitably once confirmed as viscount, Jonas requested possession of Barstowe Hall. This sparked another storm from Roberta, who eventually moved with ill grace and at Jonas's expense to a pleasant villa in Richmond.

After they left Barstowe Hall, Sidonie decided for the sake of sanity to live apart from her sister. Her birthday had passed and she'd received her legacy. Her own establishment was finally a possibility.

But the actions to make that establishment a reality had proven beyond her.

Staying with a former governess in Paddington provided a stopgap. Each day Sidonie intended to make plans. If only about where to live. But each day passed in a pall of desolation and ended with no more concrete arrangements than at the start. She didn't want to stay in London. She'd decided to move to the north, Yorkshire or even Northumberland. If only because either was a long way from Devon. But village or city? And right now, she couldn't manage the journey out of London to find a house.

Instead she spent too many days skulking in her room like a wounded animal, only doing the minimum to maintain health. She hated what she'd become, but didn't know how to break free of regret and guilt and longing. Hester, her hostess, had attempted to draw Sidonie into her social circle. Sidonie resisted, just wanting blessed numbness.

As time passed, blessed numbness proved harder to maintain. The necessity for action clamored beyond the glass wall that shielded her. Eventually she'd heed the demand, but right now, she drifted with no more conscious volition than a twig in a stream.

Trudging toward the park for her daily walk, she ignored the traffic. Her focus remained on the gray, miserable round of days since she'd left Castle Craven. The gray was almost comfortable now. In this limbo, nobody prodded her to feel anything.

She crossed to Hyde Park. While nothing offered peace, the nearest she came was here among the trees. Blankly she stared into the Serpentine's green water. She had no idea how long she stood there, not thinking, not feeling, before the hairs on the back of her neck prickled.

These days, such awareness of her surroundings was unfamiliar. Vague annoyance more than anything made her raise her bonneted head. She surveyed the area. The oily surface of the pond. Swans. Ducks. Seagulls squabbling over a crust. Children wrapped against the cold like round dolls. A trio of nursemaids gossiping on a bench.

Still that uncanny sense that someone watched her.

Reluctantly she turned. She wasn't surprised to observe Jonas leaning against the trunk of an elm several yards away. His arms were folded over his powerful chest and he was better dressed than she remembered. While she couldn't read the expression on his face under the stylish beaver hat, she could tell he wasn't happy to encounter her.

Still she didn't feel anything. Grayness permeated her soul to the point where even seeing Jonas didn't bring her alive.

Jonas waited for Sidonie to start or gasp or run away. But as her eyes rested upon him, she seemed calm. Uncharacteristically calm. She was deathly pale and her face was drawn. Only now that the crackling energy was absent did he realize how essential that quality had been to the Sidonie he remembered.

"Jonas," she said evenly as if continuing a conversation.

"Good morning, Sidonie." Through seething anger and his damned invincible, unwelcome delight in her mere presence, he struggled to keep his voice neutral. He didn't want to frighten her away.

"I assume you're looking for me." Her manner betrayed no trepidation. Purple shadows under her eyes hinted she'd slept as little as he had since their rancorous parting. "It seems too coincidental to run into each other."

She sounded distant, uninvolved. She didn't sound like the vibrant, exciting woman who had shared his bed. This woman was literally a shadow of her former self. She'd lost weight. He couldn't see her body under that ghastly cloak, but her cheekbones protruded and hollows formed in her neck.

"I followed you from your lodgings."

Not even that admission seemed to bother her. Her gloved hands clasped loosely before her and her shoulders slumped. "I suppose Roberta told you where I was."

That wasn't all Roberta had told him. "Yes. She came to visit me yesterday."

Dull brown eyes examined his features as if trying to discern his thoughts. With difficulty he kept his expression cool. "You said you never wanted to see me again," she said flatly.

"I didn't," he said equally flatly.

"So why are you here?"

"Circumstances have changed."

"They've changed for you. I hear you asserted your claim to the title with minimal fuss."

After deploring his disinheritance all these years, he hardly cared anymore whether he was Viscount Hillbrook or plain Jonas Merrick. Both were pitiful sods. "Once the clergyman's signature was confirmed, all barriers crumbled."

"Congratulations," she said with no warmth, although with no spite either. It was as though she didn't care. This new Sidonie didn't seem to care about much. "Is being a viscount all you expected?"

"It has its benefits." He couldn't immediately think of any when he stared at the woman he wanted but could never have. "It means dealing with a lot of toadies and sycophants."

"So it's not worthwhile?"

He shrugged. "It's what I was born for."

"Yes."

An awkward pause fell. He'd descended upon her certain of what he meant to say and how he meant to say it. But this wan, impassive girl vanquished his domineering intentions. He'd thought Sidonie vulnerable in Newgate when he'd played the bully fit to rival William. This woman before him now was so fragile, she looked as if she'd shatter into a million pieces if he so much as touched her.

She sidled toward the path, carefully keeping her distance. "I'm glad you got what you wanted, Jonas. I'm glad you've reclaimed your name and your parents' honor is no longer in question. I wish you well. I know you won't believe it, but I only ever wished you well."

She must think him the biggest slow-top in Creation. Fragile or not, he wasn't letting her go like this. "Not so fast, *bella*."

The endearment slipped out inadvertently. He cursed his reckless tongue. He'd promised himself no matter how livid he was, he'd be calm and reasonable and treat her as a beautiful stranger. He'd persuade, not coerce. He'd prevail without unleashing either rage or hurt.

Jonas should have known she'd shoot good intentions to hell. She *always* shot good intentions to hell.

He mightn't trust himself to touch her, but nonetheless he reached for her arm. Through the cloak, he felt its thinness. His grip gentled, although he'd meant to be stern with her, not tender.

She didn't withdraw. He had a horrible feeling she hardly noticed his touch. She'd always noticed his touch. Three months apart had turned her into someone he barely recognized. She stood docile under his hand as if nothing united them, as if that tumultuous, radiant week had never existed, as if they were indeed strangers.

Anger stirred but he ruthlessly reined it in. He had a task to accomplish and losing his temper wouldn't help. "Don't you have something to tell me?"

She didn't look at him but her face under the ugly bonnet went deathly white. "No."

"Don't lie, Sidonie."

"I have nothing to say to you, Jonas." Slowly she turned to him, her eyes glassy. Trembling in his hold, she raised her free hand to her bloodless lips. "Please let me go."

"Not on your life," he said grimly, tightening his grip.

"Please...I beg of you." To his alarm she started to sway. Her complexion developed a green tinge to rival the Serpentine. "Please."

The Sidonie he'd known would defy him, insist he remove his hand. This woman spoke in a faded voice that made him want to smash something.

"Hell, Sidonie, you break my bloody heart." He caught her as her knees crumpled and she slumped toward the dry winter grass.

Chapter Twenty-Nine

Sidonie basked in warmth and safety. She knew imme-diately that Jonas's arms held her high against his chest. How she'd missed this feeling. She'd been cold, so cold since he'd gone away. With an inarticulate sound of contentment, she pressed her cheek into the fine wool of his coat. If this was a dream, she didn't want to wake.

Reluctant awareness pricked like a knife. Jonas only carried her because she'd collapsed at his feet. How humiliating. How distressing. How...*revealing*.

Her beautiful fantasy where Jonas wanted her shat-tered into bitter reality. She cursed her weakness. She'd tried to eat breakfast, but she'd felt too tired and ill to do more than swallow a few mouthfuls. Last night, she'd forced herself to eat but hadn't been able to keep any food down.

Why, oh, why hadn't she gone north immediately after leaving Wiltshire instead of staying within Jonas's reach? But she was so sick all the time, the long coach journey wasn't feasible. And she was grimly aware that if Jonas wanted to track her down, the likelihood was that he would.

"Put...put me down." For the sake of the pride that was all she had left, she wanted to command, but her request emerged as a breathy whisper.

"No."

He sounded harsh. When he'd caught her in his arms, she'd fleetingly imagined he sounded like the man who whispered endearments as he took her to the stars.

She'd never hear that man again.

Her heart raced with fear and distress. "Please, Jonas, I can walk."

"All right."

Abruptly he stopped and set her on her feet. Immediately her head began to swim. She sucked in a jagged breath to curb the roiling in her belly. She couldn't be sick. Not now. Not in front of Jonas. That would be too mortifying. Anyway she'd need food in her stomach to be sick. Bile flooded her mouth. She started to tumble headlong down a black tunnel.

From far away, she heard Jonas swear as he swung her into his arms again. She tried to stiffen in protest, but her muscles remained as floppy as wet muslin. In her heart, she was still strong and determined, but her body let her down. She waited for him to say something snide but he kept silent. This time, she didn't fool herself she was anything other than an inconvenience.

"Where are you taking me?" she asked, once she gained temporary control over her unruly digestion.

"To my carriage," he said shortly.

She told herself it didn't matter that he hated her. Only building a secure future mattered. Over the last months, that grim thought alone had kept her trudging ahead. It lost its comforting power when Jonas clasped her tight in a cruel travesty of how he'd once held her.

"Are you taking me home?"

"No."

Without the strain of staying upright, she began to feel marginally more like the old Sidonie Forsythe. The Sidonie she'd been before her life disintegrated. She hoped so. She had a sinking feeling this meeting was about to become very uncomfortable indeed.

Her mind worked frantically. Jonas said he'd spoken to Roberta. She could imagine what her sister had said. Especially as he'd then set out to find Sidonie. After all, he could have looked for her any time in the last three months and the silence had been telling. Even when he'd offered her an allowance, the correspondence came from his secretary. Refusing the generous payment had sparked fleeting satisfaction. Until she'd realized her response had probably never progressed beyond some industrious underling's desk.

"What do you want?" she asked.

"We need to talk about that." He waited while a footman opened the door to a large town coach. "Among other things."

"Jonas, I . . . I don't want to go with you," she said, suddenly afraid. This smacked too much of abduction. She wriggled without effect. "I'd rather walk home on my own."

"Too bad," he said uncompromisingly. But his touch was gentle as he placed her inside the carriage. He climbed in after her and the footman closed the door with a click that to Sidonie's oversensitive ears sounded like prison doors slamming shut. The scents of leather, Jonas, and confined space flooded her senses, but her troublesome stomach remained quiet, thank goodness.

"You have no right to bundle me in here like a parcel," she said mutinously, then fell mute as Jonas wrapped a rug around her so carefully, it was as if he protected a crystal vase from breaking.

Instead what he broke was her heart.

Except her heart had broken months ago. No wonder she remained so lifeless despite all her bracing little lectures to herself to look to her future. Nobody could live without their heart.

"Stow it, Sidonie. And don't even think of running. In your current state, you couldn't walk across the road. I'd just have to pick you up again." He slid onto the bench beside her and turned to lift a bottle of brandy and a glass from a leather pannier on the door.

"I'll be sick if I drink that," she said with a spurt of resentment as the coach rolled forward.

He shot her an unreadable look. "It's for me."

"Am I so terrifying that you need Dutch courage?" she asked with false sweetness.

He didn't smile. "Definitely."

He splashed golden liquor into the glass and downed it. Then he returned the bottle and glass to the pannier with a deliberate slowness that played on her nerves. As she was sure he meant it to. When the silence extended, Sidonie could bear it no longer. "Roberta told you, didn't she?"

Another of those unreadable glances. "When we were together, you made me a promise."

"Then you told me to get out of your sight." Those words had rankled for months.

"It didn't alter your commitment." The inscrutable mask cracked and briefly she glimpsed his real emotions. He was angry. She'd known that from the first. He'd tried to hide it, but the muscle flickering in his cheek betrayed him. Worse than that, he was hurt. Hurt beyond bearing. Her belly twisted with remorse and regret and useless, agonizing love.

Shame kept her quiet, although there was little point concealing the truth. When he mentioned her promise, she knew the game was up. Blast Roberta for an interfering witch.

"So you still won't tell me," he said grimly. "What must I do to make you confess? Get out the thumbscrews?"

What use putting off the evil moment? She met his eyes, iron gray in the shadowy coach, and spoke with a defiance she hadn't felt since she'd left him. "I'm pregnant."

"I know."

"I ask nothing of you."

"That's hardly the point. No child of mine will be born a bastard."

"You don't want to marry me."

She wondered if he'd deny that. She almost wished he'd lie.

But of course, he didn't lie. His jaw set in unforgiving lines. "No."

She struggled to maintain an argument. It was difficult when she felt so weary and sick, and this meeting with Jonas reminded her of everything she'd lost. Shortly after their last acrimonious encounter, she'd discovered she carried his child. Most of the time since, she'd felt sick. Morning sickness seemed to be a twenty-four-hour-a-day affair. At least nausea stopped her stewing on how she'd botched her life. "I told you I'd never marry."

"And you said if you conceived my child, you'd become my wife."

She hadn't. Not in so many words. But her actions had given tacit consent to his ultimatum. She couldn't pretend he accosted her today under false pretenses.

"You can't force me to marry you." Her voice shook because right now the easiest decision seemed to be leaving all decisions to him. Then a nasty thought struck—her statement wasn't entirely true. "You wouldn't cut off Roberta's allowance and the boys' school fees, would you?"

Reading his mind in this if nothing else, she watched him consider claiming such intentions. Then he shook his head. "No, this is between us." He paused. "Or rather between you and your honor. You more than anyone know the miseries of my childhood. Surely you won't visit that torment on your son or daughter."

"People needn't find out I'm not married," she mumbled, tugging the rug up to shield her against his remarks and the conscience that until now self-pity had silenced.

"People always find out," he said uncompromisingly.

She had an unwelcome inkling he was right. One hand cradled her belly. She hardly showed yet, but in a few weeks, her secret would be a secret no more. By then she needed to be away from London, settled where nobody knew her. She needed to be able to travel more than a mile without casting up her accounts, too. The journey from Wiltshire to London had been bad enough. Right now, her stomach behaved, but of course, Jonas's carriage was the first stare of comfort and hardly jolted at all.

Decisions she'd been too miserable and frightened

to make screamed for attention. It was all very well to plan an incognito future as a widow with a child in some northern hamlet, but the prospect of living a lie until the day she died made her shudder. The pathetic loneliness of doing everything alone without the man she loved was too cruel to contemplate. When Jonas mentioned his boyhood sufferings, he cut straight to her dilemma. She didn't want her baby to be a fatherless waif. She wanted her child to grow up with two loving parents.

Once she'd almost accepted Jonas's proposal. Then she'd trusted his regard. Could she bear to marry him knowing he was furious with her? Perhaps one day, he might forgive her for sacrificing him in favor of Roberta. Nor did she mistake that he viewed the secrecy about her pregnancy as another betrayal.

Because they both knew it was a betrayal.

The very air vibrated with his repressed emotion. How she wished she'd kept her head in the park. She'd rather conduct this conversation in the open. The carriage, for all its luxury, seemed suffocatingly cramped when so much lay unspoken between its occupants.

"Sidonie, we have to marry." He sounded sad but determined.

She blinked back tears. This was a million miles from the proposal she wanted. Of course there was that sweet moment at Castle Craven when he'd asked her to be his wife, but later memories tainted that recollection.

"You're such a bully," she burst out as the jaws of her fate snapped shut. Her hands fisted in the rug.

His sigh was unutterably weary. "Think what you wish. No child of mine will suffer abuse because of our sins. Get used to it."

"I don't have to like it." She winced at how childish she sounded.

To her surprise, he gave her a cold smile. Until she realized she'd conceded victory. "Good."

Jonas leaned back in the corner, stretching his long legs into the well between the seats. He seemed to occupy all available space. Sidonie shrank into her blanket and told herself without conviction that what she did was for the best. She was far from sure. Life with Jonas when he didn't love her promised disaster, whatever legitimacy it gave their baby.

"Now will you take me home?" she asked with resurgent strength, although it was too late to do any good. She was trapped like a fly in a spider's web.

"No."

She tensed with resentment—and a healthy dose of dread. "Just where are you taking me?"

When she felt the coach slow, she realized she was about to find out. The curve of Jonas's lips indicated triumph but no pleasure. "To St. Marylebone. To pledge your troth, my faithless love."

She winced. The insult hurt like a razor drawn across her skin. "I only just—" She straightened. "I haven't agreed to marry you."

The coach drew to a stop and Jonas seized her hand in a grip that brooked no resistance. "Close enough. I won't countenance any scenes at the altar either. It's all set, Sidonie. You must have known it would be, once I learned you carried my baby. After Roberta told me, I bought a special license. You and I are about to be united in holy wedlock, *amore mio*."

Appalled, Sidonie stared at him through the dim interior. Stupidly, although it was hardly the most significant objection, she couldn't help thinking she wasn't dressed for a wedding in her secondhand blue gown and faded cloak. "N-now?"

That daunting smile lingered. "No time like the present." His voice hardened. "If I let you go, I have a disagreeable feeling you'll disappear again."

Shame and regret formed a rancid mixture in her belly. "You still don't trust me."

"Not an inch."

The footman opened the door and Jonas stepped out, clutching her hand as if afraid she'd bolt. But she was too heartsore to delay her fate.

Jonas had won.

She welcomed the return of familiar numbness. Jonas was strong. Jonas was certain. He'd make sure her child was safe. For herself, she cared nothing.

"Come, Sidonie." Through her wretchedness, she heard a hint of kindness.

Kindness was more dangerous than bullying. If he was kind, she might start believing he'd care for her again. "Very well," she said in a clipped voice that concealed dizzying turmoil.

As she stood outside the church and stared at the door through which she'd enter a spinster and leave a bride, she faltered. It was all too much. She turned toward the street, ready to run.

Jonas's hand tightened. "Courage, Sidonie." Briefly she heard the voice of the man she'd fallen in love with.

She inhaled on a sob. Her destiny was set. She married Jonas, for good or ill. Staring at the pavement, she battled the nausea curdling her stomach. She wanted to suggest they go somewhere to eat first. Through the buzzing in her ears, she heard Jonas click his fingers, a few soft words then the clink of coins.

When she looked up, Jonas stared at her, his eyes opaque. His mouth was unsmiling and a muscle twitched in his scarred cheek. He extended a bunch of daffodils toward her and she realized an old lady in ragged clothing sat on the church steps, selling flowers.

"Sidonie?" he prompted when she didn't accept the humble bouquet.

"Oh." Without thinking, her fingers curled around the flowers. Their bright, joyful yellow was a piercing reminder of everything she'd never have.

Courage, Sidonie.

Enough of this. For heaven's sake, she refused to shuffle into her wedding like a beggar. She'd march in on two feet and face whatever fortune tossed her way. She blinked away tears and stiffened her spine.

She could do this. God help her. And Jonas. And their unborn child.

As if recognizing her reviving spirit, Jonas released her. He extended his arm with a courtly gesture. After a slight hesitation, she hooked her trembling hand around his elbow. He glanced down at her and she caught a flash of something in his steely eyes that might be torment rivaling hers. Then his stony expression descended and she realized she was mistaken. Her fingers clenched around the daffodils.

"Our wedding awaits, Miss Forsythe."

"Yes," she whispered.

As they mounted the steps, the flower seller called out behind them with a cheerfulness that made Sidonie want to scream. "Heaven bless the bride and groom!"

*   *   *

Sidonie remained quiet as Jonas escorted her inside Merrick House. She knew the place well. Roberta and William had spent more of their married life in the London residence than at Barstowe Hall. Still she paused, surprised, when she entered what was once a dreary, dark hall to find light-filled space.

Jonas didn't give her time to admire the changes in the house's fussy décor. Instead, after a footman took their outer wear, he entered the library, little used by either her sister or William in the past but now clearly the center of operations.

"My lord." A young man set aside his pen and rose from the desk beneath the windows. A larger desk new to the house must be where Jonas worked.

She'd never seen evidence of his business activities. At Castle Craven, he'd been a man of leisure. She supposed now, as his wife, she had a vested interest in his financial affairs. Sadly she doubted he'd ever trust her enough to confide details of his work.

Jonas gestured her toward a brocade chair near the fire, then turned to the man. "Warren, you may finish for the day."

"Thank you, my lord." The man, obviously a secretary, bowed to Sidonie. "Felicitations, my lady."

She murmured a reply, piqued that Jonas had been so sure of her that he'd told his staff he'd return with a wife.

Once they were alone, Jonas strode to the far side of the desk. "I'll leave George Warren here with you. He's a capable young man who will help establish you in town. He'll contact me if need be."

Sidonie stiffened and turned slowly to face this man

she'd wed against her instincts. She spoke with the desperately held control that she'd maintained since recognizing that marriage was inescapable. "Why on earth should he need to contact you?"

Jonas was occupied with checking the desk drawers. "If you need funds or there's a problem with the house."

She noticed Jonas didn't mention the baby, when surely if she needed to communicate with her husband, the subject would be her pregnancy. "Why should I go through Mr. Warren, efficient and obliging as I'm sure he is?"

He slid a leather folder across the desk in her direction. "Everything you need is here, including details of personal and household accounts I've opened for you at Child's Bank. The amounts should be adequate, but I have no intention of being a parsimonious husband. Ask Warren if you need more." He cast a dismissive glance at her outdated merino dress, which even she recognized as inadequate to a viscountess's dignity. "I'm happy to give you any money you like for a new wardrobe."

"I know I need clothes—"

He spoke over her as if she hadn't interrupted. "You'll need a doctor. Have you anyone in mind? As my wife, you should have no difficulty being accepted as a patient. The fellow can forward reports to me."

The flood of information passed over her head like a skater across thick ice. Instead her mind fastened on the implications of what he said. She stood and frowned in confusion. "Jonas, aren't you going to be here?"

He didn't meet her eyes. Instead he stalked over to the window and stared out as if fascinated by the leafless trees in his garden. After a pause that made her blood run colder than the church where she'd just married him, he spoke without looking at her. "Sidonie, I have no plans to live with you."

"Ever?" She shouldn't be shocked. Today he'd worked hard to maintain his distance. She'd already wondered if he'd want her back in his bed now that she was his wife.

"Ever," he confirmed in a voice that invited no argument.

"Then why marry me?" she asked bitterly. She withdrew her hands from the hearth and wrapped them around her waist to hide their shaking.

He turned but kept a rein over any emotions. "You know why. For the child."

She staggered back and curled an unsteady hand around the edge of the mantelpiece to stay upright. Every time she thought she'd plumbed the full pain of this love, she discovered yet another layer of agony. She was torn between shock and distress. "So you won't try to forgive me? Even now we're tied together for life?"

His lips tightened, she wasn't sure whether in anger or regret. "Sidonie, I won't live with a woman I can't trust."

"You can trust me." She released the mantelpiece and ventured nearer, although the tension in his body warned her not to touch him.

His laugh struck like a whip. "Where the devil is my good sense? Of course I can trust you. You've proven yourself so eternally on my side."

She flinched at his sarcasm. "You know why I kept the marriage lines secret."

The hard-won neutrality drained from his expression. Her stomach cramped with guilt as she realized how profoundly the rift between them wounded him.

"Yes, I do." His voice was even, as if he discussed a

balance sheet and not their life together. "I know why you hid the pregnancy, too. You're not the beacon of impossible perfection I once believed, but you're not evil incarnate either. Your reasons even make sense."

This should have sounded like a concession. It didn't.

Pain held her motionless. It hurt to breathe. The way he spoke, it seemed likely she'd never see him again. Over the last bleak months, she'd struggled to accept that outcome, to plan a life encompassing her and her baby. Now that she and Jonas were married, the prospect of parting forever was too devastating. Even when he loathed her.

She stretched out a trembling hand, wanting the connection, but wanting more to ease the fierce loneliness in his eyes. "Then for the sake of our future, our child, won't you try to make this a real marriage?"

He stared at her hand as he'd stare at an adder baring its fangs. "No."

She sucked in a choked breath and took the ultimate risk. "Jonas, I love you."

He whitened, making his scars stand out like beacons. She felt him withdraw beyond reach, even though he didn't shift a step. "Until something new claims your loyalty, you probably do."

Dear God, she'd thought he was kind. She was wrong. Shaking, she grabbed the back of the chair he'd offered her. Her knees felt as substantial as jelly. "That's unjust."

"Perhaps."

"Don't you want what we had at Castle Craven?" Her voice cracked. She wouldn't cry. She wouldn't cry.

That muscle flickered in his cheek, indicating strong emotion under even stronger control, but the eyes he settled on her were ice cold. Gray ice. The fissure through which she'd briefly glimpsed his agony had knitted together. He returned to acting the inscrutable monolith. Or a glacier grinding its way down a mountain, unstoppable, destructive, frozen.

"What we had there was a lie."

"No, it wasn't." The ruby ring weighted her hand.

His smile made her shiver. Her grip on the chair tightened until her knuckles shone white. "It doesn't matter whether it was or it wasn't, my darling."

No soft Italian sweetness for his wife. What she'd give to hear a *bella* or a *tesoro.* He went on, his voice implacable. "I can't spend the rest of my life waiting for you to betray me again. You've done it twice. Twice you've damn near destroyed me. I'm not reckless enough to put myself through that again."

"Jonas, don't..."

Despite her determination to stay strong, tears stung her eyes. She'd hurt him so badly and he didn't deserve it. Even if she counted his less than angelic plans when they'd first met, he didn't deserve an ounce of the pain she'd caused him. She felt sick with despair and remorse.

Without looking at her, he headed toward the door. "I wish you a happy wedding day, Lady Hillbrook."

He bowed with a chill that made her flinch and stalked from the room.

Jonas strode into the gaudy, gilded bedroom in Castle Craven, the room that had witnessed those glorious nights in Sidonie's arms. Immediately after abandoning his wife to sole possession of Merrick House, he'd left London. He'd ridden hell for leather to get here, far enough from any temptation to recall this was his wedding night and if he sodding well wanted to fuck his bride, he had every right to do so.

Mirrors reflected him over and over. Tall, ugly as sin, dressed in black riding coat and boots. He looked as Satanic as a man could this side of hell. If she saw him now, would his wife claim she loved him?

The nearest mirror beckoned him closer. He was filthy and dog tired. His eyes were dull as tarnished tin. At the best of times, he wasn't a pretty picture. Now he'd scare the horses. He looked as though someone had done him a deathly wrong. He looked as though his best friend in the world had died. He looked like he had no interest in life and no hope for his future.

He looked a bloody disaster.

"Damn, damn, damn," he whispered, because if he spoke too loudly, his control would snap. Even here, observed only by the battery of looking glasses, he couldn't allow himself to break down.

Without thinking, he reached out with both hands and wrenched the gold-framed mirror from the wall. It took more effort than expected, but eventually he held the large glass between his hands. The mirror had cracked in the removal. Broken glass distorted his scars but couldn't make him any more repulsive. If some angel of doom swooped down the chimney at this instant and accosted him with retribution for his sins, he'd welcome annihilation.

In the reflection, he observed his mouth thin, then a flash of what looked like madness in his eyes. As if he watched someone else complete the action, he hoisted the mirror and smashed it hard against the wall.

The crash of shattering glass filled him with satisfaction. His lips curved in a rictus smile as he turned to the next mirror, then the next.

After an hour of ear-shattering mayhem, the only mirror remaining in the room was the one above the bed. Out of reach, bugger it, although he'd struggled hard enough to haul it down. Deadly shards covered the floor. In the corner, the remains of exquisite gilt frames piled one above another like firewood. The plaster walls were bare and marked where he'd flung the mirrors against them.

Without moving from the center of the room, Jonas surveyed the devastation. How he wished he could trample his heart to bloody smithereens amongst the debris.

But his heart, damn it to hell, kept beating.

Chapter Thirty

Storms split the heavens the night Sidonie Merrick arrived at Castle Craven, determined to seize her destiny with both hands.

"Oh, it be 'ee," Mrs. Bevan said without surprise when she eventually opened the door.

"Good evening, Mrs. Bevan." Sidonie removed her new cloak and bonnet and passed them to the woman. Nerves jumped like hungry frogs after dragonflies, but she kept her voice steady. Thank goodness her stomach had remained mostly under control for the way from London. Physically she was as well as she'd been for months. "I've sent my coachman to the stables. Can you see he finds a bed?"

"Aye." Mrs. Bevan stumped ahead into the hall. "'Ee'll be wanting maister."

"Yes."

"Good." Before Sidonie came to terms with Mrs. Bevan expressing approval, however laconically, the woman continued. "Maister's cranky as a bear with a sore head this last week. I'd watch my step if I be 'ee."

"I will." Strangely the news of Jonas's grumpiness was encouraging. Sidonie straightened her shoulders. "He's upstairs?"

"Aye. Will 'ee be wanting supper?"

"Not immediately, thank you."

The woman lumbered toward the kitchens. The hall was, as ever, ice cold. A lit candelabra stood on one of the oak chests, its light feeble against the darkness. Again, Sidonie felt the breath of old, hostile ghosts.

Compared to what she faced, mere ghosts couldn't daunt her.

It was late. She'd intended a less melodramatic entrance in daylight. Storms had made that impossible. Fielding, her coachman, had begged her to stay in Sidmouth and continue her journey on the morrow when, even if they had rain, at least they'd have light. She'd forced him on through the filthy weather. He must think his new employer mad. How could he know she mustered her last reserves of courage to beard Jonas in his den? Any delay might send her scuttling back to London with her tail between her legs.

No, she wasn't running away. She'd come too far to give up. Whatever Jonas did to her, it couldn't be worse than her last five days wandering Merrick House, knowing that she could remain a bride but not a wife forever.

With sudden purpose, she grabbed the candelabra. She'd wasted enough time feeling sorry for herself. She needed to reach for what she wanted.

But as she mounted the shadowy stone staircase, she was bleakly aware she might be too late for new beginnings.

*   *   *

Sidonie made for the bedroom. Where else would a man be at this hour? Surely if her husband was awake, he'd come down to see who called so late.

The door was ajar and the room was dark. Although she'd spent all week longing to see Jonas, her pace slowed. Carefully she pushed the door wider and stepped inside. No mirrors reflected her candles. She took another step and something crunched under her half-boots.

Puzzled, she glanced down. The floor was littered with a carpet of jagged and sparkling debris. Slowly she raised the candelabra.

"Dear God…"

The room was a complete shambles. The ornate mirrors that had once lined the walls lay smashed against the floor. The bed linen and curtains were ripped and tattered. Something about the willful, wild destruction struck her as unbearably sad. As though the man who wreaked this devastation wrenched free of human control until all that remained was animal violence.

Oh, Jonas…

She illuminated the bed. The mattress sagged, half off its base. She'd known when she came in that Jonas wasn't here. The empty bed confirmed it.

Turning, she found herself under her husband's assessing scrutiny. He leaned against the doorframe, a half-filled glass of wine dangling from his right hand. In spite of the gulf between them, her heart danced with joy at his presence. He wore the familiar breeches and loose white shirt. The last time they'd met, he'd been attired as Viscount Hillbrook. Sidonie didn't know Viscount Hillbrook, but she knew this man in his untidy clothing, with his hair tumbling over his forehead. This man had greeted her upon her arrival at Castle Craven over three months ago. She knew his cool eyes and lethal tongue and preternatural attention to everything she did.

"Spectacular, isn't it?" Jonas drawled, lifting the glass to his lips.

"If you wanted to redecorate, you could have had the mirrors carried down to the cellars."

His beautiful mouth curved, although his eyes remained watchful. "Seemed quicker to take care of matters on the spot."

With theatrical thoroughness, her gaze swept the destruction. "You definitely took care of matters."

He straightened without shifting toward her. On the other hand, he didn't shift away. She took what encouragement she could find. Nor, she was relieved to note, did she sense the distance he'd maintained between them in London. He didn't seem angry or hostile. He just seemed... wary.

She stared directly at him. "You're not surprised I'm here."

He shrugged. "I heard the carriage arrive."

"It could have been someone else."

He cast her an unimpressed glance under thick black eyelashes. "No, it couldn't."

She supposed not. Although the possibility existed that since he was no longer considered a disreputable bastard plutocrat, the neighbors had taken him under their wing. Except it was the middle of the night. Except a gale blew. Except Castle Craven was just as eccentric in décor and staffing, and its welcome was as frosty as ever.

She struggled to hold her course. His coolness was

unsettling. As he intended. "You don't sleep here, do you?"

His smile broadened as though he enjoyed a grim private joke. "How wifely to enquire after my slumbers, my love."

Sidonie didn't wince at the sarcastic endearment. She'd expected resentment. So far, she'd got off lightly. He could have had her barred from the house. "Where do you sleep?"

He sipped his wine, his silvery eyes unwavering. She couldn't read his expression and not only because of the uncertain candlelight. "I don't sleep much at all."

What could she say to that? She hadn't slept much lately either. "Are you going to offer me a glass of wine?"

Over the miles from London, she'd sworn she'd remain stalwart no matter what he said or did. Thank heaven during the last week, the morning sickness that had dogged her so long had ebbed. She'd been such a feeble creature the day they married. No wonder Jonas had abandoned her. If she was strong, if she demanded what she wanted, Jonas couldn't ignore her. She was his wife, she had rights.

Except now she was here, she didn't feel nearly as unassailable. She'd forgotten how tall he was, how his presence commanded, how the merest sight of him set her heart beating so fast, she turned giddy with love.

"Of course. I endowed thee with all my worldly goods. That includes my claret."

She bent her head. "Thank you."

"Will you join me in the library?"

"Is there nowhere closer?"

"No," he said shortly and prowled toward the stairs, assuming she'd follow.

Of course she'd follow. She wasn't letting him out of her sight. He knew what she was up to. There was never the slightest chance he'd misinterpret her reason for encroaching on his exile. So far sardonic remarks kept her at bay. She had no doubt he'd hunt out sharper weapons if she assailed the stony ramparts protecting his emotions. She'd come prepared for the beast to rend her limb from limb.

Arriving so late, there had been a chance of surprising him in bed and an even remoter chance that nature would take its course. Providing nature meant he still wanted her. Her very skin ached for his touch, but perhaps he'd forgotten those radiant moments when they'd joined together so profoundly, she didn't know where he ended and where she began. She swallowed to dislodge the inconvenient lump clogging her throat.

There was a couch in the library. And the desk. All was not yet lost.

In the library, Jonas poured Sidonie's wine and waved her to a chair. The fire crackling in the hearth indicated he hadn't retired for the evening. He'd already admitted sleep proved elusive. Despairingly she wished that confession of vulnerability made it a scrap more likely he'd listen to her.

He refilled his glass and wandered to the window to stare broodingly at the stormy sea and sky, lit sporadically with lightning. Sidonie sat and watched his profile, checking minute indications of temper. He looked tired and moody. Over the last days, he'd shored up his defenses. His anger was buried so deep, if she hadn't known him so well, she wouldn't have recognized it.

"Tell me why you're here, Sidonie." His voice held no trace of the familiar sardonic humor.

She set her untouched wine on a side table. She'd imagined they'd fence with words a little longer. She'd hoped they would. Once she made her play, if she failed, she had nowhere to go but back to London and life without Jonas. God help her, this was more frightening than offering herself to a stranger to save Roberta. The next few minutes threatened to shred her heart and pulverize her soul to ash.

She straightened in her chair, told herself to be brave, and stared directly at Jonas. "I want a real marriage. We can't have that when you're hunkered down here like a bear in a cave."

To her surprise, he smiled faintly. "I see you've rediscovered your spirit since the wedding."

She tilted her chin, although he didn't look at her but across the blustery landscape. "I intend to fight for you, Jonas. For my sake. And for...our child."

He took a sip of his wine. "Very laudable, my dear."

She waited for more but he remained silent.

After a long pause, she frowned. "Is that all you have to say?"

He still didn't look at her. "Yes, apart from wishing you a safe journey back to London in the morning."

She flinched. "You're cruel."

"No. I merely reiterate what I said last time we were together." His shoulders tensed as if he forced himself to continue. The betraying gesture bolstered her quailing courage. "I'm sorry you traveled so far and in such weather to hear it again. I will never live with you as your husband."

"I don't accept that." Her hands fisted in her lap.

He shrugged. "You will." He paused again. "Eventually."

"Jonas, is there no way to solve this?" She longed to be proud and strong, but faced with his intransigence, she couldn't contain her desperation.

His eyes were flinty as they settled on her. "No."

He left no room for maneuver or negotiation. Curse him, had she really failed? After all the love and joy and anguish, must she face a future without him? Impetuously she said the one thing she'd sworn she wouldn't. "But you love me."

She braced for denial. Instead he smiled again, this time with a hint of warmth. "Of course I love you."

The swift admission soothed her aching heart like balm, although his calmness negated the statement's significance. She surged to her feet with sudden hope. "Then we have a chance."

He shook his head and turned away. "No, we don't." His voice deepened into an austerity that fell like acid on her ears. "Not a chance in hell."

Desolation weighting her stomach, she shifted closer and realized he watched her in the window pane. Reflections had mediated so many of their interactions. It was time for them to meet face to face. "Jonas, I love you. You love me. Why should we be apart?"

She dared to touch his arm. He jerked as though she'd scalded him.

"Don't."

"All right." She lowered her hand, but his violent rejection proved her presence left him far from unmoved. "Answer me."

His jaw was so tight, it looked as if it might crack. "Because we can't be together."

Her frail attempt at dignity dissolved irredeemably.

She spoke in an urgent rush. "I know I hurt you. You can't imagine how much I've regretted what I did. I'm...I'm sorry I didn't tell you about the marriage lines." Despite her best efforts, her voice broke. "I'm sorry I didn't tell you about the baby."

"Sidonie—"

Before he could reject her apology, she hurried on. She had to make him forgive her. She had to. "I'll never keep secrets again. I'll never lie or deceive you. I'll be what you want."

"You are what I want." His voice was so low, she strained to hear. "You've always been what I want. But living with you will make me wretched. Be kind, sweet Sidonie. Leave me to my solitude."

Anger vanquished misery. "Your solitude will kill you."

"Pray God it does," he said bitterly.

"Don't send me away." This time when she touched his forearm, she clung when he tried to withdraw. "Give me a week. That's all I ask. I gave you a week. A week where we're lovers as we were before. A week to remind you what we are to each other."

He remained still under her hand. His pallor indicated how agonizing he found her entreaties. If she'd been one ounce less desperate, she'd back away purely for compassion's sake. "I don't need reminding."

"A week, Jonas." She moved nearer and breathed deeply of his clean masculine scent. The pain of having him so near yet so far away in any real sense was excruciating.

"You say you love me," he said as if discussing the weather. But he trembled under her hand as if his blood slowly turned to ice.

She moved close enough for her breasts to brush his arm. "You know I do."

With ruthless tenderness, he pried her fingers off him. He stepped away and faced her. His skin was ashen and his eyes were flat gray like the sea under rain clouds. "If you love me, you'll leave. You'll go back to London and your own life. A life in which I play no part."

She'd struggled to contain her tears but it was impossible. "You're the father of my baby. You'll always be part of my life, whether with me or not."

"I won't be with you." He stepped behind the desk and she recognized he used it as a barrier against her. When he set down his wine, the gesture's finality slashed at her heart.

She stared into his scarred face, more compelling than mere handsomeness could ever be, and recognized he was immovable. Nothing would change his decision. The strength of character that defied the world's cruelties turned fatally against her. She'd hurt him too deeply. He wouldn't allow himself to be vulnerable to her again.

Dear God, she'd failed.

They loved each other but love wasn't enough.

He must have recognized her surrender because the tension seeped from his shoulders. His voice emerged more naturally. "Sleep in the dressing room. I won't inflict my presence on you tomorrow."

Inflict his presence? Didn't he know his merest word was sweeter than music?

"This is good-bye, then?" she whispered, hoping against hope she'd discern some sign of relenting. There was nothing. Just stern implacability and what looked like impatience to bring this awkward encounter to a swift end.

She'd faced him down in this library once before when he'd been determined to send her away. On that occasion, she'd prevailed. This time it was clear that she'd lost. The knowledge struck like a blow, threatening to knock her to the ground.

"Farewell, Sidonie."

"Will you... will you kiss me one last time?" she asked shakily.

His flash of irritation made her cringe. "No."

She approached the desk, clumsily tugging the signet ring from her finger. If they never saw each other again, he should have it. It didn't belong to her. Very gently, she placed the ring on the blotter before him. The ruby shone like blood against the dark green leather. He didn't move to touch it, but neither did he suggest she keep it.

For a long time she studied him, imprinting every last detail on her mind. She struggled to tell herself that the war wasn't over, that she could fight again and perhaps win. She didn't believe it. "God keep you, Jonas."

She turned to collect the candelabra and took a step. Another. Her feet felt weighted with lead. The door seemed ten miles away across rocky, difficult terrain. She sucked in a breath and forced herself to take another step.

That's all she needed. One step after another. This year. Next year. Through a barren lifetime.

One step. Another step. Soon, she'd be in the hall. Then upstairs. Then in the dressing room. Tomorrow she'd head back to empty, echoing Merrick House. It was a purely mathematical issue, surely. Her heart might break but if she kept walking, eventually she'd escape this room.

At last she reached the door. She touched the handle. It turned easily and the door swung open. The world continued on its clockwork way, even if Sidonie Merrick's soul was sucked dry and barren as the Sahara.

She fought the urge to turn and beg Jonas to reconsider, to think of their child, to let his love speak rather than his fear that she'd wrong him. Better to retain a shred of pride. Better to leave him with the impression that she was strong enough to endure. Better not to be a pathetic, weeping woman pleading with him to stay with her.

One more step and she'd be in the hall, cold and dark like a foretaste of the coming years. She reached to pull the door shut and heard something. A bump. A thud. But soft. Perhaps only a quiver in the air.

She frowned and turned slowly back toward the library. Jonas stood behind the desk. He was pale, paler than he'd been all night, and that erratic muscle jumped and jerked in his cheek.

"Jonas?" Although what was the point of spinning out the agony?

"Go," he gritted out. The silver eyes were blind and his right hand fisted so hard around something that it shook. She needed a second to realize the ruby ring no longer lay on the blotter.

"Oh, my beloved," she said in a raw voice she didn't recognize. "Don't do this to yourself."

In a few swift steps, she covered the distance between them. She set the candelabra on the desk. She'd need both hands to take hold of her destiny.

"Don't touch me," he said hoarsely, backing away.

Recklessly he'd let her glimpse his despair. Everything she wanted hovered so close, she could taste it. Abandoning him to his isolation was the worst thing she could do. "It's too late, my darling. I'm not leaving."

"You must."

"You've been a fool, Jonas." Tears blurred her vision and she smiled. "So have I. It's time to stop this nonsense and start our life together."

She watched him struggle to repair his defenses. "You make a lot of assumptions." He stood against the wall now. Unless he pushed her out of the way, he wasn't going anywhere.

"Don't I just?" She cradled his dear, scarred face between her palms. He tried to break free, but she didn't release him. "Kiss me, Jonas."

"No." He raised his hands to remove her from his path but at the last minute didn't touch her.

Her smile broadened, although her heart ached for him. Her betrayals were only the most recent of hundreds of betrayals, large and small, starting with his father, that had taught him to mistrust love, hope, and happiness.

She meant to teach him otherwise.

Thank God and every angel who offered sinners a second chance, she had an inkling she'd get her opportunity. No matter how he fought. No matter how near she'd come to letting him dismiss her. "Then I'll kiss you."

She stepped so near, her breasts skimmed his chest. Immediately her nipples puckered and her blood swirled with need. She ignored the siren call of pleasure. This battle wasn't about desire. Desire they'd always had. This battle was about trust which needed time to build. A lifetime.

She could hardly wait.

He was still shaking, and the hand holding the ring dropped to his side. His other hand splayed against the white wall behind him. He could easily push her away but he didn't.

Holding his poor, disfigured face, she rose on her toes to press her lips to his. His mouth remained unmoving. The skin beneath her hands burned as if a flame devoured him from inside.

She wasn't discouraged. She'd been taught seduction by a master. And she'd always been stubborn. Poor Jonas was about to embark on married life with a difficult woman. She smiled against his mouth and kissed him again, nipping lightly, tracing the seam with her tongue.

Still he didn't relent.

Nor did she. She could kiss him like this all night, she thought dreamily, warmth seeping through her for the first time in months.

"Leave me alone," he muttered, pulling a few inches away.

"Never."

"I can't trust you."

"Yes, you can." She stared into his eyes, hoping he could see her eternal, steadfast love, a love that would never let him down.

"How the hell do I know that?" he asked savagely.

"Look in your heart, Jonas. Your heart knows the truth but you have to trust yourself first." She sucked in a shaky breath. "You have to trust yourself as I trust you. Forever."

His expression remained forbidding. But she wasn't giving up. She fought for her life here. And his.

She leaned in to kiss him again. He placed his left hand on her waist. It tightened and she braced for rejection.

For the space of a breath, the world stopped turning.

Almost imperceptibly his touch curled into a caress. The pressure changed from pushing her away to pulling her forward. He made another sound deep in his throat. This time it sounded like delight.

Finally the stern mouth relaxed, then parted so her tongue flicked into the interior. "Damned witch," he groaned in surrender.

"Oh, Jonas," she whispered and yielded to his kiss as he sagged against the wall and dragged her into his body. Under her hands, his cheeks were wet, and she'd long ago given up any attempt to stop her tears.

He kissed her endlessly. He kissed her as though he never wanted to let her go. He kissed her as though he loved her more than his life was worth.

Slowly, still kissing, they sank to the Turkish rug. Eventually he pulled away. He grabbed her left hand with a roughness born of extremity and shoved the ruby ring back on her finger so clumsily that he bruised her. She didn't mind. The unashamed need in his silvery eyes flooded her heart with love.

"Stay, *bella*," he choked out.

"Always, my love."

Epilogue

Merrick House, London, August 1827

Lamplight glowed soft and golden on the woman sitting up in the bed. Jonas stepped quietly into the room, his eyes on Sidonie and the child she cradled so tenderly to her breast.

She smiled at him, the beautiful smile that always made him feel like a king and not a scarred disaster. He didn't care what the rest of the world thought. Sidonie loved him. Now, he prayed, he had a daughter to love him, too. Because he loved both of them more than he could ever say.

"Jonas, come and see. She's perfect."

He'd ventured in earlier after an excruciating day of waiting downstairs. His wife had been tired and drawn but happy. The baby had been small and black-haired and inclined to scream. The nurse had chased him out, insisting she needed to prepare Lady Hillbrook before she saw her husband.

Good thing he was used to difficult women.

As he looked down into his daughter's tiny face, he knew that here was another stubborn female to trouble his peace. The baby yawned without opening her eyes and settled to sleep. Jonas's heart lurched with an astonishingly powerful tug of love. He'd protect this child as long as he lived.

"You're both beautiful." When he leaned down to kiss his wife, Sidonie stroked his scarred cheek. The caress had become so familiar, he hardly noticed it anymore, although the first time she'd touched his scars without revulsion it had moved him so deeply, it nigh broke his heart.

"You've had a terrible day, haven't you?"

He laughed softly and turned his head to kiss her hand. The ruby signet ring glinted in the lamplight. The sight of his ring on her hand always filled him with satisfaction. She was his heart's blood after all. "I suspect yours was worse."

"I'm not sure." She spoke quietly so as not to wake the baby. "At least I was busy."

"You were, at that." He looked down at his daughter again. "With good purpose."

"I'm rather proud of myself."

Jonas kissed her again. "So you should be. She's quite the masterpiece." His voice lowered. "I love you, Sidonie."

She stared at him, her eyes glowing. "I love you, Jonas." She blinked. "Curse these tears. I hoped once I had the baby, I wouldn't be such a watering pot."

Very carefully, Jonas perched on the edge of the mattress, never shifting his gaze from his wife and child. Who would think he'd turn into a family man? Who would think love could transform a life as barren as his?

Sidonie had created a miracle when she arrived in his life—turned a desert into a lushly flowering oasis. He'd never been so happy as he'd been since she'd forced her way into his house last February and fought for her love.

He thanked God every day for difficult women.

"Have you thought about names?"

She contemplated the baby with a tenderness that made him ache. "Of course. Haven't you?" Her eyes glinted with teasing humor as she looked up. "Richarda? Camdenette?"

"No." Although among the rich threads in this new life was the privilege of calling fine men like Camden Rothermere and Richard Harmsworth his friends. "And not Roberta."

When it became apparent that Roberta's offer to stay and care for Sidonie during her pregnancy translated into a return to the gaming tables, Jonas had denied her room in Merrick House. Roberta had retired in high dudgeon to her villa in Richmond, where apparently she now dazzled a rich merchant. Over the last months, she and Sidonie had re-established a frail connection that he hoped, for his wife's sake, would strengthen over the years. As far as he was concerned, he and Roberta would never be friends, but he wished her well. As long as she didn't intrude into his life, he was happy to let her go to hell her own way.

Sidonie muffled a huff of laughter. "Not Roberta." She paused and her expression sobered. "I thought we'd call her Consuela after your mother."

The breath wedged in his throat. One by one, Sidonie healed his old injuries. Now she healed another. He tried to smile but was too moved to succeed. "That's…that's perfect, *bella*."

To prove his true birthright, Sir
Richard Harmsworth must steal a
medievel relic—now in the hands of
the beautiful, scholarly Genevieve
Barrett who hates nothing more than
a thief...

Please turn this page for a preview of

*A Rake's
Midnight Kiss.*

Chapter One

Little Derrick, Oxfordshire, September 1827

D amnation!"
       A loud thud followed by a low masculine curse
stirred Genevieve from deep sleep. Even then she needed
a few seconds to realize she was slumped over her work
table in the vicarage library, her candles had gone out,
and the only light in the room was the dying fire. By that
low glow, she watched a dark shape below the window-
sill lengthen and rise until she recognized a man's form
blocking faint starlight from outside.

   Choking fear held her motionless. Fear and outrage.
How dare anyone break into her home? It felt like a personal affront. Her father was out, dining with the Duke of
Sedgemoor at his local estate. She'd been invited too but
she'd wanted to stay and work on her latest article. The
servants were away for the evening.

The man at the window remained still, as if confirming that the room was empty before he started his nefarious activities. The charged silence extended. Then she saw the tension ease from his long, lean body and he stepped across to the fire. From her dark corner, Genevieve watched him bend over the coals to light a candle.

Blast his impudence, he'd soon learn he wasn't alone.

Quickly her hand slipped down to the desk's second drawer and tugged it out, not bothering to mask the noise as she reached for what lay hidden inside. The candle flared into life, and he turned his head sharply in her direction. Genevieve lurched to her feet. As she stepped toward him on shaky legs, she forced a confidence she didn't feel into her voice. "You'll find nothing worth stealing in this house. I suggest you leave. Immediately."

Instead of reacting with the horrified dismay she desired, the man took his time straightening. He raised his candle to illuminate Genevieve where she stood beside the desk. His face was mostly covered with a black silk mask such as people wore to masquerade balls. Not that she had any experience of such events. "You're dashed well protected if there truly is nothing worth stealing."

Her hand steady, she raised the gun. "We live on the edge of the village, as you no doubt noted when you chose this house for your depredations." A horrible thought struck her and she waved the pistol at him. "Are you armed?"

He stiffened with apparent shock, as though the question offended him As if to demonstrate his lack of violent intentions, he spread his hands wide. "Of course not, dear lady."

This rapscallion was a most bizarre burglar. Her knowledge of the criminal classes was limited, but this man's easy assurance in her company struck her as remarkable. He spoke like a gentleman and didn't seem particularly concerned that she pointed a weapon at him. Her lips tightened and she firmed her grip on the pistol. Nerves made her hands slippery. "There's no 'of course' about it. In your line of work, you must be prepared for opposition from your victims."

"I make sure the house is empty before I start work."

"Like tonight," she said coldly.

He shrugged. "Even master criminals make the occasional mistake, Miss Barrett."

Her belly lurched with dread and this time not even her strongest efforts kept her voice steady. "How do you know my name?"

The lips she could see below the mask twitched and he stepped closer.

"Stay back!" she snapped. Her heart banged so hard against her ribs, surely he must hear it.

Ignoring her pistol with insulting ease, he lifted the candle higher and subjected her to a lengthy and unnerving inspection. Genevieve's sense of unreality grew. Everything around her was familiar. The shabby comfort of her favorite room. The jumble of articles spread across the desk. The pile of pages covered in her writing. All was as it should be, except for the tall masked man with his indefinable air of elegance and his smile of indulgent amusement. She had an irritating inkling that the reprobate played with her.

Sucking in a shaky breath, she made herself study him as she would one of her artifacts. Although with his face covered, she'd never be able to describe him to the authorities. The candlelight glinted on rich gold hair and found fascinating shadows under the open neck of his loose white shirt. He wore breeches and boots. Despite this basic clothing, his manner screamed rank and privilege. And while she couldn't see his face, something about the way he carried himself indicated he was a handsome man.

A most bizarre burglar indeed.

"A good thief does his research first," he said, answering the question she'd forgotten she'd asked. "Although research sometimes lets one down. For example, village gossip had it that you attended a soiree at Leighton Court tonight."

"I wanted to..." She realized she responded as she'd respond to any polite enquiry. The hand holding the gun showed a lamentable tendency to droop, pointing the barrel harmlessly at the floor. She bit her lip and raised the gun in what she prayed was a menacing gesture. "Get out of this house."

"But I haven't got what I came for."

He shifted even closer and with that movement, she felt more at risk than she had since he'd appeared. At risk as a woman was at risk to a man. She hadn't missed how his shadowy gaze had lingered when he'd inspected her. She started to back away before she recalled any show of vulnerability would give him the advantage. She pointed the gun directly at his chest. "Get out now or I'll shoot."

He frowned as if her threat of violence pricked his sense of decorum. "Dear lady..."

She stiffened. Somewhere she'd lost control of this encounter. Which was absurd. She was the one with the gun. "I'm not your dear lady."

He bowed as if acknowledging that she'd scored a point.

"As you wish, Miss Barrett. I've done you no wrong. It seems excessive to menace me with murder and mayhem."

Shocked amusement almost made her laugh. "You broke into my house. You threatened me with..."

He interrupted her. "Doing it too brown. So far, any threats have emanated from your charming self."

"You mean to steal," she said in a low, vibrating voice.

"But I haven't. Yet." The expressive mouth above the intriguingly firm jawline curved into a charming smile. "Temper justice with mercy. Let me go free and seek redemption."

"Let you go free and find some other poor innocent to rob," she said sharply. "Better I lock you in the cellar and summon the local magistrate."

"That would be unkind. I don't like small, confined places."

"In that case, you've chosen the wrong profession. Somewhere someone's going to catch you and lock you up."

Disregarding the gun, he took another step toward her. "Surely your compassionate heart smarts at the thought of my imprisonment."

She retreated and realized he'd boxed her against the side of the desk. "Move away or I swear I will shoot."

He lit one of the candles on the desk and blew out his own, dropping it smoking to the blotter. "Tsk, Miss Barrett. You'll get blood on the carpet."

"I'll..."

Words escaped her on a gasp as he reached out with surprising speed and strength to grab the hand gripping the gun. A few nimble turns of that long body and he caught her against him, facing the open window he'd climbed through. With her back pressed hard to his chest, she was overwhelmingly aware of his casual masculine power. His leanness was deceptive. There was no denying the muscles in the arms holding her captive or the firm breadth of the chest behind her. He embraced her firmly across her torso, trapping her arms. She still held the weapon but couldn't shift to aim it at him.

The barbed but oddly flirtatious conversation had calmed her immediate dread, but now fear surged anew. What in heaven's name was she thinking, bandying words with this scoundrel? Almost as if she enjoyed herself, when if she despised anything in this world, it was a thief.

She caught her breath and began to struggle against him. "Let me go!"

His arms tightened like straps, controlling her with mortifying ease. Genevieve was a tall, strong girl, no frail lily, but the thief was taller and stronger. She'd never before had to measure her strength against a man's. It rankled how easily he restrained her. "Hush, Miss Barrett. I give you my word I mean you no harm."

"Then release me." She was panting and her writhing had achieved nothing but the collapse of her never very secure coiffure.

"Not unless you put the gun down."

She struggled to elbow him in the belly but the way he held her made it impossible. "Then I'll be at your mercy," she said breathlessly.

He gave a grunt of laughter. "There's that to consider."

His body was so close that his amusement vibrated through her. The sensation was uncomfortably intimate. A couple more of those blasted deft movements and she found herself without her weapon. He placed it out of reach on the desk.

"I'll scream."

"There's nobody to hear you," he said carelessly, and in that moment, she truly hated him.

"You're despicable," she hissed, trying and failing to free herself. Her heart galloped with fright and anger. With him, and with herself for being a stupid, weak female, victim to an overbearing male.

"Sticks and stones, dear lady."

He drew her tighter into his body and took a sliding step backward. She was suddenly conscious not just of his size and strength—those had been obvious from the moment he caught her up against him—but also of his enveloping heat and the fact that he smelled pleasantly of something herbal. Fresh. Tangy.

This was clearly a ruffian who took the trouble to wash regularly.

He reversed another step and opened the library door with a rattle, holding her under one arm with humiliating ease. She wrenched against him and tried without success to sink her fingernails into his powerful forearm.

"No, you don't," he huffed, pressing her closer to his tall body.

"I'll have your liver for this," she hissed, even as his pleasant scent continued to alert her senses. What was that smell?

"You'll have to catch me first," he said, and she wished she didn't notice how laughter warmed that deep, musical voice. Any angry response died in furious shock as he brushed his cheek softly against the wing of hair that covered the side of her face.

"*Au revoir,* Miss Barrett," he whispered in her ear, his breath teasing nerves she didn't know she possessed, then he shoved her hard away from him.

By the time she'd regained her footing, he'd slammed the door and locked it from the outside with the key he must have palmed when he fiddled with the latch.

"Don't you dare ransack the house, you devil!" she shouted, rushing forward and pounding on the door. But the vicarage doors were of good solid English oak and hardly shook under her determined assault. "Don't you dare!"

Panting, she stopped and pressed her ear to the door, desperate to work out what he was up to. She heard a distant slam as though someone left by the front door. Could her mere presence have daunted him into abandoning his plan to rob the vicarage? She couldn't imagine why. He'd had the best of the conflict from the first.

Her hands closed into fists against the door as she recalled his barefaced cheek in holding her so...so *improperly.* "Improper" seemed too weak a word to describe the sensations he'd aroused when he'd captured her like a sheep ready for the shears. Like that sheep, she was about to be well and truly fleeced. She was in no position to stop the villain from taking what he wanted from the house. There was no hope of help until her father returned from the duke's, and heaven knew when that would be. The Reverend Ezekiel Barrett adored hobnobbing with the quality. He'd be there until breakfast if Sedgemoor didn't throw him out first.

Tears of frustration stung her eyes and she felt as jumpy as a cat on a stovetop. It was illogical, but she could feel the radiating heat of his body against hers. It was as if he still touched her. She wasn't afraid anymore, at least not for her person. If the burglar had wanted to hurt her, he'd had plenty of opportunity. Her principal reaction now that fear and unwilling fascination ebbed was disgust at her behavior. She'd acted the complete ninnyhammer, the sort of jittery female she despised. She'd had a gun. She should have been able to force him out of the house. Blast him, even now she wouldn't surrender so easily. She could climb out the way the knave had got in, using the old elm tree outside the window. Once she'd caught her breath, by heaven, she would.

The ominous silence extended. What was the blackguard up to? Would there be anything left by the time he was finished? She glanced over to the desk and thanked the Lord that the only genuinely valuable items in the house had escaped his notice. For a sneak thief, he wasn't very observant, although he hadn't struck her as a man deficient in intelligence. Or, she added with renewed outrage, impudence. Nevertheless, any professional would have immediately pocketed the gold objects scattered over the blotter, objects she'd been sketching for her article.

Something landed on the carpet near the open window. Curious, Genevieve grabbed the candle from the desk and lifted it high. Lying on the floor was the key to the door. She rushed to the window, but darkness and the elm's thick foliage obstructed her view. In the distance someone started to whistle. A jaunty old tune. "Over the Hills and Far Away." Appropriate for an absconding thief, she supposed. Not that he seemed in a panic to flee. Again, his confidence struck her as puzzling. The music gradually faded as the whistler wandered into the night.

With shaking hands, Genevieve scooped up the key

and balanced it on her palm, her thoughts in turmoil. One completely unimportant fact threw every other consideration to the wind. She'd finally identified the smell that had tantalized her when he'd held her close.

Lemon verbena.

THE DISH

Where authors give you the inside scoop!

♥ ♥ ♥ ♥ ♥ ♥ ♥ ♥ ♥ ♥ ♥ ♥ ♥ ♥ ♥ ♥

From the desk of R.C. Ryan

Dear Reader,

When my daughter-in-law Patty came home from her first hike of the Grand Canyon, she was high on the beauty and majesty of the mountains for months. Since then, it has become her annual pilgrimage—one that fuels her dreams, and feeds my writer's imagination. I've wanted to create a character with the same passion for the mountains that Patty has for a long time, someone who experiences the same awe, freedom, and peace that she does just by being in eyesight of them. And with JOSH, I think I finally have.

Josh Conway, the hero of the second book in my Wyoming Sky series, is truly a hero in every sense of the word. He's a man who rescues people who've lost their way on the mountain he loves in all kinds of weather. There's just something about a guy who would risk his own safety, his very life, to help others, that is so appealing to me. To add to Josh's appeal, he's a hard-working rancher and a sexy cowboy—an irresistible combination. Not to mention that he loves a challenge.

Enter Sierra Moore. Sierra is a photographer who comes to the Grand Tetons in Wyoming to shoot photographs of a storm. At least that's what she'll admit to. But there's a mystery behind that beautiful smile. She's come to the mountains to disappear for a while, and being

rescued—even if it is by a ruggedly handsome cowboy—
is the last thing she needs or wants.

But when danger rears its ugly head, and Sierra's life
is threatened, she and Josh must call on every bit of
strength and courage they possess in order to survive. Yet
an even greater test of their strength will be the courage
to commit to a lifetime together.

I hope you enjoy JOSH!

R. C. Ryan

RyanLangan.com

❤ ❤ ❤ ❤ ❤ ❤ ❤ ❤ ❤ ❤ ❤ ❤ ❤ ❤ ❤

From the desk of Anna Campbell

Dear Reader,

Wow! I'm so excited that my first historical romance with
Grand Central Publishing has hit the shelves (and the
e-waves!). I hope you enjoy reading SEVEN NIGHTS IN
A ROGUE'S BED as much as I enjoyed writing it. Not
only is this my first book for GCP, it's also the first book
in my very first series, the Sons of Sin. Perhaps I should
smash a bottle of champagne over my copy of SEVEN
NIGHTS to launch it in appropriate style.

Hmm, having second thoughts here. Much better, I've
decided, to read the book and drink the champagne!

Do you like fairytale romance? I love stories based on
Cinderella or Sleeping Beauty or some other mythical

hero or heroine. SEVEN NIGHTS IN A ROGUE'S BED is a dyed-in-the-wool Beauty and the Beast re-telling. To me, this is the ultimate romantic fairytale. The hero starts out as a monster, but when he falls in love, the fragments of goodness in his tortured soul multiply until he becomes a gallant prince (or, in this case, a viscount, but who's counting?). Beauty and the Beast is at heart about the transformative power of true love—what more powerful theme for a romance writer to explore?

Jonas Merrick, the Beast in SEVEN NIGHTS IN A ROGUE'S BED, is a scarred recluse who has learned through hard and painful experience to mistrust a hostile world. When the book opens, he's a rogue indeed. But meeting our heroine conspires to turn him into a genuine, if at first reluctant, hero worthy of his blissfully happy ending.

Another thing I love about Beauty and the Beast is that the heroine is more proactive than some other mythological girls. For a start, she stays awake throughout! Like Beauty, Sidonie Forsythe places herself in the Beast's power to save someone she loves, her reckless older sister, Roberta. Sidonie's dread when she meets brooding, enigmatic Jonas Merrick swiftly turns to fascination—but even as they fall in love, Sidonie's secret threatens to destroy Jonas and any chance of happiness for this Regency Beauty and the Beast.

I adore high-stakes stories where I wonder if the lovers can ever overcome what seem to be insurmountable barriers between them. In SEVEN NIGHTS IN A ROGUE'S BED, Jonas and Sidonie have to triumph over the bitter legacy of the past and conquer present dangers to achieve their happily-ever-after. Definitely major learning curves for our hero and heroine!

This story is a journey from darkness to light, and it allowed me to play with so many classic romance themes.

Redemption. A touch of the gothic. The steadfast, courageous heroine. The dark, tormented hero. The clash of two powerful personalities as they resist overwhelming passion. Secrets and revelations. Self-sacrifice and risk. Revenge and justice. You know, all the big stuff!

If you'd like to find out more about SEVEN NIGHTS IN A ROGUE'S BED and the Sons of Sin series, please visit my website: www.annacampbell.info. And in the meantime, happy reading!

Best wishes,

Anna Campbell

♥ ♥ ♥ ♥ ♥ ♥ ♥ ♥ ♥ ♥ ♥ ♥ ♥ ♥

From the desk of Katie Lane

Dear Reader,

One of my favorite things to do during the holidays is to read *The Night Before Christmas*. So I thought it would be fun to tell you about my new romance, HUNK FOR THE HOLIDAYS, by making up my own version of the classic.

> 'Twas four days before Christmas, and our heroine, Cassie,
> Is ready for her office party, looking red hot and sassy.
> When what to her wondering eyes should she see
> But the escort she hired standing next to her tree?
> His eyes how they twinkle, his dimples so cute,
> He has a smile that melts, a great body to boot.

There's only one problem: James is as controlling as Cass,
But she forgives him this flaw, when she gets a good look
    at his ass.
He goes straight to work at seducing his date,
And by the end of the evening, Cass is ready to mate.
Not to ruin the story, all I will say,
Is that James will be smiling when Cass gets her way.
Mixed in with their romance will be plenty of reason
For you to enjoy the fun of the season.
Caroling, shopping, and holiday baking,
A humorous great-aunt and her attempts at match-making.
A perfect book to cozy up with all the way through December,
HUNK FOR THE HOLIDAYS will be out in September.
For now I will end by wishing you peace, love, and laughter.
And, of course, the best gift of all… a happily-ever-after!

Katie Jane

♥ ♥ ♥ ♥ ♥ ♥ ♥ ♥ ♥ ♥ ♥ ♥ ♥ ♥ ♥

From the desk of Hope Ramsay

Dear Reader,

I love Christmas, but I have to say that trying to write a
holiday-themed book in the middle of a long, hot summer
is not exactly easy. It was hard to stay in the holiday
mood when my nonwriting time was spent weeding my
perennials border, watching baseball, and working on my
short golf game.

So how does an author get herself into the holiday mood in the middle of July?

She hauls out her iPod and plays Christmas music from sun up to sun down.

My husband was ready to strangle me, but all that Christmas music did the trick. And in the end, it was just one song that helped me find my holiday spirit.

The song is "The Longest Night," written by singer-songwriter Peter Mayer, a song that isn't quite a Christmas song. It's about the winter solstice. The lyrics are all about hope, even in the darkest hour. In the punchline, the song-writer gives a tiny nod to the meaning of Christmas when he says, "Maybe light itself is born in the longest night."

When I finished LAST CHANCE CHRISTMAS, I realized that this theme of light and dark runs through it like a river. My heroine is a war photographer, who literally sees the world as a battle between light and dark. When she arrives in Last Chance, she's troubled and alone, and the darkness is about to overwhelm her.

But of course, that doesn't last long after she meets Stone Rhodes, the chief of police and a man who is about as Grinch-like as they come. But as the saying goes, some-times the only way to get yourself out of a funk is to help someone else. And when Stone does that, he manages to spark a very hot and bright light in the dead of winter.

I hope you love reading Stone and Lark's story as much as I did writing it.

Ya'll have a blessed holiday, now, you hear?

Hope Ramsay